PERSEPHONE'S ESCALATOR

by

Joe Taylor

First published by Sley House Publishing 2024

First edition

ISBN: 978-1-957941-04-2

Editor: Lillian Ehrhart

Interior Design: Jeremy Billingsley

Cover Design: Ranxvrus

ACKNOWLEDGEMENTS

I would like to thank Patricia Taylor for her insights into the many early revisions of this novel. I would also like to thank Richard Derus, who worked hard as an agent and friend with the novel's early stages. Lastly, Jeremy Billingsley and Lillian Erhart offered invaluable advice on its final draft. My thanks to all involved.

PROLOGUE TO AN EPILOGUE

Proposition 1a.

There are scientists who could have measured precisely how far below the earth's surface lay the cavern in which Abel crept, precisely how many kilograms of hate-filled flesh supported his vast, slothful body, precisely how many liters of his brother Cain's blood he planned to spill in revenge for that first, sad death. And there are scientists who could have measured precisely how few nanoseconds it took Cain to sense Abel's hateful presence and viciously repel his attack to once more slice him down.

For man is the measure of all things. All things, that is, which he—or she—is willing to believe measurable.

Proposition 1b.

After all, even as Cain's rock ax, for the myriad-eth time in history, crumpled Abel's body to that cavern floor, even as Cain gloated over oozing blood, and even as underground sycophants glowed in uncanny ivory hues and cheered his ax onward—*Down! Down! Down!*—it was the simplest thing to measure the altitude of one Delta jet leveling at 12,232 feet to catch the dawn's rays on a flight from Atlanta Hirschfield to Tampa International.

Nikki Ryan was serving a Martell cognac to a silver-haired passenger in the jet's first-class cabin. *She* could have measured the weight of Cain and Abel's endless hatred, for she was a scientist… of sorts. But being a new witch in an old order, she herself was not ready to believe. Close though, for her neighbor and sister in the Matrix, Alice Fairbain, had for nearly a year turned the night sky north of Tampa a Chernobyl pink until every sister witch in Florida complained about spells working sidewise or backwards—when they worked at all.

Wait, Nikki cautioned herself time and again on spotting that pink sky from her back yard. *Wait; impatience is for wizards.*

Her teenage alter-ego had no such restraint and bawled inwardly even as the jetliner hit an air pocket: *We can't wait. Fairbain's a bummer. We need to do something about her. As soon as this damned jet lands, Mommy-o…*

"No, Night. No."

The passenger looked up from his cognac. "I beg your pardon?"

"Sorry, sir. I was daydreaming."

"I suppose that's all right for a woman as young as you, as long as you're not flying the plane, dear."

The man was a distinguished late sixties. Nikki smiled gratefully at him, knowing his paternal presence had cowed Night back into her subdued, subconscious form. Still, mulling over the man's comment about her youth, she hurried to the cabin's service area, pulled its thin blue curtain and took out her compact: gums much too pink for her thirty-five years, plus a smooth teenage brow. She hissed at the mirror, "Not now, Night. Never on a flight, I've told you. Go back and daydream about that hunk of a physics teacher you have."

Fairbain's onto us, you know.

"No, she isn't."

Yes.

Outside, the jet engines roared. "Give me a week," she whispered.

Maybe. Not too much time or I'll go over there and blast her and her house and that stupid Aaron man of hers with a globe of destruction that'll make Hiroshima look like small cheese.

Nikki snapped her compact shut. That was precisely the kind of talk that worried her about her migration. Witches who underwent migration were supposed to be specially chosen by the Matrix for their wisdom and maturity, for their ability to carry on tradition, like the Dalai Lama and the Buddha. Why else would the Matrix allow a mortal to live 150 to 300 years? But this teenager Night inside her babbled more like a power-crazed alchemist than a witch on the cutting edge of tradition and maturity. Hearing a cough from another stewardess, Nikki felt her brow. Good, worry lines and wrinkles had reappeared. She realized she must be the only woman in history glad to feel them.

Proposition 1c.

On Alice Fairbain's land twenty miles north of Tampa, Annie Kirby fired a kiln with the coming false dawn. Her movements were clumsy, as if she were a newborn unused to life. She *was* unused to life, not because she was an infant, for she clearly wasn't, but because she was of the walking dead, a zombie in a land that didn't believe in zombies. Over her head, crawling along open eaves and looking down on the kiln, a rag doll with cherry tomato freckles dotting its cottony white face shook a vial of clumped maggots until they fell down onto Annie's hair. Watching the wriggling white forms disperse from where they'd dropped into strands of sandy hair, the rag doll quivered with so much merriment that it lost its grip and fell, scampering with a laugh to avoid Annie Kirby's clumsy dirty bare feet.

"Pie? Pie, where are you?"

The rag doll tossed the empty vial under Annie Kirby's heel, causing her to stagger against the hot kiln; then the doll ran happily toward its mistress's voice.

Proposition 1d.

Cain! Cain!

Dean Kirby awoke to a yellowish haze pervading his room. In the mirror on his apartment's desk, a stranger with ivory skin as smooth as the side of a refrigerator sat intently writing.

"Who… what… are you doing here?" Dean wheezed his question out, fighting the sweaty sheet that wound about his groin, while looking for something heavy he could use to strike out.

Cain! Cain!

The stranger dropped his pen with a tic. "You're awake. How sad. I'll leave you to yourself—for what that company's worth. But don't forget: I'll be back."

The stranger stood, his skin shining, Dean decided, like a dumpy kitchen appliance from the 50's. Remembering a commando knife he'd recently bought, Dean fumbled in the desk's drawer for it; then he lunged, connecting with the stranger's left leg, burying a good two inches of blade. But the stranger simply smiled his refrigerator smile:

"I'll be back. And when Cain calls, we must free the boy and take him to the Fairbain woman. Don't feed him anything on the way. His liver must be pure. Do you understand?"

Writhing, Dean collapsed.

When he awoke mid-morning, pain burned his left thigh and he fell, bashing his chin and biting through his tongue, expelling blood that tasted like swamp water. He hobbled to the desk and saw a dozen or so pages, all filled with the word "Cain!" in minuscule, cramped writing. The word must have been written several thousand times. He started to sweep the pages into the trash, but hesitated and then folded and placed them in his pocket as he dressed, ignoring his throbbing leg. He telephoned a taxi for St. Veronica's Center. On hearing it honk outside his apartment, Dean tucked the knife in his waistband. *Bobby; must free Bobby*, he thought. He was afraid to speak, afraid of what might overhear him if he did. But then, what if it could read his thoughts?

Proposition 1e.

"Can't you see? Can't you? My mother's alive; it's my father who's dead!"

Dr. Martin Edmonds tapped whatever was closest to him—this time it was a paperclip holder that gave an empty pop—and he cursed his habit, for a psychologist should have more control.

"You'll be seeing your father today, Bobby. He's visiting this morning, at eleven."

"How? He's dead! He's dead!"

Proposition 1f.

At the University of Kentucky in Lexington, a professor stood motionless, eyes glazed. Her class tittered, thinking: typical absent-minded academic. She smiled. "Where was I? Oh yes, the medieval Catholic Church. Much wiser than we credit, that institution not only allowed for the irrational in astrology and saintly relics, whose bones represent sympathetic magic at its best, but it also edged very close to worshipping a female deity through the many Mary cults. Any random glance at the Old Testament tells us that blustery Jehovah was in sore need of a little female balance." *Will that clock ever reach eleven?* A graduate student raised his hand and Jewel Dawn let him take the floor. With any luck, he'd talk until the period's end. She had other problems to worry about. Something was wrong with the Matrix, deadly wrong. Deadly wrong, and the Supreme Executrix of the North American coven hadn't the faintest idea what or why.

Proposition 1g.

The world *is* all that we know, but all that we know isn't necessarily all that is.

A RAY FROM HELL

(three weeks later)

"Yet he hath ever but slenderly known himself."
King Lear

1.

Before St. Veronica's Psychiatric Center came about, there was the forest primeval. After St. Veronica's came Atlanta, then Sherman. Sherman torched Atlanta, but even that fire couldn't destroy St. Veronica's. Such was the myth its staff espoused, for no one seemed to know exactly when the mental facility was founded.

Dr. Martin Edmonds, firm Jungian believer in myth, massaged his eyes on entering the green foyer. Not just green, but split pea green—ancient, scaling split pea green. Could any client hope for recovery here? But the Board of Directors, mystic czars from a far-off planet, insisted the facility had no money for mere "facial improvements."

As always, Martin was conscious of the sound of his footsteps on the green granite. He nodded at the receptionist behind her grandiose mahogany counter. A prune-faced gargoyle, she silently frowned at some imperfection in his attire.

"Morning, Doctor."

Martin startled at the cheery voice to his right, which emitted from the only male nurse St. Veronica's had ever hired. Martin smiled at him, glad for an excuse to avoid an encounter with the prune. Some rumors had it that *she* had founded St. Veronica's, having come over with Leif Ericson.

"I hear our wraith acted out again," the male nurse said, matching Martin's stride toward a stairway. "Have you ever thought that maybe his kid's right and we should requisition some voodoo charms from Haiti?"

Martin rolled his eyes and groaned as the nurse abruptly cut away for another corridor.

"Wraith" was what Bobby Kirby called his father Dean. A wraith was a dead man returned to life for some special purpose, a zombie, in a sense, though a self-appointed zombie, not a victim like those in Haiti. And while there just might be some believable chemical basis for Haitian zombies—blowfish poison administered until a deathlike trance ensued—there was no such counterpart for wraiths. They were completely supernatural, completely mythological. Martin knew this because he'd looked the word *wraith* up in the musty encyclopedia in the foyer near the musty receptionist. It gave reference to poor dead—read murdered or abused—dairy maids haunting barns; baleful eyes summoning the living to their doom; foul mists befuddling townsmen. Wraith. And when he'd turned toward the receptionist after reading the definition he'd understood the concept immediately.

Odd to recall, but the judge who heard Kirby's pre-trial three weeks back, before remanding him to St. Veronica's, had referred to Kirby as a "ray from hell." The judge had twittered his hands and said the city jail just wasn't up to detaining such… *rays from hell* as would attack their own son with a knife. A son, senselessly committed, the judge further chattered, when it was the father who needed psychiatric care. But that decision about the son remained to be settled, and Bobby was still in St. Veronica's, though in a far-distant and locked ward from his father's own locked ward.

Martin stopped mid-stride. Yellow papers jutted from his in-house mailbox—incident reports. As he unlocked the door, light from his window blasted the mailbox, so he glanced to see Dean Kirby's name listed prominently on— "I'll be damned"—all four reports. Four on a single client had to be a record. He trudged his office's floor planks— painted forest green, of course—to start his window air unit. From it he looked out onto Atlanta street life below. The Beautiful People weren't up yet; garbage collectors, winos, and street cleaners still held the field. The air conditioner rattled and Martin sniffed. He'd been asking maintenance to change its filter for three months. *Give it up, move to Montana,* he told himself.

Instead of packing, he read the reports. One nurse had tried to give Dean Kirby a sponge bath—all they dared do since the man previously scalded himself and two nurses in the shower. *Pt began rambling about home. When asked where home was, Pt laughed, forcibly knocking nurse away. Pt's voice altered noticeably, deeper. Pt grabbed basin, threw water, tore basin in two.*

Tore? Martin pictured the tubs used for sponge baths, tubs of thick, considerable plastic. He tried to imagine simply tearing one in two, but unless Hulk Hogan was… he skimmed the other reports. Kirby had broken two restraints, been administered 100 mg of Nembutal, ripped his bed sheets "looking for the body" (Kirby's words). *Upon being asked what body, Pt replied "Mine."* So another 100 mg of Nembutal. Kirby then lay in bed for nearly an hour chanting "Live, Evil! Live, Evil!" until the staff finally administered a third dose of Nembutal. Three injections of Nembutal? The man could be comatose. Martin inhaled sharply and phoned the North wing.

"Have you checked on Mr. Kirby this morning?"

"You want to hear him?" It was the male nurse.

Martin heard muffled shouting, as if from a distance.

"That's our boy. Wraithing on out. You coming up to see him?"

At that question, Martin's stomach rebelled, remembering he'd skipped breakfast. The trouble was that Kirby constantly emitted a gangrenous odor, a rotting, cloying wetness that wouldn't leave your nostrils. They'd had an infectious disease specialist over twice to run tests: nothing. Whatever the reason, the odor came in acrid waves and clung to anyone and everyone's hair and clothes.

"No, I think I'll see him after lunch."

"He'll be here unless the voodoo doc—we'll take care of him, Doctor." The nurse's voice turned singsong.

Martin smiled at the abrupt change; some patient's relative must have approached the nurse's station. He hung up and went to grab a pastry from the snack machine and begin his rounds. Coming back two hours later he saw the receptionist's emerald smock wisping from his office. He waved feebly, but she and her pre-Sherman gray hair disappeared. *Twilight Zone* at St. Veronica's. Entering his office he saw a bright green card Magic-Marked, "Doctor Edmonds! Important!" The card was folded into a tent and erected over an Express Mail package from Wesley Chapel, Florida. Wasn't that where the Kirbys were from? He opened the package and read, in an elaborate, turn-of-the-century penmanship, this letter:

June 15
Alice Fairbain

Dr. Edmonds:

I'm too old to be dealing with these things. No, that's not true; just writing to a psychiatrist has me defensive, you see. Truth is I'm barely middle-age halitosis. And the other truth is that I'm normally too involved with my sculpturing to become entangled in people's affairs. That's why when Annie Kirby first asked me to undertake the legal guardianship of Bobby, I resisted. His father, Dean, frightened me, you see. Then I realized that I'd only become guardian if his father were… were to die or become incapacitated. So I signed the papers (my lawyer will contact you) making me Bobby's legal guardian.

I suppose I never really thought I'd be called on—though Bobby's a pleasure and I will happily do my duty. I just never thought it until I read this diary, the one I've enclosed. I found it yesterday at Dean Kirby's house, which I bought months back. I skimmed it and immediately phoned the Atlanta police—far too late, as you know.

Frankly, I believe Mr. Kirby will attack Bobby again. You may have heard that I formed a fond kinship with the boy's mother. You may also have heard that the father blamed me for Annie's death. I beg to differ. His wife didn't die under normal circumstances, as you're surely aware. But are you aware that her grave was robbed and her body never found, and that the Kirbys soon after left for Atlanta? This on top of a poor little neighborhood girl who was decapitated… Well, missing bodies and gore are out of my realm; I'm an artist, not a ghoul.

The boy knows who really caused his mother's death. That's why his father is under your care. The enclosed diary will convince you Bobby should be released to me, as his mother desired. I'm not really sure why Mr. Kirby even kept this diary, but why did Richard Nixon record his White House conversations? Who can tell?

I realize this letter rambles. But there's rambling and there's rambling. Just read the enclosed diary to see how true that is.

A.F.

Martin confirmed that a loose-leaf diary was in the package; he then opened the white

linen envelope placed on top, and a voucher for a first-class, two-way airline ticket from Atlanta to Tampa fell out, along with a second note in that same turn-of-the century hand:

A check for two thousand dollars also awaits you. Sir, the money's not meant as an insult. You're a professional and the last thing I want is to insult you. But I'm desperate. Could Dean Kirby have discovered I am to take care of his son? I understand from a friend in Atlanta that Kirby committed himself and thus can leave anytime. Someone else told me that a judge remanded the man to your care. Obviously, I don't have all the story. Here's why I wonder. Last night I received a call: "Look out your window," a voice says. Click. So I lift a pistol from my desk and edge to a window. The local moo ranchers claim that my children (my sculptures) walk the lawn at night; I never deny that fancy since any publicity is good publicity. But something was walking. And when I opened my front door a six-foot rattlesnake coiled from a basket. Please, please use the enclosed voucher and let me tell you all this in person. There's something else—something I want you to see before the police do—something very interesting.

Sincerely,

A.F.
Alice Fairbain

P.S. One more thing: Kirby thought his wife and I were having an affair. Because I'm near middle age and single, farmers think I'm a witch, academics think I'm a lesbian. What do you think, doctor?

What did he think? Being a good psychologist (not psychiatrist, damn it), Martin kept what he thought to himself. And that self told him to hold judgment until he read the diary purportedly belonging to Dean Kirby. He pulled it out; it looked genuine, in Kirby's cramped neurotic script that so resembled a bug's inky trail. From the first entry, Martin could see that the diary—if genuine—was a year old, from about the time when the Kirby family's problems began.

DIARY
PROPERTY OF PROFESSOR KIRBY

Wednesday, Aug. 8

Bobby was the most excited about our move to Florida. This surprised Annie and me, for fifteen-year-olds aren't supposed to be excited about anything their parents instigate—it's against the law. But he was between girlfriends (which meant we caught him on an off-week) and unhappy with his teachers (which meant *plus* ça *change, plus c'est la même chose.)*

Annie was second-most excited. Florida. Ah-h-h. Where the rules are different. When I eked out a job at a small Catholic college (I'm not Catholic, but Episcopal, which must count for something in these days of materialism) she immediately landed a nursing job at a prestigious new university hospital in Tampa with plenty of room for advancement—a far cry from her hospital in Kentucky with battle-axes who never seemed to age, though they voted for Prohibition and probably personally ran in at least one Derby.

Me? Well, I was semi-excited. If Daddy wasn't going to be the breadwinner, he could at least put potato chips on the table.

We had two surprises: First, every piece of land in Florida doesn't border the ocean (in fact, Tampa wasn't anywhere near an ocean, though Tampa Bay and The Gulf of Mexico fooled this Kentucky boy). Second, any anorexic parcels that do touch water sure aren't affordable for a small-time college teacher and his registered nurse wife and son. But it wasn't bad; we opted for eight acres of semi-swamp at the end of a long, mostly deserted, whale-bone white road.

"Spoo-ky," Bobby exclaimed next to me in the cab of the rental truck. I hit a pothole and worried that U-haul would charge me for a new shock absorber or whatever these monster trucks have.

Bobby's comment concerned the Spanish moss drooping from skeleton cypress. And the water: I'd never seen black water before. I mean like ink that they used to dip pens in— or, say, drive your car an extra fifty thousand between oil changes and see what comes out. That's how black this water was.

Now I swear this is true, and it's a good thing our family has a sense of humor, or we might have turned around. The last thing Annie did after the real estate closing was to put up one of those cute green plastic mailboxes that look like a barn. *Green Acres*, get it? It was out of her character, as she'd developed a tough veneer from working the Emergency Department, but who isn't out of character now and then? On top of her Green Acres mailbox as we drove up perched a vulture, what I later found out was called a turkey buzzard. It appeared to weigh thirty pounds, looked as black as if it'd dived into the nearby swamp water for a bubble bath, and oh yeah, globbed around its nasty eyes flapped enough red gummy skin to make an orangutan in heat blush.

"Look at that sucker!"

The vulture just stared. Not at us. Vultures don't have eyes for the living. It just stared. We were about fifty feet from the driveway and the mailbox.

"That's a vulture," I said, showing off my Ph.D.

"Now are we gonna get a gun?" Bobby asked.

That had been his first comment on learning we were going to move onto eight acres at the end of a deserted road, onto one of the few land developments in Florida that had failed. He never minded repeating his comments for my further edification.

The vulture flew off at this suggestion, evidently not a member of the N.R.A. I admit that an ugly beauty graced its flight, its wings flapping with slow inevitability.

"Spoo-ky," Bobby drawled once more for my edification.

I pulled into the drive, between tall cypress and pines, heading toward the house. Before I even stopped the truck Bobby jumped out and was running back to catch sight of our bird friend. Edgar Allen Poe I'm not; screw the bird, I wanted the house. Behind, from our car, Annie's passengers tumbled out too. Our mixed breed lab chased after Bobby, knocking the cats and their cage onto the grass.

"What kind of bird was that?" Annie asked as she righted the cage, knowing better than to scream at a running teenage boy.

I think she knew what brand of bird it was. She's strange in this way; working as an ER nurse since I've known her, watching people kill themselves, kill others, be killed, maimed or any other delightful variation on the medical scene—doing all this gory real-world work, but when she's home, I'm Mr. Experience. Me and my 1,728 books. Humans, can you beat them?

"Some kind of blackbird, I think." Sure, I lied. "You know, Quoth the blackbird, 'Nevermore.'" After my cheap Poe imitation I gave Annie a hug, feeling her thin waist, smelling her sandy-silk hair. Damn, why didn't we get a separate hotel room for Bobby last night?

The cats stared at me. Their prerogative. Mine was to leave their cage in pine needles, fire ants, and sand till sunset. I don't like cats. But Annie took them to the house, telling me to make sure the windows were closed so kitty-kits couldn't run back to Kentucky. Hell, Colonel Sanders was welcome to 'em. The minute we walked inside the house, both cats backed into a corner of the cage and hissed. Typical.

"Just put their water and food in the cage; they'll come round. Better than getting all scratched," I suggested.

But Annie wanted them out to enjoy their new home. As she bent I could still hear my voice echoing that funny way that empty houses make a voice do. There was a loud rap at the window. We jumped, not so much from the rap, but from turning to see Bobby's macabre grin in that filmy window…

Look, when I was a graduate student in humanities my hero was a philosopher named Wittgenstein—all his numbered propositions falling into a very certain place, beginning with that granddaddy "The world is all we know." Yeah, take that you churchies. Take that, you popes and your nine classes of angels. Take that, Falwell, Billy Graham. This world, she's it, t'ain't nothin' mo' out there, bub.

But I'm telling you that as I turned to see my son, I wasn't so sure. His teenage face was still in need of Clearasil, his white arms still skinny enough that a bully might mistake them for chalk sticks. I saw this, I saw him holding a scrawny kitten. Nothing alarming, right? But damned if something didn't make me jump. Maybe his mouth was too black, like it was opening beyond tonsils and adenoids to drain into that inky swamp water and connect in some primal way. Maybe his eyes blurred the way eyes in post office mug shots do, photos of murderers lolling and waiting for an opening, a weakness—in you. The eyes of Cain. Listen: I could swear he was thinking of killing us. My son, relishing the thought of our deaths.

The kitten in his hands let out a fierce yowl as if he were crushing her neck. This seemed to shake him out of whatever fugue he was in, and he yelled through the pane, "It was after this kitten. That vulture." He jerked his head, indicating the vulture while rubbing the kitten's ears. He was our son again.

"That's what the babies are afraid of." Annie ran out the side door to help Bobby hold the newfound kitten, who was wide-eyed and backing from the house into Bobby's chest.

Afraid? Yeah, that's what's so scary, a third damned cat to trip over. Still, I watched Bobby, who in turn stared over my head as he tugged at the kitten's ear. I turned: Nothing but an empty room, four white walls and the wooden staircase I stood by. I glanced up it: nothing. When I looked back, the window filmed my view of Annie, rendering her yellow with dust, like she'd been laid in her grave a century or so. Her hand, a collection of wired bones, jerked. The two cats, still in the cage near my leg, hissed wildly. It was then I heard the stairs creak and felt something brush my hair. I snatched—Christ!—and momentarily held a hot, callused finger. The rest of the hand pressed mine conspiratorially, not with more fingers but with talons.

Did I scream? You bet, St. Theresa. Even tripped over the cat cage. When I looked up from the floor there was nothing but the stupid white room we planned to paint a stupid peach. The staircase was empty, not even a dust mote or mite. Then came a tap at the window. "What's wrong, Dean?" My palm was bleeding and torn. I looked at my wife's still skullish head, then back to the room's sepulchral emptiness.

OK, Wittgenstein, do your stuff, I thought, squeezing my bleeding palm and glancing at the empty stairwell: Proposition 1. The world is all we know. Proposition 2. Florida has these nasty brown bugs called palmettos that can substitute as aircraft carriers. 2a. That's what you felt. 2b. That's what scared the cats, too. 2c. That's what cut your hand.

"Nothing. A bug flew into my hair."

By now the cats were hissing at the hallway connecting the laundry room and what would soon be Bobby's room. I stood from where I'd tripped and edged to the window, feeling more comfortable near open spaces. Was that a dirty footprint on the carpet?

"Our moving party's got an uninvited guest," Annie said, her voice vibrating the glass. I started, then saw she meant the kitten. I looked back at the staircase then the hallway, thinking, *Palmetto bug, palmetto bug.* I nodded and dumped the cats from their cage—if anything lurked, let it get them first. Gobble, gobble. Hiss, hiss. But the cats scrambled back into the cage. By then Bobby and Annie came charging in the side door to my left, Annie pointing to the hallway.

"Wow! My room's back there?" Bobby forgot the kitten and dropped it on the kitchen counter.

"Bobby! Stop!"

∞

A brief aside: In case you ever wonder as you watch a horror movie, How come no one believes the pretty girl in the skimpy yellow outfit about the vampire? How come no one believes the nice kids about the slimy bald monster? Let me tell you, the movies have it wrong: It never gets that far, because no one tells. I don't know; maybe before old Wittgenstein, something like this might have happened:

"Morning, Frank."

"Morning, Zebe."

"You know, I saw the durndest thing out by the cow shed last night."

"That so, Zebe?"

"Yep. There was this floating brown finger grabbed my hair and give it a tug, then disappeared like a flash. Lookit my cut finger here. And afore that you know what?"

"What, Zebe?"

"My boy was a-staring through a cob-webbed window and looked all weird-like."

"Whatcha mean, 'weird-like'?"

"Can't tell. Just weird-like."

"Well ain't that somethin'."

"Yep."

"Come on into town, let me buy you a red-eye gravy breakfast. Sounds like you had some strange happenings out on the farm. Think maybe there's another witch around? That young blonde widow people've been talking about?"

—Wittgenstein, he stopped all that.

❧❧

"What's wrong, Dad? Why'd you yell *stop*?" Bobby turned to look at me.

"I just think we should go through the house together. Besides—" I walked to where Annie had laid her purse on the kitchen counter and retrieved her mace while avoiding the kitten— "I thought I heard a noise back there. Could be a raccoon."

"Neat!" Bobby said, rushing off.

Neat. I ran after him.

Monday, Aug. 28

At breakfast we found the kitten and our male cat, Zeus, dead outside our screen door. There were clots of blood in their sides as if they'd been bitten or stabbed. Annie insisted on taking them to the vet's for an autopsy. Bobby'd named the kitten Chance. No other comment needed. We're keeping Hera strictly inside.

Thursday, Aug. 30

School begins for me and Bobby both. Coming home I stopped at the vet's. She gave me the oddest look when I walked in.

"Your cats were both killed by a puncture wound to their hearts," she said. "An old-fashioned hat pin or a syringe."

"Maybe some kind of snake?"

She shook her head. "Do you have children, or maybe

neighborhood kids coming around?"

My face flushed with anger and I left.

Thursday, Sept. 6

Bobby had joined a cross country team right off and was at a meet in Orlando. "Watch out for the rabid mouse that lives there," I told him this morning. He just frowned. I have to roar at his lousy jokes or I don't understand teenage angst; mine can sink into the Silent Sargasso Sea.

So Annie's and my ships were scheduled to cross at 4:45, the approximate time she came home from work. Like most mildly amorous parents we planned to make the best of our offspring's rare absence. Run, Bobby, run. Hump, Mom + Daddy, hump… So I was lying in bed with a pair of black Hanes' bikini briefs—posing as the hottest professor since Nietzsche. (Poor guy went nuts from syphilis.)

To pass the time I was reading a detective novel, so when I heard the kitchen door open *sans* accompanying car sounds, I wasn't worried; I hadn't heard Annie's car arrive because I was entranced over Hans murdering Monsignor Caspar with a candelabrum.

"Babe? Come meet your maker," I yell. (You do without for a month and see if you come up with a better line.)

No answer. Shit, she's had a hard day. "You okay, hon?" I hear her coming up the steps—Wait! That is, I hear, but I don't hear *her.* These steps are deliberate and mean, like they want to make peach paint blister, planks screak, nails bend. So just what do they have in mind for me? I'm off the bed, looking frantically at the door, which is blocked open by three huge boxes we never unpacked. Why didn't I listen to my son? Why didn't I buy a damned pistol or shotgun? Even a candelabrum! I did buy a second can of mace, so I reached for it, opening the bed's headboard as quietly as a man in black Hanes could. Those steps weren't quiet, though; they were as insistent as a smoker's cancerous cough.

I pressed to the wall, finger on the mace, ears hearing *Su-reak! Su-reak!* I was shaking and cold, and either had to pee or did so as the steps closed in. The top of the stairs has a small landing four feet from our bedroom door. The footfall reached the last step; I could actually feel its vibration and—a low breathing?

"Fuck you, suckface!" I yelled, diving around the corner and spraying the mace—at nothing. Nearly, in fact, tumbling in a head-dive down the stairs. As I held back I saw muddy footprints on the light oak steps leading up and I heard a whimper-laugh behind. *Cain*, it laughed. I twisted and sprayed again: at nothing, again. No, that's not true. There was a musty smell like a pantry of ferrets had been loosed, and I spotted long ivory fingers closing the door of the study across from our bedroom. Click, went the door's lock. I sprayed stupidly at the door, but my eyes were already watering from the mace. *If you stay up here, you won't be able to see to protect yourself.*

I was down the stairs and out of the house, hacking from the mace. A breeze on my back reminded me that I was nearly nude. Twisting about and about to look at the upper floor windows, I resembled an out-of-season toy soldier from a porno version of *The Nutcracker.*

What's behind me? Nothing. *What's beside me?* Nothing.

When I sprinted around the side of the house, keeping lots of space between me and everything, I saw muddy tracks on the carport, the kitchen door ajar. The tracks came from either the swampy cypress stand or the barn. My heart was beating so fast my eyes ached. Something touched my hand

and I jumped: It was Blackjack, our dog, licking blood dripping from my arm. Somehow I'd cut myself. Then a window broke in Bobby's room. Blackjack growled lowly, his hair bristling.

Until then, I didn't realize how still the land we lived on was. I called Blackjack and we backed toward a storage shed near the road. In the distance a peacock cried. I thought of eyes spreading on its feathers and twisted to check what was at my back, feeling especially vulnerable in a pair of black briefs.

Ten minutes (600 very long seconds) later, Annie pulled into the drive. Holding an ax from the storage shed, I ran for the car, Blackjack following behind. She slammed on the brakes; I could see her stare transfixed at the house even as I got in. Blackjack ripped over me into the back seat.

"There's something inside our house, isn't there?"

The car was in reverse and she was already backing away. Some*thing*, not some*one*.

"Something," I agreed.

So it came that on the way to the Circle K convenience store to find cell service and phone the police, we both told what we'd been afraid to tell. Here's my anti-Wittgensteinian list, followed by Annie's:

1. The night we moved in, I awoke about 2 a.m. to hear Zamfir's brother playing pan flute outside.** I thought it was Bobby watching a late movie, but from our bedroom window I saw him standing outside near three tall pines, staring at a glow near the old barn. Go back to bed, I told myself. Swamp gas. You're just tired from the move, and the kid's just excited from it. He's out whistling in the dark.

2. A week later I heard the flute again, went to Bobby's room and found him staring at a wall, hands very empty

though the flute had played until I opened the door. He claimed he hadn't heard a thing.

*** Dr. Martin: This just might have been me. I play a flute when I'm restless at night, and the swamp carries sounds unbelievably around here. A.F.*

3. The kitten and the cat. I finally told Annie what the vet had said. Before, I'd told her it was a snake.

4. Assorted noises, chalky pale movements, muddy footprints—plus of course, what just happened in the house. I told Annie about the ivory fingers on the door, and grabbing what felt like a finger the day we moved in.

Annie's turn:

1. The day I drove the empty U-Haul truck back, she'd heard Bobby talking in his room. She listened, then decided he was talking on the phone to a Kentucky friend. ("But," I said. "That's right," she agreed. "His phone was lost in the move.")

2. She awoke five nights before, thinking she'd heard the barn door open. When she'd looked out the window, yellowish lights glowed in tree limbs and streams of fog were moving from the barn toward the swamp. Chilled, she noticed fog actually enveloping her inside our room. Next morning she awoke near me, under the covers. "It was like I'd been drugged. And the strangest dream, Dean-o. I dreamed of wobbly little white elves sweeping and dancing inside the barn."

3. She too found muddy prints around the house. They were hoofed, the size of a good fist. Bobby told her they were deer, but a doctor at work told her deer never get that size in Florida.

4. Assorted noises and chalky pale movements that under any other circumstances she would have ignored.

5. Our surviving cat, Hera, awoke her every night, hissing toward the barn. One time Annie looked out and thought she saw a thin, pale woman being prodded along by a tiny rag doll. The vision was so quirky, and came in the middle of the night after we'd shared a bottle of champagne, that she figured she was half-dreaming.

ᙡ

That's it, our anti-Wittgensteinian list. It looks as if the world's not all that we know.

By this time we'd reached the main road in the car. Dressed as I was, I ran a good chance of being picked up for indecent exposure or being shot by some irate Florida cracker. Annie remembered a blanket in the trunk and retrieved it. Great, cat-hairs-in-a-blanket, my favorite thing next to cats. We drove to an orange stand-turned-emporium off the I-75 exit and bought a pair of too-big swimming trunks and a Florida Souvenir T-shirt for me to wear. Annie called and the sheriff's office said someone would be out. "What I really want to buy is a shotgun," I commented on the way back, still sneezing from the blanket. No argument from Annie, just tight, white knuckles on the steering wheel and a set jaw…

Pasco's like a lot of counties in Florida: Fifty years ago the sheriff himself might have come out, spat tobacco juice on my roses, kicked my rooster, petted my dog and concluded: "Coloreds. Or maybe Yankees." But despite our specific failed land development, nearly every county in mid- to south Florida owns some "fastest-growing" statistic. The fastest-growing school district in the nation. The fastest-growing housing. The fastest-growing boat registration. The fastest-growing crime rate. So that wasn't how the high sheriff came. In fact, he didn't come at all, but sent two sleek cruisers, one with a tired-looking female, the other with a cherry-faced, crew-cut blond male. I've heard that police shifts overlap. This was living proof, for the woman cop hung back, her eyelids searching for a bedspread, while the guy cop asked questions and cased the house. You can be sure the floating lights and the pan flute weren't mentioned, but I did tell him about the fingers on the doorknob and Annie did mention our punctured cats and "some strange noises and footprints." We actually had the young guy thumbing his holster guard when:

"Hi, guys. What's going on?" It was Bobby, opening the front door. "Huh! Nice outfit, Dad."

Behind me, I could hear the woman cop's eyelashes click in a yawn.

"How long have you been here, son?" the male cop asked.

Bobby looked from the policeman to me and his mother. *Go ahead, Bobby, we didn't raise you to mistrust the law, did we? Answer him.*

"About an hour."

The hairs on the back of the woman cop's palm loudly tucked themselves in bed.

"An hour?" I asked—a little too harshly?

Bobby flinched. "The track meet was canceled. It's raining in Orlando. I walked upstairs to tell you, but you were asleep. I heard you yelling five minutes later and went and saw the mud I tracked. I cleaned it all up, though—honest. You can go look."

The woman cop was doing everything but snoring now. We signed a field report and they left after one more droopy look from the female. I privately hoped she'd fall asleep and drive into a ditch…

"Where were you when I screamed?" I asked Bobby. We

were all three inside now, and Hera was crawling along his shoulders, looking for a place to perch, eyeing me with her green-yellow devil eyes.

"In my room talking with the cat."

I didn't like the word "with," but let it go.

"Something was in the house, Bobby. Or someone. Didn't you smell the mace I sprayed?"

"*That's* what that was." He rubbed his hand over his nose.

"Your father thought he saw something… an albino animal."

I straightened—maybe that *is* what it was, escaped from one of the three million tourist attractions in the state. Fastest-growing albino population in…

"Neat," Bobby said.

Neat. Round two.

Night clamped like an evil grin. Each window was staring in at me, a lengthy ivory finger waiting under each sill, scraping, sharpening itself against the concrete foundation, waiting, waiting… The moon rose yellow, full. There was a smell that clung to the upstairs. Not the mace, that's biting like a snort of ice-cold pepper, but a ferret smell, a deep musk halfway on the side of nasty. For some reason, I thought of a shepherd looking at the moon and petting his dog. Baa, baa, baa…

But then, where was the wolf?

Thursday, Sept. 27

Three insomniac weeks later: tired, apprehensive, relieved that Annie was beside me—as if something was ready to snatch her away.

Thursdays are my short days; I get home about 1:30. Like I've said, the road to our house is desolate. Its blacktop's been bleached by the Florida sun and there's a half-mile stretch to the nearest house, another half-mile before three more, and all this peppered with cul-de-sacs, cypress trees, swamp, and litter from good old boys too cheap to hire a garbage service, too mean to burn their own.

My half-mile neighbor (I'd seen him mowing on a small tractor) stood in the middle of the road, waving me over. His little gold glasses, which Annie said made him look like a bit actor in a Nazi movie, gleamed with anger. I figured someone had dumped milk cartons on his land and he wanted me to help lynch them.

"I'm your neighbor," he told me, walking around to the driver's side. "My little girl's missing."

"Oh no. I'm sorry. Do you want me to—" I stopped, at a loss for words, and looked around stupidly as if I might spot her for him.

"I saw her playing with your boy the other day. Robbie. That his name?"

"Bobby. When was that?"

"Tuesday afternoon."

Tuesday. Christ, he was supposed to be at another cross country meet. Is that all it does in Florida, rain in the afternoon?

"I'd like to talk to your boy," he said. "My little girl's just twelve."

His face looked like cast concrete. This could turn much more serious than anyone would like, much faster than anyone would like. "How long's she been missing?" I asked, turning off the car engine.

"Since some time last night. She wasn't in her room when Lucy went to wake her."

I wanted to defend Bobby, say he's an honors student

(that doesn't carry far in America) and a good athlete (which might get him somewhere, but then what about the missing cross country meets?) Instead I asked, "Have you called the police?"

"Right away. They've been and gone hours ago."

"Do you have a picture of her?"

"Lucy's having duplicates made right now."

Again, I looked around: Not a pretty place for a child to be lost. Of America's four types of poisonous snakes, Florida has four and a half. Plus alligators, bobcats, scorpions, spiders, fire ants, swamp, swamp, and swamp. "You've searched everywhere?"

"People from church are coming. Lucy and me've been nearly everywhere…" he paused to look in the direction of my house at the end of the road.

"Do you want to—" I faltered, for a car stopped behind. A woman with greenish blonde hair got out. I suppose she'd been good-looking in high school, even a prom queen, though she was a country beanpole now and her eyes were deep-set, worse than a fashion model's. Well, if Bobby disappeared, I don't suppose Annie'd be running for Lady Gaga look-alike on hearing the news. The woman walked up with a handful of photos, so I got out of the car and nodded.

"Our neighbor," my neighbor said. "Lucy, my wife," he finished.

"Dean," I told them both. "Dean Kirby."

"Mr. Kirby just asked if I'd like to look down on his land for Cristy."

Well, not really, he didn't ask. But he was getting ready to, so we'll let that go.

"… So you wait here, and I'll go," my neighbor, whose name I still didn't know, told his wife. She nodded, then handed me a picture of her daughter Cristy, as if she were passing communion at a service.

"Pretty girl," I mumbled. And she was, but what twelve-year-old isn't unless they're on an ice cream and cookie diet? We got in my car.

"Didn't catch your name," I prompted while driving.

"Didn't throw it," my neighbor answered, as if that response were scrolled into his brain. "Ralph," he relented, remembering he'd invited himself onto my property. Such etiquette. He even opened the farm gate to my yard.

"Just put that up?" he asked, getting back in.

"A week ago."

"Gonna put in some livestock?"

"Just keep things out."

He gave a snort that I suspect meant I was a fool for thinking a gate would keep out Florida wildlife.

Up until then, afternoon green in Florida had been a lovely color, but this afternoon looked dusty and wrong. We stopped at the tool shed to check if she'd gotten locked in. I suppose that made sense. As Ralph looked, I glanced to the house, remembering three weeks before when I stood in my skivvies with Blackjack. Where was Blackjack? I called, but no answer. Neighbor Ralph was evidently satisfied that the shed was empty. He came to my side:

"Medium-sized black dog?"

I nodded and called again.

"Your boy had him when he was playing with Cristy."

I really wanted him to stop associating Bobby with Cristy. What *was* Bobby doing talking to a twelve-year old girl, though? We started toward the house. For a second I recoiled, thinking someone was inside again. Then I recognized Blackjack's nose pressed against a window. He'd gotten locked in. But how? I was everything but philosophically sure I'd let him out. I'm not philosophically sure I have a wife and son, or even a body, if you catch my drift.

I let Blackjack out and got myself and neighbor Ralph a Coke. He'd been eyeing the barn a hundred yards behind the house. I'd only been there twice myself, once before we moved in, to be sure (not philosophically!) there weren't termites; once after we moved in, to be sure there wasn't an antique Packard hidden in a stall, or a cache of Confederate money in the loft.

Urp. A quiet one, but the Coke's carbonation was taking hold. We were heading through embarrassingly high grass, with the sun working its way into a real good heat.

"Need to be careful about this," Ralph said, indicating the grass. "Lots of snakes."

It wasn't really on cue, because we took about fifteen more steps and Blackjack had gone tearing after a rabbit when we heard a low buzzing. Ralph grabbed my elbow and pointed ten feet ahead. A little brown and tan beauty—almost bone or ivory—its triangular head flicking a forked tongue, its tail vibrating nervously.

"Watch this," Ralph said, his red face beaming. He pulled a cigar from his shirt pocket, sheaved between several nerd pens stuck there, lit it, gave a few puffs, and flipped it at the snake. I saw a shivering of grass where the snake slithered away, while the cigar lay six feet off where it'd been knocked by the snake's strike.

"Damn."

"Faster than two bolts of lightning hitting one another." He walked over to pick up the cigar, dropped and stomped it. For this I was grateful, for that stogie's manufacturer had used canceled foreign stamps instead of tobacco leaf. Snake venom could only have improved the smell.

We reached the barn. Ralph looked hopeful when he saw the loft. "Cristy! Cristy!" he called. "She could've climbed up there and been afraid to come down," he explained.

Blackjack sniffed, curious.

"Cristy! Cristy!" he yelled again, spying the ladder and heading up. I watched him climb, his country pants loose as a woman's skirt. He slowed near the top—probably the same dark vision had come to him as to me—maybe something was up there that he didn't want to see. Then he went on. I could see his head bob, could hear a few mud daubers hum excitedly. I noticed something in a stall and walked over. A pitchfork jabbed in the corner, but what... a rag doll. For a moment I worried it might be his child's, but a scaffolding of spider webs covered the pitchfork's handle, so unless the doll had dug under and stuck itself to the prongs, someone had done this long ago.

"Nothing up here!" he shouted down. "You still there?"

"Yeah, I'm checking these stalls." I kicked old straw over the doll—no sense in him seeing something like that with a kid missing.

By the time he climbed down I'd checked the three other stalls and stood in a storage room. It looked different from when we first moved here: neater, tools hung and cleaned. Had Bobby gotten a wild hair? It was damned sure I didn't, and I couldn't see Annie sweating out here. An out-of-place hint of chalk dust hung in the air. I know that smell well— white lung disease being a professorial hazard.

"Hellfire."

I turned to see my neighbor in the door. He took off his Nazi gold glasses and cleaned them.

"This is just like it looked when old O'Hara owned the

place."

"The man that had it before me?"

"Naw, that guy just kept this place just to show off to his girlfriends. He wouldn't know a cow-pie from an apple pie less he took a bite. A city fella."

I tried not to be offended.

"Old O'Hara was the first person to figure you could pasture cows in Pasco County. Takes an Irishman to break the ice. He owned quite a bit of land around here. His house was two hundred yards up the road. This was just one of his barns." While he talked, he picked up the strangest wood implement I've ever seen: It looked like a four-foot smoking pipe, except its bowl was solid, as was its stem.

"I remember the old man carrying this. He called it a 'shy lilah,' said it was to beat off any pretty girls that come around." He turned it over; it spun on its own, since its bowl threw it off balance. "S-H-I-L-L-E-L-A-G-H—That's how he spelled it. If you ever think of getting rid of this—"

Blackjack began barking, so Ralph replaced the whatever-it-was on the wall, and we went outside. A police car was at the gate, with two policemen inside. No, one was a woman, the sleepy-time gal—I recognized her. I called Blackjack and motioned them to come in and held his collar. The male cop got out and opened the gate.

"They told me they'd stop this way when you got home," Ralph said. "Guess my wife told them you were home."

I noticed Ralph had a way of addressing the sky behind me. "That's all right. I'd want the whole neighborhood fine-combed if my boy were missing too."

"That shillelagh. If you ever want to sell it, I'd pay."

I nodded. Why in the world's he so worried about a stick when his kid's missing? Blackjack jerked my wrist, lurching.

"That old man, was he a friend of yours?" I asked my neighbor as the lady cop drove the police car through the gate.

"Up until his grandson got killed and his daughter burned the house across from mine down."

"Killed?"

"Pitchforked. A little boy pitchforked in the middle of a dirt road."

I snapped at Blackjack's collar, remembering what I'd seen in the stall.

It *was* the woman deputy from the other day, though much fresher. She even managed a nod. They wanted to search the area and the house. Fine, I told them. We all four went inside: nothing. Completely boring, though my dirty underwear stuck out of the hamper, not the black ones, at least. Still, the woman cop snickered.

Since Ralph and I had just searched the barn, the cops let it go, just giving the vicinity the once over. We joined in a few courageous shouts: "Cristy! Cristy!" Our voices already sounded forlorn and I wondered how soon shouts would be replaced with grim, plodding footsteps and downcast eyes. Not a pleasant activity, searching for a child. Neighbor Ralph let out a last sad croak, then walked out the gate, refusing a ride from the police, calling Cristy's name as he walked up the road. The cops turned to me.

"His church is going to search the area tonight, did he tell you?" the woman deputy asked, nodding toward my neighbor's slumped receding back.

"Maybe there's something you should see. Come on."

When we got to the stall the rag doll was gone. I called Blackjack, figuring he'd taken it, but of course he wouldn't come—he's obedient like that.

"There was a rag doll under that pitchfork. Cobwebs all over it like it had been there years. O'Hara's grandson. Wasn't he pitchforked like that?"

"O'Hara? Old man O'Hara?" the male deputy asked, looking at the pitchfork, which was rusted on the business end.

I nodded.

"My dad was sheriff then, drove him to Chattahoochee. Said he howled like a dog all the way."

The woman looked across to another stall. "There it is."

We walked over. The rag doll slumped against the stall's back wall just as if it had been staring at us. It was perfectly clean of holes or any marks. The woman cop bent.

"Damn!" she yelled, dropping the doll. Blood flowed down her palm and she gave the doll a kick through a rotted board into the next stall. "A hat pin stuck me." She grimaced and held her wrist. When her companion pried her fingers loose blood spurted.

"It did a bang-up job and hit your radial artery," he said, pressing her finger back.

They left for the emergency room and I went back into the stall for the doll. No dice. I did find a long black hat pin, though. It was still sticky with the woman's blood and looked as if it had penetrated a full inch. How?

⊱⊰

Annie, Bobby and I did join the church group in searching that afternoon. The preacher gave a prayer, and we performed the penance of holding hands. I say penance because a short-haired Teuton vice-gripped my right hand. This woman weighed three hundred pounds and must have thought my hand a wiener schnitzel the way she squeezed. Prayer done, we padded off, keeping a two-arms' stretch between us. Most of the men had broom handles to scour the ground and scare off snakes. We looked like the Village from Hell. I'm sure if we had found the poor girl she would've run the other way.

After half an hour, our house came into view. How disappointing that sight must have been to Ralph and Lucy Settles, for it meant that one-half the search had passed without finding their Cristy. There was shouting down the line, a jumble of words and gasps and high notes.

"My God, someone's been snake-bitten," Annie said.

Bobby's eyes protruded as he looked in that direction.

"No, it's just Maureen Jackson," a nearby woman told us. "She's got the gift of tongues."

Everyone hurried to Maureen. To my horror I saw that she was the Teuton who'd done so much damage to my hand. I felt certain she was having an epileptic seizure, but Annie shook her head. We caught the tail-end of her act, which included shouting nonsense and gesturing wildly. A brown, spindly woman wiped spittle from the Teuton's mouth, then held the handkerchief in front of her own thin lips, as if tasting it, to intone: "What the Lord said through Maureen was that we shouldn't double back. We should go on over there." She vaguely pointed to a spot in our land that bordered a swampy area.

No one seemed to doubt that inspiration was better than logic. So we stumbled in that muck for fifteen or twenty minutes before two people shouted "Over here! Over here!"

A robin's egg blue blouse with white lace frills was floating in tar-black water.

"Cris-ty!" Mrs. Settles sunk to her knees and grabbed the blouse. Her husband put a hand on her shoulder and she wailed even louder, "Cris-ty!" blowing us backward with her anguish.

Bobby was sticking closer to his mother than he had since grade school, so I knew that this salivating made an impression. We trudged on. A girl about Bobby's age was helping out; Leslie, we later learned, was her name.

"NE-YOW! NE-YOW!" The shrill noise stopped me and Annie dead.

"It's just peacocks," Leslie told us. "This is the back of the witch's land."

The girl said 'witch' so matter-of-factly that I did a double take: She was medium height for her age (fourteen or fifteen), had sandy hair bleached from the sun (in a ponytail), and was a lot cuter than I'd expect a child from this church to be (her pug nose aided immensely). But to believe in witches?

She must have caught something in my appraisal, for she added, "She's not really a witch, she's a sculptor. She does magic tricks for little kids, so everyone calls her a witch."

By this time our spacing had thinned because of the swamp water, despite the supposedly dry season. A group clustered near our fence. They were staring quietly ahead, several with crossed arms. One man spit tobacco juice very purposefully over the fence. I asked Leslie:

"Don't the neighbors like this woman?"

"Less than they like teenagers."

When we reached the fence, I saw why: Ahead, in a well-cut lawn of two acres or more, amid drooping Spanish moss and oak and cypress and pine, were over a hundred white statues of fairy book creatures standing anywhere from one to twenty feet. Annie grabbed my arm and nodded to a spot to our right; a fanged, white frog the size of a chair dared anyone to climb the fence. Evening echoes of a big bullfrog added to the statue's fierceness. Some statues had greenish moss covering them. In particular, a trampish figure doffing his hat and standing on one leg struck me.

"You shouldn't be looking at this," an older woman told Leslie.

What? I wondered. *A tramp?* But then—yes, there were naughties stuck amid the fairyland creatures. Things much worse than dragons, dearie—penises and mammaries and exaggerated asses.

Bobby laughed as Leslie whispered in his ear. He ambled over to me and his mother. "Leslie says there's a six-foot tit in the middle of the yard."

"Bobby!" Annie exclaimed with embarrassment.

But two men by the fence had already turned sharply.

Kids say the darndest things.

The Teutonic woman warbled some more, so we circled around, and neighbor Ralph and his wife and the preacher walked to the sculptress's door and knocked. We were about twenty yards away, close enough that I could see that on answering she was somehow amused at the motley crew, though Annie later swore to me that the woman had been staring at her the whole time.

Fairbain evidently agreed to their coming on her land, so we all walked among the fairy creatures—and yes, the huge breast, which turned out to be two huge breasts. Ralph and two men descended in a gap between them that looked like the mouth of a cave. Annie and I stopped, curious, and the creator of the bosoms joined us. She was rather tall, with dishwater blonde hair, but what stood out most about her were her hands. They were huge and red, from all the sculpting she did, I presumed. For a moment she stood silently, working those huge hands as if massaging them, but when the three men started back up she let them drop to her side and turned to us and smiled. "You two are the ones who bought the old O'Hara place, aren't you? Why don't you stop by for dinner sometime next week? I'd love to talk under more pleasant circumstances."

Monday, Oct. 1

It was a cinch the Victory Assembly of Ever-lasting Life or whatever it was called wouldn't be visiting with fried chicken after news spread about Bobby's comment. I even half-expected a cross burning that night when we left Fairbain's property, but the young minister with the crevassed forehead surprised me by shaking my hand as if it were a milk cow's tit. No doubt he later dipped his palm in cleansing waters when he heard what my son said. If there's one thing worse than four-letter words, it's a three-letter one.

So that left Alice Fairbain, the witch sculptress, for our local social life. Annie and I did go over for dinner on Monday. Even in October, Florida's heat bore down on us as we walked over the tiny bridge to her house. I say bridge, though it was no more than three culverts with blacktop drizzled over them.

"Everything's still so green," Annie commented.

We spotted only one shrub with the slightest hint of autumnal coloration—nothing like the oranges, reds, purples, and yellows that seasonally splash up North. I noticed what I thought was an albino deer standing along the creek bed.

"Did you see that deer?"

"It was a goat, Dean. Didn't you see its beard?"

"A goat? That's your fantasies."

In reply, she turned to bat those eyelashes of hers that can dance a circle of laughter.

The front of Alice Fairbain's land was bordered by an eight-foot iron fence. Through it, her statuary glowed ghostly white, especially in early evening. For a mailbox she'd constructed a small dragon's head with two claws for pedestals. We both stopped.

"Not so long in our country's past, this woman could have been burned as a witch," Annie commented, her fingertip hesitating before the dragon's head. Annie had already commented that Fairbain's gaze made her uneasy, though we wrote this off to the circumstances of the previous week. That girl was still missing. The police had come back in force on the second day with all shapes and sizes of sniffing dogs. But the dogs hadn't accomplished any more than the Teutonic woman, for they homed in on the same spot where we'd found the blue snatch of dress.

Annie at last touched the dragon's head mailbox, even rubbed it on a lark, and we opened the gate and walked in, to the immediate barking of a very large dog chained near a kiln by the house, and the squalling of peacocks. While poor Blackjack had been cowed by the troupe of German shepherds the police had brought on our land, I doubt very much that this dog had been. I'm not much more on dogs than cats, but it looked like some type of mastiff or maybe a Great Dane. About 180 pounds' worth. The dog hadn't been out when we'd been searching for poor Cristy.

I say 'poor Cristy,' but her parents are whom we see suffering. Her mother was walking the deserted whalebone roads just last night, calling Cristy's name; following was the father, pleading with his wife to come home. Their wailing counterpoint filled the swampy air, silencing even frogs.

I suppose Cristy's disappearance lent the statuary a gloomy cast, despite some comical statues: an impish four-foot roach begging for food, a bearded old man kissing a young virgin's astonished breast. We didn't have time to evaluate, for the huge dog bounded from the kiln. It was a dirty yellow-orange and shaved like a lion. If it hadn't been so big and galumphing toward us, I would have laughed.

"He's friendly," Alice Fairbain's pleasing, deep voice assured us. She stood by the kiln—even from there her large-boned hands stood out, twisting once more, as if working a spell. She stepped from under its eaves to call the lion-dog, whose tail was wagging furiously, which posed more of a threat, considering its size, than its teeth. I had forgotten—I don't know how—another particular about Fairbain: Even in the reddish evening sun her eyes showed such a clear blue-gray that I could perceive individual fibers in her iris. Those eyes and her high cheeks captivated me. Only determination let me again notice the ironic twist in her lip—as if she made a practice of laughing at the world. Her hands took Annie's hand and squeezed; I watched Annie's impressed reaction— to Fairbain's grip? To her gray eyes? To some animal magnetism? When my turn came for a handshake, her dog growled. Speaking of animal magnetism. The antipodal type, that is.

"Rex. It's okay." She turned to us. "I was just out checking the kiln's temperature. Would you care to wander about the yard? It'll be a lot more pleasant than last time, I promise."

She promised pleasant, but the more we trod on that strange, springy Florida grass called St. Augustine, the more I felt an underlying grotesquery, even menace, hovering about the statues. An otherwise cute pixie, for instance, was graced with a razor-sharp grin edging toward rapier-point ears. And the pervading ghastly white of all the statues added a sepulchral pall, relieved only by occasional greenish mold.

"That green," Fairbain explained as I rubbed the slight fuzz, "is purposeful. I soak them in buttermilk and wrap them in rags for two weeks until *Voila!*" One of her red slippers (encasing heavily veined feet that matched her heavy hands) nudged a greenly drunken leprechaun several times, almost as if she were chastising it for being out of line. There were loups-garous, vampires, gargoyles, Assyrian griffins, and various depictions of the devil mixed with playful pixies, fairies, and occasional dinosaurs.

"Where do you get all these ideas?" Annie asked.

"Tea."

Not Fairbain's answer, but a grunt emanating from a walking, talking hulk who completed the yard's panoply of myth: the original Jewish golem, come among gentiles to wreak destruction with tannic acid and caffeine—better known as tea. Annie tightened her hold on my arm and forced a smile at the man, who no more acknowledged it than would have a statue, say the pale Robin Hood fifty feet away. We sipped

the tea, and the golem ** disappeared. I mean this literally;

Annie asked for sweetener but he was gone—off on silent wheels, like some movie ghost, with Alice Fairbain left holding the service tray in her callused hands.

** *Dr. Martin: Aaron Wasserstrum ("the golem") escaped from Hitler's Germany while in the womb. He certainly has reason to hulk, for his father wasn't so lucky as his mother and never made it to New York. Could Mr. Kirby be revealing a wee prejudice against the Hebrew race? such a delight on top of his academic cynicism.* A.F.

Annie tipped her cup toward the largest sculpture, the infamous concrete breasts that our beloved son spotted. Were they truly under an apple tree? In Florida? Our hostess led us forward. I blushed at their tinted pink nipples. Close by them again—and this was a surprise—I saw that actual steps descended between the breasts, not sloped earth as I'd sup-posed when Ralph and the two men had walked down.

"I call it 'Persephone's Escalator.'"

Annie and I laughed.

Half an hour later, Fairbain explained over dinner—I blanched on discovering we were eating barbecued lamb—how delighted she was to find someone who even knew who Persephone was. "The locals—you've met them—they all wrinkle their noses on seeing statues looking like graveyard monuments. To them, Persephone must be some communist aunt I'm hiding, instead of the ancient Greek goddess who ruled Hades and was responsible for our seasons. You should have seen the roving deputies the day before yesterday—they all were itching to write me a ticket for obscenity. Corrupting their bloodhounds, I suppose."

The inside of her house—did I say? I suppose not—the inside was as full of her "children" as the outside. "My chil-dren" is the term she uses for all her works—admittedly, the woman is quite an artist. Most of these household "children" were toddlers; that is, they ranged from inches to two feet in height. But they were everywhere: hung from the ceiling with fishing wire, scattered on shelves, in nooks and crannies, in-between the stairway banisters. Their subject matter was more realistic than those outside: all human forms, though some single emotion eerily dominated each tiny face and body. All in all, hers was not a house I'd choose to live in, but then I'm not driven by artistic compulsion.

Dinner continued, and I found myself wavering about Fairbain once more; she was entertaining and cosmopolitan in many ways. I didn't find myself wavering in the least about her golem of a servant, though, even if he did serve a fine Irish coffee.

One other thing about that visit. As we were drinking those after-dinner coffees, the lion-dog began howling outside. I just said that the interior statuary was smaller and more realistic; not entirely so, for by the entrance door squatted two griffins nearly eight feet apiece. As Fairbain got up to see about the dog I noticed that both griffins seemed changed. Where they'd sat like obedient overgrown pups before, they now extended claws five feet into the air, as if ready to shred anything that walked in. I whispered to Annie, but she was unsure what they looked like when we first entered. I let it go, for the dog, Rex, came slinking inside, tail between its legs, hiding behind Fairbain's hippie-time skirt with its purple and gold paisley eyes. Funny, but she had barely bothered to look out to see what upset pooch.

"Someone coming?" For I thought I'd heard a car door slam. But then, maybe the golem had lurched into a tree.

"Just a raccoon. Rex is afraid of raccoons ever since he was bitten."

I found that hard to believe considering Rex's size, but there he was, whimpering.

"We really need to get home. Our boy will be wondering, even though we left a note," Annie said.

"Yes, it is late." Fairbain switched the porch light on and off, on and off—Nervousness? A signal?—and we said our goodbyes and left for a dark but uneventful walk home amid fog rising from the local swampland.

We reached home to learn that Bobby had come in second in the 6K run. I'd rather he won a journalism award, and no doubt Annie would rather a pre-med scholarship, but these days a parent whose kid doesn't drop out has plenty to crow about—no need to worry why he stays in.

Monday, Oct. 8

Columbus Day, but no new continents for the Kirbys.

After a second dinner visit with Alice Fairbain, an odd thing happened: Annie went into a sneezing fit, so long that both Bobby and I tired of saying *Gott gesundheit*, even though it's a pet family superstition. After two Contac, she still sneezed. I swear she sneezed even in her sleep.

She's been back to visit Alice Fairbain at least three times, maybe more. It's good to see her develop a friend so quickly after our move, but… am I jealous? I haven't made a single friend. The professors at St. Dominic's fall into two camps: old farts who think Milton's a contemporary, and the young and upwardly mobile who think, in their heart of hearts, that *Northern Exposure* is a timely literary statement.

Wednesday, Oct. 10

How to write about today? From the beginning, I suppose. In the late afternoon Annie called from Fairbain's house. I recognized her voice even before I'd heard it because of the omnipresent sniffle she'd developed. But I have to say that if it weren't for that sniffle, I might not have recognized her voice because it droned with a virus-like tiredness. "Alice has asked me to stay over and model for a full-size sculpture. You and Bobby can go out to eat later, can't you?" / "Yes, if I can find him," I responded, "But with your cold, do you—" / "Try the neighbor girl he met on the search: Leslie, remember? Her phone number's on the calendar in his room." / "Okay, I love you," I said. / "Okay," she answered.

Okay?

Bobby wasn't at Leslie's when I called. Sunlight swam with a hot ambiance that left me feeling about to drown. Hanging up the landline phone I shouted for Bobby, then for Blackjack. No answer. Something was in the air.

You know how your eye catches movement and your neck bristles as if Cro-Magnon hair was growing from it? I was standing in the kitchen and thought of the mace, but damned if I wasn't afraid to go upstairs in my own house. Then Blackjack nudged the back screen. I skipped toward his friendly muzzle, but he took off like a *Lassie* sequel. I followed. Outside, the cedars and palmettos glowed with the sun's blood red. As Blackjack neared the barn, Bobby called. His tone made me run double-time.

At the barn's entrance, its dirt floor and stall walls were bathed in the sun's same blood red, and a smell of musty hay bit my sinuses. *Maybe this is what's bothering Annie…* but I didn't get beyond that thought, for Bobby whimpered "Dad," more like a wheeze than a word, his voice coming from the stall where the pitchforked doll had been. I ran, catching my shirt and ribs on a nail in the stall's door. Bobby was backed into a corner, staring. Holding my side, I turned to see the same damned doll, again pronged by the pitchfork, but now squirming (yes, squirming!) as if to free itself. Broken pieces of plaster and a maroon/black blood spattered the stall's straw. The doll twisted to stare angrily at me, then back to my son.

"Dad…"

"Come here, Bobby. Get out of there." I talked low, like I always imagined a snake-whisperer would.

The doll shifted its gaze to my right side. I realized the nail had put a good-sized gash there as I felt blood pooling around my waistband. The doll knocked the pitchfork against one corner wall, then another, still keeping its eyes on my side and the blood.

"Come here, Bobby. Come on out."

"I'm afraid."

(*No kidding. Me too, son.*) "Bobby."

He edged toward me, and the doll—at least I think it did this—tippled the pitchfork. We both jumped. Blackjack scooted between our legs and snapped at the doll. He must have tangled up the pitchfork, for it wound up in his side and when we tried to pull it out he got scared and flipped a prong into my right foot. At least that's what Wittgenstein, Bobby, and I told the vet where Blackjack got some antibiotics. Did the damned rag doll twist the pitchfork around somehow? I don't know, because we ran from that barn like it was an infested snake hole.

After the vet's and the Emergency Walk-in clinic we took a trip to Wal-Mart. A 12-gauge shotgun costs $198.98, plus $7.53 for shells on Mastercard or Visa, your choice.

Driving back, I had visions of the doll's mouth opened in a scream, and maroon/black blood dribbling down its dress.

"Dad, watch where you're driving."

"Dad, I want to tell you something. Did you buy some statues from that Fairbain woman? Because there's ten of them in the loft now."

"Dad, slow down."

"Dad?"

I couldn't answer. All I thought of was how the trigger would feel on my finger. I've never shot a gun in my life and needed to prepare myself.

Blackjack wouldn't come near the barn when we went in this time. But the doll wasn't staring or twisting. It lay limp, exactly as I'd seen it two weeks or so before when Ralph came over, when the police looked at it. In fact, its dress was still bunched where the policewoman had pinched it. I had to do something. After trying to put the shells in backwards and fumbling for the safety, I shot the goddamned doll. Shreds of cotton puffed, then settled on the dirt. The face, the damned smiling face, remained intact, looking not the least bit friendly. And I swear this is true: The smile had twisted into a snarl. Bobby took the gun and finished the face with a direct hit that drove it into the dirt. We heard Blackjack hack outside and remembered the vet warned not to let him get excited. On leaving the stall we heard faint scratching. A rat, we told each other. A rat.

Wittgenstein, the world's pressing in… Are you sure we really know it?

Saturday, Oct. 13

Annie said she was going to spend the night at Fairbain's.

"Why, in god's name? I thought we were going into Tampa."

She coughed. "I told you: Alice is sculpting a model of me. She wants to have it finished by tomorrow afternoon. She has a show Monday."

"Mom," Bobby whined from the bottom of the stairs.

Annie peeked out of our bedroom, rubbing her lovely neck that I haven't touched in two weeks—since we met Fairbain. I thought I saw skin slough off under her hand, like a bad sunburn peeling. The only thing, she was as white as a cloud.

The Settles' girl was still missing. Once in a while, I'd hear dogs barking, but it wasn't the police. They think she was kidnapped and are busy running profiles through computers.

Friday, Oct. 19

Annie has had a bad cough for two weeks. She went to the hospital's employee doctor, but besides an accumulation of fluid in her lungs he could find nothing wrong and has recommended an allergy specialist. I'm hoping the cough is what's influencing her attitude, which has been weird enough that Bobby and I decided to keep the encounter with the doll away from her, though she heard the shots even from Fairbain's and saw the shotgun the next day. We said we were shooting a snake—and missed.

How strange: I'm as worried about Annie as I was about Bobby when we first moved down. She seems to have acquired all his oddity, while he himself has returned to normal. I attribute his change to Leslie. If I were fifteen, I'd cake on Clearasil and talk on the phone to her every night for an hour or so, too, because she's cute as a button. I spotted them in our yard this afternoon. She looked like a tropical flower weaving about a rainforest. Lately I've been giving him lectures about another dirty three letter word (s-e-x), hoping to allay that flower from blossoming into a premature pod.

But back to Annie. She's been downright spooky (to steal Bobby's favorite word). Staring out the windows at night, staring at me when she thinks I'm not looking. I don't mean a love look, I mean staring like, 'Who is this creature and why is he on my planet?' If I didn't know better I'd think she was having an affair. With the resident doctor they have now? But she hates doctors. With Fairbain? We are facing the new millennium, after all. But Annie? No way.

I'm writing this while she's asleep, while she's coughing and turning, as well she should be after what happened this evening:

She had gone to the convenience store, saying the fresh air would do her good. We needed eggs for a cake. She said baking a cake would do her good. Anyway, by the store is a house, and by this house were a fire truck and two police cars. It seems that the woman who lived there, a retiree from some vague city up North, had phoned because two (not just one) of her cats had climbed a tree. My favorite animal, up to its old tricks. The medievals certainly had things right by labeling cats as witches' familiars. Anyway, Annie, being a normally curious human being, watched from the fence as a fireman rescued the first cat, then ascended for the second. She didn't notice the old woman creeping toward her. Suddenly—Annie's never seen this woman before—the woman scratches Annie's right cheek, screaming so loudly that the fireman, who by now has gotten the second cat, drops it and falls himself. The other firemen rush to help him. Meanwhile the cats both run off and the woman pulls out a small pistol that she waves at Annie, shouting something about the mark of Cain. She fires and misses. She cocks the trigger and… the young policeman, Annie says, had no choice. He shot the old woman. Her body, Annie says, arched in a hiss, then dropped flat.

The police drove Annie home. She told Bobby and me all this and showed us the three fingernail marks in her cheek. Her blood had dried as dark as the local swamp water. She described again how the woman jerked and slumped, falling at her feet like a bundle of dirty laundry. "Like dirty laundry," she repeated, while rubbing her cheek, almost slashing it herself. I reached to stop her, but she pulled away with a wild look. "Like dirty laundry." Did she spit this at me? She climbed the stairs for bed. Blood in the form of a handprint marred her tan slacks, evidently from where the mortally wounded woman had grabbed her.

Later I walked from our study to peek in the bedroom after hearing an especially hollow cough. She was tossing, sweating though we had the air-conditioning igloo cold. One hour later, I checked again: This time no sweating, despite her tossing under a sheet and three blankets. I touched her forehead—cool, as if body heat was seeping out, and her skin was slick, as if oil was oozing from her pores along with that body heat. Her hands clutched wildly at a blanket and her legs worked like they were climbing. Her pants with the bloody handprint lay tossed over a chair, and I thought of the still-missing child. Annie's legs began thrashing. Should I awaken her from the dream, I wondered. No, she'd only remember the nightmare around her.

Saturday, Oct. 20

As I laundered the pants the next morning, Leslie's older sister, Abby, knocked on the door. When I answered, Blackjack sat calmly on the porch by her as if she were his master, not anyone in the Kirby family.

"You must have quite a way with animals."

She ignored me and introduced herself, saying that she heard Bobby talking about my specialty being folklore. I opened the door to the little charmer.

Tuesday, Oct. 23

She's been back every day now and she's read a borrowed book every night—God knows she couldn't be doing any homework. And God knows if Annie weren't spending all her time at Fairbain's—despite her sickness—she'd wonder about the persistence of this teenage girl, whose hair bounces curls on curls of brown and whose cheeks glow rose, if cheeks (not makeup) ever deserved to be called that color.

Annie excuses her absence by claiming there's something on our property that's making her sick. Bobby and I mucked up the old hay and burned it, but this only sent her into hacking convulsions in the night.

Wednesday, Oct. 24

Two hunters found Cristy Settles' body in a pond on Fairbain's far back land. I'm sure that the police had already dragged the pond once. Although the Pasco sheriff and the newspapers are tight-lipped, the rumor mill at the local convenience store has more than enough grisly gossip. The hunters found her at the edge of the water, half under a log. Crosses were branded onto the child. A turtle or alligator had eaten through the rope pinning her at the bottom of the holding pond and she'd floated upwards—minus her head. Driving on into work, I kept seeing the photograph of that child, her healthy cheeks reflecting the camera's flash, a last baby tooth missing and ready to grow, that ridiculous pink country bow in her hair. I thought of Lucy Settles wandering and wailing like a banshee, her husband Ralph dogging her steps like an overworked zombie.

ℂ℟ℜ℠

I know this is cowardly, but when I came home that evening I wanted to sneak by their house unnoticed and even thought about putting the car in neutral and coasting. When I passed, the windows were closed and shades were drawn—but hadn't a shade lifted?

Unpleasant thoughts occurred as I drove on: After the Settles' house were only our house, Fairbain's, and Leslie and Abby's house. Then there were Fairbain's "children" and her pond. There was Abby and her insatiable curiosity about folklore—well, witchcraft is what her conversation always turned to, odd aspects such as voodoo and mind control. "Fascianato," I told her, feeling prissy and doctoral. She commenced to tell me more than I'd ever known about the Evil Eye. Abby… there were certainly enough bizarre oddities on Fairbain's property to attract a Manson-type personality. I sat in my car staring at my gate, picturing Abby's schoolgirl eyes. Impossible. She was too kindly… I opened the gate and drove in, to ponder well into the night, barely listening to Bobby as we had TV dinners. (Annie was, of course, at Fairbain's posing for a yet another sculpture. "A bigger, more spectacular one. Life-size. I think—ka-huh, ka-huh—my cough's clearing a little.")

"They'd dragged that pond twice," Bobby said as I chewed a Salisbury steak, scraping the aluminum tray for dirty gravy. "Once just four days ago when Leslie and me fished in it."

I looked to my son, his pink eyes. "Leslie and *I*."

"Hell, Dad, aren't you listening? They dragged the pond for the second time four days ago. That Cristy girl was alive four days ago. Leslie's sister Abby heard she was killed with a pitchfork. She heard there were cement scrapings under her fingernails." He paused, munching on the TV Dinner. "I think you should do something about mom. Leslie's sister Abby thinks—"

"Do something? She's been to four doctors." I was pretty sure I knew what Abby thought, but I couldn't see how it would do any good for Bobby to think his mother the victim of someone's Evil Eye, or worse, that she was becoming a South Florida zombie. Even a folklore specialist has limits where he bows to modern psychology.

I looked to Bobby's pink eyes. He didn't avert them but stared angrily.

So much for psychology.

Saturday, Oct. 27

Cristy's funeral was today. Bobby and I went, and I saw Annie with Fairbain in the back of the church. Both of them wore tinted glasses. Fairbain pointed to a pew and my wife entered obediently, stumbling as Fairbain gripped her arm and pushed her in. Annie coughed through the first half of the service. When I looked back later, neither she nor Fairbain were there.

Monday, Oct. 29

Are my feelings for Abby preventing me from seeing something? Still reading a book a day and visiting me nearly every day, she's taken to cooking dinner for us. I'm not sure this is right, even though her sister's here with Bobby. My wife, of course, is posing at Alice Fairbain's. Forever posing. Forever. She's been calling in sick. Now, I too must wonder: Is she drugged? Hypnotized? In love? What?

Halloween

Tomorrow is a religious holiday in the Catholic Church. Other professors tell me that a lot of the kids will come to class with ashes on their foreheads: "Remember, Man, that thou art dust, and to dust thou shalt return…"

Saturday, Nov. 3

A week after Cristy's funeral I was awakened at night by a single scream and looked out our second story window to see flames shoot from the Settles' house. I phoned 911. When I ran downstairs, Annie was coughing fluidly while staring out the front window. Frankly, I was happy she was home, so I tried not to listen too closely to the cough. Bobby ran out from his room.

"Let's get in the car and go," I said, pointing to our kitchen's fire extinguisher.

That fire extinguisher felt stupid by my side as soon as we turned the corner, for the blaze was as high as the surrounding cypress stand. When we got out, the house was too hot to approach. I even had Bobby move the car back, fearing cinders would land on it. Annie and I skirted the yard, seeing nothing, keeping half a view on that mesmerizing glow that was once a happy home. We were in thick brush and palmettos were stinging—neighbor Ralph didn't much follow his own advice to keep the grass low—but it seemed important to keep looking—what if one of them were out in the yard, half on fire, unconscious, whatever? Near a chicken coop I saw someone—

"Ralph? Mrs. Settles?"

But whoever, whatever, it was gone.

"Did you see that?"

Annie, wide-eyed and open-mouthed, was walking toward the fire, hypnotized.

"Annie!" She collapsed. A siren sounded. When they arrived there wasn't much for them to do but resuscitate Annie and put out brush fires. The Settles' house was completely demolished. With oxygen, Annie came to, though the paramedic was concerned with her blood pressure and pulse, saying she might go in for a checkup.

How many checkups can a person have? I wanted to ask, but held my tongue, looking at Annie's ashen face. Leslie and her parents showed up. Was it her I'd seen? No, she and her mother had on dark clothes, but I was sure it was a woman I'd seen. Abby?

The wind shifted and a rancid smell stopped everyone. Several firemen exchanged glances and I surmised what that meant: The Settles, at least one of them, had died in the house. Annie got sick, and Bobby, wincing at his mother's retching sounds, said he'd walk back. I made my courtesies to Leslie and Abby's parents—a Tom and Vera Beasley—and took Annie home.

But the night wasn't over. Back in our own yard I saw what I thought was a smoking tree or bush. Turning the car's lights in that direction revealed a smoldering body, its arm elevated and pointing toward Alice Fairbain's house. Annie slumped with a groan.

"Ralph!" I ran from the car, but wind gusted through the cypress leaving what had appeared to be Ralph Settles scattering into ashes, blowing over me, the yard, the house and the car.

Annie was on the ground, wheezing. I carried her inside, saying I'd run and get the paramedics again, but she wouldn't let me go and tore into my wrist, her nails slicing at my veins. We knocked over a lamp. In the afterglow from the Settles' fire from our windows I could see her face. It had the same damned leer that rag doll in the barn had. She whispered something about Bobby; I leaned to hear and she slashed at my throat with a razor and killed me.

DESCENDING TO LOWER DOMINIONS

1.

Martin reread the last line in Kirby's diary: "I leaned closer to hear and she slashed at my throat with a razor and killed me." *Now that*, Martin thought, *is a hard act to follow.* Just how many psychologists can claim to have a client who thinks he's a freshly killed corpse? Dr. Oliver Sacks, move over.

Martin thought of Dean Kirby, a slender man who always seemed to be mocking with typical academic cynicism. Well-shaven, well-kept for a professor. Worried about a job and supporting his son now that he had to leave Florida. Upset by his wife's death, of course. Nothing particularly clinical, certainly nothing enough to explain the last entry. So what was happening? Did he really try to kill Bobby? Or was he attacking some hallucination that wanted his son for an evil ritual, as he claimed? A mid-age crisis bursting into some religious experience? Certainly, resurrection of the dead has been claimed before and no doubt will be again.

Of course, this might not be Kirby's diary at all. It might be a forgery by this Fairbain woman. To what end? To get control of Bobby? To what end?

Martin thumbed the pages. They were Kirby's, all right. Until the last entry they read with that Kirby-esque stance of practiced irony. And Martin remembered Kirby telling him that he kept a diary, remembered him tilting his head like he was looking over bifocals to intone there were things in it that would shed a great deal of light on Bobby.

Martin studied the handwriting before him, a nervous scatter of letters that sprouted tiny ink thorns every half-centimeter—mimicking Kirby's mind. Still, if it hadn't been for the knife attack on Bobby three weeks ago, he would have sworn in a courtroom this diary was a forgery. Curious: Fairbain inserted comments a couple of times, so why didn't she comment on this ludicrous end? Had she simply skimmed for passages concerning herself or Aaron? And why would Kirby leave a diary like this in his house, especially as he must have suspected (though the deal could have been hush-hushed through lawyers and realtors) that Fairbain would buy the land? To frighten her? Because she *could* become legal guardian for Bobby?

For the briefest of instants—the time it might take a quark to skit through a Kleenex—Martin thought of confronting Bobby with the diary. But those last lines… that wouldn't do. Only a month ago the staff finally convinced Bobby that his mother had actually died. It would take another month to convince the boy his father wasn't some zombie or wraith from hell come to haunt him. This diary's last entry would hardly help.

Martin thought of forgery again. Maybe he had the right

tree, but the wrong branch. Could Bobby have faked his father's handwriting? To what purpose? Even a twisted mind needs a purpose.

So how about taking everything at face value: Annie Kirby died under mysterious circumstances, her body was stolen from a grave three days later; understandably upset, Dean Kirby left Florida with his son and moved to Atlanta within a week. The son reacts, refusing to believe his mother is dead. Instead, he believes the father is dead but resurrected for some evil (?) purpose. The son's delusions become so serious that he is committed. The visiting father cuts the son, supposedly defending them both. A friend (?) of the family offers to become guardian of the son. This same friend implies that the father killed the mother. Why would Kirby kill his wife? He was hardly living high on the hog from the insurance money. And as far as women, the most Martin had seen the man do was smile at a blonde nurse. Could he be playing possum, letting the heat—*Good Lord, man, listen to yourself. The heat? Next thing you'll do is fly to Florida, spade in suitcase, to exhume Annie Kirby's body at midnight. Enough is enough, Martin Edmonds.*

Martin stood from his desk, carefully placed the diary in a drawer under lock, then left for the North Wing and Dean Kirby…

… who was sitting lotus-like amid his mint green institutional sheets, resembling a dollop of whipped cream on pistachio custard, meticulously ripping a paperback, piling tiny shreds of pages over the bed. Martin walked near to see that the piles were dictionary entries. Oblivious to Martin, Kirby pressed his fingernail into a page. Then a slow, careful rip and voila! The word *gab* joined the slender pile of G's.

"Your son's doing fine, Dean. He asks about you."

No answer. Just a finger pat for *gab*. The male nurse raised his eyebrows in an "I told you so."

"The sun's out today, Dean. You still have time to get in a good game of racquetball. Didn't you say you played that?"

No answer, though Dean's nail, which had returned to the dictionary, skidded to a halt. Martin looked at that nail, horny and yellow beyond Dean's years. It reminded him of his granddad's big toe, the one a horse stepped on. His granddad used it to scare the kids, saying he'd send it up to their beds if they didn't behave. Martin looked at the new word Dean was now tearing out, forcing himself past Kirby's rising odor that crossed somewhere between a Georgia paper mill and a sauerkraut vat. *Gag* was the word. The nurse suppressed a laugh then spoke:

"I bought this dictionary for him on my lunch hour. He hasn't talked since. He'd been screaming all morning for someone to bring him one."

Martin nodded and was about to speak when Dean shouted, "It's a damned lie!" and began hitting a word he'd torn out, thrusting the torn scraps on the bed upwards in a snowstorm.

Within minutes, he was under sedation. Before that, though, he'd dislocated the male nurse's shoulder and given Martin a puffed lip.

∞

Martin was at last able to get away to the fourth floor. He found Bobby sullen, as if some magnetism was sinking him into the depths of the floor below.

"My dad's acted out again, hasn't he?"

This was the first time Bobby had referred to his father in anything other than the past tense or with some qualifier such as "the thing living in my father's body." Martin nodded, studying the boy's pocked face and wet blue eyes. "How'd you know?" Martin asked, wondering suddenly.

Bobby was sitting at a dresser in his room. He stood and walked to a corner to place his ear against a pipe painted a seaweed green. "Through this. I heard him shouting that he's going to kill me."

"He's *not* going to kill you, Bobby. That's not what he really wants, and even if he did, we wouldn't let him."

"You just don't understand. How are you going to stop him when he's not really alive?"

One step forward, one step back. "All right, let's talk about something else. Do you know a woman from Florida named Alice Fairbain?"

Bobby's face looked like an undertaker had attached a suction machine to his carotid. Tears welled then streamed over his fluorescent skin.

"Bobby, she says your mother appointed her legal guardian."

Bobby's eyes, perennially pink around the lids, roamed to the barred window on the far wall, then to the door. Martin leaned forward. "You're staying here as long as you want; you won't have to go unless you want."

Bobby wiped his eyes. "I want my mother. Why can't anyone understand that? Why'm I here? She's in Florida. She's not giving me to Alice Fairbain. I want to be in Florida with my mother."

One step forward, *two* steps back. Martin patted the boy's hand. The reason Dean Kirby had moved from Florida to Atlanta was that Bobby had constantly driven to his mother's grave, insisting she hadn't really died. On two occasions the boy tried to dig up the gravesite, once with his hands, once with a shovel he'd stolen from a nearby hardware store. The hardware store's owner and the cemetery caretakers were as understanding as they could be, but…

"All right, Bobby. You're going to be all right. Will it make you feel better if we move you to a different locked ward?"

Nodding pink eyelids. "Can I call my mother at least?"

"We'll get you in a different ward. How will that be?"

"Can I call my mother then?"

"Did your mother like Alice Fairbain?"

Martin spent an hour talking with Bobby about Alice Fairbain, not finding any specific reason why Bobby's mother wouldn't have declared the woman legal guardian, not finding any compelling reason she would. They were neighbors. Bobby had worked for Ms. Fairbain for two weeks, explaining that he finally quit because she was "weirded out to the max." He said that all the kids in the area called her Mrs. Kruger, from *Nightmare on Elm Street*. She made statues for a living and she talked to them all the time, asking them how they liked this, how they liked that. "She always asked them how they liked me, and she'd make me stand in front of them when she did, and she'd hold their hand or neck when she asked. I told her it was because of school that I had to quit, but her and Aaron being so weird is really why. Then Mom started going down there all the time, every day. Dad didn't care until it was too late. Then he thought they were lesbians or something." Bobby's pink eyelids twittered.

"And how did you feel about that?"

"About what, Dad or Mom?"

"About either."

"How would you feel if you thought your dad thought your mom was queer and your mom thought your dad was a loser and your neighbors thought you'd killed their little girl and another neighbor thought her statues were in love with you and a track coach thought you were on drugs and your girlfriend's sister kept warning you about 'zombies' and your girlfriend was strung out and wouldn't let you touch her because you once worked for a witch? How would that make you feel?"

"It's good that you're expressing your anger, Bobby."

With that ridiculous answer, Martin left, promising himself not to read psychology journals for a month until he learned to become human. But after all, maybe it *was* good that Bobby was expressing anger instead of fantasizing about wraiths and resurrections.

◈

That afternoon Martin received a phone call from Fairbain's lawyer, who said he wanted to have Bobby transferred to Horizon Hospital in Tampa.

Not so fast there, Buckaroo.

"We understand that the father's incompetent, dangerous, even."

No comment on that as yet, Buckaroo.

"Well, we'll see about that. I have friends in Atlanta."

Don't kid me, Buckaroo. Lawyers don't have friends, just connections. Martin did inform the lawyer that he would take Alice Fairbain up on her offer to come to Tampa—for the $2500 ante the lawyer mentioned. God knows he could use the money. He made arrangements with the administrator for four personal leave days, and told the other staff members, Bobby, and even the receptionist in her gray-green study who answered,

"Florida, huh? Most people go there in the winter, not summer. I went there once."

Was it a state then or a Spanish colony? Martin wanted to ask.

2.

Martin was on a plane to Tampa, reading Dean's diary. Not the one Alice Fairbain had sent, but the one Dean gave him on learning of the trip to Florida. This happened when Martin made his last rounds. Logically enough he and the nurse assumed Kirby was still sedated from the Nembutal and Martin was explaining about going to Tampa to see this Fairbain woman. Kirby suddenly broke a restraint and grabbed Martin's shirt. "In my suitcase… a key to my apartment. Take it. In my bedroom closet… a blue box and notes. Read before you go. Promise."

Martin heard his shirt ripping from Kirby's grip.

"I promise," Martin said. And as simple as that, Kirby let go. It was one of the sanest moments Martin ever experienced at St. Veronica's. And since he'd decided to be human for a month, he actually kept his promise, even though none of the red tape had been signed permitting him to enter Kirby's apartment.

So far though, the diary was a disappointment, repeated ramblings about the purported Annie/Alice lesbian affair and occasional whining about St. Andrew's, the college where Dean taught.

The ticket for the flight was first class, a luxury Martin had never experienced, so when the stewardess offered a drink before "debarkation," he simply asked for hot tea. She gave a quizzical look then got his tea. He watched her hips. She was an imperious woman whose shape, stature, full lips and high forehead left her betrayed in time—she should have been Egyptian royalty, say Cleopatra's daughter. Or better, Nefertiti herself, with those angular cheeks and that haughty gaze.

The teas were as fine as the woman: Earl Gray, English Breakfast, Darjeeling, Blackcurrant. Martin picked one and pocketed the rest, looking back for that high forehead before he did. It wouldn't do to have Nefertiti think him a scurrilous miser.

There were only four other people in the first-class cabin, which left it over half empty. A young tan couple sat in back, probably on a honeymoon, but who could tell these days? Maybe they were whiz kid college graduates hired at 80 grand a year. In front of them was a serious looking executive drinking a martini and spreading papers importantly. Across the aisle from Martin himself was a perfume heiress. He didn't know this for a fact, but simply assigned that role to her as most likely considering her bored look, her emanating odor, and the way she sloshed down Manhattans—she ordered her second as he dipped his tea bag. As the stewardess walked back, the businessman ordered another drink too. The race was on.

Martin played between reading Kirby's diary and squeezing his tea bag until the plane took off. Then came another first-class ritual: the steaming towel offering. Martin wiped his hands, glad it wasn't his $899 paying for this charade. The stewardess was consoling the perfume heiress over something—not enough ice in her drink or the cubes were clattering too loudly. *Egyptian*, Martin thought, studying the stewardess's legs and ankles.

Maybe Kirby's diary was why he referred to her as Egyptian. He looked at it and shivered. Accidentally, the page had flipped and in blood red—real, crusted, finger-smeared blood—were the paired words, *ROOD-DOOR*.

He flipped to find more paired words, all written in blood. *AND-D.N.A. EVIL-LIVE. PART-TRAP. PIN-NIP. PAR-RAP. PIT-TIP. TAR-RAT. DOG-GOD. NOT-TON. MEET-TEEM. NOW-WON. TUG-GUT. GAS-SAG. GAT-TAG.*

Just like on the bed. What was Kirby up to? Reversals, as

in personality? Better question: What was he doing writing in blood, and whose blood was it? Martin closed his eyes to picture the child who disappeared near Kirby's house, what she must have looked like before… but all he saw was after, and the picture wasn't pretty. Removing his hand from the diary to feel the warm tea through his cup, he still couldn't keep his eyes from the page.

Rood to heaven?
Door to hell?

"Your patient looks like he needs help pretty desperately."

Martin started and looked up, closing the diary. The stewardess smiled at him, a smile so large that it could never be false.

"Are you a psychiatrist?"

"Psychologist."

"I once took folklore in college. Did you know that witches write in blood when they're making a pact or binding a curse?"

"No, I didn't. In their own blood?"

"Of course; it's much more effective that way."

"Much more infective, too."

The stewardess smiled again, and Martin caught himself holding his breath. Her teeth were movie-star quality, though she was a tad too old for the current dental mania for braces and large bills. Her hair glowed from a bun of black, the true purple-black that ravens strut in cornfields. Her eyes were a soft gray that could lead a man anywhere. Egyptian royalty indeed.

"*Rood* means the cross of Christ, by the way."

Martin flipped back to the page where he first encountered the blood. "Rood to heaven? Door to hell?"

"Are you from Tampa? Do you take patients outside the area?"

He closed the diary, sickened at the flakes of blood on his lap and hands and imagining a future HIV test.

"Let me get you a towel." The stewardess returned in a moment and handed a second steaming towel to Martin.

"Thanks. No, I'm not from Tampa, but Atlanta, though I keep a Florida license since St. Veronica's where I work plans on opening in one of the major cities. Ordinarily I don't take out-of-state patients. I'm on a bit of a busman's holiday this time, I suppose."

"I'm from Wesley Chapel. I have a teenage girl who needs a good psychologist, or just a man. Growing up without a father has created its problems; she's a trifle anxious to develop a serious relationship and nothing Mother can say can dissuade her."

With that, Nefertiti walked to calm the honeymoon youngsters, who were forgetting the FAA had regulations against loud, obscene wet sounds. Not to mention acts.

Martin did a double take on his notes: Yes, Wesley Chapel was where Alice Fairbain lived. He looked back at the stewardess bribing the youngsters with sweet talk and champagne. Maybe he should read up on Jung's theory of synchronicity. How else explain that the stewardess was from the very town he is going to? Now that his feelings had a theoretical foundation, Martin gawked at her long legs and quickly sank to the lower dominions. He could see her left eye watch him. Well, it's not like admiring a woman's figure is dysfunctional. Not like he was catcalling or hooting. Her lips curled; vaguely, Martin wondered how a fish felt being reeled in.

Two teas later—five Manhattans to three martinis, the perfume heiress won hands down—Martin was disembarking. He'd stopped reading Kirby's manuscript because an inner voice told him to, and he always listened to inner voices—his bow to Jung, his snub to Freud and Skinner and cognitive therapy. Nefertiti had elicited a promise that he'd wait for her in The Palmetto Lounge. So he carried his suitcase and briefcase into the airport lounge and ordered a Diet Coke sans booze after reminding himself this was a business trip, not a tour of the Valley of Kings and the pyramids. Nefertiti walked in, out of uniform. Every male eye and maybe some female ones turned. *At least I'm not alone in my infatuation*, Martin thought.

"How about a deal, Doc?" Nefertiti said, easing her long body onto a bar stool. "In exchange for a brief meeting with my daughter—just to let her know psychologists don't strap scalpels under their sports jackets so I can persuade her to visit one—I'll give you door-to-door service to Alice Fairbain's."

Martin started. Had he mentioned Alice Fairbain on the plane? No, he remembered he hadn't needed to because Nefertiti had seen Kirby's name and mentioned Fairbain, which led to the fact that he was going to see her.

"You know," Nefertiti said, lifting her royal chin to reveal a long, royal throat, "that besides being a sculptress she's also a witch. I'm one too, but a gray witch, not a black."

Gray, not black? Anything she said was fine with him. His forty-three-year-old personality had dissolved to teenage wereboy.

"Do you want a drink before we go?" he asked.

"I don't drink… wine." She laughed and ordered a Diet

Coke. She thanked the bartender and left a tip that was equal to the price of the drink, turning to Martin as she did. "We're not supposed to be in here. The company turns its head when we're out of uniform though. Still, I like to keep everyone happy and on my side."

"You're a witch; you can't hypnotize them?"

She looked over her straw. Her gray eyes could be portraying a winter sea before a storm. "Some," she said, quite seriously, "but not all. Look, you're a psychologist, so let's talk in psychological terms and forget what you think of as mumbo-jumbo."

Martin started to protest but she stopped him.

"I know Alice Fairbain through… mutual acquaintances. I've spoken with her once or twice at… mutual gatherings. She's… let's say forceful and cunning, okay? And you'd better be a damned good psychologist because I'm not a good enough… not forceful or cunning enough to be much help. My daughter, though… you *will* see her in trade for this little info-fab and rent-free limousine service, won't you?"

Martin nodded, shaking off the bartender who wanted to get him looped on caffeine and Nutra-Sweet.

"My daughter has quite a forceful personality. As I'm beginning to think does your Dean Kirby."

"What do you know about him?"

"It's a small world, an even smaller Wesley Chapel. Not like Atlanta. His wife's odd death followed hard on a little girl's sensationalized murder. Besides, my vision tests at 18 over 20, and you leave your notes open. If you do the same with cards, we'll have to play poker before you leave, preferably for very high stakes." Nefertiti gave a smile and slurped the last of her drink through her straw while gazing at him with those gray eyes. Martin was in serious danger of falling off his barstool.

"Just what is your name?" he asked. "*My* vision's 18 over 20 too, but there's a zero behind both numbers. I've been thinking of you as Nefertiti. The *N* is all I could make out on your name badge."

"Nefertiti. I'm flattered. My name is Nikki. It's not my real name—my real name is Nyx, because I was born at midnight. My father taught classics and gave me a Classical Greek name. I had my revenge by naming his grandchild Night."

"Night, like the opposite of day?"

"Night, like the daughter of Chaos. Or maybe the mother," she added.

Martin looked to a pay phone across the way, where a hulking man in an army green raincoat had been standing ever since Martin had been in the bar. They finished their drinks and walked out, and the man turned to talk in the phone, hunching over it like a kid whispering a secret.

Outside over the airport's parking lot, an ugly cloud was blowing off the Gulf. It grew even uglier and its cooling raindrops became pelting hail. Soon it was an absolute green— almost Martin thought, like a genie's face. He felt the hair on his arm rise and he reached for Nikki. A bolt of lightning threaded onto a safety lamp, dropping a twenty-pound hunk of glass and metal approximately where Nikki would have stepped to get in her car. Martin could feel his heart thump; Nikki gave the debris of the lamp a glance, then looked at Martin. Behind her, far back under one of the drive-up awnings, Martin noticed the man in the green raincoat. By the time Nikki walked around to climb in the passenger side, the man was sitting in a pick-up five parking spaces away. He turned aside when Martin noticed him.

Nikki followed Martin's gaze and looked out her window

to the shattered lamp. She reached into her purse, not for keys but a vial of—

"Salt. Can you toss some outside in the air for me? I don't like touching it."

Martin raised his brows.

"A superstition. Humor me, would you, and I won't make any comments about the packets of tea you pocketed."

Martin grinned, though rolling down the window in this storm wasn't the most pleasant option he could have thought of. Still, anything for those gray eyes. He threw the salt, much of which flew back in his face as he expected, though he hadn't expected the fierceness of the stinging nor the howling of the wind and driving of the rain.

"Like iodine seeding a storm. Now I know how a pilot in a weather plane feels," he said, rolling up the window. He thought he noticed a bluish glow surrounding Nikki and was afraid that lightning was somehow caught in the car. Could that happen? He expected the hairs on his arms to rise again at any second, but they didn't. She started the engine and gave the rear-view mirror a little tug. The glow disappeared. The man in the pick-up had driven away.

"Was that salt for good luck?"

"A talisman. I don't believe all that much in luck."

Not far from the airport they had to pull off the road, along with several dozen other cars and trucks, because of pelting rain.

"This airport causeway cuts through Tampa Bay," Nikki explained.

"Is that why the storm came up so quickly?"

"That's why the *storm* came up, yes."

"And the lightning?" Martin found himself shivering from the combination of wet clothes and air-conditioning. Nikki turned the air down.

"We need it to keep the windshield unfogged. This won't last more than a half hour."

"And the lightning?" Martin repeated. "And the salt I threw?"

"Good. You're persistent. That might stand you well with Alice Fairbain." Nikki reached into her overnight case for two hand towels, giving one to Martin and wiping her face with the other.

"The lightning? The salt?"

Nikki smiled. "The lightning and the salt mean that you need to talk carefully with Fairbain. They could mean that I've butted in where I'm not wanted and should have kept my mouth shut."

Martin noticed how white her knuckles were as they gripped the steering wheel awaiting the end of the downpour. Outside, he could see waves beating against the beach surrounding the road. A sheet of rain covered his window and he shivered, glad to be in a royal coach with Nefertiti.

Because of the rain, it took an hour and a half to reach Wesley Chapel.

"We're going to stop for my daughter first. I can't drive you to Alice Fairbain's. Night's a mature young woman when she wants to be: You'll find her more of a conversationalist than me right now but not quite as good a driver. Tell her to slow down if that bothers you. You're supposed to wear your seatbelt anyway—"

"I know, I know: It's the law. I've seen at least twenty signs."

They arrived at Nikki's house thirty minutes later. It was a cozy wood-frame that had been built, Martin guessed, sometime after World War II. Its yard was large, and if it hadn't

been raining he would have loved to walk the dock over
the lake in the back. But it was raining again, not as hard as
before, with another storm system overhead. Nikki left him
standing in the living room after a warm squeeze of his arm
and a Nefertiti-uplift of her chin that made him lean forward, a bit ashamed and a bit… horny. He chided himself.
And he noticed he was still leaning when Night walked in
from a back bedroom. She was pale and raven-haired like
her mother. She offered her hand and it was all he could do
to shake, not kiss it, wondering how that perverted impulse
arrived.

"Mom says I'm supposed to drive you to AF's."

Martin straightened at the familiar use of initials, remembering how Fairbain initialed all her little notes. Given his
choice of Freud, Jung or Skinner as a present companion, he
would have turned them all down for J.B. Rhine and his deck
of ESP cards.

"Thanks. Your mom said a great deal about you."

The girl looked at him and smiled, lifting her Nefertiti chin
the same as her mother, and nervously clicking her keys. Her
eyes were that same lucid gray—always his favorite flavor.
At the jangle of keys, a white bird flew into the room and
perched on her shoulder. The girl fed him some seed from
her pocket.

"Skull. He'll keep us company."

Martin nodded. Damned if the bird didn't look more like
a hawk than anything. But it wasn't hooded and as far as he
could see the girl wore no more than stylish shoulder pads
where the bird perched with its huge talons.

Night drove over the road they'd come on once they'd
gotten off the interstate. Martin commented as politely as he
could on this redundant trip.

"Mr.—Dr. Edmonds, what do you believe?"

"Believe?"

"Like in 'believe in.' Like some people believe in Christ, some in the Virgin Mary, some in American Express, some in Salman Rushdie, some in Mohammed."

"Well, I don't know that I believe in anything like that."

Night gave a smile and the bird nibbled her ear, causing her to smile even more. Why did he feel he'd been made a fool of by a teenager and a Beretta reject?

"I believe in the complexity of the human mind," he snapped a little angrier than he meant.

"Answered like a true rationalist."

The girl or the parrot said that?

"And what else besides that mystical complexity?"

The girl. She had that wonderful smile on her face. And Nikki was right; she did drive too fast.

"This probably isn't up to your concept of a professional, but I believe in following my instinct; I always have."

The car slowed and Night turned toward him. "That's good; that's excellent good."

3.

Before she left him at Alice Fairbain's, Night slipped a rough hunk of metal into his hand. "Lodestone," she said. "A magnet. What does your instinct tell you about that?"

"That you want me to keep it close." He looked at the girl, her mother's daughter without a doubt. He noticed droplets of sweat forming on the upper cusp of her lip.

"And what does your instinct tell you about me?"

He blew a puff of air against the windshield. His instinct told him that he wanted to leave Atlanta and St. Veronica's and all its upper middle class substance abusers and live with this girl and her mother on a small lake until his hair fell out.

"It tells me that I'll keep this magnet close like you and your mother ask."

"Your instinct's smarter than you give it credit for. Here, Mom also wanted me to give you this: It's our phone number. She says you and her have a date tomorrow for dinner and a game of poker. Ryan is our last name, we're the only ones in Wesley Chapel, in case something happens to the number. Instinct is a wonderful thing to believe in." Night turned toward him with eyes that managed to glitter despite the still overcast sky. Before he knew what was happening, she gave him a peck on the cheek. "Don't tell my mom. That's for her, not me."

That was half an hour ago. As soon as Martin walked into Alice Fairbain's house he followed not instinct but reason and remembered that he'd yet to call St. Veronica's about what he'd read in Kirby's diary. So he excused himself and did so, and just in time too, for the staff had almost decided to let Bobby (who was off medications and walking) see his father. Dr. Edmonds elicited a promise from the caseworker that they'd not let the two come in contact until he came back—in three days, he promised, almost adding "rising like Christ." Which caused him to pause and wonder about Kirby's cynicism. Never had a client influenced him more. *Clients*, for Bobby seemed an intricate part of whatever… Hanging up the phone, he noticed that Alice Fairbain was holding out a cup of coffee for him.

"To knock off the chill," she said.

Thirty minutes after being dropped off by Night, after Alice Fairbain's urbanity, her obvious artistic talent, her concern over her deceased friend Annie Kirby and her family—after those thirty minutes, that small wooden house on the small lake with a kooky-though-beautiful mother/daughter witch combo seemed American cheese versus Alice's Russian caviar. Martin was barely aware of his shifting emotions, only an uncomfortable muscle spasm in his right leg.

Fairbain's house was pretty much as Kirby's diary described it. Martin noted the griffins by the door, though he'd been so enchanted with Alice that he'd not noticed the position of the claws. Listening to her voice (husky, but sexily so) and watching her hands caress this, then that sculpture, he didn't very much care.

"This," she was saying, pointing to a two-foot sculpture on a large wood desk, "is my rendition of Annie. Did Dean ever show you a picture of her?"

He had indeed, though the picture must have been taken well before Annie's sitting for this work, which had the absolute saddest gaze he'd ever seen, focusing on its uplifted palm as if wind had unexpectedly blown something important from its grasp.

"Go ahead, touch it. Art is meant to be fondled and loved."

As with most of Alice Fairbain's larger sculptures, this was a concrete mixture she'd bleached to snow-whiteness. Martin felt the empty palm's cool, lonely smoothness and involuntarily looked to see if he might spot what had flown off. In the back of the room, near a row of windows and hanging from the ceiling like Christmas decorations, were easily a hundred smaller sculptures. As far as he could tell, they were ultra-realistic compared to those outside. These were mundane, managerial and secretarial types, though a few clasped what seemed to be tiny daggers instead of pens. Mostly, four to six inches in length. Alice Fairbain must work with manic devotion to sculpt so many.

She led him upstairs to one of the three turret rooms in her house, one of the two facing the back. From its windows Martin could see the back yard and caught what must be "Persephone's Escalator" under a fairly large apple tree, those two earth-mother breasts being partially hidden by a different tree.

"I didn't know apples grew in Florida."

Alice joined him. "They're not very good, I'm afraid. Aaron's learned to make an apple pie from them that for all the world puckers my mouth like Key Lime. I've gotten used to it and even like it, though guests are always surprised, as you can imagine."

"You said in your notes that Aaron was a refugee from Nazi Germany…"

"A refugee *in utero*. He was born in New York City months after his mother arrived. He shows amazing resilience considering his history, considering that his father owned two jewelry stores in Germany and his mother was killed by thugs when he was fourteen. There are families that seem born to a bad time of things."

"Like the Kirbys?"

"I'm not so sure that doesn't have its source in one root: Dean Kirby. The paramedics that night of the Settles' fire, you know, told him she should be immediately taken to a hospital."

"I thought he did take her."

"The next morning. His son and I drove them both there. I came for a morning visit and felt her face, as cold as a North Atlantic clam, and we immediately drove her to the hospital in Dade City. If it had been left to Dean Kirby, she would have had frost icing her lips, though I have to admit he wasn't much better off and was admitted too. Maybe he was

avoiding hospitalization because he hadn't met his deductible.
"

"You don't like Dean Kirby?"
"It doesn't take a psychiatrist to know that."
"Psychologist."
Alice Fairbain began humming a tune in a minor key, a tune most exasperating because it employed the repetition of three notes with a tonic only after some time.

Martin heard steps behind on the stairs. Aaron, or who could be no other than Aaron judging from his huge frame topped by an oddly thwarted cranium holding 850 ccs of gray matter at most—this creature glided in with amazing quiet carrying a decanter of red wine plus two glasses. Alice motioned with a nod, and he set the decanter on a desk and began to pour.

Martin watched him give the bottle a wine steward's twist with his huge bony wrist. Aaron may as well have been a Great Dane reciting a poem:

> *I think that I shall never see*
> *A poem as lovely as a tree*
> *Bark-bark.*

"Madam, it's nearly sundown," the Great Dane intoned with a jolting baritone. Then he moved to close the blinds. The last outside scene Martin saw was Persephone's Escalator under the peaceful russet shade of the apple tree. What he saw when he looked back in the turret room was Alice Fairbain holding up a glass of burgundy. The hulk had disappeared.

"I… drink wine," she said with a short laugh.
He could neither imagine why she said what she did, nor

why she laughed. Still, he nodded conspiratorially like a good psychologist should and lifted his wine in a toast to…

"To Bobby," she said. "That he makes it through all this."

Martin nodded and drank.

"Annie posed over there." Alice pointed to a platform covered with concrete bags, paint cans and a stack of art books.

"Nearly every room in this house is a part-time studio. I even use the downstairs lavatory—it has a Jacuzzi that's inspired some very naughty sculptures, special requests, of course. I'm no Rodin; at times I've got to make money by being a vulgar whore to the muse."

"How well did you know Mrs. Kirby?"

"Not as well as Dean Kirby implies in that diary of his, I can assure you. But a lot better than he did, I can also assure you." She motioned to a chair. Martin sat, bumping against one of the dangling statues which tangled in his hair. Laughing at his contortions, Alice sat in a concrete throne with a gorgon's head growing out of its high back. Despite the gorgon's horrible countenance and snake-hair, its tongue stuck out in a childlike defiance that lent it humor. Alice spoke, and again Martin was drawn to her gray eyes.

"He didn't know, for instance, that she was pregnant."

There was a pause while Martin took the smallest sip of wine and studied Alice's face. Was she lying?

"You must be a wonderful psychiatrist—psychologist," Alice said. "That's a psychologist's job, isn't it—to listen?"

Martin nodded and she giggled, though he noticed the giggle had a smoky rasp.

"I believe in psychology, too." She scooted a small sculpture across the desk. From where Martin sat the ten-inch statue appeared mostly mouth and fingernails. The mouth contorted around goofy, rabbitlike teeth. Atop this sat a tiny brow with sparrow eyes and two uplifted hands that were talons. Only its stupidity defined it as human. "This is the soul of a boy who mowed my lawn three years ago." She plinked the talons, easily one half the length of the entire statuette. "Two years ago he killed a man and woman he found by a beachside fire on Courtney Campbell Causeway, the one that goes to the airport. After hacking their bodies in a nearby hotel room, the charming boy drank a fifth of whiskey and killed himself and a Tennessee family by head-onning their station wagon."

Martin coughed and looked around at the statues. Those not hanging from the ceiling were decidedly more grotesque, perhaps because their size allowed detail. On a nearby bookshelf a thin woman reached out plaster hands to choke some imaginary enemy. Another was staring at her own sex. Martin stared too, then discerned the head of a small penis protruding.

"You can see Freud is my major influence," Alice said with a musical laugh, similar to the tune she'd been humming.

"Everything derived from our subconscious isn't violent, evil, or sexual," Martin said.

"Oh?" she responded.

"Dinner is ready."

Martin started on seeing Aaron at the door. Alice finished her wine in a gulp. Like a ghost, Aaron had already floated away when they headed downstairs. At the bottom Martin made sure to check the griffins' claws: They were poised about the height of his shoulder.

Once seated, Alice motioned for Aaron to refill her wine. When he raised an eyebrow, she covered her glass with her palm, taking water instead.

"Your comments indicated that you took Mr. Kirby as a

threat when you asked me to come down."

"My comments. I basically skimmed Kirby's manuscript for my name or Aaron's. Actually, I skimmed half and slithered through the rest. The man was little. I don't waste time on miniatures; I leave that to dilettantes like Fabergé. If you must do them—and sometimes you must—for godsakes, do them quickly."

Ah, Martin thought: Her attitude does explain why she ignored the part in the manuscript where Kirby proclaimed himself a corpse. Martin took a goodly drink of the wine. Aaron was immediately on hand to pour more.

"What I'm worried about is Dean Kirby's violence. He might be a pygmy intellectual strutting about some college north of here, but he also has gotten it into his head that I'm responsible for his wife's death. Don't you call that transference of guilt?"

Martin nodded, adding "Perhaps" on seeing Alice Fairbain's smile.

"You don't think *I* murdered her, do you? Shrunk her down and covered her with plaster like some cheap movie? If there's anyone to blame for her death—and I'm not saying there is—it would be that lousy husband of hers who didn't rush her back to the hospital after her second attack. She basically drowned in her own sputum, though the hospital listed her as having a heart failure."

There was a silence as Martin put down his wine glass.

"I want to be sure you hear my complete estimation of Dean Kirby himself; that, combined with the diary he kept for god knows what reason, should make it clear the boy's not safe with him. And I want you to know someone called again just this morning and told me to check my front lawn: I did and there was another snake on my doorstep. I shot and froze it; you can go look if you want. I want you especially to see something at Dean Kirby's residence; that will have to wait until tomorrow."

Was she really frightened of Dean Kirby? No, he couldn't say that upon observing her queenly manner and her huge griffins guarding the door. In fact, he wondered if it weren't Kirby who should be frightened, for all her talk about Bobby consisted of pat phrases ("Such a nice boy—like his mother.") and queries ("Where is he now? I'd like to phone him, give him any comfort I could."). When speaking of him she'd study her nails or a spot on her shoe. But confidence exuded as if she were keeping some hole card back. The trip to the Kirby residence tomorrow?

"I should be leaving for a hotel," Martin commented, waving Aaron off from a second after-dinner drink. "I passed a Day's Inn at the interstate—"

"Don't be ridiculous. This house begs for company. And you've never spent a night until you've spent a night in one of the turret rooms. Of course they're haunted. What good psy—psychologist could turn down a chance to analyze a ghost?"

"*Analyze* is a psychiatric term. You're determined to give me a degree I don't have."

"Would it make you smarter?"

"My father says it would make me crazier."

"We should all listen to our fathers. And you should listen to your hostess. Spend the night. Tomorrow, if you want, I'll tell you every little thing I know about the Kirby family while we walk their property."

Alice Fairbain's lip twitched oddly in a way Martin hadn't noticed before. *Instinct. Trust your instinct and leave*, he thought as he followed Alice upstairs to a turret room. Thinking was no doubt the reason he stayed.

4.

Once Martin was alone in the room facing the back yard, he lifted Dean Kirby's diary from his briefcase, but found the day's activity, when combined with dinner and drink, became too strong a competition. Hearing a frog outside he opened a window and was pleased to find a chorus of nighttime mud princes and princesses, so he turned off the light and went to sleep, noticing the room's dangling statuettes forming ghostly white wisps that danced to the frog chorus. They pleased the child in Martin better than hopping sheep ever could.

He awoke sometime during the night to voices below in the yard. The air was still, as if awaiting a constellation to shift. Alice's dog barked, then yelped as if it had been kicked. Flute music was playing. Martin edged up on one elbow in the bed, and a couple of the dangling statuettes twisted with his movement. While the flute's tune was more varied than the repetitive nonsense Alice had hummed earlier, it couldn't have consisted of more than five or so notes. Martin counted. Da-Deeee-Da-Duh-Duh-Doh. Six notes, over and over. He looked to his door, wedged closed with typing paper he'd folded over since there was no lock. The hall light was out, he could see by looking at the doorframe's crack. He stood and walked to the window, trying to avoid the mobiles since one had left a small cut on his cheek earlier.

From the window he could see Alice seated by "Persephone's Escalator" playing a Pan flute. A regular Zamfir. All this and a witch too. Martin chuckled, though he had to admit that seeing her on that concrete bench with fog shifting about sent a chill through him. Two candles on her either side glowed and Rex, sitting at her feet, bayed. With a fluidity

Martin would never have attributed to anything but a TV sports play, something jumped from behind the apple tree to bodily throw Rex to the ground. "Aaron, no," he heard Alice plead. The figure jerked the dog up by the mane, and let it fall. Rex ran off yelping. Something slammed in the house: Maybe a pet door. "Go sleep, *Hund*," Martin heard. Then Aaron looked at the moon and descended into Persephone's Escalator.

The flute started again, unsteadily, then droned. All the while that Aaron was gone—Martin estimated twenty minutes—Fairbain played that godawful tune. The repetition— how many times? Hundreds. Then came a voice Martin couldn't make out, a voice from the "escalator," and Alice switched to a bass clef—was that what it was called? His daughter from his marriage played piano since the age of five—her mother wanting her to be a prodigy, he wanting her to be a Freud… The music continued without pause for breath as far as he could tell—Alice must have mastered some trick technique. Then Aaron's head appeared… he was carrying… someone… a nude… pale… man. Quite a large man, nearly as large as Aaron, though not as muscular. And bald? His head was the same ivory as the rest of his body. The body—no, the man was alive, for once outside he stood wobbly, concentrating on the moon.

Martin felt something tug at his pants. (He hadn't un- dressed—instinct told him not to, just as paranoia told him to wedge paper under the door.) Startled, he tumbled back- wards through what seemed to be hundreds of slashing razors and ripping fingers until he was hanging by his hair, kicking the floor to keep balance. The pressure on his hair tightened and he was pulled upwards; when he reached to free himself his fingers were slashed. He could feel his toes leaving the ground.

"*Lodestone.*"

A voice as clear as the pan flute. He reached into his pocket for the lodestone, raising it to his hair. Immediately he was dropped, and his left leg tipped something sideways. Did it squirm? Stumbling to switch on a bedstand light he saw he'd knocked over one of Fairbain's children—this one a bit under three foot in length, a foot of that being an outstretched arm that metamorphosed into a sword point. It lay in the middle of the floor, a caricature of a pirate. Its right peg leg had broken from the weight of his fall. Its face was turned toward him, teeth widely spaced in a grin that looked more like a bite. How could he have missed it before? How could he have missed tripping over it when he first walked to the window? Something trickled down his cheek and he saw his arm and shirt spattered with blood. Overhead, a statuette fell off its wire holder onto the sword to shatter. Martin realized how lucky he'd been to have kicked the pirate sideways as he fell—the probable results were funny to think about now, but disembowelment wouldn't have been too humorous to experience.

A knock. "Are you all right?"

Martin lunged for the paper wedged under the door. How embarrassing if Alice Fairbain were to discover that not only had he broken two statues but had locked her out of a room in her own house. And spied on her! But on his knees with his hand on the paper he paused, remembering the lodestone and Nikki's warning.

He could see Alice's gold slippers shifting through the door's generous crack. "Dr. Edmonds, are you—"

"I tripped, but I'm fine," he said through the closed door. "Go on back to sleep. I'm sorry to have woken you up. I'll clean up and see you in the morning."

There was a momentary silence as Alice's slippers turned to the right. Was she conferring with Aaron, someone else?

"As long as you're okay. I was up anyway, working with Aaron down in the yard on a sculpture. We'll probably call it a night now. See you at breakfast."

Her slippers stayed at the door even after he acknowledged what she said. Her dog's front paw appeared then lifted, probably to slap at her dress. Then they left. Martin stood and walked from the door to the guest bath in the room. Flipping on its light he quivered on seeing his face streaked with blood. It hadn't hurt until he saw it; now each cut ached. There was a slight clatter behind, as if the dangling mobiles were knocking into one another. He watched the mirror carefully but could see no movement. Just what the hell had grabbed him anyway? The pirate? How did it get to the middle of the floor?

Washing increased the pain. Most of the cuts were the superficial kind that paper gives, so once cleaned of blood they closed, leaving nearly no lines. But there was a welt around his throat that he could account for only by the wrapping of wire. That would explain the lifting sensation: He'd gotten caught in one of the mobiles and had actually been lifting himself by his own awkward twisting. His fingers began to ache, and he remembered they too had been cut.

Giving a last look at the mirror he saw the pirate lying on the floor behind. No doubt it had somehow caught his pants. He stalked back and stamped the pirate's grinning teeth. His foot slid and cracked the sword to reveal a haft of steel coming to a bayonet point. Inhaling, he involuntarily tightened his buttocks…

Crickets, frogs, and other night creatures of God including

an owl sang outside. With a final grimace at the sharp steel he walked to the window, rubbing the lodestone in his pocket. The moon had dropped and Persephone's Escalator was barren of movement.

A new statue, a young man, was holding a head, inspecting it after the Greek mode of Jason and Medea. But the young man's look was not one of calm Grecian pride at having defeated this monster: It was one of lascivious bloodlust. Was this the same man Aaron had carried out, the one who'd wobbled? Maybe there was a kiln down in Persephone… but hadn't Ralph Settles and his two friends descended?…

Too disconcerted to sleep, Martin glanced to the paper wedged under the door, rubbed his lodestone, and began reading Dean Kirby's diary as he'd meant to do four hours earlier.

ARIADNE'S THREAD

"Thus I found that there are psychic parallelisms which cannot be related to each other causally, but which must be connected to one another through a different principal…"

C. G. Jung

1.

Dr. Edmonds put Dean Kirby's diary down with a sigh. If he'd had this earlier, he might have foreseen the attempt on Bobby's life. Kirby was working himself into as fine a multiple personality as one could want.

He looked out the window—rather *at* the window, for the moon had disappeared and his vision was blocked by dark reflecting glass. He thought of Nikki. Had she mentioned dinner? No, it was Night, her daughter: "Mother expects you for dinner tomorrow. She'll pick you up at six here."

Just as well: He wouldn't be welcome past breakfast once Alice Fairbain found out he'd broken two statues under his not so lard posterior. Martin looked at the statues still hanging. They'd untangled themselves—thank God for small favors. He looked back to Dean Kirby's manuscript:

Ka, Ka, ka.

Damn Kirby and his humanities Ph.D., anyway. What the hell is ka? *I know, I know:* ak *spelled backwards.*

Martin set his alarm watch and let out a yelp as cuts along his cheek and neck split. After a few minutes of less than manly whimpering he went to sleep…

Not even into a good REM pattern, he heard noise overhead. Flicking on the light, he saw a statue that looked for all the world like an office secretary sitting at a desk with crossed legs, twirling about. He imagined her nervously tapping her feet on the floor, flipping her glasses and yanking paper from her printer. As he did, another swung near her like a beau. Then another.

Then they twisted to face him.

He grabbed for the lodestone and pressed it tightly. Clinging to the stone was Night's perfume, which was her mother Nikki's perfume also. Overhead, another statue swayed softly, but didn't manage to turn.

2.

While Dr. Martin Edmonds was dining with Alice Fairbain, Dean Kirby simply walked out of St. Veronica's and hailed a cab. Atlanta's evening air was cool since a storm system from the South threatened, so until hard rain came, everyone was taking advantage of the July break.

"Where to?" the driver asked, hanging his arm across the seat in a friendly gesture as Dean opened the cab door.

"Wesley Chapel."

"You're going to have to give directions." The driver flipped the meter and started off.

"It's right off the I-75 exit. State Road 54."

"54?"

"Between Zephyrhills and Land o Lakes."

"Where's that?"

"Who's the cab driver, you or me? It's 16 miles north of Tampa."

The cabby slid the car to a halt. He turned and looked to a blank-eyed man with thick glasses and a blonde crew cut. The man's forehead glowed tomato-red.

"Tampa, Florida, right?"

"Right."

The cabby noted the guy had to snap himself to attention to answer the question, as if the raindrops beginning to fall had entranced him. Then he immediately slumped back to press against the window, leaving a grease spot.

"Right, wrong. You think I'm going to drive you all the way to Florida? I get off at eight tonight, my friend, and my lady will be mad if her lasagna overcooks. *Comprende?* Out. Go on back to St. Veronica's or wherever you crawled from. That's O-U-T for you *Sesame Street* fans." The driver gave a jerk with his thumb, then banged the Plexiglas divider. "Out, out, fruitcake, before I have to wring you out like a duck. Hurry and the rain won't wash away any more of your brain cells."

But the man just sat staring at the rain that now pelted the window, so the cabby himself got out and pulled the back door open, intent on tossing the fare. Instead, he found himself rolled like a lover's tryst into the back seat, underneath this skinny maniac with a pit-bull grip on his throat.

"Where am I?" A wet, colicky voice demanded.

"Peekssstrt," the cabby answered, gagging from the rotting breath and trying to kick free. The grip only tightened as the question was repeated. He held still, indicating he would answer.

"Peachtree Street. Atlanta." He looked at eyes so black that they were totally pupil, so he added, "Georgia."

A woman knocked on the window, wanting a cab, and the driver kicked, trying to get away. Dean Kirby's hands squeezed until he heard vertebrae snap. When he looked up, the woman dropped her mouth into an O. His fist smashed the window to grab her, but she ran off in the rain. He followed until he found a car with its engine running. Getting in, he pulled away, stopping two blocks off with a coughing spell. Recovering, he was on I-75, heading toward Florida.

"You shouldn't have killed the cab driver."

I had to. I'd be back in that cell if I didn't.

"You could have tied him up—"

You watch too much TV.

"I found the car for you; it was easy enough. I'm the one who'll take care of business in Florida. He's my son; she was my wife."

You? You're nothing, a has-been college professor. If you'd summoned me sooner—

A car pulled off an entrance ramp and Dean Kirby had to brake, barely managing to keep his briefcase from falling. His face broke into a manic smile as it looked into a side mirror and saw itself wink.

Two hours later, he was heading out of Tifton, turning the heater on full blast until sweat ran in a steady stream down his face.

You think it's hot in Georgia, Professor? Georgia's an ice box. Wait until we hit Florida's heat. Heat is lovely for passion. Lovely passion is why you summoned me, ain't it?

Valdosta 46

Valdosta 33

Valdosta 26, Gainesville 97

Dean watched signs pass. Why wasn't there any air? His throat jammed. It was all he could do to roll down the window and turn off the heater. As he did, he heard manic laughter. Then there was even more heat.

3.

Nikki Ryan sat in her back yard throughout the night once Martin Edmonds was delivered, deposited, dropped—she hoped not deceased—at Alice Fairbain's. The afternoon's storm had moved north and she occasionally saw heat lightning as the moon ascended through cypress and cedar. Had she made a mistake by leaving Martin alone? What else could she do? Alice Fairbain and her clunky servant were too powerful at this point. The weakness she hoped for had yet to materialize, though Dr. Martin Edmonds' appearance could be a harbinger.

"Patience, patience," she counseled, her foot tapping the soggy grass as the moon rose. She stroked the bird Skull shifting on her shoulder, digging its talons in until she winced. "Patience. He'll be back tomorrow. He'll be back."

She'd invited Martin back for practical reasons: He had to be extracted from Fairbain's influence within a reasonable time; he could give inside information on her; and he'd unwittingly capture some essence from her house, an essence that would cling to his clothes, hair and skin—an essence of particular use…

But there was an impractical reason too. She found herself attracted to this Dr. Martin Edmonds in a most ridiculous way considering the situation, considering his occupation, hers. It wasn't that the old wives' tale about love or tears breaking a witch's power was true. On the contrary, emotions were essential to the workings. For instance, that wonderful emotion, Belief. Lack of emotion was a sorcerer's game, what made them an extinct breed in an age of science. Still, only a fool would deny emotion's downside: With either romance or lust, judgment could become blurred, slowed.

೮ଃ୫ଠ

A little before midnight she saw what she'd seen for six months—a pink glow eight miles east, over what she knew was Alice Fairbain's house. Instead of gathering into an ochre ball as it had every night before, the pink simply vanished. Something was going on. She worried for Martin and eyed Night's Trans-am, pushing herself forward on the lawn chair. Then a youthful, tinkling giggle interrupted her. *Instinct, Mommy-o. Not machinery.* The giggle was so relaxed that Nikki sat back to concentrate on the word *instinct* and Martin's face. She imagined stroking his beard, rubbing her hand over his chocolate-y eyes and his worry-line brow. *Instinct, instinct.* With each pulsing thought, Skull pecked the night air as if nabbing mosquitoes…

Well before dawn, Nikki heard an alligator bellow on the lake. This awakened her from an easy slumber that had settled with the fog. She stood to go in her house, light-footed, for she knew she'd won, this time, anyhow. Martin had heard her and used the lodestone as a talisman. As she walked, her skin transformed into that of a teenager: Night could go to school today—no ridiculous recording informing her that her "daughter" missed another class.

4.

Martin fumbled with his wristwatch, trying to turn off its built-in alarm, wondering how much this new invention would increase the neuroses already plaguing modern society.

He looked at the ceiling and sat up: the statues had completely straightened themselves. Were they all facing him? He peeked over the side of the bed and reddened on seeing that the major damage to the pirate had occurred when he angrily stomped its arm. Getting out of bed, he tilted the pirate upright. Molasses splotches ran from each major break, like blood. What in the world did Fairbain put in her statues that could cause that?

"Breakfast will be in half an hour, sir."

Martin fumbled, nearly knocking the pirate over again as he looked to Aaron in the open door.

"An accident, sir?"

"Yes. I hope this wasn't Alice's favorite."

"Ms. Fairbain has no favorites in the house but the griffins guarding door. You didn't break them, ja?"

Martin gave Aaron a second look. Could it be possible that those hands the size of a basketball, that brow curved as a hoop, that brain as porous as netting, had combined to make a joke?

Aaron gave a wet snort that reminded Martin of a bull his grandfather had raised in Georgia. "I will take that all to the workshop. It can be repaired." Aaron stepped inside then turned to the bed. "*Nu*, I see Pauline was in the fracas too. Kaddish, Pauline."

"Pauline?" Martin asked.

Aaron pointed to the bed's headboard where a squat secretary had landed upside down in the night. Her pen stuck nearly an inch into the wood. He yanked her up and crushed her in his fist into a powder over a garbage can. "Bad *Fraulein*. You could have hurt *Herr* Doctor." Aaron's grin was nonstop as he stooped for the pirate on the floor.

Martin's eyes watered thinking of the secretary's spearpoint pen falling two small centimeters forward. He sniffed.

"Believe me, *Herr* Doctor, you make more of this than it merits. Besides, Ms. Fairbain, she already knows."

"How?"

"What else could the last night noise have been? You interrupt our nightly frog concert." With that, Aaron lugged the pirate away.

Martin stood at the door and watched him descend the steps, glimpsing a last crooked smile before Aaron's head disappeared beneath the banister, a smile that unsettled Martin. How had Aaron gotten in? He turned to see why his paper trick hadn't acted as a lock. It wasn't there, that's why. He found it beside the wastebasket, gripped by two of Alice's statues, with their tiny hands. *Very funny, Herr Aaron.*

Brushing his teeth Martin realized he'd formed a dislike for Aaron, if not a downright hatred, with almost as much vitriol as Dean Kirby had. The thought of Kirby tumbled Martin from the bathroom to give a glance to the last thing he'd read in the diary: *Ka, ka, ka.* He turned the page: *AK* in bold letters filled the whole sheet. Kirby had borne down hard enough to snap the point of the pencil he was using and actually tear the paper.

Martin packed the manuscript in his briefcase, locking it. Paranoia: the sane twentieth century alternative. As he walked down, Alice appeared shocked at the cuts on his face and hands. Martin waved off her concern, even as his neck stung. He sat and sipped coffee in a bay window overlooking the apple tree and Persephone's Elevator. "I don't know if Aaron told you, but I'm afraid I got these cuts in the process of breaking two of your—"

"Don't worry about that. Someone's already working on Billie the Sailor. And Pauline?" Alice gestured with her right hand to indicate *Poof!* "The world's full of Paulines, it's better off without another. Are you all right? That's what concerns me."

Martin nodded and ate a patty of sausage. "Nothing worse than I'd get shaving on New Year's. What do you do with all those little statues?"

"The same thing I do with the big ones. Sell them. The little ones go to little heads who want to own original art. I told you I'm a whore—the only difference is one can't contract VD or AIDS from my wares." She laughed huskily, that same undertone he heard last night coming through strongly.

"Still, I'd like to pay for what I've done."

"You can pay by keeping Dean Kirby far away from me, and from his son. Maybe his son will grow up to be something besides a second-rate, pea-mind academe that way."

Something—instinct?—told Martin to listen. It was, after all, what a good psychologist should do, as Alice had pointed out. But the rest of breakfast was sedate, the only surprise being the large helpings of pancakes, sausage and bacon, scrambled eggs, and biscuits, plus sliced tomato and melon.

"Aaron can't believe it either," Alice commented good-humoredly. "That a young *goyische* girl can eat so much. If you have to eat pig, he says, at least do it in the morning so I won't know I'm cooking it."

If Aaron heard Alice's comments, he pretended not to. She seemed disappointed there was no response, and Martin recognized a tart's teasing tone in her voice. He watched the hulk bump against the door and trundle to the kitchen and wondered if they were lovers. Sausage caught in his throat and he didn't know whether to choke or laugh. They finished half an hour later, after coffee cake. Martin felt as if he'd been through a five-course dinner instead of breakfast.

"How strong is your stomach?" Alice asked as she pushed her cup and saucer away for Aaron to clear.

"How full or how strong?"

"How strong." She raised her chin to look at him.

"Well, St. Veronica is in the middle of Atlanta, not far from a wino district. I've seen knife fights, a shooting…" he shrugged.

"I ask because I know that all I've given you to go on is my word, though I'm sure your own appraisal of Mr. Kirby will testify that he's dangerous." Alice looked out the window, tapping it for some reason. Martin started. Was that whatever Aaron had carried out last night, lying by the apple tree in a clump like a fallen Greek hero?

Alice turned back: "Follow me."

They walked into the kitchen. Martin was surprised, for the view through the door belied its true size. It held a restaurant's eight-burner stove, two ovens underneath, with a double tier more overhead. Its walls were lined with glass-enclosed shelving that reached the ceiling, holding myriad dinnerware and serving trays. Alice, no doubt used to gawking guests, grabbed his elbow and led him to a box freezer. Opening it she pulled out a ten-gallon soup kettle, giving a grunt. When the kettle thudded heavily on a butcher's block, Martin realized how strong she actually was.

"You tell Mr. Kirby, when you get back, that I'm saving this for him." Removing the aluminum foil, she motioned to the inside of the kettle. Martin recoiled on seeing a very large rattlesnake frozen in water. The snake had been shot directly behind its head.

"Remember what I told you about the calls? One of these coiled on my porch each morning your patient called. I ate the other one. You can tell that to your patient too."

"Did you tell the police?"

"The police and I don't get along since the Settles' girl was found in my holding pond. They're here more than enough already. That's why I called you, to show you this and what's over at the Kirby house. It's a lot less appetizing than a dead rattlesnake."

Martin nodded as she replaced the foil. With a fearful premonition he wondered if she were going to show him Annie Kirby's body. "If what is over at Kirby's is anything indicating illegal action, I'll have to report it, of course."

"Of course. You're still not completely convinced about Kirby, are you? And you're still not convinced that Bobby should come here either."

Martin shrugged.

From her blouse, Alice pulled out paper. "To show you there's no hard feelings." She handed over the $2500 check as the lawyer had promised. "But I do advise keeping an open mind until we reach Kirby's old house. Let's go see what we can see."

"I need to brush up first."

As he walked to the stairs he almost reached out to touch one of the griffins but held back, imagining a tendon tense in its front leg. He stopped. Both legs were pointing down, near his kneecaps.

A flash popped and he jumped to see Alice Fairbain laughing, holding up a camera. "The griffin pose! Of all the merry poses my guests perform, that's my favorite. Hurrah! The griffins are wired electronically, of course. Now hurry upstairs: I promise not to sneak my camera into the bathroom."

⊂Ω⊃

Brushing his teeth over a gargoyle wash basin, Martin decided it was good that Fairbain had art as an outlet, for she was a classic manic-depressive personality. As an artist, her mood shifts came off as "creative temperament" and probably enhanced her reputation rather than alienated her friends. He zipped his bathroom bag and tossed it onto his suitcase. Maybe it'd be smart to take the briefcase along. He didn't want to leave Kirby's diary unguarded, and he'd need to take notes if Alice showed him what he more and more feared: the exhumed body of Annie Kirby.

One last look outside at Persephone's Escalator—no movement, so he looked upwards. The sky was a wonderful bright blue. Alice's dog ran below and Martin chuckled at the silly haircut that made it look like a miniature lion. He was sure the manicured dog added to her artistic mystique, and he was also sure Alice was businesswoman enough to tax-deduct the pet's grooming. How else would she have been able to fly him down first class and pay such a ridiculous fee? Especially after he said Bobby might not be released to her care. But then, what if it *was* Annie Kirby's body she was taking him to see?

Rex was sitting now, watching Alice's kiln. In front of the kiln, a woman arranged statues on a metal rack. When she turned to pick up another, Martin bumped his nose against the warm windowpane. The frame rattled and she looked up. He backed from the window. Her hair was waist length; other than that, for all the world she looked like photos of Dean Kirby's deceased wife.

Hanging statues twisted throughout the room. Maybe the air conditioning had started—maybe it hadn't. He ducked well out of their reach and grabbed his briefcase and suitcase, hunching over and feeling foolish. Once outside, he straightened to assess the room. *They're just statues*, he assured himself.

Alice and Aaron were waiting at the bottom of the stairs.

"If you want to know the truth," Alice said, "I think it's just a matter of very short time before Dean Kirby finds his way down here. So Aaron's staying close by."

Martin nodded, noticing Aaron reach for a large suitcase—an old one with fat, square sides that resembled a box. He irrationally imagined the rattlesnake thawing inside.

A SUMMONING

1.

$\mathcal{J}$ewel Dawn sat staring out her office window, realizing she couldn't even remember what the young graduate student who'd just left had wanted. She remembered the girl's looks, a talcum paleness topped with nearly white hair spun like old-fashioned Christmas angel hair, and she remembered signing some form. Had the girl dropped a class, added one, transferred to Harvard? Any number of things. Jewel quit the window for a Triple A map of Florida that hung on her wall.

Florida had been on her mind for a year. The faculty kidded her about early retirement, but that wasn't it. Nothing to do with the university at all. In her capacity as Executrix of the American Coven she'd received letters from many Floridian Sisters, complaining that everything from simple herbal potions to grand spells were being thwarted, working backwards, or simply flubbing. And the problem was spreading: Sisters in New Orleans, Mobile, Birmingham and Atlanta were writing. It made sense that witches would be the first to feel a twist in the Matrix, but a twist this strong would soon be felt by non-believers. A twist like this could be fatal.

She told this to the Grand Council and they, in grandly bureaucratic fashion (yes, witches have that problem too), suggested waiting, studying. They suggested not jumping to conclusions, not firing a cannon into a molehill, not, not, not… She'd held her tongue like a good politician and gathered a private council. If gravity suddenly began repelling instead of attracting in one area of the earth you'd be damned sure physicists would flock there, wouldn't you? Whether the Grand Union of Physicists gave them travel vouchers or not. So several Sisters had agreed to help unofficially.

Jewel locked her office door, then looked at the map. From her purse she took two packets of NutraSweet and formed a powdery circle around herself on the floor. She grinned, thinking how many young witches would be offended she hadn't used animal blood. That was why she was Executrix: she understood not only that the Matrix changed, but that it *had* to change to stay vital. Not that NutraSweet worked as well as blood in rituals—not yet, anyway—but it worked, and there was a certain *je ne sais quoi* added to the power by inventing new methods. Maybe the Matrix has a sense of humor, who could tell? She spit on her left index finger three times and looked at the map, angrily noting the copyright date—two years before. Damn Triple A.

Damn yourself, Jewel. Concentrate.

She took two more packets and overlapped her Circle of Power, repeating the ritual in case her lack of concentration flawed the previous one. She again spit on her left index finger and watched the spittle fall.

"Burn not me." She repeated this three times.

"*Nolle me incende*," she added, passing her finger over the map, using the Latin more from sentimentality and habit than any real enchanting power that dead language contained. She watched as her finger made its pass: nothing over the Panhandle. Her finger felt oddly cold over Gainesville. But cold wasn't what she was looking for. Damn that grand council of fools anyway, didn't they notice all the quirks bounding through the Matrix day after day?

Her finger slid down the eastern coast and a blue arc popped from across the state's west coast—a good ten inches on the map. Not only did it knock her backwards, but the map flamed.

She recovered enough to slap it out, burning her hand. The arc had its origin to the north of Tampa. A burn had never been that prominent in this type of summoning, and certainly one had never jumped in a spark. Had she procrastinated too long? Some Executrix she was—no wonder her time was up.

Her phone rang and she was tempted to ignore it.

Answer.

She did.

"You've found it, haven't you?"

It was Anne Marie, the woman once preened to inherit the Executrix position, though they both knew that was no longer so, even if the other Sisters didn't. Jewel had been more disappointed than Anne Marie—why should some unknown upstart take the position, for an upstart it must be, as none of the other eleven at the Grand Council's meeting had shown the slightest interest once the serpent crawled up Anne Marie's leg to lie in her lap ten years before. Such strong affinity wasn't to be denied or even questioned. At least it seemed so at the time. But as Jewel knew too well, the Old Religion was no less infallible than new ones, no less than technology, no less than the Pope. And just what was the reason? Jewel supposed that time, as always, would tell. So, despite the serpent, not Anne Marie, but some unknown was slated to replace Jewel as Executrix.

"Yes. Or it's found me," Jewel looked from the phone to her finger, burned despite her invocation. "We need to prepare at once. Come over tomorrow at ten."

"Blood and Birth," Anne Marie said.

"Blood and Birth," Jewel answered, cradling the phone, hoping their ancient greeting would weigh toward its latter, not its former half. But she was grave with misgivings. It came to her that the student had wanted to add a course in the Fall: *Witchcraft, Women and Medieval Politics.* It was a course Jewel feared would never be taught, at least not by her. Despite her frilly forays into NutraSweet Circles of Power and Bisquick voodoo dolls, she knew the future wasn't in her, nor in Anne Marie. Anne Marie had pledged a dual-death rite when she found out: She wanted to follow Jewel into "wherever." But Jewel argued that Anne Marie would be needed, especially if this new Executrix was as young as they feared. The power structure would be wobbly, no matter how strong the Matrix was in this new creature. And assassinations weren't unknown among witches' grand councils…

She hadn't erased her Circle of Power before answering the phone—not the first time lately she'd muffed a ritual. She bent to scoop the powder in her palm, hearing bones pop in her knees, ankles, back, and neck. I'm a walking percussion instrument, she laughed, blowing the dust into the air, sensing a sudden invasion of her taste buds with the sweet powder. NutraSweet was a definite improvement over pig's blood.

Driving home she spotted a billboard depicting a young woman impressing a male by smoking a cigarette. Where'd all his smoke disappear to? Into her expensive evening gown? Her full lungs? And preachers worried about the Devil… ridiculous. After the 1700s the Old Religion had given up on the Devil. That male fantasy had only gotten tens of thousands of Sisters burned and maimed. Modern Sisters knew there was no Devil (male, of course) just as there was no God (male, of course). There was the Matrix. Jewel smiled at the word's Latin origin, *mater, mother.*

She braked sharply as a teenager in a pickup spun into a street not forty yards ahead. She turned the same corner, thinking of tossing off a good bust-a-tire spell, but noticed a deathly black aura growing around the truck, enveloping its fancy chrome, and knew she needn't bother: the child would cause much more serious pain for himself soon enough. It wasn't always fun having the power to see…

She drove on home. Colleagues jokingly referred to her house as "antediluvian." Twelve years before, Paul bought her a three-foot representation of the ark, which she placed by the door. Paul, the department chair then, joked that if the Great Flood came she could curl up in it with her cat and one hundred cans of tuna and weather the forty days. Jewel now stroked a ten- inch figurine of Noah standing at the ark's bow. She thought of Paul's wondrous, smooth hands as billowy and soft as a violet. That billow she so loved was his downfall though: he died of a heart attack six days before summer solstice four years ago. Of course she was an emotional disaster on the solstice, but the Matrix had been its usual stubborn self and she had to repeat the ceremony six times to get even a flop effect. As much fog as a pond would spew and a small familiar manifested—a parrot or cockatiel, she forgot which. One initiate was so charmed with the bird that Jewel gave it to her. Sesuj had given the bird a good swat, then settled into licking his paws. Most indecorous for an Executrix's familiar. While many members of the Grand Council and the coven empathized with her ineptness, she could see blame erupt in some older Sisters' eyes: *If you hadn't become involved with a man, this solstice would have been spectacular.* Left-hand thinking or jealousy? Was there a difference?

She gave Noah a friendly rub and wondered what role Paul had assumed in the Matrix. A good one she was sure: some creatures would follow the right-hand-path until the second coming of Chaos, just as some would follow the left-hand-path that same period of time. This thought told her she'd better make a few preparations against Bethsheba, a.k.a. Beth. The pretensions of the woman's name were as high-handed as the woman herself. At least, Jewel thought, I came by my name honestly. Her mother meant to name her Judy Awle; *Judy* because she liked the name, *Awle* because of a pioneer friend. The midwife misunderstood it as Jewel Dawn. It was a high-spirited daimon that twisted the air between her mother's tongue and that midwife's ear. Names, as everyone knows, have the power to move. *And move Sesuj and I have for over 150 years.*

In the kitchen, Jewel began a large crock of cinnamon potpourri. This alone would throw her highness Beth off for three days. But Beth, reeking of garlic, would no doubt come to the house. So Jewel started an extra pot. She then reached for her purse. Cinnamon was nice, but bullets bite. She broke down a two-shot derringer and kissed both bullets. *What an efficient little witch you are,* she thought, tucking the gun into her apron.

But there'd be more than enough of the left-handed way today to keep Beth happy. Jewel's real problem would be convincing all six women to go. She wanted at least a Pentad of power, plus two, herself and one other. Beth could be either asset or hindrance, depending on her mood, so Jewel and Anne Marie had worked on a young girl named Becky, promising to pay her way. Thank the stars they were going to Florida: how many could she have gotten to go to Nebraska?

She pulled dough from the refrigerator to let it rise. Cook tonight; eat tomorrow. What was that ritual trying to teach? Be prepared? They could join the Girl Scouts for that. No matter, once all seven of them had eaten, she'd sit easier: the bond would be formed. Then all they had to do was go to Florida. All. She started, realizing her cat Sesuj was watching from his perch on the counter.

"Eavesdropping again?"

Sesuj licked his paws then jumped to sniff the rising dough. He meowed, nudging the bowl with his head and pit-patted to the spice shelves, hopping to the third one. Jewel obligingly moved the rising dough underneath. *I shouldn't be so snippy about Bethsheba's name*, she thought. *After all, I named my familiar with an acronym for Jesus Christ—both pretensions are astounding, and I had only the excuse of youth.*

Bump, bump, bump. Sesuj knocked off cayenne pepper, cumin and curry powder—all for strength. Jewel added a quarter teaspoon of each, but the cat howled, so she doubled the recipe, her tongue cloying at how the rolls would taste. She looked up. Since she'd built the shelves to accommodate the cat's roving he could hide well in the back if he chose, which he was doing at present. She could see only the white of his paw lifting to his face, then the pink of his tongue.

"That's all then?"

She wouldn't mention to the Sisters that Sesuj doubled the potion. She kneaded the dough, still cool, then formed eight large rolls, leaving an extra as she always did for the unexpected—be it guest or enemy. Another spice fell. Jewel stared at a tin of bay leaves. A mistake. The embalming herb. Still, an unfortunate omen. She replaced the tin on the shelf. Sesuj knocked it off again.

"Are you sure?" Her voice rasped like a smoker's cough. Sesuj purred. Jewel nodded and went for a vanity mirror, this being one incantation she didn't want to muff. Propping the mirror behind the rolls and under Sesuj (who was leaning over the shelf), she walked to the refrigerator and pulled out a jar, her stomach curling. The blood of a slaughtered pig, kept liquid by the modern science of refrigeration and a nudge from the Old Religion. She popped the vacuum lid and an immediate gag reaction set in. Good old pig's blood. Her hands shook as she placed the container on the counter.

Sesuj licked his paws and stared. "I know, I know," Jewel answered. She stuck her tongue in the blood, holding her breath. It tasted awful, like vinegar and iron, and when she finally did breathe, it tasted worse. She poured it about her on the floor, careful to make the circle as round as possible, as thick as possible. With little less than half a pint left, she surveyed the circle and poured more on a thin spot, her own feeling for the ritual being that patching was tolerated more by the Matrix than prideful ignoring—no human nor witch was about to pour a perfect circle the first try. A few tablespoons were left. She bent her head back, opened her mouth and drank, spilling half of it on her face, forcing what went into her throat to stay down.

She placed the jar between her legs and began to chant, watching her lips in the mirror, seeing them as they were when she was barely a teenager in her second soul/body migration and Thomas Edison was inventing the incandescent lamp. Her first menstruation had come one month before.

Veni, mors. Veni, mors. Veni, mors. Seeing her lips move, she realized she wasn't using the church pronunciation of "V," but the classical pronunciation *Weni.* She trembled, feeling all of her 154 years. In the mirror, clouds, then Paul's fluffy hands reached for her image. She blinked back tears, though she'd been certain this would happen, as it had before. *Concentrate:* "*Weni, mors. Weni, mors,*" she repeated. A mere child when he died—at least to someone who'd lived three lifetimes, though no one but herself and a handful of Sisters would ever know it—his face appeared in the mirror, lissome and mischievous as a teenager's, though a surprising robustness filled his chest and arms. He beckoned. She remained chanting "Come, death. Come, death." How many times had he appeared in the middle of some ritual, attracted no doubt by her psychic energy? Always, always, she had to hold him back from something that was terrible for them to resist: to touch again, at last. If he did step from the mirror would those hands afford the same cottony feel?

"No, Paul!" she sobbed. She saw him smile and withdraw even as she opened her right eye widely to keep a tear from falling. She stood motionless for three minutes. The tear subsided; it had not fallen. Nor had they touched. But soon they would. *Soon, Paul.* She resumed her chant. "*Veni, mors. Veni, mors. Veni, mors.*"

Sesuj placed a paw over the edge of the shelf and scratched the wood. Jewel reached uncertainly for a bay leaf. This she placed on the nearest roll. She looked back: the paw was still out. She picked another. And another, and another. Sesuj withdrew his paw, leaving four claw marks. So. Four would die. Seeing something scurry on the floor, Sesuj hopped down, driving one leaf deeply into a roll. She understood. She would die and three of the six others would die.

That brought Paul nearer… But a fifty-fifty return wouldn't make it easy to get volunteers. Jewel looked at the circle of blood: *No reason to stay inside it now—the Matrix has made its decision.* She stepped out and wadded paper towels to wipe the blood before it dried. *Disgusting, even, for a witch to die and leave her house in this shape.*

As she cleaned, she took inventory of the Sisters coming over. Anne Marie would go. She felt a duty to be where Jewel was and would certainly feel this duty now. Beth would go: Her left-hand habits would see to that. The young bubbly girl, Becky, would go. Death holds no fear for the young. The red-haired woman named Nancy? Who could tell? Adventure might call and she might go. Probably, Jewel told herself. Ah, the two married women, both with children? If anyone should shirk, it should be them. What if she herself had met Paul fifteen years earlier in her third cycle at a child-bearing age? Would she have renounced the powers of the Executrix? In the stupefied mid-seventies she might have. Of the two marrieds, Tiffany would go if Beth did. Tiffany was such a little tease—with men *and* women, and Beth had such an irredeemable fascination for the wench. Jewel lifted the blood-soaked paper towels and tossed them in the garbage. She glanced at the extra bread roll and was glad she'd made it. An adventuresome guest, the type to drop over unexpectedly, the type who could on a moment's notice take off for Florida was the oddity needed for a strong Pentad.

Six o'clock. In two hours the rolls would rise and be baked. She needed to keep quiet about the bay leaves. Time enough for bad news tomorrow at ten. At six-twenty, Jewel perused her library, pulling books she would take, though the stars only knew that if she hadn't gotten things down by now, no book would help. She had just decided against *Malef-*

icus Maleficarum because of its tedious spells and over-detailed amulets when her doorbell rang. Sesuj was already sitting there.

"You seem awfully sure of yourself today," Jewel commented. The cat blinked his gold eyes and she opened the door. For a moment she recoiled at the paleness of the girl. Not only was her skin white, but her hair was too. If not for a pair of splendid blue eyes, Jewel would have guessed her an albino. It was the student from this morning, the one who'd pleaded to be let into the course that would never be. It had been those blue eyes and an effervescent seriousness (delightful oxymoron!) that convinced Jewel to let her sign up. She simply didn't have the heart to say no, especially as the girl had already read half the books. So Jewel had handed over a reading list, thinking the girl would at least get the benefit of that.

"Come in."

The girl took an audible breath, clearly impressed with the house.

Jewel was preparing a quick speech about expecting company when Sesuj began rubbing against the girl's snow-white leg.

"I need to go with you tomorrow," she said. "A voice told me as soon as I left you this morning. I tried to ignore it, but it only got stronger when I touched the reading list you gave me. I see bad things; I try to block them out, but they only peek around the curtain." She rubbed her hand on Sesuj's back and sharply drew away. "Death's involved, isn't it?"

Jewel had learned caution over her 154-year life span. "I'm not at all sure I know what you're talking about, child."

The girl—young woman—bristled at the word "child." It was a slip Jewel occasionally made. She once called the Dean of Arts and Sciences that—and why not, he was forty-six at the time, while she was 131, though appearing to be in her late fifties. Paul had been able to brush the joke off—she herself was barely aware she'd made a mistake. The girl's scowl disappeared as easily as it came.

Jewel forced a smile. "Well. Since death isn't a particularly enlivening subject, why don't we talk about you. Would you care for some hot tea?"

"No, nothing to eat or drink."

So the girl was on her guard too. Still, Sesuj was in her lap the moment she sat on the couch. There certainly was no doubt in his mind that she was friend, not foe. Jewel relaxed at this, looked at her wall clock—half an hour for the rolls to rise—and took a seat.

"I'm a math major," the girl said mundanely.

"You told me this morning you were majoring in history."

"I lied because I've been—*interfacing* is the word I adopted—I've been interfacing with the various you's for two weeks."

"The various me's?" If this girl somehow knew about her three migrations… Jewel rubbed the derringer tucked in her dress's waistband.

"The you as a professor, the you as a lover—"

It was Jewel's turn to be offended: The only way she'd been a lover since Paul had died was through memory and occasional self-stimulation that she wasn't eager to share. It couldn't be healthy, even for a witch, to envision sex with a dead man.

"I'm sorry," the girl said. "The interfacing has been so powerful that I haven't been able to control it. I quit high school because of this. Five, six people's thoughts would rush at me like a wet telephone line mixing conversations.

I took drugs so I'd be committed, but that was even worse, so I ran away and worked as a waitress in Corbin. After two years I learned to control what voices came to me. But when I moved here to Lexington, I found things out of control again. The city is too large." She stroked Sesuj.

She thinks Lexington is too large? Jewel thought.

"What's his name?"

"Say-sooj," Jewel replied. "And you should be extremely flattered. Sesuj doesn't make many friends." *Not more than ten in 142 years.*

"Is he really 142 years old?"

Jewel stared at the girl. A telepath. Jewel had only met two others in all her years. She stopped herself from thinking about them and turned to the girl.

"If you want me to like you as much as Sesuj does, you will have to stop doing that. I find it more than rude, I find it dangerous, if you follow my drift."

"You will kill me like you killed the German man."

"You're good. Better than he was: I didn't even *consciously* think that. But you *will* have to stop using your power on me. You can control it that much, can't you?"

The girl nodded as light from a lamp caught her pure white hair.

"Good. Then do you promise?"

The girl continued petting Sesuj. "Yes, I promise. Do you know that I've never met another person with this power? For five years I went to fortune tellers. The only one even vaguely aware was an old man who told the future by scattering matchsticks. He had me touch them, then he didn't even bother to drop them on the table. He just said I couldn't possibly need an amateur's help. He said that he would pray for me. It was strange that a man—the others were women—

that a man could come closest. And using matchsticks, too."

"Sometimes the Matrix doesn't make sense."

"The Matrix?"

A complete naïf—*I'll kill her now*—or a complete and exquisite liar. Jewel purposefully interposed the thought of murder. But there was no reaction: The questioning look stayed, so the girl was being honest about not using her telepathy any further. Of course, that didn't mean she'd stay honest half an hour down the road.

"Do you believe in God?"

"Of course… I guess," the girl said, backing off a bit.

"The Matrix is like Providence, like God's all-encompassing plan for the universe."

"And we don't always know God's complete will?"

Jewel nodded, mindful of Nietzsche's Zarathustra and his parting words to an old hermit who still believed in God: "What could I have to give you? But let me leave quickly before I take something from you!" *Could it be possible*, Jewel mimicked in a Nietzschean voice, *that this child hasn't yet heard God is dead?*

For the remaining hour, Jewel tested the girl. Her parents lived in Cincinnati, an hour and a half north. She was indeed majoring in math—more to escape the illogic of ever-invading thoughts than any Pythagorean love of numbers. Too bad, Jewel thought; just as mathematicians made good musicians, she suspected they'd make excellent witches. Enough medieval men had dabbled in both areas, that was for certain. Jewel was amused to find out the girl (name: Lori) was a virgin, though how the subject had been broached she hadn't the faintest idea. A twenty-four-year-old virgin was nothing to sneeze at. A lesbian? Jewel searched for signs but found nothing other than a fawning teacher-student attachment.

All this time, Sesuj refused to leave the girl's lap. *Girl, girl, what are you getting into? Go home and work out some calculus equations.* At fifteen after seven, Jewel stopped Lori's running autobiography. "Now I need to tell you some things. I'm not sure how clear your 'interfacing' as you call it is, but there is indeed danger—mortal danger, death—in the cards—in the bay leaves—for half those who go tomorrow. And the bay leaves are seldom wrong.

"And once you break bread with the Sisters, you're bound to go. I don't mean that lightly like a date, like going steady or even getting married—" Jewel remembered the girl's virginity and rethought her similes. "Let me put it this way; unpleasant things are bound, bound like steel cable, like strapping wire, unpleasant things are pledged and obligated to happen to a person who breaks bread then breaches her promise. I normally send everyone off with a glass of brandy to a room— this house has more than enough—to let her think the consequences through. Those who wish to continue meet at a prearranged time; those who wish to leave do so through the front door without any loss of face, especially in this case. I fully expect two women not to go."

"They won't," Lori said.

Jewel took a breath; there was no doubt the girl's powers would be an asset. But so young, so untried. A virgin, by Mary's Lower Beard. A thought niggled Jewel. Could this be the one? Could she be the new Executrix? Surely not. Too many things were missing in the pattern. But what was she? A lonely telepathic virginal waif? The Nine Names of God help us, then.

2.

Alice Fairbain had gone moody on the brief drive to

Dean Kirby's old house, so Martin took in the landscape: the area certainly could turn someone's mind given the right circumstances. Bald cypress trees loomed like forlorn giants with frazzled hair and beards. Jet black water stood in deep drainage ditches, just as Kirby described. For Martin too, that hue was a novelty, and not a particularly attractive one. He glimpsed the cinder core of what must have been the house where the farmers (Settles, wasn't it?) lost first their daughter, then their lives. He imagined the heavy woman Kirby described as a Teuton screaming in tongues as she trudged through the surrounding sharp palmetto like a suffering saint.

They pulled into the drive, and he noted with surprise that Fairbain hadn't bothered to remove Kirby's name from the mailbox. Living here a grand total of three months and the wife dies suddenly, the son is investigated for murder, for graverobbing, then withdraws into depression—Kirby'd had a hard time of things, and his friendly philosopher Wittgenstein hadn't been much help. A dog barked deeply as Aaron opened the gate, its black shape then running through the yard to the back of the house.

"The Kirby's dog came back?" Martin asked. Dean and Bobby both had told him that it ran away.

No answer.

Martin shrugged, glad he would be spending the evening with Nikki. Fairbain's artistic temperament was wearing thin, and jokeboy Aaron was downright gaseous. They got out at the house. Martin looked in the front window: What he presumed was Kirby's furniture was still there, though Fairbain's statues were scattered inside. Since he'd seen the woman who so resembled Kirby's wife working at the kiln, the vast output of statues wasn't a mystery. Alice had taken her tack from Henry Ford and opened an assembly line.

"Are you going to use this house as a showroom?"

No answer. Alice Fairbain didn't seem to hear, and the human wall lurched behind as incommunicado as ever. Spotting Aaron's reflection in the window, Martin realized that he may have been the man in the green raincoat hanging about the airport. Martin suddenly doubted that Fairbain had anything substantial to show him.

"The house isn't really what I want you to see," Alice said in encouragement.

They walked to the barn. Inside it, instead of a pleasant odor of hay, a layabout rot permeated the air.

"Something large has died in here," Martin commented.

"No doubt," Alice said.

Martin saw a blur to his right. Then his body met the barn's dirt floor.

"There, didn't I tell you this would be important?" Alice Fairbain gave Martin Edmonds' jaw a kick. "Put him inside with the others, Aaron."

The human wall moved, a hint of a smile cracking its plasterboard.

3.

While listening to her history teacher talk about Lincoln, Night shifted her legs so that a boy sitting with his head on his desk and his mouth half open couldn't see up her dress. Suddenly she felt a coolness pervade her body. Something was blocking her contact with Martin Edmonds. She'd been too sure of herself with the lodestone and her simple spell, though she had managed, as Nikki, to draw a circle of power around him, a subtle circle she'd been refining since then. It would keep Martin from serious injury and make his survival seem an intrusion of chance, not protection from the Matrix. *Pride, Night, pride. That's why you're here listening to this teacher and hiding your green panties from a Clearasil bozo. Don't be so sure of your powers against Alice Fairbain; that glow over her house isn't coming from a satellite dish.*

"Mis-ter Taylor. Maybe you can tell us about Lincoln and the Emancipation Proclamation."

The boy who'd been staring at her legs straightened with a salute. "Yes sir, anything you want to know."

"Well good. When did it happen?"

The boy rolled his shoulder like a weightlifter—in what was supposed to pass for thoughtful expression. "Uh, I read about it yesterday in the paper, so he did it Friday, right?"

The class tittered. Fools and saints, Night thought, are often one and the same. But this acne punk who'd been looking up her skirt was obviously only one.

"In the paper yesterday, hmm? Just what paper is it that you read, Mis-ter Taylor?"

Night closed off the rest of the charade after giving the clock a glance. Enough humility for one day. She felt a sharp pain in her cheek. At first she thought one of the boys was shooting paper clips; then she felt an amazing thud on her head and knew she was in contact with Martin. He was having a tough time of things. She concentrated, feeling a tickling along her back: was he being dragged? Her heels thudded, as if being yanked over a sill then dropped.

"Ms. Ryan?"

Night reluctantly looked at the history teacher. From the way the class was giggling, he'd already called her several times.

"Ms. Ryan, Mis-ter Taylor suggested that you knew quite a bit about Lincoln and that you might be able to fill us in."

She stared at the teacher, the assistant wrestling coach,

who looked every bit the part. He was a nice enough man, but his assured look bugged her today.

"I once met a woman who'd met Lincoln. She said he had the saddest eyes she'd ever seen."

The teacher stared angrily, turned and began his lecture. She hated to do it to him, but what the hay, it was true: *Saddest eyes I'd ever seen* was word for word what her spiritual mentor Jewel Dawn had told her about meeting Lincoln. Twice. That is, Jewel had told the story twice. Night tittered. She'd gone to Jewel for initiation into the Sisterhood two times, both as her mother and as herself, and no one was the wiser… But to the business at hand: her mind felt for Martin. He was evidently unconscious. She let her breathing change to his, her leg stiffen… breathe, breathe… hay, she smelled hay. And something was crawling, no, dragging itself toward him. Something warm and wet, like breath, over his face. A hand stroked his forehead, gently, despite its calluses. Then only the smell of hay. No, another thing: a low humming, a song, and though she couldn't make out the words, the voice was a pleasant baritone.

The school bell rang.

"I think you almost had old What's-His-Face believing you about knowing Lincoln."

"Not me. I know someone that knew Lincoln. And I do."

"Right, Night. And my mother's Cleopatra." The girl flitted her eyes and went to her locker.

As Night you're getting quite a reputation as an eccentric, Nikki thought. *That's okay: it'll come in handy someday.* She walked out the hall and off campus, waving at a security guard who turned the other way, thinking she was a teacher. She needed to get home: the transformation into her mother had started and Night/Nikki could feel clothes tightening in all the places teenage girls want them to tighten. Besides, she needed to help Martin pronto if she wanted to have a dinner date tonight. Or ever see him again, period.

She started her Trans-am, thrilled by its immediate rumbling—*Pride, Night, pride.* Her physics teacher walked to his classroom window and shook a finger at her, giving his crooked little smile and laughing with his beady eyes. Too bad he was married, or maybe big momma Nikki would visit during PTA and make a pass or two.

It was less than four miles to home and a good part of the curving road appeared deserted, for its houses were built far back near the lake and their frontage was overgrown. She gave the gas a punch but braked on seeing a bird fly directly for her: Skull. She pulled over and lowered the window so he could land on her shoulder. He did so and shifted nervously from claw to claw, like a human making a decision. Night—nearly Nikki now—saw and felt her dress splitting in two embarrassing spots (not the stomach though, she noted proudly) and checked her rear-view mirror while patiently waiting for Skull to make some sign.

Then, in a heat-dazzle ahead on the road, stood Jewel Dawn. She was evidently talking to someone, several some-ones from the way she moved her gaze. She was completely unaware that Nikki was watching. A car blared its horn and passed, speeding directly through Jewel, who didn't seem to mind the intrusion in the least but continued talking, gesturing. Nikki saw her turn for a piece of chalk, stamp her foot in a small curse when she found none, and continue her talk. It was one of many things that endeared her to Nikki—this absentminded professor always unable to decide whether she was addressing a coven of witches or a classroom of college students. As Nikki watched Jewel go through her motions—

very animated, so something important was up—she re-membered being initiated into the Sisterhood a second time, under the name of Night Ryan. She remembered watching a mourning Jewel fumble the ritual five, six times before getting a response from the Matrix. While some Sisters had been resentful that the death of a man should interfere with their solstice, Night-Nikki had been touched—also im-pressed that the Executrix could shuffle such high emotion and ritual at all. Not the easiest thing in the world to do.

Skull ruffled his feathers in excitement.

"That's right, there's Mommy," Nikki commented. May-be, just maybe, Jewel's emotion that night had added to the power of the Matrix, for Skull had been born a changeling like Nikki-Night, with unlimited shape, from hummingbird to Condor. A very powerful ally as far as familiars go. From the moment she'd seen him prance from Jewel's cat, not even deigning to fly or fight back, she'd known Skull was meant for her. Before Skull she'd had a black cat—which showed just how simple-minded she was.

Another car passed, from the opposite direction. The driv-er slowed then sped on. Nikki glanced at her dress and was glad the car door covered most of her body. She wouldn't be as lucky if a cop passed. Yet what could she do? Run over her twice-mentor's image? It was there for a reason, after all.

She could see Jewel pouring brandies. One… two… eight. So she could be traveling with up to seven others. That would assure a Pentad Plus—Nikki heard a noise and glanced to her rear view, but this car pulled into a driveway—a Pen-tad Plus was nothing to scoff at and the brandy indicated the Sisters were being given a choice. Which meant either that the purpose of the Pentad was of debatable morality or held a possibility of death.

Jewel poured herself a glass—a formality, Nikki was sure—and turned. Jewel spilled some brandy and Nikki knew Jewel had at last seen her too.

"Blood and Birth," Nikki mouthed.

Jewel nodded and disappeared. Had she returned the greeting?

"What do you think, birdie?"

Skull bit her ear as a car approached. Time to move. She respectfully drove over the roadway where she'd just seen Jewel Dawn stand. Arriving at her house, Nikki honked cursorily at her next-door neighbor, Agnes Thompson, a friendly old woman who'd missed her chance to be a babushka. Though she didn't want to be seen getting out of her daughter's car in half torn clothes, looking like she'd been dancing at a nudie club, Nikki was anxious to get inside to share in the brandy that Jewel was drinking.

Unlike other Sisters, Nikki believed that the Matrix was subject to chance (Heisenberg's Imp, her physics teacher called chance). But this particular vision was no chance. So she poured herself a Martell cognac—working for Delta at least taught her good taste—and went with Skull to sit on her dock. For the next few minutes, she sipped the cognac, aimlessly dropped bread to the fish, and wondered if Dr. Martin Edmonds owned a fishing rod. As Night she'd invited boys over, but all they'd wanted to do was go skinny dipping, drink beer, and screw. Skull was a big help in discouraging their young male paws, which she taught him to peck, hard.

As she dropped bread, a five-foot alligator swam nearby. From the safety of the dock, she bounced a twig off its nose. It turned, looking as if seaweed were growing on its teeth; alligators don't have much of a sense of humor. She checked her watch: ten minutes left for them to make the decision.

Some Sisters may have left Jewel's house by now. If so, they were two steps ahead of her, for she didn't even know what the decision involved.

A splash sounded: the alligator had opened its mouth and was swimming backwards, disgorging eight white kittens. Their frantic cries skimmed the dirty water. Eyes wide, Nikki jumped and reached for a pole. But the alligator recaptured four kittens and partially submerged. Not even thinking, she stepped off the dock into water above her waist and scooped up the remaining kittens while Skull frantically dove at the alligator's retreating hide. She placed them on the dock and pulled herself up. Skull gave a last hit at the water then perched on the dock's handrail. Looking back, she hardly believed what she'd done, and gulped her Martell to hold the kittens as she shivered and they mewed.

A sign: the Pentad wasn't a matter of morality, of dubious choice between good and evil; it was a matter of life and death. Of course it would be that: Jewel Dawn dealt almost exclusively with the right-hand path, what most people call white magic. Nikki couldn't say the same for herself, nor did she really wish to. A little revenge was good for the soul.

Three minutes to make her decision. The kittens were crying, their wet hair standing from their bodies like wire, their eyelids opened as wide as if stretched. It's not every kitten that gets to descend like Jonah into the belly of the beast and come back.

Two minutes. How could she commit herself to Jewel Dawn when she was already committed to at least extracting Martin Edmonds? Skull squawked in answer and Nikki remembered the solstice four years before when the bird had been given to her by a distraught, lovesick witch if ever there was one.

"Okay, okay."

She took the kittens inside, Skull flying close by, and broke the bread she'd quickly prepared.

"Blood and Birth, Jewel Dawn."

This time, she could swear she heard her old mentor answer back as the kittens and Skull fought over crumbs.

4.

Bobby Kirby was lying in a hospital bed watching TV when what appeared to be two male nurses walked into the room.

"We're going on a trip," the taller one told him.

"Neat."

When he was escorted past the physical therapy room, he stiffened.

"We're going outside this time. A walk on the streets in the sunshine will do you good."

"Neat."

Half a block later they were panhandled by a sixty- or thirty-year-old man—impossible to tell through layers of dirt and smell. The nurse on Bobby's right stiff-armed the bum so hard that his head bounced off a building's brick wall and he slid down the side coughing.

"What'd you do that for? He just asked for money." Bobby said, pulling away as the nurse tried to recapture his elbow. No answer. Instead the two men jerked him into an alley and toward a waiting car, muffling his scream with a chloroform-soaked rag.

Thirty minutes later, one man looked in the back seat to see that the knife-wound stitches in Bobby's arm had pulled loose and the boy was bleeding. The man climbed over the back seat and stanched the bleeding.

"Where the hell you get that, kid?"

"My dad."

"Yeah? My old man was an asshole too."

5.

"How could you be so stupid?" It was the 88th time Dean Kirby had asked this question, give or take a few hundred. And for the 88th time—give or take a few hundred—the only response was a constricting forehead and a rush of heat. The stolen car had run out of gas and Bubber had simply coasted onto the shoulder to bang the steering wheel until Dean emerged from his mental shell. *Bubber* was the name Dean had given the voice that took over his body. Bubber was what he had summoned with young Abby's magical spell the same night that his wife had killed him. Now he sorely regretted summoning whatever it was. But then if he hadn't summoned Bubber, would he be dead? Was he dead anyway? "Move over, Bubber, and let me handle things for a while."

Feeling Bubber recede, Dean got out of the car.

An hour past dawn he managed to hitch a ride from a college student heading toward the University of South Florida. *Why don't you let me do the talking, Bubber, and we might not have to walk?* A visceral snort was his only answer.

"Going to summer session?" Dean asked the young man, coughing to cover the snort.

"Naw, Dad gave me money to get an apartment early. Tampa's a bitch to get a decent place to live if you arrive in August. Besides, I'll get a head start on all the waitresses that way."

Dean felt better. He smiled at the student's pop eyes and burr haircut and asked what his major was.

"Business. I want to make big bucks when I graduate."

They passed into Florida; the Florida sign made Dean queasy. The kid kept talking about easy waitresses, beaches, and big bucks. Two hours of that and a six pack of beer later:

Can you pull off ahead by that river? I've got to piss.

The student tilted at the sound of the voice, which grated now, where it had held a humorous nasal whine before. "There's a stop ten miles ahead. This Panosuckee Lake or whatever is too creepy. There're alligators."

Just pull off here. I'll buy us some beer at the stop.

The student shrugged and pulled to the side of the road. "Guess I might as well tinkle too."

Tinkle, you asshole.

As the young man walked down the swampy bank, Dean's alter-ego tripped him from behind and held his head under water, avoiding the flailing arms until they were still. Bubber had re-emerged.

6.

"Feed him. I've got work to do," Alice said.

When Fairbain turned to leave the barn, Aaron scowled and gave Martin a kick, tossing the leather briefcase on top of his head. Beside Herr Doctor there was a Black man who groaned and rolled to face the stall's far wall, and three bodies in various states of decay, two being efforts at Alice's dabbling in voodoo zombies. The oldest consisted of bones whose cartilage barely held together. The second was desiccated so that its skin draped like cloth over abandoned furniture. The third was puddled with flies, maggots, and roaches. How Fairbain had ever managed to zombify the Kirby bitch was beyond him. These two came afterwards, and look at them. Aaron smiled, glad that Ms. Fairbain had found something much better than voodoo: the *ka* and *ak*. Glad because of the power he would soon have. But he was sad, too, because the idiots didn't survive nearly long enough to be tormented, unlike the Kirby bitch. Still going strong, even with the maggots in her hair.

He sniffed at the smell in the stall, then inhaled. Of the three, the puddled one had been his favorite: a neo-Nazi skinhead he'd picked up off the Tampa streets. Such a disappointment that there wasn't more of a fight. Ms. Fairbain simply slipped the punk a narcotic and they dragged him here. Then the fun began: all those spa muscles and that shaved head melted to little boy tears in this stall as Aaron hit him and the rag doll worked overhead making the punk's likeness. Such a tiny *ka*, though. The rag doll had extracted a four-foot midget model whose only use was for simple tasks like mixing concrete, not even as much as the Kirby zombie could handle. The punk's alter-ego was devoid of the rebelliousness Ms. Fairbain had hoped for, though she swore that the *ak* and the *ka* would give them unlimited power.

The Black man moved a foot as Aaron shut the door. This *Schwartze* had been a fortunate find. His *ka* would be wild. The rag doll was making his likeness nearly life-size. Unlimited power. Aaron nearly giggled at the thought, then left the stall to mix oats, water, and sprinkles of dieffenbachia leaf to deaden the vocal cords. When he came back he peeped through a knothole. Everything was the same. He opened the door and set the bucket inside.

"More food, *Schwartze*. It won't be long. Soon you'll have stronger than ever. You'll be meat, not oats." He waited for a reaction, but there was none. Did the *Schwartze* have something in his hand? No, nothing. Aaron looked to Edmonds, the briefcase still over his head.

"I'll be back later, *Schwartze*, to feed your new *Freundin*. Lots nicer than your other companions, *nu*? You don't know how nice it is that you're getting a statue made for you. Much better than being a zombie. New, improved—that's what you Americans say, *nu*?" He closed the door, sliding a heavy bar through and padlocking it; then he walked out of the barn, also shutting its heavy door. A week after buying this place from Kirby, Fairbain directed him to soundproof the barn, saying, "The time is coming." He'd smiled and worked ceaselessly, surprising both himself and Ms. Fairbain. "Ms." Fairbain would soon get another surprise, he thought as he checked the lawn, deciding he'd better mow it to keep neighborhood kids from creeping about looking for work. Another surprise, all right, for her damned rag doll and all her black magic were nothing compared to the hate he'd built since birth, since before birth. He sometimes could feel the rocking boat on which his mother had fled from Germany. He sometimes could feel the poking and laughing hands of the two Huns who raped her—in exchange for safe passage on that boat. "*Anpflazen sie eine jüdische Frucht? Denn sie mochst kauft zwei Fahrkarten.*" Are you growing a little Jewish fruit in there? Then you need to buy two tickets. And they made her come back that night to entertain them again.

He could feel it. Whenever he walked into Persephone's Escalator, he could feel tingling hate making him powerful. He pictured Persephone's fire-hot walls glowing dusky. Fairbain had no idea how they laughed at her there, in Cain's Land. He'd been pleased to find that the Jewish legend was true: Cain and his descendants banished to live beneath the earth where they toiled, sweated, and waited. Not even procreation was allowed. Destruction was all, except for the entrance of new souls every minute of every day, something no one in Cain's Land had been able to explain. Not that it mattered. Cain's Land would provide more golems than the Hebrews had ever imagined, and each golem would redress a thousand thousand wrongs. Their glow gelled below the surface until the day they would walk out **über** *alles* and create an Armageddon beyond any tiny Florida witch's dreams. He alone, Aaron Wasserstrum of the living, had seen them. He alone would learn to control them and gain vengeance for his people, his mother and father, their mothers and fathers. Hate made Cain's orphans listen. Hate was what they were built for. Hate had isolated them, now hate would bring them out.

Aaron opened the tool shed. Spotting the open suitcase, he hesitated. The snake curled inside frightened him, for it was completely under her bidding, unlike both the zombies and the *ak's*, which were easy for him to control, too. Supposedly the snake wouldn't awaken until nightfall; still… he found a rake and prodded. No movement. He stepped gingerly around, keeping the rake between the snake and himself. On reaching the shed's back door, he opened it, then hopped on the riding mower. He relaxed as the engine started and the snake still lay lifeless. A Weedeater hung in the tool shed, a high torque model that would cut even small branches. He nodded as he rode under it: If Ms. Fairlybright wasn't more careful of her magic props, she shouldn't be surprised if they got chopped into little snake tidbits.

After ten minutes on the riding mower in the sun, his smile reappeared, for after hatred, what made him happiest was feeling sweat drip from his chin and forehead.

QUESTIONS

1.

ewel Dawn turned from pouring the last of eight brandies when a vision came to her. The bookcase faded to
a brown unimportance while a sun-filled road with a
red sports car emerged. She leaned to see the car's driver, but
a white bird momentarily fluttered at the windshield before
perching on the driver's—shoulder? Jewel watched. The face
came into focus and she could see Nikki, a Sister she'd initiated twenty-five years before. Suddenly the bird fit in too: it
was the bird she made for the initiate Night. Jewel could see
Nikki giving her the Sister's greeting. Jewel nodded, hesitating
before returning the greeting… then she was staring at her
bookcase once more.

"It's time for us to go consider," she said, urging the Sisters in the room to find their separate crannies in her house.
"Twenty minutes." She nodded at the grandfather clock.

They left and she waited, looking at the bookcase and
wondering if the vision would return. Nikki was in Florida,
the last she'd heard. Could she have something to do with the

rippling of the Matrix? Surprised to find her brandy snifter containing a drink, Jewel bent and breathed its warmth. The bookcase was firmly in place now, the vision gone. She was a bit off-hoof because the gift of seeing wasn't exactly her forte; in fact, in her three lives totaling 154 years, she could count the waking visions she'd had on one toe, that toe being named "Moments Ago."

She glanced to the grandfather clock. Its built-in barometer had been broken for a week, so a sad drizzly face continually looked back at her even though the skies had been sunny. The clock was the last investment she and Paul made. Its four-foot pendulum swung, and steps squeaked as someone descended the stairs. The front door opened and shut. That would be Denise, always quick to decide. Considering Denise's two children, Jewel could hardly fault her. Seven minutes passed. She looked from the clock's drizzly blue face and crossed Denise's name off.

Lori's name caught her eye and Jewel flinched. Not that she was ashamed that consoling had turned to caressing during the night. Her 154 years smoothed any scruples about lesbianism to no more than crinkles in old wallpaper. And it could easily be that her contact with the girl precipitated the vision she just had, which meant it was an overall good decision to allow the girl along, despite her status as a novitiate's novice. "Overall good"—a lovely phrase to hide the very real possibility that Jewel's seduction of the girl was not only an initiation rite into adult life, but into death. "That's what the poets tell us, isn't it? That sex and death are intertwined."

Sesuj looked up at her from the clock. She was irritated that he'd caught her talking to herself once more; she was irritated with herself for the habit that had started one year to the day after Paul's death.

"Sesuj, I suppose you're right: old time's a-flying and I better do some thinking about the vision."

Where had Nikki's last letter come from? Somewhere above… she looked to the map that she'd spread on the table to show the Sisters. Somewhere above Tampa. The spot that had burned yesterday morning? And what of the girl Night, whose familiar had flown into the vision? Her letters had come from several states—never Florida. And always typed, something odd for such a young girl. Still in her teens, surely. Could she have met Nikki Ryan?

"Sesuj, I want you to think about something very hard. I want you to remember twenty-five years back: that's right, you were an old cat then. It was before you took another life. I want you to remember a dark-haired girl who went by Nikki but said her real name was Nyx. Remember how pretty she was with those high cheeks and that tilt to her head? And remember how well her hands worked the magic?" The cat licked Jewel's legs, its tongue scratchy.

"Not that kind of magic, dirty-mind, I'd just met Paul then. You're letting last night carry you away. And you're tearing my hose."

The cat rubbed Jewel's leg where it had licked with its barbed tongue.

"All right. Now, I also want you to remember not so far back. Four years ago. Remember a girl named Night? Remember Paul had just died and I was upset and it was summer solstice and…"

The cat walked to its Scrabble box and began shuffling letters. Jewel took her brandy and watched.

"G-R-E-E-K. Greek. Sesuj, you've written with your paws in at least six of your nine lives. Don't you think you could give an old woman a break and just form a sentence instead of puzzle-words?"

The cat simply nudged the letters.

"Greek. All right, Nyx is Greek—" Jewel stopped and took a sip of brandy. "Nyx is Greek for *night*. Nikki is Night's mother? She would have told me that. Both she's."

The cat flipped out a *Y*.

"Yes, Nikki is Night's mother or yes, they would have told me that?"

Sesuj flipped out another *Y* and pawed both.

"I might as well fly to Egypt and interview the Sphinx, Sesuj."

Sesuj batted around the pile. As he did, the stairs creaked once more, the door opened once more. A slight smoker's cough told her it was Sarah. Well, who could blame her— newly wed to one of the last river boat pilots in America? Romance like that couldn't be ignored. Jewel mentally wished her well, then looked back to Sesuj after checking the clock. Six more minutes.

"O-N-E? One?" Jewel looked from the word *GREEK* to the two *Y*'s to the word *ONE*. "Nyx means night. One. Nyx *is* Night? Is that what you're telling me?"

The cat flipped one of the *Y*'s closer to Jewel.

"Honey, I hate to doubt twice in the same week, but are you sure?"

The cat simply licked its paws, refusing to even look up.

"That's a lot of ectoplasm flowing from one young witch, Sesuj."

The cat kept licking.

"Is she the reason we're going to Florida?" Sesuj routed among the letters and flipped out a blank, then scampered after a fly, leaving Jewel to look to the clock: five minutes.

She crossed off Sarah's name. That left six, if you counted Lori, which you couldn't because Lori wasn't a Sister. But she did have telepathic powers, which were a hell of a boon. She'd already indicated to Jewel that Beth was harboring no specific evil thoughts when she entered the house. Jewel loved Lori's qualifying word *specific*. Lori had certainly pegged Beth quickly enough.

If no one else quit, they'd have their Pentad of five. If Nyx was as powerful as Sesuj said, if she could split into a separate identity then return to—who knows, split into both at once? If she were the reason they were being summoned to Florida, she would make a powerful enemy. And a very deceitful one, considering. But no, Nyx was golden. Jewel had faith.

She again pictured Nyx in the red car. Now that she thought about it, the face had been thin and young, almost like she remembered Night. Did Nyx transform into Night? But Nyx couldn't be more than 37, 38. Jewel herself hadn't accomplished her first migration until she was 52, after the death of her Virginia plantation husband—may his soul be picking cotton in hell under the watchful eye of the blackest meanest inhabitant therein.

Migration was not a technique every Sister could master—one in a thousand—just enough to assure continuity of the Matrix. For the first time, it occurred to her that she should contact the International Council. Sesuj let out a yowl. "You're right, honey, the red tape would be deadly."

The half hour struck and she dashed off her brandy and folded the map so the table would be clear except for the plates. Then she stood behind the head chair, waiting.

Anne Marie came in first, her gray hair transformed to silver, her shoulders straighter than Jewel had remembered them for eight years (since the time they both learned by chance that Anne Marie wasn't to be Jewel's successor). Becky came next, as gangly as ever, her lips open to reveal her gat-toothed smile. Jewel always thought that if ever a woman were born in the wrong age, it was Becky. Her imposing build, her spacious teeth would have made her the town beauty in the Middle Ages. And her lively laugh would have kept her out of trouble; if not, her knowledge of the Matrix certainly would. Nancy and Tiffany came together— no surprise since Nancy was awed by Tiffany's femininity, and Tiffany was more than willing to tease, though she was a confirmed heterosexual. All of them stood behind assigned chairs and eyed the four empty spots. No doubt they'd heard the door open and shut; and no doubt their own feet had tingled each time, urging them to get while the getting was good.

There was a pause, and Jewel feared that she'd become so involved with the mystery of Nyx and Night that she'd missed someone's leaving. She'd have to call the whole thing off, if so. Suicide missions just weren't the North American Sisters' way.

Then in walked Lori, followed by a smiling Beth. Of course, Beth would want to be last. But smiling? Jewel studied her as she took her place behind a chair. She knew something: Jewel mumbled a quick plea to Circe that Beth hadn't found out about Lori's ESP. Beth gave a sultry glance to Lori, then Jewel, then vulgarly ran her tongue over her lips. It was all Jewel could do to keep from laughing. *Wonderful. Lori, you are Jewel's jewel.* Smarmy Beth will spend so much time with that piece of sexual gossip that she'll never question why you're accompanying us. Jewel, still avoiding Beth's eyes, motioned for the plates at Denise's and Sarah's settings to be turned over. They were getting ready to hold hands when

Tiffany's tiny voice called:

"Jewel?"

Jewel saw Tiffany point to the extra plate that was face up. The air-conditioning chose that moment to shut off with a *thunk* and everyone laughed nervously. Tiffany started to turn the plate, but Jewel stopped her.

"No, the Romans had a statue for an unknown god, we'll leave a setting for an unknown Sister."

"Do you think it's wise to leave an opening for a person not with us? How can we be sure she has good motives?" Beth asked.

"*She* might even be a warlock," Nancy joked.

Jewel was glad Nancy cut in, for it let her bite her tongue about being unsure of the good motives even of those present. Still, Beth's point was well-taken: an open plate would leave a chink in the Pentad unless it were filled by someone they could trust. They needed to decide quickly: once the ceremony was initiated its power built to a certain point, then began to drain.

"Anne Marie, Becky… Beth. Do you remember the initiate Night four years ago at the solstice ceremony? The one who took the bird?"

They nodded, one by one.

"A judgment, quick. Anne Marie?"

"She made me sad. I thought she was the most beautiful girl I'd ever seen when she took the bird in her hand."

"Becky?"

"The bird flew by me. I wanted it, but my hands wouldn't move. The girl had talked to me earlier and made me laugh about something. She tucked in the zipper to my skirt."

"Beth?"

"I didn't like her. But I was mad because you'd taken so

long with the ritual. And I was mad because the bird went to her: everyone else thought the bird was unworthy of solstice, that you'd scattered the ritual's power. But each time I looked at it, it changed: an owl once, an eagle, a robin. If you think she might be the one somehow taking that plate, I warn you: I think the child is very powerful. A powerful child is a dangerous companion."

Jewel nodded. "No, I don't think it will be exactly her, maybe her mother, whom only Anne Marie and I vaguely knew."

Anne Marie looked up.

"Nyx Ryan. She went by Nikki. Do you remember her?"

"The one who writes you from Florida?"

Jewel nodded and Anne Marie shrugged. "A nice enough woman—more of a beauty queen than a Sister. I always thought being a stewardess a fitting occupation for her. Didn't she have a black cat as a familiar?"

Several of the women tittered at that, for black cats were immense bad form among those in the know. Tiffany's hand was still poised over the plate.

"Leave it." Jewel said, huffing air to finalize her decision. She lifted her hands palm up, to indicate they should start. Then she lowered her eyes, sensing hesitation.

"Until I raise my eyes, the covenant has not begun. Thirty seconds. You may still leave." It was only fair. She'd thrown a new pattern into the quilt. It could drastically change the odds—not very pretty as they stood. She counted to thirty then raised her eyes. They'd all stayed. Nodding her thanks, she took Anne Marie's and Lori's hands. The others joined in the circle, Becky and Tiffany holding the extra plate between them. She could feel electricity fishing through her hands, bumping her heart. This was probably the fiftieth Pentad she'd formed in her lifetimes and was easily the strongest. She was pleased that Lori did not break the power, being a novitiate. Maybe her telepathy gave her insight into the Matrix.

Jewel heard Tiffany squeal, then saw a jolt pass from the empty plate along each woman: Nancy and Beth grabbed for breath, Lori shivered and Anne Marie's fingernails cut into Jewel's palm. Sesuj began to yowl. Jewel received the jolt from each direction, then blacked out…

She heard their voices; when she looked to their faces, she felt cold. For a moment, in the presence of those she trusted most, plus the cool white face of Lori, she wanted to die. But something (Anne Marie's stabbing nail?) made her sit up, with Lori's help.

"The bread," she managed. She shook them off and stood, wobbly, against the table and reached for the basket, holding it high as she passed it to her right.

Lori, who drew first, balked on seeing a roll with a bay leaf imbedded on its crust. Jewel suppressed a moan. Anne Marie spoke:

"Some Sisters think it's good luck to draw the bay leaf because you're forced to face death at that moment and build your courage. They say you won't be asked to face death twice in the same Pentad."

Jewel managed a nod when Lori looked at her for confirmation. *True, but not true. Y and N*, she thought, *the blank Scrabble piece, The Hanged Man—knowledge through defeat.* She hoped Lori was keeping her promise not to invade her mind again without an express invitation.

Nancy and Tiffany drew their rolls, trying hard not to show relief when they revealed a shiny brown egg-white finish.

"Becky, it would be best if you drew for the plate and yourself."

Becky nodded, giving a big smile just like she had been asked to frost a cake. She drew a shiny egg-finished roll for the plate and a bay leaf for herself. Jewel was amazed: the girl smiled her happy gat-toothed smile at the leaf as if it were a laurel.

"Well, not too auspicious odds, are there?" Beth said, taking the basket. "It's only fair to tell you that some Sisters," she added loudly in Lori's direction as she stuck her hand in, "think that drawing the bay leaf means just what you think it means, being as it was a main ingredient for Egyptian embalmers." She gave the basket a brisk shuffle and sent it on, looking somberly at the egg-finish on her roll.

Anne Marie drew the inevitable bay leaf, leaving the roll Sesuj had stepped in for Jewel—no accident since she'd buried it under a fold of the cloth lining the basket.

They sat and silently ate the bread, being attentive to crumbs and keeping their eyes on the plate between Becky and Tiffany.

"Who knows?" Beth said, speaking for all of them. "As powerful as that surge was whenever Ms. Whoever joined us, her bread just might up and eat itself."

Tiffany and Becky were too close to the plate to appreciate the thought, while Nancy laughed. When everyone finished Jewel invited them to get their bags, but Beth spoke. "I've taken the liberty of bringing some things along. I'd like to distribute them now if we've got time, Boss."

Jewel gave a nod. It was the closest Beth had come to familiarity in the fifteen years she'd known her. "Maybe a few things from the left-hand-path might be appropriate," Jewel said.

"Nice of you to acknowledge the fact." Beth went to the hallway and returned with a black suitcase made of the skin of some animal. Besides being a black witch, she was an actress who never missed her chance to put on a show. Jewel watched her rub the suitcase before opening it. With a flourish she produced what appeared to be a butter tub and motioned them to come forward. As they did, she handed them each a tub.

"Graveyard clay," she smiled sweetly, "from Henry Clay." She paused at her pun, then continued. "That ground contains the most prominent nearby Kentuckian in my grasp. Poor man's buried in a mausoleum and not the least happy about it—he told me so—"

"Beth…" Jewel's finger pointed out the grandfather clock.

Right, Boss. Short and to the point." She turned to the butter tub in her hand. "Okay, this really is ground from around Clay's mausoleum. Besides the dirt, there's two things inside: instructions for a zapper of a curse plus its antidote." Beth nodded to the empty plate: "Since we're not all sure we can trust one another, I advise you to start the antidote right away. It's time-release, isn't science wonderful, so you need only take a capsule a day. Two weeks' worth in there. The curse's rites—don't make any sloppy circles of power, because misfires are hell—are deceptively simple. All you do is form a figurine in the shape of the target, wrap it in paper— toilet paper adds a nice touch—and wet it down once, twice, five times a day—depending on how quickly you want things to act and how severe you want the reaction to be. Anything from a cold to the Big Chill.

"Aren't I sweet to be giving you something like this?" Beth curtsied. "It works over immense distances—much more efficient than a voodoo doll. Some special herbs and spices make it that way. I really would recommend taking the pill, by the way." She pulled one out and popped it in her mouth. "Sorry for the taste, but when you work with the left-hand path you get used to things like that."

Jewel took a pill and Lori followed suit right away. The rest couldn't get them in their mouths fast enough.

"You didn't need to take one, Jewel. I've already tried to kill you and it wouldn't work."

Beth laughed, but Jewel daren't look at Lori's reaction: dipping in Lori's well too often would give the secret away. It also might make for a sad life. She decided to treat Beth's comment as levity: "I'm glad to hear my shield's up."

"Oh, it's up all right, dear. I was sick for three days when my spell bounced back."

One of them gave a start. They turned to see Denise's plate had flipped back over and now held half a roll with blood spattered on it and the surrounding tablecloth. Becky pointed to the far plate that had been between her and Tiffany. Its roll was broken neatly in half, the plate white and shiny as a movie star's teeth.

"We've got to catch our plane," Jewel said dully, trying not to register the ache in her stomach.

"Shouldn't we warn Denise?" Tiffany asked.

Jewel thought of Oedipus. Being warned hadn't done him a damned bit of good. Arguably, it had forced his hand and made killing his father and marrying his mother possible in the first place.

"Knowing an oracle only drew Oedipus the King deeper into the trap," Lori said.

Jewel started. Had she read her mind despite her promises? But the girl just shrugged as if she were embarrassed to have spoken about something academic.

"You're learning the Matrix fast," Anne Marie said. "Lori's right. If it was a fluke of misguided magic, maybe all of us subconsciously wishing the bay leaf on someone else, then we're just putting Denise in danger by telling her. And if it's in the Matrix strongly enough… we all know there's little we can do when the Matrix has moved."

Jewel winced at Anne Marie's tone. Jealousy and anger. Did she think Lori was to be the next Executrix? Was that why she was showing an anger she hadn't for eight years, since finding out that her plans to succeed Jewel were negated by the Matrix itself? Jewel raised her eyebrows and herded everyone from the room. Next stop would be the airport, Blue Grass Field. The less they looked at that bloody plate, the better off they'd be.

2.

At nearly the same time Jewel and the Pentad were toasting, Martin Edmonds awoke to a throbbing in his leg and head. He also awoke to a piercing fetid odor and a chalky-hued Black man slapping at his face. He raised his hand and gagged, nearly passing out again from the smell and heat.

"Sh-h-h. The Frankenstein monster still outside mowing."

Martin realized the man was talking about Aaron.

"Man, I planned on busting out of here today: I didn't expect any company coming along." The man nodded up to what Martin could see was a very small opening or window on the wall he was propped against. Outside, a lawnmower was running. "And I didn't expect Frankenstein to take a sudden interest in lawn manicure."

"What the hell is that smell?" Martin asked, gagging again.

The Black man had been squatting very close to him. "You're going to have to see it sooner or later when we leave—and we are going to leave. What's behind me isn't pretty. I've been here twelve days and it ain't got any prettier." The man held up his hand as Martin shifted. "There's two skeletons and a rotten body behind me, so brace your stomach."

Martin looked the man in the eyes. They didn't shift, they just seemed tired, with a yellowish tint.

"Okay," Martin said.

The man nodded and leaned against a wall… Martin let out a groan. On the closest body, hair had grown in sprinkles over what had once been a shaved head. Its eyes were wet sockets and its teeth leered through decaying flesh. The body was completely nude. One fly landed then lifted off. Why?

"They spray it, man. With insecticide. Frankenstein wants to preserve it. Ain't that the kinks?" the Black man said as if he'd read Martin's thoughts.

Next to the corpse were two skeletons. Martin could see ants working in a line over the hip bones of the farthest.

"Is the water from that bucket any good to drink?"

The Black man nodded and poured some into Martin's own cupped hands. Martin drank, not taking his eyes off the bodies.

"My name's Walter Brown. I came here twelve days ago…" The man was talking and staring out the window. "Not here, really, but some rinky-dink fat woman's place at the front of this mess they call Quail Hollow. And Frankenstein out there just happens by while I'm mowing her lawn and asks if I want to make a clean hundred mowing two and a half acres. It sounded good, so I drove back, following him. The fat woman waddled out, warbling about witches, like she was nuts. I should've listened.

"Frankenstein took me to a tool shed out front of this

place and damned if there wasn't a five-foot rattlesnake inside. We both jumped and I went to my truck for a machete.
Frankenstein was real pleased when I whacked its head off,
he got a giggle out of that, he did. Then I started mowing
while he was toting boxes into the house. He left three or
four times and come back with a carload each time.

"Finally he motions me to stop the mower. Says he's got a
job that needs help in the barn. And boom, Cousin, just like
you, I'm out.

"My truck's in the back. I hear him start it every other day.
So are you ready for the odd part?"

Martin looked up at Walter.

"Oh yeah, three murders, a kidnapped nigger, and hosing
down a stiff with bug spray ain't odd enough yet. Shoo no.
Look up."

Martin did and saw wire mesh stretched over two beams.
Staring down through the mesh was a white, nearly life-size
sculpture—the beginnings of one at least… Martin moved
his eyes to Walter.

"Except for skin color it do make a nice likeness, don't
you think?"

Martin could hear the lawnmower outside and imagined
Aaron sitting seriously on it as he destroyed grass and smiled.
And in her off hours Alice Fairbain would come over for
whatever weird reason and climb to the loft and peer down
and chip away at a sculpture of a Black man, two skeletons,
and a rotting corpse.

"That nice lady with you and Frankenstein. She used to do
the sculpturing up there; now I just hear her talk."

"Who does it now?"

"That's the double weird part. We'll move right into triple
weird soon." Walter broke into a cough. "I don't expect this

is the healthiest environment ever."

"I don't expect so," Martin answered.

"And the food," Walter lightly kicked the bucket over. "Drugged so you can't talk and can barely move. Yeah. So how am I…" he walked to lift the farthest skull. "When I came I had four candy bars in my pocket. I'm a chocolate addict. It's one of the vows I've made: if I get out alive, I'll stroll into Bern's Steak House down in Tampa, past all them red velvet wall coverings and fancy White waiters, head up to the dessert room, and eat Death by Chocolate and drink hot cocoa until the maître d' takes me to the emergency room, pumps my stomach, and lets me begin again." Walter had been holding the skull at an angle; he let it drop. "Until then I eat whatever this slop attracts: ants, roaches, ten or so mice and one rat. The rats tasted better in Vietnam. I was prisoner of war there for four months." He turned to Martin: "Some folk have all the luck, don't they?" Walter shoved his palm hard into the wall. Martin could feel the vibration against his head, so he sat forward.

"So who does the sculpturing up there?"

"I was letting that go, Cousin, since I didn't want you to think you were sharing this hotel suite with a loony."

Walter walked over and leaned down in Martin's face. "Look, tonight's gotta be the night. You're fresh and I've still got strength left. But the closer that statue gets to being done, the weaker I get. I can feel it. Are you with me?"

Martin noticed that his briefcase locks had been broken.

"Sorry about that, man. Had to see if you had anything useful like a gun or food. You're a psychiatrist, right?"

"Psychologist."

Walter nodded. "Well I'm a philosopher, and the privacy of one ain't near as important as the life of two. I'd have got us both out of here if you had a saw or crowbar folded away in there."

"Don't worry about it."

"I read some of your papers while I splatted water on you. If I'd read them two weeks ago I would have voted for locking that Dean friend of yours up in a double-pad, double lock cell. Now I just want to call and give him an invite to the party. Man, I've seen a walking rag doll, so why not?"

Martin tried to push himself up, slumped and grabbed his head immediately.

"Yeah, Frankenstein don't go easy on his knockout taps. You better just ask questions, not jump around. We'll need that later."

"Okay: rag doll. Did you read that in my papers?"

"No. I only read ten or so pages, where you had the paper clip."

"Mean anything to you?"

"Maybe. *Ka.* I think that's what Frankenstein tells me I'm gonna be when the statue's done."

The lawnmower outside again, nearer, and they both held still. Then it faded.

"You asked who did the sculpture up there. Not who, but a bunch of whats. When I first got knocked out, that kid was alive. I was tied up like you were. I'd been conscious about an hour watching him just staring at me with that bald head. I don't expect he liked keeping company with a Black dude, but neither of us had a hell of a lot of choice. Anyway, it was about an hour when I heard shuffling overhead. The kid got a real scared and scrunched against the wall. That first night Miss Nice Lady came. There wasn't any wire up there then—that was later when I tried to get away and busted my first statue. It was only about two foot high, not as big as that one. Anyway, Nice Lady leaned over and called: 'Danny. Wake up. I'm going to lower a bucket to you, Danny. It's food. Before you eat it, I want you to ungag your friend and feed him. Leave his hands and feet tied. Do you understand?' He nodded and did. That's when I found out that the food made you unable to speak. 'Danny,' she went on, 'one more night and you'll be stronger than ever. You can leave your weak body for a new one of stone.' He had a statue up there too, you see, maybe four foot high. And his was damned near perfect. She chipped on it and he'd give a jerk when she hit her mallet extra hard.

"You're a psychologist, right? Then tell me what they put in that oatmeal trash to make me vision a damned rag doll scamper over and watch the kid feed me mush. And the next night was worse. 'Feed him, Danny. Then untie him,' Nice Lady said. 'Tonight's your special night for a wonderful trip. Two weeks waiting will seem like no time, Danny. The real you will come out tonight.'

"I'm trying to get her voice down, understand. Real calm, like you'd talk to a nut. And Danny there, he was acting the part. When he fed me he just watched his hand and my mouth like they were the two most important things in the world. Whenever Nice Lady wasn't looking, I spit out the food. Danny didn't mind, just shoveled more in. Then he untied me like she said and I laid there, figuring that was the smart thing. Danny just crawls to lay his lanky bald body down and she's up there chipping away.

"'All finished, Danny,' she said later. But he wasn't having none of it. I thought he was flat dead, laying there with his eyes not blinking. 'Walter, just twelve days for you. Just wait till you see how Danny turns out. You won't let a little White fascist like him outdo you, will you? We've got great hopes for you, Walter.'

"The damn bitch kept stroking that statue of the kid. Then she left to drag something over, a new block of whatever they were using—concrete, plaster—I couldn't tell. And she starts tapping away after staring at me for a minute. I knew I shouldn't yell, because of the drugged oats, but I let out a gurgle. She looked down. I guess she thought it was the kid 'cause she said, 'Danny, sweetheart, don't die just yet.'

"Next thing I knew, she'd come down and was inside the stall. She gave me a kick and I managed not to say anything. That might have given away that I'd spit out most the mush. She knelt by the kid and slit his throat—it happened so damned fast and I wasn't expecting it: I don't think I could have done anything anyway since mush from the day before was still in me. She caught about a half pint of blood in some Tupperware. Then she flipped his hand up on his lap and left him there.

"I could hear her climb the ladder outside and soon she was by the statue of the kid again. She poured blood on its head, dabbed some in its eye sockets and mouth, then tilted it—I think so it would look down on the kid."

The mower outside stopped.

"Shit, man. If we gotta do it now, we gotta do it. Look, I'm going to put the gag back on you and just flip the ropes over your legs. If Frankenstein come in, we'll have to try him. Okay?"

Martin nodded and watched as Walter did as he said, then stooped to dig in the sandy floor to retrieve a screwdriver. "I'm going to ram this in the bastard's stomach. You've got to help me though. We'll push him outside this stall in case the bitch comes with him."

They heard footsteps outside, then an engine starting.

My truck, Walter mouthed, pointing to himself. Martin nodded. The footsteps passed and they heard the barn door shut. Minutes later, a car started and drove off. Martin even thought he heard a gate opening and closing.

Walter let out a slow sigh. "You hear how damned far sound travels over this wetland?" he whispered. "We got to be careful and talk quiet as mice. It's good he left. I'm not so sure we could have taken the bastard as sick as I am and bashed as you are. Second plan's the best. But I got to prepare you." Walter walked over and untied Martin's gag and tossed the rope aside.

"A week ago I started loosening that wire by standing on the window. I could stand there maybe a half hour a night before the wobblers started to crawl out."

"Wobblers?" Martin took the screwdriver at Walter's prompt, then stepped into his cupped fireman's ladder palms to be hoisted onto the window's small ledge. In the loft overhead, through afternoon motes of dust, he could see the entire room was filled with figurines similar to those at Fairbain's. He caught a glimpse of one of the boy Danny with its left arm torn off. Then he noticed something strange: the room was moving.

"Jesus, they're all breathing."

"Lower your voice," Walter said, giving his leg a shake. "Those are the wobblers. And for godsake be quiet getting those last screws worked out. I counted only four more—immediately in front of you."

Martin began on the nearest one, grimacing at his still throbbing head. The angle was awkward, and it took much longer than he expected to get a single screw out. And there were three more. He could hear Walter below, doing something.

"How'd they ever let you keep this screwdriver anyway?" He was on the second screw now, and it was coming a bit easier.

"I stole it from one of the wobblers I knocked over."

Martin stopped screwing and looked under his arm to see Walter gathering dust to put in his pockets.

"Get me on a couch later, Doc. Just keep your eyes open."

Martin did that very thing. The third screw was a complete bitch. Before he had it loose Martin was convinced he'd seen several statues move—a sudden tilt of a head or motion of a hand. Danny's statue now faced him, where it had been looking at a wall before. He told Walter. Walter nudged his leg and showed him a fistful of sand.

"If it comes toward you, move your foot twice. I'll pass this up. Don't say nothing, just keep screwing and reach down for this to throw in its eyes. They see, hear and feel like we do; they just don't talk. And my man, they're absolute nuts: they'll do anything from kill you to wiggle their ass and grin. Promise you won't be trying no psychobabble on these babes, okay? Just throw dust in its face when it's close."

Catching movement from a statue, Martin looked down at the completely serious face of the Black man. "Did you escape from prison in Vietnam?"

Walter nodded, placing a hand on Martin's shoe, holding sand in the other.

The third screw came out. Two statues moved, and Danny's was in the process of bending for something. Martin started the last screw as quietly as he could, but the eyes of Danny's surrogate opened to reveal a black liquid night. He screwed hard, his hands fumbling because of sweat and cramps. The little Danny walked with comparatively long strides and was five feet away when Martin dropped the screwdriver. He stomped twice and frantically held out his hand, then felt Walter squeezing his fingers together to hold the sand from the stall's floor.

As the statue of Danny bent and took a swipe with a knife, Martin threw the sand. Half of it came back in his face and he tumbled. When he looked up, Walter had sprung onto the windowsill and pushed the wire to catch the statue's leg. Martin stood and steadied Walter on the sill; seconds later, Walter broke the statue's remaining arm and jammed the screwdriver into its eyes. Black blood dripped through the mesh as little Danny went rigid.

Within a minute Walter finished the last screw and moved the wire. He hoisted himself up and Martin lifted him his briefcase. Walter made a face, but Martin insisted. He nodded, took it and helped Martin up. Before Martin even managed to get to his feet Walter had stuffed pictures of himself and Martin that were tacked on an easel into his pocket and was hitting the head of his likeness with a hammer. Martin could see statues jerking all around them. He grabbed Walter's arm. "You've got to stop! You're waking them up."

"If I don't destroy it, it'll destroy me." Walter's eyes went to some tools hanging on a wall. "Hacksaw," he whispered, and Martin ran for one and a mallet.

He was halfway through the neck when Martin saw two small statues open their black eyes. With the mallet he smashed one, though the other stabbed his leg. He managed to smash it and black liquid oozed from the wound. But others were moving now.

"We've got to get out of here!" He tugged Walter's shoulder. Walter nodded and with the hammer gave his likeness a sharp smack where its neck was almost cut through. It cracked. He hit it again and the head fell. They could hear shuffling throughout the loft.

"Behind you, Doc!"

Martin turned to see a small white face with an evil leer made more evil by oil-spill eyes. But its palms were cast upward in a "Why worry?" gesture. Martin's arm descended in fury and the mallet smashed the statue, splattering black blood over the loft floor.

"Doc, don't stare; let's get the hell rolling!" Walter had tucked his ersatz head under his arms and was pointing to the loft's ladder.

But as soon as Martin started to run, he tripped, dropping the mallet. The prankster statue had tied his shoelaces. He tried to break them but couldn't. Kicking off his shoes he ran to Walter, who'd evidently jumped, not even bothering with the ladder. Martin's foot caught on a nail, and he hopped to toss his briefcase down to Walter. He felt something tug his belt and spun to deflect a stab from what looked like a pen. He yanked at the statue holding it, a young woman, but couldn't break her grip. Everywhere he could hear the slow shuffling of feet.

"Just jump down with her, man. I'll get her with the hammer."

Martin did, landing in a squat, the pale woman ripping into the skin on his stomach. He heard two *thunks* and felt her hit against his back, then slide off. When he turned, black blood spattered his face and shirt.

"My truck!" Walter yelled.

They ran for it at the back of the barn.

"Great! Frankenstein left my keys." Walter started his truck as Martin scrambled in the passenger side. Through the windshield they saw a line of statues descending the ladder. The truck caught; Walter gunned the engine then ran over four small statues of ditch diggers, complete with shovels. One chalk lawyer or businessman complete with attaché jumped from the ladder to the bed of the pickup. Martin could swear that a cloth doll's hand leaped from a stall window to grab onto the truck's side too. He was about to say something when they crashed the barn's door and the windshield smashed. The businessman, at least, was halved by splintering timber.

"Hold on. We're hitting the damned front gate the same way."

Looking back, Martin could see lights go on in the barn. Thirty or forty statues ran out, falling over one another and the splintered door. Checking the back of the truck, he saw only tools, a lawnmower, and a broken plank. No rag doll. They hit the gate, knocking it over. Somehow they managed to keep from going into the swampy ditch on the other side of the road and were soon squealing a right-hand turn onto the road leading by what was left of the Settles' house.

"There's nothing behind us, for now."

"*For now's* two real big words."

Walter floored the gas, though they were going too fast already considering the state of the road and their visibility with only one headlight. Martin's head hit the roof as the truck hit a pothole.

"Walter, that last statue. It tied my shoelaces. A joke."

"Wouldn't have been very funny if another one slipped up and cut your throat, would it?"

Martin heard movement in the bed of the pickup. Another statue? But his head hit the roof again. They spun sideways in taking a left, then they accelerated. Again, a noise, and no bumps in this new road, just a ribbon of silver with palmetto stretching on either side.

"I think one got in the truck bed."

"Well, the little wobbly fucked up then." Walter reached under the seat and pulled out a machete. "You take the mallet. We'll get it from both sides. But first I'll give it a bit of a ride, so hold on."

Martin nodded as Walter jammed the brakes, screeched into another right, accelerated a hundred yards, then stopped. They both jumped out. As they did Martin heard Walter scream and saw him fighting something around his neck. Martin ran to help; from the light of the cab he could see Walter tugging at a large snake. Even after he struck the snake's head with the machete, it managed to bite his ankle then slip off into the water-filled ditch alongside the road. Martin caught Walter as he collapsed.

Walter managed a smile. "Some folk got all the luck, don't—" His body jerked then slumped. He'd been bitten at least twice in the neck.

The truck's engine stopped and Martin saw a rag doll jump from the driver's side. It turned briefly to smile and give a jangle of keys. He grabbed the machete and sprang, but the doll ran under the truck. By the time he got to the other side, all he could see was vague motion in the palmettos. Frogs croaked loudly on either side of the road.

Over the swamp water, he heard a car, then spotted its lights. By the time it turned onto the road, he was crouching behind a palmetto, glumly feeling warm water creep up his pants leg, thinking of the wounded snake that had crawled off. He watched the approaching car and the body of Walter, the man with all the luck.

3.

During all the time when Nikki felt her powers growing

immensely she'd told only one close friend—actually, a young friend of Night's—and even her she'd not entrusted with the truth of her dual existence. This friend was a strange sort named Abby Beasley, who'd collared Night their sophomore year and asked if she knew where there was a coven—not your typical opening question to secure a lasting friendship. But it had worked, even though the only nearby covens Night knew were the ones she was in as her mother—unacceptable on all counts. So Night and Abby formed their own coven and held weekly meetings for a year, wondering like the children they were at "tricks" Night could do.

While they wondered, Nikki worried. This power was becoming too much like sorcery, a man's game and a game of which she didn't particularly approve. Witches dealt with people, and people after all, comprised the earth. Love, revenge, personal wealth, good luck—these were what witches worked at proudly. Sorcerers dealt in ideals, and ideals killed—often as indiscriminately as a drunk driver. Joshua, invading Canaan and blasting down the walls of Jericho to slay everything inside, even cattle and sheep; Merlin the kingmaker, so concerned with his coming king and social order that he instigated a battle and allowed the rape of a woman; Asphodelus, who raised an army in 1123 to destroy a village where a pope whose Papal Bull he didn't care for was born. Lovely ideals, all of them.

But the power of sorcery wasn't enough for men. They resorted to the power of technology to enforce their wondrous ideals. What sorcerer could top the atomic bomb? None, but technology and Mr. Edward Teller could invent a hydrogen bomb which used the mere atomic bomb as a detonator. Lovely. Nikki considered: while her powers weren't atomic, they'd grown far beyond amulets and temporary spells or potions. Unfortunately, Night was also coming to understand this, and even more unfortunately, Night was not always as mature as Nikki. Some small part in the transformation left each personality partially excluded from the other.

"What's the biggest thing you can make disappear?" Abby had asked Night one evening.

No! the mother Nikki in Night shouted. But Night had already given a flourish. "*Evanesce,*" she said, and a bolt of lightning destroyed an acre of palmetto before them. She heard the squeal of a family of boar, the cries of mice and quail caught in the senseless fury. Nikki held back from migrating for a week after that, and of course kept Night from as much school. When Night did go back, she didn't talk with Abby for a week.

"I'll never ask you anything like that again," Abby promised, passing her in the cafeteria line at lunch.

That had been near Easter a year ago. And Night's power was growing unbelievably. What would happen now? Five acres? More? Then came today's vision of Jewel Dawn and the hazy feelings that Martin Edmonds was in danger. Telepathy was not in the usual witch's realm. It wasn't in the usual sorcerer's realm. Where was it coming from? On four occasions she'd become Martin's eyes and seen: 1. A Black man bending. 2. A white, menacing stone face peering down. 3. A dead body and two skeletons, which she could even smell, and which prompted her to abandon awaiting Martin's phone call and drive over to Fairbain's house. On that drive she envisioned: 4. A wire cage? The image blurred; she presumed driving dulled her concentration.

The sun was setting when she neared the Settles' house. Abby lived around the corner, beyond Alice Fairbain's. Should she get her? Not as Nikki, Night's mother, that would never do. She pulled into the Settles' drive behind the still-standing storage shed. The charred skeleton of the house gave her the creeps. Skull, who'd sat on her shoulder, flew up and began a transformation that finished in half a minute. He was now a large white owl, ready to attack. Nikki took cue and tossed bone dust from a pouch into the four wind directions to summon the guardian angels of Hebrew lore. She could feel protective power descend and saw a faint blue glow settle over her.

She leaned against the shed to assess the night's sounds. Frogs, crickets, rustling palmettos, owls. Then a heavy splintering, followed by metallic banging and squealing tires. A truck careened around the corner. Martin was inside as the passenger; a Black man drove. She ran for her car to follow but Skull swooped to prevent her, then flew to a charred timber and perched. Seconds later she heard a clopping like a small herd of unshod horses on blacktop; they turned the same corner the truck just rounded—fifty or so bleached midgets, disgusting in their unsure wobbling, their footsteps giving off the hollow clonk of porous material. They held knives and hatchets—an army of pygmy statues, leached of color. In the moonlight she could make out their intense black-eyed stare, filled with obsessive hatred. One spotted her and started wobbling over the grass. Skull dove and left it eyeless, dark blood covering its moonlit face.

Nikki raised her left hand, thinking to destroy them, but a flap of Skull's wing bade her hesitate. Stragglers rounded the corner: she guessed the whole troop's number at a hundred, probably too spread for a globe of destruction to work. She motioned for Skull, who hovered as she instructed him to follow Martin first, the wobbly creatures second.

They are both going to the same place.

"Yes," Nikki answered, hardly surprised that Skull's thoughts had directly transferred—so vivid had been her telepathic powers lately. "I'm going to see where they came from. I won't be long."

The owl flapped its wings.

"I'll be careful."

With a low hoot, Skull was off.

The last time Nikki tried to conjure a cloak of invisibility was as Night. She had glowed a hot pink like the underclothing she wore. "That's some disappearing beacon you created," Abby had commented. Abby was good for cooling her pride. Still, Nikki took a piece of a dried bean Abby had given her, placed it under her tongue, trying not to think where it had been. If Abby used the same preparations she was familiar with, they required fermentation in a human brain.

"Night come, Sight go. Night come, Sight go. Night come, Sight go." She could see grass around her slowly lit by an orange haze.

"That's some disappearing beacon you've created."

She turned, still glowing, to see Abby, braces and all.

"You're not much better at invisibility than your daughter, Mrs. Ryan."

Nikki had felt guilty about lying to her friend and had wondered how long she could keep it up. Not long, evidently. The girl motioned her behind the shed, even as another wobbler's footsteps sounded on the road.

"The way you're glowing, those things will see you."

"You saw them walk by?"

"I've seen them before. That's why I was out here, to keep tabs. I think they drowned Cristy, the little girl who lived here. At any rate they pulled her from the pond and began cutting at her neck and I ran away."

"Why didn't you—"

"Sh. You've got to undo that orange glow, Ms. Ryan. Lots of those things walk round here at night. —You at least know how to unfix your mess, don't you?"

Nikki thought of cuffing the seventeen-year-old. Instead she chanted, "Come Sight, go Night. Come Sight, go Night. Come Sight, go Night." The orange glow subsided, but she was suddenly snatched backward five feet and fell to her knees. Abby smirked.

"I was going to tell you tomorrow that I figured out why this was misfiring. I tried it a bunch this afternoon and it worked fine, so I thought: Night's a lot more powerful than me, so how come she can't do this? I've given her what she needs. Then I figured: The Matrix is like a computer sometimes. It puts out just what you put in. Night's name is Night, so the Matrix is making her so bright that people can't see. *Come Night, go sight.* As Mrs. Janson says, 'Isn't language wonderful?' I bet Mrs. Janson could fix the spell up for you in Latin with the proper objects and verbs in no time. And just now, it snatched you backwards. 'Go Night,' is what you said. So you're Night."

"That's ridiculous, Abby."

"Is it? Remember what she told us about case endings making Latin more precise like math than any other language?"

"Yes, so? I—" Nikki realized she'd just been had. Licking her lips, she asked, "How long have you known?"

"I wasn't sure until now. But I suspected when Skull changed into an owl and you sounded so much like Night a minute ago while you were chanting, 'Come Light, Go Night!'—Go Night? Gosh, you're lucky you're not on the moon. I think you should really rework the spell before you do it again, Mrs. Ryan."

"You can't tell anyone all this, Abby."

"There's a million things I can't tell anyone. I told those two hunters about the Settles' girl's body, but I couldn't tell them how she'd been killed. I can't tell anyone about the wobbling statues, I can't tell anyone about the Black man who disappeared into the Kirby barn two weeks ago and who I thought I saw lying dead in a stall with a corpse and two skeletons, but who just now drove off—"

"You said you thought he was dead."

"I guess not. I mean, I don't know for sure—"

"Come on, let's find them. I've got a special interest in the passenger." Nikki motioned to her car and they both got in. They drove a mile before slowing.

"Where are the white things? They couldn't be traveling fast enough to get away." Nikki looked to Abby, who shrugged.

"They usually don't go along the roads. I see them in the palmettos all the time when I astral project."

"You astral project? Keeping other secrets too, aren't you?"

Abby smiled. "It's not like I hop to Bombay or anything."

Nikki pulled to the middle of the road and rolled her window down. Palmettos rustled to her left. Ahead, maybe a quarter mile, glowed the lights of a farmhouse. She could hear a dog barking there, echoed by another dog in the distance.

"Abby, have you ever learned to summon a shield of defense? Other than drawing a circle of power or using a talisman, I mean."

"That's what that blue around you was, wasn't it? I can barely see it now."

"It's still there; it stays for one rotation of the earth. The glow disappears."

"Neat."

Nikki looked at Abby.

"A saying I picked up from my sister's boyfriend." Abby squeezed her mouth like it held a lemon. "I guess I'm going to have to grow up if I want to be your friend anymore, Ms. Ryan. Are you still going to be Night?"

"If we live through this night, I'll be Night, yes." Another dog joined the first two and a floodlight snapped on at the house ahead, spraying light across the road. "Let's hurry. Get out and I'll circle you with a shield; it won't be as powerful as if you'd done it yourself, but it'll be okay, especially if you use your power to disappear—how long does that last?" Nikki asked before getting out.

"I don't know. The grimoire I used didn't say. I should tell you this: once I'm invisible I can't move many things. I tried but could just scatter paper and ruffle grass. Oh yeah, I made our dog sneeze."

"Hold still," Nikki said when they were in the road. She opened her pouch and tossed garlic in each of the four wind directions.

"How's that supposed to make me—"

"Abby!"

"Sorry."

Nikki began again. She saw Abby shiver and knew the shield had taken effect when a light blue haze enveloped her. "Okay. Now make yourself invisible."

Abby swallowed a bean and half-turned to mumble some words. Nikki smiled. Within a minute Abby had all but evaporated. There was only bluish smoke left.

"I don't suppose you can talk," Nikki asked.

She felt a draft tickle her right ear: "Naa well."

"You're not kidding. And you smell like seaweed. Come on, wisp in and let's go."

They drove past the floodlight and toward another house.

"Keep an eye out for Skull. He's following the men in the car. I—" She broke off, seeing the owl ahead. He swooped at a stop sign, then headed left. Nikki turned and drove as fast as she dared, then felt pressure tickling her foot on the accelerator. "Stop that, Abby. You're not driving with Night—at least not completely." A crispness ran up her calf, which Nikki translated as laughter. Skull flew into a road leading right. Turning down it she immediately saw the taillights of a truck a quarter mile ahead.

"I'm not going to say anything else to you until we're out of here, Abby. Okay? Just brush against me now and then to let me know you're around. Keeping our secret this way will do us both a much better service. Okay?"

"Okaaaay," Nikki heard whispered in her right ear.

When she reached the truck she saw the Black man lying in the glare of its single headlight. She was almost sure he was dead. A snake wriggled ten yards away from him; she recoiled, seeing it was headless.

"Martin?" she called, getting out and looking around.

A crash in the palmettos made her turn to see Skull ascend with something in its claws. As he flew by, she could see the headless snake striking at him. Skull dropped it before the truck, where it fell on its back, then twisted to coil and strike at the low-flying owl in the truck's still lit headlight. Nikki raised her left hand to snap a globe of destruction. Surprised when nothing happened, she snapped her hand more powerfully and the snake burst into flame. She heard Skull screech, then saw him come back, dropping the shredded snake's head over the ashes of the body. She destroyed it too, and Skull perched on her shoulder and she grimaced. "Not so tight, not so tight."

But he didn't ease up even as she bent to feel for the Black man's pulse. None, so she closed his eyelids, then jumped as palmetto fronds clacked in the dark distance, making entirely too much noise for one animal or human.

"Martin? Martin, are you around here?" She double-checked the truck.

"Nikki?"

She heard sloshing water and saw Martin Edmonds emerge from palmetto scrub, briefcase faithfully clutched in one hand, a machete in the other. Nikki gave a short laugh. But a hundred yards behind, fronds clacked, consistently approaching.

"We need to get out of here."

"Can we take Walter with us?"

"Walter?" She saw Martin nod at the man on the ground. "It would mean questions with the police, Martin."

"I don't want to leave him for the wobblers. He's seen too much of them already. Look, what you did to the snake, could you—he's single, without a family."

Nikki nodded, raised her hand and burned Walter into ashes. She felt something cool enclose her as she did, encircling her arms, and knew it was Abby. Nikki pointed to the ashes.

"Okaaaa. I'll tryyyyy."

Martin stooped to the ashes, keeping one ear cocked nervously toward the palmetto and crumbled a last bone. "God bless, fellow." As he stood, Abby flew about, swirling the ashes into the surrounding swamp. Palm fronds were crackling wildly.

"Let's get the hell out of here."

Overhead, tucked quietly in the high limb of a bald cypress, behind silvery moonlit curtains of drooping Spanish moss, a rag doll with limpid black eyes watched as they drove off.

4.

Cain! Cain! Cain!

The center of any sphere lies directly under any and every point of its surface. Directly underneath Martin, Abby, Nikki and Skull, the grating and howling name gave pause, unaware and unconcerned with what happened above.

"Is he risen?" each voice whispered. In the silence—so odd for these caverns—neighbor glared with hate and distrust at neighbor, yet held club, fist or stone in abeyance to await the answer to that single question. "Is he risen?"

He was. They could feel it. The cave walls cooled from fiery orange to cherry red. Rest for now. Wait for the first command. What will it be?

Cain! Cain! Cain!

5.

Dean Kirby had changed the name of his alter ego from Bubber to Bruno, tiring of that joke as much as he was tiring of the constant battle with Bruno. Why, Bruno? Why did you have to kill? Trapped in a corner of his own brain, Dean felt like a burglar creepy-crawling his own house, casting tentative queries into long spun axons or neurons instead of kitchen drawers. The memories he snagged were frightening. What, oh what would friend Wittgenstein say?

1. The world ain't all you know.

1a. You don't even know you.

Dean tried to remember the recent past, starting with this morning, in Florida, not Georgia. So he had driven last night—he meaning Bruno? He'd driven till he'd run out of gas. Was that why Dean had been able to take over for a period? Confusion? After all, Bruno didn't especially seem the brightest of all God's creatures.

Okay: 2. Bruno quits now and then.

What before that, pushing things back along a Cartesian timeline? Killing the cab driver. So, Bruno can take over and seems to do so especially when anger is involved. In fact, Bruno seems to grow on anger.

Okay: 3. Bruno wins now and then.

Then he remembered a hospital. Along with that came an image of his wife baring her teeth as she slit at him with a razor. So she *had* tried to kill him. He remembered his throat being sliced… one… two… three… he began to feel queasy… four and five times. He couldn't have lived through that.

He didn't live through that. That came to Dean with unsurpassed clarity. He felt his neck, running his finger carefully over several paper-thin scars, hoping not to alert Bruno. How had he healed?

No answer. Just more mileage signs: Tampa 86.

Wait a minute. The world is all you know. You talked to the strange older sister of Bobby's girlfriend. Remember her braces? And how she wanted to borrow six or seven books and you told her: "Any one. When you finish it, I'll loan you another." *That's what you said to her, isn't it? A slight little smile, showing those braces. You remember. And what did she borrow?* The Egyptian Book of the Dead.

"Did you know that the Egyptians thought each person was accompanied on this earth by a *ka*, a sort of force that would help them in this life and prepare them for the next?" she had asked. "What if the Egyptians only had half of it right? What if there's an *ak* too? An evil life force, an evil double? I mean something that exists apart, is born when a human is born, but doesn't necessarily die when the human dies. Like anti-matter for matter. What if someone had found a way—" *found a way to give this ak, this evil double, entrance into a resemblance of its once living body, say into a statue.*

That was what she'd said, while browsing an odd little book about Jewish golems.

"How would someone accomplish such a feat?" you asked.

"The Egyptians believed that the *ka* would hang around after death if a lifelike image was buried with the body," she answered. "A little statue, for instance. It wouldn't have to be but a few inches high for a soldier or priest, though it would have to be larger to hold the *ka* of a princess or pharaoh."

"About the size of Alice Fairbain's tossed-off statues would do for most of us, then?" Oh, the brace-filled smile that flashed when you said that.

"Just about that size."

And where was Annie all this time? Annie, your honor, was at Alice Fairbain's house day and night, posing for a statue. A statue, you say? And hadn't Annie mentioned that Fairbain had wanted to sculpt a statue of Bobby? *Yesyesyesyes.*

So the girl with braces—Abby, she had a name, after all— came back two days later and put into your hands the very process to summon forth the *ak. Where'd you get this, little girl? From one of my books?* Those braces glinted in answer.

"If a person dies while he clasps his image and recites this rhyme, his good and bad will merge for a second chance at life. But within one year he must break the chain and become one or the other, *ak* or *ka*, before he truly dies. It's a great gamble. It's only for people who expect to die before their time."

And just why had she turned those teenage eyes on you, Dean-o?

"I've written this for you." She'd pulled out paper in one hand and a sturdy statuette of old Dean-o himself in the other and shoved both toward you, hadn't she? She pointed to the paper: "If you read that aloud and hold your hand over a candle—you have to burn the flesh—and be sure to keep the statue close everywhere you go, then maybe you can help Bobby even if—can I borrow this book?" And she'd grabbed the first thing her hands touched, then ran out the door.

In your hand a scarab of a dung beetle and two amulets, one a heart and one a hawk with a human head. Under the heart, in Abby's neat handwriting: "I shall not eat the cakes of Osiris on the eastern shore, nor shall I sail the dark river. May my mouth, my arms and hands and legs overthrow my foe." Under the hawk: "Hail Annui! If my soul should tarry at the time I call, bring it unto me!"

Realizing you'd already started the ritual, you burnt your hand (brave man!) and recited the nonsense poem three magic times, hadn't you, Dean-o?

> *Beware, beware!*
> *Live is evil*
> *Dog dies a god*
> *God dies a dog*
> *Pan may nap*
> *A saint may taint*

Certainly tainted enough with two murders on his hands now.

Okay: 7. There will be a fight, but you can control Bruno at times.

With his last thought Dean began to concentrate on his breathing. He felt his neck ease and oxygen circulate as he slowed from 85 to within the speed limit. He saw road signs and heard cars and trucks pass. *His own* hands held the steering wheel. *HIS VERY OWN* hands.

Driving into Tampa two hours later, he parked on a side street where the car wouldn't be noticed, then counted the money Bruno'd lifted from the dead college boy: over $400. Had he managed to get his own wallet from St. Veronica's? He felt his hip pocket. Yes. So he'd rent a car. By the time the police found this one, he'd have done with Alice Fairbain. For it was her he had to stop. She was making a statue of Bobby. She wanted to do to him whatever she'd done to Annie. He rented a car and drove to a pawn shop where he bought a shotgun. He felt something stir at that. *Sleep, Bruno. Sleep. Your time will come.*

6.

Alice Fairbain slapped Annie Kirby, knocking her against the loft's ladder. "It's hard to comprehend, but you're even stupider now than when I first met you and you were married to that asshole professor. Don't you appreciate the trouble I went through to dig you up? Aaron had blisters for a week. This is the second thing you've botched. You somehow managed not to kill your asshole husband and you've somehow managed to let Aaron's favorite pet *Schwartze* and your son's psychologist get away. What were you doing?"

"She was walking in the house," Aaron said.

"Walking? In the house?" Alice turned to face the barn full of her children wobbling from foot to foot. She pointed out six of them. "Take her into the stall."

Annie murmured inarticulately and her eyes widened.

"If you were walking in the house, you must have been on a sentimental journey remembering the good old days with Deanie and Bobby-pooh. Is that it? You're not Annie, dear. You're E-inna. It nearly rhymes with hyena. Keep telling yourself that."

Six of the children were pulling at Annie Kirby's legs. She tumbled, and two grabbed her hair to drag her toward the stall that Martin and Walter had recently escaped.

"Remember, dearie: E-inna. Keep saying that to yourself. Say it now."

Annie Kirby was crying but her mouth moved, trying to form the name "E-inna," after a kick from one of the children.

"Shove her on the little neo-Nazi boy," Alice directed. "To remind her what she'll look like if this happens again." Alice turned to the mass of white before her, its hundreds of black eyes uplifted in expectant reverence. "Almost time, little ones. Your big brothers will be coming out soon, and you have to help." She motioned with her left hand and they walked from the barn into the light of a half-moon thirty degrees on the horizon. She directed them to a stand of cypress already mucky from summer rains. "Dig. Aaron says it should be ten feet deep and fifty feet in diameter."

Alice shook one taller female *ak* by its shoulder and pointed. "See?" The chalky woman nodded. Shorter ones were already handing muck and debris to their helpers. Some were in water that came up to their eyes and still walked back with handfuls of muck. Alice watched.

"Ms.?"

Alice caught a nasty tinge to that word and turned to look

to Aaron as he herded a second group from the barn.

"I've directed those in the house to come and help. There are nearly a thousand."

He said this with some surprise, Alice noted. Good. She didn't like his aura lately, darker than usual, and she didn't like his scowls, and she especially didn't like depending on him for information. How many times had she caught herself saying "Aaron says"? Too many. But she had a surprise for Aaron when he finished this second escalator. She would descend into the underearth and consolidate her power.

"Good. E-inna has at least done one thing competently. I told you it'd be worth keeping her as a zombie." Alice nodded toward the house. "Let's take ten of the children and find good doctor Edmonds."

"You should have kept the puppet here instead of trusting that Kirby zombie."

"Pie is a rag doll, not a puppet. You were raised speaking English; show it. And isn't it strange that you should suddenly take Pie's part—I thought you hated her."

Aaron gave a snort as they got into the pickup. Alice glowered, directing ten of her children to climb into the truck bed. She pointed toward the gate for Aaron to drive. Every day she moved her surprise for Aaron forward, but every day the Jewish bastard would counter with some problem inside the escalator. Of course he was right: The Kirby woman had been such a failure that Alice had given up hope of any zombie replacing Aaron, though she had held hopes for the *ak's* of Edmonds and the gardener named Walter. Now that was thwarted, for Pie told her minutes before that the good doctor was footloose and the gardener had been killed by the snake. More incompetence: the snake was supposed to stun, not bite in the damned jugular. She looked at Aaron as he drove: his face was as hard as ever. This wasn't a good time for her magic to work in half-measures.

Just off the property, one of the children ran in front of the truck and Aaron slammed on the brakes, but too late. Alice motioned ahead with her left hand. The back tire thumped once and they drove.

Alice squinted at an approaching farm's safety lamp. "It's too bad Edmonds was so nosy last night up in my guest room. He saw. I was anxious to test the first large child we pulled up. Why did he look so weak, Aaron? The little ones have walked out, but you were carrying him. Was my music all right?"

"Your music was fine. The large ones need time. Patience. They've been down longer, they've gotten more accustomed to the deep."

More delays. Alice moved Aaron's surprise date back to Christmas just after she'd jumped it to mid-July. *Wait!* She shut off the air-conditioner and rolled down the window, indicating to Aaron that he should slow down. While most witches (Alice hated the usage "Sisters") kept animals as familiars, she used a nearly indestructible doll whose life spark floated outside the body, pulling it like a puppet. In this respect Aaron was correct, though he had no idea why. It was Pie who used animals like a marionette.

"Stop," Alice said, reaching her hand out the window. The animal approached awkwardly in a way Alice had never seen any of Pie's mesmerized messengers act. She laughed: Pie had hypnotized a bat. The bat landed on her outstretched hand, loosed a small roll of paper, then fell to the road, dead. Alice gave Aaron a withering look, hoping the bat's death was not entirely lost on his thick skull.

Hurry, the tiny scroll read. *Intruders. Take a left, a right.*

"We need to hurry. One left at the end of the road then a right."

When they reached Walter's truck, the children were bashing it, having dismantled all four fenders and broken the glass and flattened the tires. Pie stood in the road clapping. Aaron and Alice both scowled when it was clear that Martin Edmonds wasn't around.

"What happened?" Alice asked Pie when she got out.

Pie stopped clapping and looked at Aaron, who went to retrieve something from the pickup's bed. As he did, the children jumped up as if the idea hadn't occurred to them, and they began scattering tools.

"*Desiste!*" Alice shouted when a hammer landed near her.

The children froze, their blackened eyes staring blankly ahead in every direction like angry guard dogs. Pie finished scribbling and handed Alice the note which she read by the headlights of her truck.

Nyx Ryan destroyed snake with Matrix. Then took Edmonds away and destroyed body of gardener. Her new familiar is an owl, and she knows how to use the Shield of Defense. She is powerful.

"Powerful? She was an airline stewardess seven years ago, Pie. She still is. Don't you remember?" Alice pulled Spanish moss from the doll's head.

The rag doll nodded.

"And you still think she's powerful?"

Another nod.

"She replaced that black cat I ran over with a cockatiel, and now an owl. Who would choose a familiar that could only fly at night?" Alice was speaking to Pie but looked at Aaron, who was waiting close enough that he might have heard, especially in this damp. "What do you think?" she asked.

He shrugged. "We might as well take these back with us and let them work on the second opening, *nu?*"

"I mean about what I just said to Pie."

"You told me not to listen to your conversations and I don't."

Pie pinched Alice's ankle and glared at Aaron. *I know, baby. I know.*

"Well, Pie thinks it might be a good idea if we used these as guards around the Kirby place, so let's get them loaded and back. It'll be about eleven. Do you need to rest before going down tonight?"

"I don't want to, but I think I'll have to."

"Sleep. I'll drive us back and take care of these children. Pie will wake you at midnight."

⚛

While Aaron rested once they got home, Alice consulted her files on the local covens. There were three: one south in Lutz near the nudist colony, one in Tampa, and one in St. Petersburg, though that one was filled with doddering toothless hags intent on love potions for doddering toothless grandpas. She'd quit all of them after she got her information. Bland do-gooders interested in the right-hand path, though she had been cautious enough to attend under a pseudonym and disguised with thick make-up and a wig, which worked a magic of its own, she supposed.

She found a card under the Lutz Coven: *Nyx Ryan. Tuesday meeting, 8:10 p.m. March 4, 1991. Approximate age: 30-32. Occupation: airline stewardess (!). Rank: common member. Comments: The most witchly asset this fluff has is her looks. Why didn't she run for Miss America where she could wield some real power?*

Alice heard a noise: below at the oven, Annie Kirby inserted statues for firing. Alice stuck her head out the window and heard the woman weeping and gargling something that vaguely sounded like, "E-inna," as she situated the statues for firing. Alice grinned and went back to the files.

Another card under the Tampa Coven: *Nyx Ryan: Thursday meeting 8:40 p.m. July 16, 1993. Approximate age 30-34. Occupation: airline stewardess. Rank: common member. Comments: Our little lady spent her time talking about leaving for Kentucky to try for custody of her daughter. Buy her a subscription to* Vogue *and a Hallmark Good Riddance card. A black cat for a familiar? And bring it to a sabbat so every sister can paw its fur for future influence? What a dork.*

"See how much of an impression she didn't make, Pie? I didn't even remember having met her at the Lutz Coven two years before, so I made a second filing card."

The rag doll sat motionless.

"Okay." Alice riffled the third file, the Saint Petersburg one: "Nothing, Pie. Maybe our stewardess is afraid to cross a bridge; maybe she thinks water will rob what little power she has."

Pie walked over and pinched Alice's ankle. "Okay, if you insist." She picked the rag doll up so it could search the files. She watched as Pie pulled out a card.

Date: June 2, 1995.

"I forgot I was attending those silly things that recently."

Late for sabbat because of collecting blood at a delightful wreck. Absolutely the most inane minutes any coven could endure: big discussion the previous week about efficacy of cinnamon versus nutmeg in love potions for men over sixty. How about cayenne pepper, girls? So bored that I peeped around to spot one old granny with a voodoo doll—not a nice thing to be holding at a sabbat, dearie. She was staring at a younger woman two rows ahead and jabbing away without the least affect. I involuntarily flinched when she poked the doll right in the eye. Checked my own aura to be sure my Shield of Defense was active. Granny really go-

ing at it. Then noticed a hag to her right doing the same, evidently aiming for same victim, one of a group of young women. A purple-haired spinster seated behind leaned to say something. Then all three joined hands to plunge a single needle in one doll. There was a scream—not from their intended but from the purple granny. "Jeannie's had a heart attack!" A doll with a pin lanced in its heart lay on the floor. One conspiratorial crone pocketed it, giving the other a frightened look. I turned to spot their target, but the five young women were all vaguely familiar. Three of them I could identify: Marianne Smith; Pauline Jackson; Lou Anne Timmons. The other two were nondescript, one with dark black hair and a beauty-queen look, the other with a thick nose that belonged on a boxer—dog. Until I'm certain what happened, none should be underestimated. The meeting adjourned when the ambulance came...

Pie took a stubby pencil from its apron and scribbled after the first beauty-queen description: Nyx Ryan.

"Do you think? All right, Pie. We won't underestimate Ms. Ryan, will we?"

Pie pointed to Alice's watch.

"Yes, it's time to wake the slumbering giant. We won't underestimate him either, will we?"

Pie pinched Alice's forearm and jumped onto the file cabinet to hop a goofy dance imitative of Aaron's walk.

"You want to wake him? Go pinch his ear. He hates that, doesn't he?"

Pie clapped and ran. Alice looked out on Persephone's Escalator. A red glow reflected from the kiln. She opened her desk drawer and withdrew a leather pouch of bone dust, sprinkling it to the four directions. She'd never known if a double Shield worked any better; it certainly didn't work any worse. Then she pulled a .32 from her drawer. *Never put all your eggs into one magical basket.* From another part of the house Aaron yelped and she smiled.

CRSO

Aaron himself wasn't smiling. He reached for a glass of water by his bed and threw it at the rag doll, missing as usual. *Someday*, he thought, *maybe I connect with a glass of gasoline—then, poof! How will your magic puppet hold up then, Ms.* goyische *bitch?*

He waited until the rag doll scampered out of his room, then checked his watch. Fifteen minutes. He went to his closet. No sense in being foolhardy: he ran his hands over a bulletproof vest's webbing. He also donned a belt holding a hatchet he'd had chromed, for down below they appreciated something shiny. And for those that didn't, he had three clips of bullets for a semi-automatic Walthers. He put on high-topped, steel-toed boots, a K-Mart special, and began winding himself with bandaging to thwart any weak knife cuts at his knees and below. Hot as Gehenna, but necessary. He walked to the kitchen and heard Alice outside, already playing her pan flute. He eyed the refrigerator and bolted a chunk of lox and a bagel, nearly choking on the latter so he could get out in time.

Outside, Alice didn't even look up, though Pie was eyeing him. To his left the Kirby zombie was working away, muttering. The glow called. What was it about the glow which made him feel as if he could chew a dozen Heinrich Himmlers on his back teeth, spitting their bones at a dozen Adolf Hitlers? He gave a last look at Fairbain and her rag doll. *Smile*, he told himself, giving a friendly wave.

But the moment his foot touched Persephone's, bones in his spine popped erect. Not twenty steps past Fairbain's ridiculous shield of illusion that had fooled the cops and those three cracker bozos he passed an *ak* heading upwards to inhabit its statue. He could see its eyes resting on his shiny chrome ax, and he could see it hug the far wall. This one was missing a left ear. Amazing. Fairbain had said that in the entire geography of once-living mankind any possible combination of face would exist, and she was right: no more than a handful of her statues hadn't attracted an *ak* from below. She was right except for their size. He was the one who told her of much larger *ak's* in the deeper confines of Persephone. Hence the newer statues at Kirby's barn.

He'd toyed with giving her family photos. Any moment he hoped to meet the double of his aunt's gnarled form, which he would take great pleasure in hacking through and through. Would he find his father, his brothers, whom he'd only seen from yellowing photos? Those he would try to convince to ascend with him, though he knew reasoning wasn't easily accomplished in the escalator. Still, he kept looking for them among the *kinder*, as he called the *ak's* since they so looked like children except for their vicious fighting.

So vicious and so many. Fairbain's *kleinlich* eyes were aglow only with her *kleinlich* pantry of helpers. She had no idea how vast the network was. As many as she had above, he had ten times more waiting, fighting in two caverns he'd led them to by recording Fairbain's pan flute—recordings, which she had assured him would never work: the magic had to be living. *Ja*, so much for the great witch and her gingerbread theories. Two entire small towns stared at two tape recorders like children to pipers. How many more would come? He had no idea, though his idea was better than Mistress Witch's. He made a face and stomped happily on a second small *kinder* who walked too close to him. They'd soon be crunching underneath his boots like seashells.

Two more *kinder* passed, paying no notice for they were banging one another with rocks. It was that way each time he encountered two or more. The single ones spotted his ax and walked on, at least the small single ones did. Some larger *kinder* would attack, but they were easily stopped by a nine-millimeter.

He walked twenty minutes; he could feel small ones crunch underneath regularly, or occasionally stab at his boot and cuff. The heat made him breathe shallowly and filled his head with a pleasant spinning. He hopped delightedly on a cluster of small *kinder*, so that his boots crushed them with a happy sound that moved through both his legs and his ears.

The voice would start soon, maybe another five minutes. He'd never understood what this voice was saying, though it repeated over and over and seemed to drip from the very walls and ceilings of the caverns. Ms. Witch had never heard it from her safety, and he had never told her about it, for the voice, he was sure, held the key. Several *kinder* passed, all eyeing his glinting ax. He heard a skirmish and turned to see one *kinder* chase down three smaller cousins, bashing them with a rock.

Aaron was surprised by a new opening; from its glowing red walls he could hear the faint crying voice he'd been awaiting. This descent looked steeper, and he stopped to listen.

"Aagh!" He grabbed his leg. A *kinder* had stabbed him with a makeshift rock knife. Aaron dodged a second blow and yanked his ax from its scabbard so that it gleamed in the glowing tunnel. The creature's black eyes focused on the chrome and backed away, itself glowing chalky white compared to the walls.

"Too late for that, my dove." Aaron smashed the *kinder*, nearly severing its head. Blackish phlegm oozed from the wound. Aaron backed against a wall to inspect his leg. This one had cut right through the thick wrapping. They were getting stronger, a good sign. He'd have to be careful to leave the ax visible, maybe just carry it: a drip of prevention is worth a waterfall of cure, *nu?*

Another *kinder* stepped over its dead brother, kicking the head loose, eyeing the ax Aaron held. Aaron watched the *kinder* ascend, heading for the music, which remained quite clear. He could still see the main corridor where another group were ascending and fighting. He heard scuffling and looked to see the decapitated head's mouth wetly call out to its torso. There were many things he hadn't told Fairbain, among them the fact that down here death was only temporary. No matter how smashed the body, it would crawl back together and stand. Within an hour, this one would be pawing for its rock knife. Aaron walked over and kicked the head farther away. Make that two hours.

He decided to continue along this new tunnel. Its descent was much steeper—did that mean anything? After a few minutes the voice became loud enough to cover Alice's pan flute from above. This tunnel seemed to multiply a garbled cry more than the others. He paused to look back: three hundred yards separated him and the main corridor. Though he could still see figures walking there, the glow might soon render them invisible. But tonight he wanted to go deeper than he ever had. He searched ahead: still no *kinder* in sight. Mice are afraid to play where there's a cat, *nu?* He walked on, keeping an ear out for Ms. Alice's flute. Fainter? Soon he might have to loop his spool of fishing line over a rock to make his own Ariadne's thread.

Not thirty steps later he stopped, for the flute had disappeared to be replaced with that terrible voice. This never happened. Had he been this deep before? This tunnel was easily twenty degrees steeper than the other three he'd taken. He caught sight of two *kinder*, fighting as usual. They stood to his chest, a half foot larger than the others. He watched one trip the other, then lift a rock, missing his foe's head. They grappled, edging toward the music they still must be able to hear. But the thread. To be safe, he should put that down. He saw a rock jut ahead. As he bent to loop the line, his fingers touched the warmly glowing rock:

"*Cain! Cain!*"

He pulled away and the cry again became garbled; indeed, he could again hear Fairbain's flute. Seeing another *kinder* approach he made a gesture with the ax, then purposefully placed his palm on the rock.

"*My brother Cain. Cain! Cain!*"

The cry made him dizzy and angry. Sweat broke from his brow.

"*Cain did it! Cain! Cain!*"

Aaron jerked and swayed, accidentally touching his head to the wall. The voice screamed:

"*CAIN! CAIN!*"

He hit at his ear and lurched, fishing line playing out behind. The name *Cain* whispered without stop. How he hated Fairbain! Her damnable art, her damnable dog with its hair cut like a lion's mane, her damnable taunting foul pork breakfast, her damnable breasts and thighs, her damnable male hands, her damnable blue-gray eyes always laughing at him, her damnable ass wagging around the yard and house, her damnable deep voice…

"Why are you here, mortal?"

Aaron raised his ax. Two full-sized men and a woman stood abreast in the corridor. Some thirty feet behind them two *kinder* were fighting. The trio ignored them, though, to stare at Aaron.

Cain! Cain! Cain!

"To give you freedom."

"Why would we want that?"

He couldn't tell which was speaking. All three? Or was the voice coming from the walls?

"You can have more power outside. Up." Aaron pointed backwards. At first they seemed disjointed, not even aware of one another, but as the two *kinder* behind closed in, the three moved like neon tetras, splitting rank to let the two pass— still scuffling like spinning, glowing tops and heading toward Aaron, who also let them pass.

"And how is it that you're going to give us this power?"

"I'm creating two openings. They're heading for the first." Aaron nodded toward the two clawing *kinder*. "Hundreds of them are topside now, waiting. And three thousand of the very little ones."

"The little ones are nothing. Petty evils and pranks."

Cain! Cain! Cain!

Aaron grimaced, moving his elbow that had accidentally brushed the wall of the tunnel. "But hundreds of thousands of them and yourselves to command them…"

"And what do you get from this?"

"Revenge." Aaron saw a smile simultaneously cross their faces and again thought of neon tetras in a tank. "Twelve million of my people, my father and brothers I never saw except in pictures, were killed. I want revenge." Heat paced his chest. Each time he descended he felt power. Down here he was able to lift rocks he couldn't even roll above. Revenge. He would be the Messiah, the new Abraham for his people. He stared at the three large *kinder* before him—an army of true golems for him to direct.

"The strength you take from here will make you rulers beyond your dreams. And we have machines to help kill. Imagine being able to fly through the air over the entire globe above, wherever you want, in hours. There's so much to see up there, so much to kill."

Their smiles remained fixed and he was unsure if he should continue, if he should tell them about Alice Fairbain. He decided he better show more power than a glinting ax.

"Above, my assistant has powers to kill with a twist of her hand. Powers that make this ax look weak. What do you have for weapons down here? Rocks and your bare hands. Look what this, the weakest of my weapons, can do to your rocks." He swung the ax high and brought it down against a stalagmite's side, cutting cleanly through with an ease that surprised even himself. "This weapon I will give you—and others even more powerful. Not this." He tossed the stalagmite club to their feet.

Their smiles disappeared and all three scrambled for the club, gouging one another with rock knives they'd concealed. Oily blood spewed and Aaron noticed for the first time its acrid, hot odor. The three tumbled for minutes until a victor emerged with the stalagmite. He glared at Aaron's ax, then lunged. Aaron clipped him neatly on the shoulder, leaving his arm dangling and the stalagmite rolling down the inclined stone floor. *Cain! Cain! Cain!* the walls shouted until Aaron had to hold his ears and stomp to allay the sound.

The stalagmite thudded against something Aaron could hear but not quite see. Then came a hollow, deep snort that a bull might give on a hot day, and the clumsy footfalls of many *kinder* running below. They appeared in a reddish glow. He pulled out his pistol, but the *kinder* paid little mind and ran past. Then ominous quiet.

Aaron saw movement: the large *kinder* he'd killed was congealing quicker than he'd seen any do before. *Cain! Cain!*

Cain! The walls cried as blood crept to enter the neck wound and the arm worked back to the shoulder, flesh fastening to flesh. With surprise, Aaron looked at the other two, who were already facing him. They stepped forward.

"I am pleased. You have brought light to Cain. Build not two but three of your openings and many more of the likenesses will come and they and I will bring dark to your world, as you want." All three were talking together again.

"Can you come up with me?"

Had he asked that? He wasn't sure. He only knew that he ascended Persephone's Escalator hours after he'd left, alone with two spent clips from his gun, and that both he and Alice Fairbain looked down to a sea of large *kinder* eagerly awaiting statues for their *ak's*.

DOWSING

(July 2, very early morning to July 11, midnight)

1.

From a daytime flight, Florida looked pleasant. Lori joked that they could use a good spy satellite and Ann Marie frowned, but Jewel agreed. Why not? Technology might well be the witchcraft of the future. How many witches of the left-hand-path could boast of doing even a tenth of "Little Boy's" damage to Hiroshima? How many witches of the right-hand-path could boast of accomplishing even a tenth of oral polio vaccine's good? But then again, untold little miracles made both possible, didn't they? Well, leave that for the next Executrix to sort.

When they landed, Jewel blew part of her life's' savings she carried in traveler's checks—even witches won't leave home without them—to rent a van so the Pentad could ride together. They stopped at a motel on Bearss Avenue because of a strong tug there. The double *s* in the name? Witches, as everyone, could be influenced by incidentals. By one a.m., looking out at a vague glow in the sky's aura, they knew they'd made a mistake. So they moved in the middle of the night to a Day's Inn at Wesley Chapel, thirteen miles north.

"Instead of getting two rooms, why don't we take three?" Beth asked. "I'll pay for it: magic," she said, showing a credit card to the check-in clerk at the registration desk.

Jewel sniffed the air: she was familiar enough with Beth's exudates, the faint vinaigrette which made her smell like a health salad. But this was a much danker smell—iron, like a profusion of blood. "All right, as long as we can get rooms next to one another. Not even one room separating us." She looked at the clerk, a heavily made-up blonde woman, who checked her board and found three rooms on the second floor facing the pool.

Great, Jewel thought, *if I get tired of fighting Beth I can jump from the balcony into the shallow end.* Tiffany and Nancy took a room together; Jewel could imagine Tiffany taunting Nancy all night, changing nightgowns and hinting she might leave her husband to form a lesbian alliance. Beth, Becky, and Anne Marie roomed together: if someone had to watch Beth, Anne Marie was the surest. Which left Jewel and Lori. *That* rooming combination raised eyebrows with Beth and Nancy quickly enough. Let them think what they want, Jewel thought… as long as the Pentad isn't made ineffective.

It was a quarter after two as they carried their luggage into their rooms. Jewel noticed Beth staring over the railing toward the sky.

Beth coughed. "I think it would be wise to convene tonight before going to sleep."

"That won't make anyone happy."

"I know. But I do think it would be wise."

Jewel looked from the sky to the ground fog and nodded.

She knocked on Tiffany and Nancy's door. Nancy opened it; behind her Tiffany was modeling a skimpy teddy.

"We need to get together tonight, Nancy. Ten minutes?"

Nancy nodded, her liquid brown eyes appraising Jewel's face. Tiffany pouted and picked at her teddy. Jewel hadn't particularly cared for bringing Tiffany along, but you gotta do what you gotta do, she thought, that being as philosophical as she cared to get at 2 a.m.

She spotted movement below, but on facing the pool saw only a fountain with the most lewd cupid she'd ever seen spouting water from its drawn arrow. She could swear a bulge for a man's penis puffed its white, loose-fitting garments. A local artist's creation—she'd forgotten the artist's first name, though Fairbain had stuck because of a pun Nancy made on seeing the bulge: "No Fair Maid's Brain hung that tool on this kid's body."

Four other statues guarded the four corners of the pool's iron fence. Wood nymphs at a Day's Inn? Jewel became mesmerized by the trickling water and the shifting underwater lights refracting through the turquoise pool. She imagined the four statues running, giggling while Cupid shot little love arrows. Dancing to a waltz. But one nymph screamed as an arrow hit her. She fell, black blood oozing from her wound. The Cupid prepared another shaft. He drew his bow to aim not at a nymph but Jewel herself, for two shining black eyes—

"It's time."

Jewel jumped from her imaginations, twisting her foot in the railing.

"I'm sorry; I didn't mean to scare you."

It was Anne Marie. Jewel looked from her to the five blithe spirits below, holding their steady-state love poses.

"Jewel? Beth's inside preparing an herbal broth to make us more perceptive to dangers and enemies."

Jewel shook her head as she gazed down on the pool's sylvan nymphs posed in eternal ecstasy, its Cupid daintily peeing water from his arrow and his quiver.

"Silly, aren't they?" Anne Marie asked.

Jewel gave a frown, then went inside, smelling Beth's portable hot pot purging itself of past concoctions.

Since Lori was becoming the darling of them all because of her youth, and since she'd already proven she didn't diminish the Pentad, Jewel indicated she should sit around the bed with them. Besides, it was advisable to keep the same arrangement from that morning (not far from twenty-four hours ago, Jewel thought, blinking to fight sleep). So they held hands, still keeping the open plate between Becky and Tiffany, while Beth scattered in a handful of dill seed. The smoke was almost pleasant, it was so light. Then Beth dropped in mustard seed and covered the pot. Lots of popping, no appreciable change in the smell. Still, Jewel knew it was coming; ah, there in the sinister left hand. A flask of cider vinegar. She winced, waiting. With a hiss, the smell arose, and Jewel could feel Lori's hand tighten as she tried not to sneeze from the vapor. Beth unplugged the pot to pour the mixture into saki cups.

At a nod from Beth, the others began to talk.

"Doesn't she have to chant something?" Lori whispered to Jewel, who was herself surprised Beth didn't take the opportunity for the floor, even if the particular potion didn't call for incantation. So many surprises at the end of life. Maybe it's not the end, she chided herself. She sipped the mixture and grimaced: Beth might have slighted Lori's expectations by not chanting, but she sure hadn't on the taste of this crap.

"This is supposed to make us see enemies clearer, right?" Nancy asked.

Beth nodded.

"Well, it's already making me think twice about you, Beth, for making me drink it. Haven't you ever heard of Sweet n Low?"

"Bitter seeks bitter," Beth answered.

Slowly, one by one, they faced northwest, the same direction they'd faced in the other hotel, except now they were much nearer to the ominous whatever they were facing. They sat some ten minutes listening to the roar of trucks on the interstate and occasional night sounds—a laugh from the hotel, a breaking glass.

"Enough's enough," Jewel said at last, turning to face inside the room. As she did, an odd flicker hit her eyes—from someone's aura? She shrugged it off: "This is only getting us nervous. Let's join the Pentad in a shield of defense and go to sleep. Tomorrow will be just as long as today."

After performing the ceremony and ushering them out, Jewel glanced at the pool below: a chair had been shifted to face their rooms. She rubbed her head, tired from the flight, tired from many things. *Paul, will you come tonight to my dreams? Will you, Paul?* She heard Lori fumble with the light switch and welcomed the dark.

2.

Abby, in the guise of pale smoke, clung to Nikki all the way home. Nikki realized their relationship would never be the same now that Abby knew Night and Nikki were one, for age hath its privileges even among witches. It would be *Mrs. Ryan* for quite some time. Too, Martin was throwing in a cog she hadn't expected: she felt an animal attraction that might prove dangerous. Well old gal, these are modern times: witches can not only cry, they can love. Besides, the power of sex was nothing to be scoffed at. In fact, it was time young Night had that experience so her own power would grow. Nikki looked at Martin sitting by the car's window, his eyes glued to the side mirror. She raised an eyebrow; it'd be a dirty trick, but…

Two logistical problems faced her once they reached Highway 54, pulling by the Day's Inn near the interstate. First, should Abby forsake her invisibility to materialize and let Martin in on her existence? Second, how would Abby get back home? It certainly wasn't safe for her now in this neighborhood. She'd just have to call Abby's parents and reassure them.

☙

"There are some things in Dean Kirby's manuscript I want you to look at," Martin said as Nikki turned the car toward her house. "It's possible he guessed what was going on over there. His specialty is folklore, you know."

Nikki nodded, feeling Abby loosen a bit in the car. That's right, Abby had met Dean Kirby—maybe even had a schoolgirl crush on him.

"We'll do that when we get home. Keep watching the mirror to be sure we aren't being followed by Fairbain or her man."

Fifteen minutes later they were home. On getting out, Nikki glanced to the sky. Redder than usual. The Tampa paper claimed it was a phenomenon like the Northern lights. She couldn't agree less. On reaching Nikki's front porch, Abby began to materialize—evidently deciding on her own that she could trust Martin.

"What's going on?" Martin asked as the porch swirled with

thick fog. Understandably nervous, he grabbed a brick from the flower bed.

"It's all right, Martin. She's a friend." Nikki touched his hand, urging him to drop the brick, which he did.

For some reason, materialization took longer than its kin dematerialization. Vapors gathered from the air, the grass, and tumbled about emitting colors and sparks. After three or four minutes a solid form stood before them, though mist still clung about Abby's body.

"It's harder if you wait long," Abby explained.

"Abby, meet Martin. Martin, meet Abby, who drove along with us in the shape of the wind—not because we were trying to deceive you, but because it seemed best to have a surprise in the toy box, so to speak."

"Understood," Martin said, bending forward to touch Abby, then shake her hand as if to assure himself. Abby giggled.

Nikki turned, then shook her head at the sky's glow. "Let's get inside."

"What is that?" Martin asked, staring at the glow.

"Maybe your Dean Kirby can fill us in. Abby knew Dean Kirby, by the way, Doctor."

Martin, still looking at the reddish glow, grabbed his briefcase. "Abby. I think he mentioned you in here. In very favorable terms."

"She's blushing, even in the dark."

"Mrs. Ryan!"

Skull flapped over the porch. "All right, stay out," Nikki said, looking at the bird. "But leave the kittens next door alone, will you?" No answer, so she turned to Martin: "If you ever become a warlock, take a familiar who isn't contrary. You don't happen to be a momma's boy, by the way?"

"Not that I know of. Why?"

"They say momma's boys or men who've never seen their father make the best warlocks. It's a dying breed, and we always need recruits."

"You'd think with today's divorce rate there'd be plenty of both."

Nikki switched on a floodlight; an immediate ruffle of feathers brought her loud apology and she flipped it back off, turning the house lights on instead. "You'd think a lot of things from statistics and textbooks."

"Can I get something to drink?" Abby asked, running her hand along the dark pine of the living room.

"Why don't you make us all some hot tea? Caffeine might help us decipher what's going on." Nikki looked to find Martin collapsed in an armchair, his hands limply hung over its sides.

"It just hit me," he said, "that that woman was going to kill me."

Nikki put her hand near his head. "I don't think so. I think Aaron could have handled that easily last night, if she wanted. But why would she go to so much trouble to get you down here and keep you here?"

"Bobby's the only answer I can come up with. Annie Kirby made Fairbain his legal guardian. Fairbain wants to adopt the boy and save him from Dean Kirby."

"Bobby hates her!" Abby yelled over the microwave from the kitchen.

"Bobby was her younger sister's boyfriend," Nikki explained.

Abby walked in with tea on a tray, evidently feeling quite adult. "She wants Bobby because she needs him for whatever she's doing with the statues."

"How do you know that?"

Abby looked from Nikki to Martin and swallowed her adulthood. "Because I've been to her place, I've heard her talk to that man and her rag doll."

"You've been there and didn't tell me?" The irritation in Nikki's voice rose to a teenage screech and she mentally cursed, hoping Martin would overlook it, but he didn't.

"How do you two know each other anyway? Through Night?"

Abby winked at Nikki and waxed eloquent: "Oh what tangled webs we weave, when first we practice to—"

"All right, Abby. One thing at a time." Nikki turned to Martin. "That's right, through Night, who's staying with a friend."

After a snort, Abby added, "Alice Fairbain asked Bobby to help with her kiln and paid him a lot of money. I know because my sister told me. But I knew something she and Bobby didn't: Old bitch Fairbain was making a statue of Bobby, a really big one. I used to sneak around back of her property: Fairbain never caught me. The statue was for magic so bad it would kill him. Aaron always kept Bobby working below her back turret window so she could use him as a model. I told my sister to tell Bobby that Aaron was Old Fag City and that he might even have killed the Settles' girl."

"And did he?" Nikki asked, looking into Abby's brown eyes.

Abby scooted back into her chair. "I think that what Fairbain's doing is so bad that she and her stupid Aaron, neither one know what it really is. No, he didn't kill Cristy, but something the two of them're doing did."

"The statues," Nikki and Martin said at once.

Abby's lips trembled and she pinched at the crushed

brown velvet of her chair. "What I told you before about Cristy Settles wasn't all true. I was out walking when I saw four of Fairbain's statues running like albino midgets carrying pitchforks. I followed to see them chase Cristy into the pond. This was a long time after the police came looking for her, so I guess they'd been keeping her and she'd escaped from them. Anyway, they caught her and cut off her head. This all happened in the middle of the night. Cristy used to sneak from her parents' house and walk her dog on the roads, which is probably how they got her in the first place, I guess. It happened so fast. I was too scared to do anything, I don't have your kind of powers, Mrs. Ryan. I wish you'd been there." Abby bit her lips. "This was before I'd learned to become invisible."

"No one ever found the girl's head, did they?"

Instead of answering, Abby looked down at the brown crushed velvet. Gripping her teacup, she looked at Nikki. "I knew I could get vengeance for Cristy that way."

"It's okay, Abby," Nikki said. "After all, being invisible has likely kept you alive till now."

Martin, not following the implications, interrupted, "Well, after Bobby quit, Dean Kirby stopped worrying about him and instead began to wonder about his wife and Fairbain." He opened Kirby's manuscript. "Now here's some really odd stuff. First, Kirby begins to see a rag doll—"

"Her familiar," Abby said, her head casting a shadow on the den's cedar wall. Nikki nodded agreement.

"Well, he sees it several times and even tries to destroy it twice with a shotgun, it says in here." Martin punched the manuscript in emphasis.

"Not many witches have either the ability or desire to keep an inanimate familiar," Nikki explained to Martin. "The advantage is that they're nearly indestructible, but they're also moronic. There's a story about one who outlived its mistress a hundred years; it sat in a tree doing her last bidding, watching whoever passed the crossroads. Every night it would strut to her house—even after her house had burned and was no longer there—and write a report out in the dirt about who'd passed. Unfortunately, the betrayer the witch had feared didn't use the crossroads but came over the river to kill her, thinking the water would waylay her curse."

"That sounds about right: this rag doll never seemed to do much but watch, according to Dean's diary." Martin jumped at scuffling on the roof, but remembered Skull.

Nikki walked to the front door and opened it, still speaking to Martin. "Watching, that's their great ability. Wonderful rote memorization and attention span, and who'd expect a doll flopped in some corner to be a spy? Skull, for instance, makes people nervous. And he gets carried away by whatever form he inhabits. As an owl, he hunts mice or kittens—which he better not be doing now." Nikki shouted this last out, then closed her front door and returned to sit down.

"What about a witch? If she's in a beautiful form will she get carried away by a man?" Abby inserted, giving Nikki a look.

"Your time will come, princess, don't fret that."

Martin blushed. "Okay, you explained the rag doll, see if you can explain this passage about his wife." He looked to the diary and read aloud. "'I leaned closer to hear and she slashed at my throat with a razor and killed me.' "

Nikki and Abby stared at one another. The frogs on the lake in the back were joined by the bellow of an alligator.

"And here," Martin said, tapping the page that had so mystified him, the page with *ka* written over and over on it, and that final reversal to *ak*.

"*The Egyptian Book of the Dead,*" Abby commented, leaning to look at it.

"Yeah, he mentions that you borrowed that book and came back with a talisman."

"Not a talisman. An incantation, an excellent scary one, part from the *Book of the Dead* and part from an old English folk song. I didn't really think it would work. He must have taken the clay model I made him and hidden it, like the spell directs. He did it because he wanted to protect Bobby. Fairbain needs Bobby."

"What for?"

Abby blushed. "She needs a virgin. And she needs one who looks like Bobby. The looks are important, for some reason I don't even think she knows. I told my sister to lay Bobby, but she's so stupid she would've gotten pregnant if she did. And she didn't anyway."

"A virgin. Why? Is she planning on raising a family of these *ka's?*" Nikki asked

"I guess. I think she may have tried zombies, too."

"Zombies?"

"I think. Sometimes I'd be so scared over there that things got confused. Sometimes I thought her statues could see me even when I was invisible, because their eyes would snap open. Once I thought I saw Mrs. Kirby, I mean a long time after she was buried and all, carrying a sack of concrete."

Martin raised his eyebrows, thinking of that morning. "Why does Kirby make such a big deal out of this *ak*? It's *ka* written backwards, so it's life force written backwards. Death? The id? An anima?"

"You're talking psychology," Nikki commented, placing her hand on Martin's wiry arm. She looked at a page of the diary with the *ak's* scrawled on it, then flipped it over to see scribbled demons, bats and screaming lips interspersed with a minuscule handwriting. "Good Goddess above, what happened to the man? Does any of this have to do with your spell, Abby?"

Abby took the diary and flipped through pages of frantic scribbling and doodling. *Cain* was written ten thousand times if it were written once. "I don't know. It's all really crazy," she said. "Just like Fairbain's place."

"What exactly would the spell you cast on Dean Kirby accomplish?" Nikki asked.

"One of its requirements was that no tears of mourning could touch the body before it turned cold. That requirement means something went wrong that needed to be righted. Then the corpse will live and have a full year to right the wrong. But—this is really important—the corpse will carry about a 'lytle daimon' in its chest until it really dies at the end of that year. That means that the body won't belong completely to the owner."

"What kind of little demon?"

"It didn't say, except in the folk song the little demon in the dead woman nearly kills her lover when she searches him out."

"And what was the wrong that this dead woman wanted to correct?"

Abby looked up at the ceiling before answering Nikki. "She became pregnant on her wedding night but was killed and raped three months later by raiding, drunken soldiers. She wanted to at least have her husband's baby and give it to him."

"I'm not sure a spell like that wouldn't be a curse." Martin commented.

"I think that's what the song was saying. The baby was born without hands or feet, and the woman died giving birth. The lover killed himself by jumping into a rushing, cold river. Then both of them roamed the riverbanks forever, on opposite shores and the baby floated in the river's mist, in the middle."

"Delightful reading, Abby."

"About like this." Abby indicated Kirby's manuscript, touching it and pulling back. "If it hadn't been for Bobby I'd never have given Mr. Kirby the spell. Wait," Abby pointed to a page of more legitimate script. All three of them huddled to read:

My name is Dean Lawrence Kirby, I will avenge Annie and save Bobby, my name is Dean Lawrence Kirby. I will take Bobby away. He thinks I killed his mother. I will take him and keep him from her grave. When the short time allotted me is done, when I turn to the rotting meat I already am under this cloak of illusion, he must be away from AF. Annie was not free. I realize that now. Only death made her free, for she'd been slave to AF. AF must die. I will avenge Annie and free myself to death. Her bones cry from the wet ground like Abel cried to

CAIN CAIN CAIN CAIN CAIN CAIN CAIN CAIN

No, I must forget Cain. My name is Dean Lawrence Kirby, Dean Lawrence Kirby, and I will live for eleven months and 29 days or until I have finished my task on earth.

Please let my son live to have a son and see trees and light like he should. Please God, let death not be like this

The rest turned to scribbling nonsense again.

"It looks like your spell worked."

"I can't believe it. I even made a little of it up."

Nikki reached to touch Abby's knee. "Maybe that's what the Matrix is about—not what 99% of the wiccans and witches with their stiff Latin and Hebrew formulas they don't even understand think it's about. Maybe it's a bit of intuition, a bit of knowledge, a bit of luck."

Martin shook his head. "Wait, you two. Let's say his wife *did* try to kill him—stress from the move or being sick… or whatever. If so, her attempt wouldn't be something he'd want to remember, especially as she died weeks afterwards. So let's say he compartmentalizes that memory, fixating on mythology: Cain. He draws up demons to accompany her attempted murder in an effort to forget it, to excuse it."

While Abby frowned at Martin's explanation, Nikki had a more neutral response. "Martin, you're saying then that he didn't really die." When Martin raised his hands in an exasperated Well-naturally-since-I've-seen-him-walking-and-breathing gesture, Nikki turned to Abby: "You did say, after all, that you'd made some of the spell up."

"Whose side are you on, Mrs. Ryan?" Abby turned to Martin, shading her eyes from a light bulb on the back porch. "What about the statues? Do you have an explanation for them killing Cristy? And the way I appear and disappear? Is that psychological?"

Martin raised his palms to slow her down. "I'm not trying to cast doubt over everything, Abby; I've become a convert to the wonders of magic and witchcraft—"

"We prefer to call it the Sisterhood—"

"Okay, okay," Martin said, raising his palms again. "But that doesn't mean that everything has to be magical, does it?

You don't use incantation to make your dinner appear every night, right? And you go to school, instead of magically osmosing textbooks into your brain. Look, Abby: in a way it doesn't matter whether Dean Kirby is a victim of multiple personality disorder or an actual—what? Zombie, possessed man, or wraith on a mission of vengeance. It doesn't matter, insofar as how we need to treat him, and that's as a very dangerous individual."

A clacking of wings sounded from the roof, followed by a hard crash. They rushed to the front door to see a two-foot plaster cast of a curly-haired boy smashed against a stepping-stone. An oily substance oozed from the ivory shards. Nearby was a small knife, still clasped in the statue's separated hand. Skull flapped overhead. With a final sweep it landed on Night's Trans Am to let out two hoots.

"Are you sure?" Nikki asked the bird. Another hoot. "It's okay," she said, turning to Martin and Abby. "There was only that one. Maybe it grabbed onto my car when we left Quail Hollow."

Abby pointed to the plaster hand no larger than a mouse edging with the knife toward its arm, the tiny fingers knuckling along, leaving a trail of black blood on the stone. Other body pieces vibrated slowly. A leg began kicking toward the body, but suddenly shook in a spasm and stopped, as did the all the shards. No further movement. It was as if the whole shebang were playing possum, waiting for them to go away.

"Do you have a hammer?" Martin whispered.

"In the kitchen, under the sink," Nikki said.

He fetched the hammer and pulverized the remaining plaster. At Nikki's suggestion, they placed the knife in the oven, careful not to touch it with their flesh, and baked it in vinegar at 500 degrees for half an hour in case it had any spells attached.

"It's three a.m. We need to wait until dawn and get Abby back home. Let's sleep till then."

Abby gave Nikki a wink, nodding at Martin and puckering her lips in a kiss when he wasn't looking.

Nikki bridled. "Martin, you take the couch."

Abby let out air, whether in disapproval or approval of the separate sleeping arrangements, Nikki couldn't be sure…

3.

Cain! Cain! Cain!
He awakes.
Cain! Cain! Cain!

4.

Dean Kirby had rented a room at Day's Inn late Sunday night.

"My name is Dean Lawrence Kirby," he told himself in a whisper as he signed the register. "And I will kill Alice Fairbain tomorrow."

As Dean's neck twisted stiffly with a tick, the clerk backed from the guest register. By the time Dean walked toward his room, his head was throbbing and his chest pulsed. He nearly tumbled on seeing Fairbain's statuary down by the pool. He'd have to be careful with Fairbain, her Frankenstein monster, and her two griffins. What happened after that didn't matter. Bobby would be safe in Atlanta, his grandmother would take care of him, and what was once known as Dean Kirby would shift into dust like in some vampire movie.

The World is all we know.

Ah, friend Wittgenstein, you'll do me a good turn yet.

At a cramped desk in his hotel room, Dean listed the steps

he'd take in the morning, writing methodically so his mind would have structure right off on waking up. This way, Bruno wouldn't have an opening.

1. Call room service and order coffee and a donut.
2. Do 50 push-ups in two sets of 25.
3. Wash face.
4. Write down your name, your wife's name, and your son's name.
5. Check to see that the shotgun you bought is loaded.
6. Drink your coffee, unless room service hasn't come. Then skip to 8.
7. Eat your donut.
8. Do 50 more push-ups, in two sets of 25.
9. Prepare a rough map of Alice Fairbain's house.
10.

Dean fell asleep, the soundest sleep he'd had since November of the previous year when his wife slit his throat and left him dead.

5.

Alice didn't like the smug way Aaron had been emerging from Persephone's Escalator. Was he forming alliances down there? She thought of killing him; it would be easy. Then she could go down and take complete control. But that thought faded as she watched him emerge thirty minutes before dawn. Or rather, nearly emerge, for he collapsed on the steps. When she ran to him she could see lacerations over his body, and she had to call E-inna to help drag him up the few last steps of the escalator. When they were done, Alice gave that drudgebag a kick and sent her to make more statues for the *ka's*. She'd drop soon anyway, Alice thought, watching E-inna trundle off. Her body smelled and flies would gather on her for five minutes straight before she brushed them off—maybe maggots were already implanted, who could tell? Death by worm would be a fit punishment for screwing so many things up. Alice turned her attention back to Aaron, still unconscious, and found a pistol on him. She hadn't known he carried any weapon besides the silver-plated ax. Finding the pistol was fortuitous: it wouldn't do for her to work a charm against ax blades and forget bullets.

She turned, hearing something. Nearly a dozen *ka's* were peeping from the steps of Persephone's Escalator. Their black eyes gave her the creeps despite herself. She quickly played her flute and pointed out the direction they were to take to reach their concrete likenesses, just across what once had been Kirby's fence line. They hesitated, then walked the way she indicated.

Why the hesitation? She didn't like that. She gave Aaron's hair a yank; his eyes opened then closed. Had his eyes been black? She slipped a dagger from her apron and mentally tracked the path to his Adam's apple before yanking on his hair again.

"What? Cain, no! What?"

Pie was nearby and Alice indicated she should fetch some water. The rag doll came back with a hose, happily spraying it every direction, but especially on Aaron. When Aaron came to, he was so confused that no amount of cajoling could get him to speak, so Alice led him inside to bed.

One good bit of news anyway. Pie added to what she'd written earlier, to relay that one of the children had slipped from the truck to hang under Nyx Ryan's car. Alice could only hope that it would cut both Edmonds and Ryan to ribbons suitable for a baby's fine hair.

But even better news was coming. Who needed Edmonds,

as the two thugs she'd hired to kidnap Bobby—at more than enough expense—had phoned to say they were on their way.

She looked from her back porch into the false dawn where the children were still waddling towards their likenesses. Motioning for Pie, she and the doll followed the children to see what E-inna was doing. Dean Kirby had been right about his wife and her being lovers, though with more premonition than insight, for it was only as E-inna that she'd taken her. During the first few months after coming up from the coffin, E-inna's skin had been so pale and cool; it was the oddest, kinkiest sensation making love to a zombie.

The children walking ahead of her and Pie now were pale too—from living without sunlight. They were barely recognizable as human shapes. They scurried toward even paler statuary, which they merged into, to take on facial features other than those blank, black eyes. But this morning, something new happened: this batch weren't shielding their eyes from the rising sun. In fact, the first batches that had emerged too close to dawn had simply melted, she remembered. Only later batches had covered their eyes and blindly wobbled. But now… what was happening down there? She had to talk to Aaron soon. For now, she watched. Everything else was the same: A *ka* would approach the statue resembling it, then clasp it, then slowly osmose its own body into the statue—fooled, in essence, into thinking it once more lived. So far, her statues had been limited to attracting *ka's* that were two-, sometimes three-feet in size. She'd tried larger ones, but emerging *ka's* simply sloughed against them in a tired trance. The closest Aaron and she could figure was that maybe each *ka* was endowed with limited energy. To see if they could change that equation, they'd been trying live human bodies like the neo-Nazi and the Black man. That route certainly seemed to be a dead end, though. Alice laughed bitterly at her pun.

All but two of the *ak's* had transformed, so Alice readied her flute to place them into hibernation. But one, probably some bumbling schoolteacher from Kansas or Alabama in her past life, clung to a male statue when her obvious match stood three statues away. The male who did match the statue knocked her down and began the osmosis.

"Over here, you stupid bitch." Alice stood by the correct statue, a railish girl of thirty. The female *ak* turned black eyes toward her, facing the rosy sun, and faltered, then gathered strength. Pie skittered from Alice's arms as the *ak* raised a sharp rock with obvious malicious intent.

"Go back and grade tests, you bit of nothing dirt." Alice dropped her flute and pulled a Bowie knife she carried to knock its butt against the concrete head of the statue she'd just pointed out. With each hit, the *ak* faltered. On the fourth hit, the concrete head fell to the ground and so did the *ak*. Walking over, Alice struck her knife to its hilt, driving through the small breast into the grass. The school marm made a clawing effort, deeply scratching Alice's right hand. Alice swung the knife up and down again, then looked to the other statues. Had they moved? No, a car had driven by on the road. She craned, wondering if it was the men with Bobby—no, they couldn't possibly arrive until mid-morning. The paperboy, then? Nervously, she played the flute lowly until the *ak's* all closed their ugly black eyes.

She gave a last glance to the broken statue and its already decaying thin *ak*. The *ak's* weren't terribly powerful without the statues—above ground, anyway, though from the shape klutz Aaron was in, they were formidable below. No matter. Above ground was what counted, and with ten thousand statues that cumulative power would transfer to topside. Then all of Pasco County would be in her pocket, from every lousy Northern bum on the make to the staid Dade City and New Port Richey meat-packing dynasties and their concomitant cattle ranches.

Her hand stung where the school marm *ak* had clawed her. Taking this last incident into account, she decided it might be smart to slow E-inna's production until questions could be answered. She thought of Aaron. With his wounds, it wasn't likely that he'd put this scrawny school marm up to an attack. What then, had happened? Alice studied the dead *ak* and its broken concrete counterpart, then picked up Pie and headed for the Kirbys' barn.

As she walked away, the school marm's leg twitched and half a dozen of the statues opened then closed their oily black eyes.

Alice could hear work coming from the barn ahead. E-inna had been plenty scared last night and would work until she dropped, which couldn't be more than a week or so. But there was another noise. Alice halted behind a young, bushy water oak and directed Pie to run to investigate. From where she stood, she could see a large mound where the children had started the second Persephone's Escalator. She looked to her left where the rising sun was taking on a yellowish hue. They couldn't still be working in this daylight, could they? But as she watched Pie bend over the hole, she could see sand being pushed up all along its circumference, tiny dirty hands occasionally showing like snake heads. Pie jumped as the fingers of one swept toward her. Two black eyes lofted over the lip of the mound and stared first at Pie, then at the sun, then submerged—evidently to resume work.

Pie ran back. Alice handed her a pad and Pie wrote down:

They're digging.

"How can they be doing that still, Pie? It's daylight."

It's dark down there.

"How far have they dug? Isn't there a lot of flooding?"

No real water, lots of wet, lots of echoes. Deep.

"Well, if the little bastards get too uppity, we can always hire a backhoe to cover them up, right, Pie?"

Pie didn't answer. "Right, Pie?" Alice asked again.

I hope so, the rag doll wrote.

Alice bit her lip, then carried Pie to the Kirby's barn, listening to the steady drone of work behind her, ahead of her. The barn door still hung loosely where the truck had crashed through. *Too bad the muscular Black one was killed*, she thought. *He could have done a lot more than pick cotton.* Near the barn Alice waved her hand in front of her nose and wished for her grandmother's snuff: the dead children attracted decay, despite their concrete bodies, and there'd been nine killed last night in the barn.

"E-inna?" Alice looked up the ladder opening. She could hear a shuffling.

"Mother of God's blood!" Alice exclaimed when E-inna peered down over the ladder. At least fifteen flies were clinging to her face and a maggot dropped from her hair onto Alice's forearm.

"Mistress?" E-inna answered. Something fell from her mouth and Alice jumped aside, not even wanting to look.

"Back off from the damned ladder so I can climb up. Ten steps back. Hurry, hurry. *Mach schnell* as Aaron says. Don't touch anything."

Alice climbed three steps, hesitating. Why was it so dingy dark up there? And why was the shuffling still going on?

"Pie, go up." Alice tilted her shoulder toward the ladder and

Pie scrambled, not in the least concerned with hygiene or danger. Alice stared toward the gaping hole. In a moment Pie scrambled back and took a pad to write:

Very dark. Lots of statues, lots of children working. E-inna just waiting for you.

"So they've learned to make themselves. Good. We won't need Wormcake anymore, will we?"

Pie shook its head and smiled, but the smile didn't carry the usual enthusiasm.

"E-inna? Come on down, dearie. And don't drip on anything."

Alice backed down the ladder and stood back. Annie Kirby came down the steps, slipping on the last rung and falling to the dirt floor, causing a swarm of flies to take flight.

"Since you've been so clever in teaching the children to do your work, I'm giving you a promotion. Grab a shovel in the tack room and follow me." Alice leaned from the zombie woman's smell and waited at the back door of the barn. She looked around: where were the nine dead children from last night?

A shuffling Annie Kirby emerged, and Alice laughed. "No, I don't think that's a shovel, dearie. That's what we call a pitchfork. But in your state I don't suppose it matters much, does it? Bring your novel shovel along and let me show you where to dig."

Alice led her to the rear of the property, near the second Persephone's Escalator. "Isn't this nice? You get a view of the house where you and Deanie boy lived. Who could ask for a better burial plot? And did you know that Bobby's coming? Yes indeed. Now don't get too weepy. Get sweepy. That's right, you stay right here and dig a six by three foot space, and if you're good, I'll bring Bobby to see you. Look,

I haven't crossed my toes or fingers or anything, so you know I'm telling the truth. Wouldn't you like to see Bobby once more?"

A rattling, wet yes emerged from E-inna's throat.

"Good. Just stay and dig and you will. Very important task for such a bright, professional woman as yourself. I'll be back now and then. Dig nice and deep and you'll get to see Bobby."

There was a wet gurgling again, and Alice indicated with a flick of her wrist that E-inna was to begin.

"Digging will at least keep flies off you, dear. Even if you do consider them pets, maggots simply aren't good for your health. Just view this as dancercise. Weren't you and Dean boy members of a spa?"

No answer, so Alice left. Pie, who rode her shoulder, looked backwards with a big grin. "What's the matter, Pie, are you jealous that I slept with her? You needn't worry about that now… *nu*?" Alice intoned heavily, in Aaron's accent.

Pie gave a tug to Alice's ear which made her laugh. She heard a shrill scream drift over the wet swampland, but found nothing unusual on hurrying to her house by the back way. Maybe one of the neighbor's girls had lost her cherry to some four-wheel driving cracker.

At her kiln area she paused, thinking she'd heard a female's voice. Nothing. The only bad thing about the Kirby bitch drooping into such lousy shape so suddenly was that she'd have to work the kiln herself for the larger sculptures. That is, if she even needed more sculptures. Pie told her the loft was nearly full, even though they'd emptied it the night before to have the new children work on the second Persephone's Escalator. She looked at her hand, which still burned. Was it safe to let the children re-create themselves? Rex ran from near the kiln, whining. Alice petted him and he whimpered again.

"What's wrong, boy?"

Sirens in the distance. She listened as she aimlessly plinked the kiln's gauge. She was too old to fire up day in, day out. The heat was too much. But she damned sure didn't want the *ak's* in on this stronger method of production too. Or the concrete, for that matter. Plaster was plenty. She thought of the two girls at the end of the block. Either could run this kiln with training, though the older one was smart-mouthed…

The sirens were coming closer and Alice's eyes widened. She glanced to her house for smoke—nothing. *By the Weeping Holy Thorns, all I need is more trouble in this neighborhood: The Water of Life, Yell It Out, Jump and Shout Primitive Baptist Church will reinstate the Inquisition with me as its main guest, not to mention another round with the police…* The sirens passed what she judged to be the Settles' house: that only left her place, Kirby's, and the What's-their-names with the two girls. She watched through her thick front hedges and iron fence. A police car sped by. Another. And another. All heading toward the What's-their-names.

She ran to wake Aaron.

6.

Nikki had awoke not liking the day. The alarm clock with its nasty electronic, insistent beep; the toilet seat that Martin Edmonds left up so she nearly fell into oblivion before she realized it; and Skull—no longer in the shape of an owl, but now a hawk. Besides all that, it was still dark out and Abby snapped at her on being roused. But they needed to get her home. At least Martin was pleasant. And without a shirt he had an amazingly lank build for a psychologist, when you'd expect an armchair spread.

In twenty minutes they were on the road and in twenty more into Quail Hollow Estates with false dawn. Nikki rolled down her window at Skull's pecking insistence and he took to the air.

"I'm going to sneak around Fairbain's house and the Kirby place today," Abby said.

"What about school?" Nikki asked.

"You think Night will go? I'll go if she goes."

"I'm sure Night is being responsible, Abby."

"Like I said, 'I'll go if she goes.' "

Nikki kept her eye on Skull and her mouth shut, deciding Abby already had one mother.

"I saw someone with a gun. What would someone be hunting around here?" Martin asked, breaking the developing tension.

"Nothing. It's out of season. Did you really see someone with a gun?" Nikki looked back quickly, worrying about Skull.

"A guy back there."

"Did he see Skull?"

"He wasn't even looking at the sky. Just plodding along."

Ahead, Skull did a swoop and flip where the road turned left and right. Nikki slowed the car. She kept getting hot flashes and wished she'd eaten something. But it was more than that.

She made the turn and spotted the faint glow of a shield of power's blue aura. What the hell would Alice Fairbain be doing up at this time? *Looking for Martin and that poor man who was killed, of course,* she thought, answering her own question.

Skull swooped under the trees arching the small bridge

before Fairbain's and Abby's houses. Nikki glanced right to see Abby chewing on a nail. So she sensed something out of place too. Even Martin was somber. Fog clung to the road around the bridge. They drove through it, past Fairbain's. There was a single light in one upper room, nothing else. From the side of the road an opossum stared, then waddled off. Another patch of fog and some scrub trees. Abby's house was a hundred yards on the right. Nikki had visited here once, supposedly to talk about their two daughters, but it wasn't much more than pure nosiness and just wanting to meet the parents of her best friend. Nice enough, normal enough. She'd noticed a family picture: the grandmother seated in front was making a hex sign with her left hand's forefinger and thumb. Some old women in the St. Petersburg coven had taught it to Nikki. So Abby came by her leanings honestly, even though she said she didn't remember too much of her grandmother on her mother's side.

Now, as they neared the large yard, actually a pasture for a single pet cow, Skull flapped back frantically. Nikki slammed on her brakes, but too late, they were at the driveway. On the other side of the fence, the cow was lying topsy-turvy, obviously dead, for its hide had been flayed. The front door to the house gaped like death's black jaws. A window, no, several windows were broken.

Abby jumped from the car before Martin or Nikki could stop her. They ran after her, puffing past the dead cow, only to hear her shrill scream as she entered the house. They came to the front door to see: inside, blood covered the walls and carpet, and Abby's sister lay propped in a chair, dead. Her father was slumped in the archway leading to the dining room, a lamp he must have used as a weapon still in his hand. Near the fireplace lay Abby's mother, cuts ascending and descending her body like stairways, her eyes staring blankly at some spot on a wall.

Martin shoved past Nikki, motioning her to take Abby outside. But the girl wouldn't move until Martin—needlessly—checked all three bodies for a pulse. Hearing a crunch he looked down as he stepped away from the mother. Pale white pieces of plaster arms, fingers, and half faces were littered among the broken light fixtures and overturned furniture.

Abby beat her head against the living room wall and threw up. Martin looked to Nikki and they both started to take her outside by her arms, but realized that the dead cow in the front yard, its hide flayed and its legs upstretched in rigor mortis, would hardly calm her. Martin did a quick check of the house and they led Abby to her room that remained relatively untouched by the fight. From there he phoned the police.

"I'll kill her," Abby said between heaving sobs.

"I'll help you, if she did it."

"Is that an oath?"

"An oath, Abby. Blood and Birth."

Abby grabbed a picture, broke its glass, then cut her palm. Nikki did the same and they mingled their blood on the floor. Martin started, but had to keep talking on the phone: "… we brought her over. She'd forgotten something for school and had spent the night with her friend Night Ryan. That's right."

"Have you thought that the killer still might be there?" the dispatcher asked. "I think you should get the hell out of the house."

"Right. We'll be in our car in the front. Right, we won't touch anything," Martin hung up. "She says we should leave the house. I said we'll wait by the car. Maybe we can go out the back door, to—"

"She killed our dogs too. Or they'd be barking." Abby worked loose from Nikki's arms and went to her closet to retrieve a black leather satchel. "I need to get some things behind the shed first. Alone."

"I don't think—"

Abby glared at Martin, then turned to Nikki. "Alone. You know what I need to get, Mrs. Ryan. It's very important."

"Okay. We'll wait at the back door. But hurry. The police will be here soon."

As Abby stumbled through the dining room she began gasping for breath in crying heaves on seeing her father lying to her right, so Nikki hurried her through the kitchen past more plaster arms, torsos, heads, and legs—she wondered what the police would make of them. Once on the porch Abby stood, shivered, and then ran to the garage after checking the back yard.

"Maybe the dogs got away," Nikki whispered.

"What is it that she's getting?" Martin asked, watching Abby take a shovel from the garage and walk to a shed.

"Some things she needs to be invisible."

"She's going to need to be invisible soon, you know. Unless she has relatives, the state will take her as a ward."

"I could have custody, couldn't I?"

"Probably. I'll see if I can help."

Nikki watched Abby skirt the shed and began to worry. "She shouldn't be left alone."

"You're right," Martin agreed.

Nikki ran through the yard toward the shed. "I'm okay," Abby said when she saw her. Abby held a shovelful of dirt. An old rabbit hutch stood nearby, though it looked like there hadn't been rabbits in it for a couple of years.

"I want you to stay with me, Abby. As long as you want, you can stay with me, do you understand?"

Abby nodded, though she hadn't stopped digging. "This is sort of gross, Mrs. Ryan."

Nikki stepped back to wave an okay to Martin, then watched Abby pull a small gunny sack from under dried rabbit dung. In it, she knew, was young Cristy's head. She turned away. "You need to hurry before the police get here. And you need to cover it well."

"They won't find it: it has a spell on it too." Abby fumbled with her satchel, dropped something in, then picked up the shovel again. "Okay, you can look, I'm finished," she said.

Nikki watched her re-bury the sack, with the head—or most of the head— still in it, evidently. Abby was right— whatever spell she'd managed, the ground looked as if it hadn't been touched since the last rabbit lived in the hutch abandoned some years ago. They walked back.

"I think we should get out of here," Martin said, shifting his eyes about.

"I agree. Yes, Abby's got what she needs." Nikki scanned the acres and acres of palmetto. "Let's get back to the car."

Martin gave another glance through a kitchen window and caught sight of Abby's father's arm—lacerated, with gaps of flesh torn from it. It could just as easily have been him lying on a back road one mile from here.

"Alice Fairbain is going to get hers—one way or another," Abby commented. "One way or another."

They heard distant sirens. Nikki noticed the leg of a dog, matted with blood, jutting from under a large azalea bush by the fence, but kept her eyes forward and her mouth shut until they were well past. By the time they reached the car, the sirens were very close. Nikki again spotted a bluish aura through the trees. It surrounded the second story of Alice Fairbain's house.

You'll get yours, bitch. Abby's right: one way or another. And you should pray to whatever cheap devil you worship that we're the ones who give it to you, not your little statue friends.

7.

Across from the burnt skeleton of the Settles' house, Dean Kirby dove into the dewy palmetto as soon as he heard sirens. A root cut his hand and his blood threaded with a black, oil-like substance…

Cain!

Calm, calm. He had to stay calm if Bruno was to be kept quiet. *I promise you'll have your time, Bruno.* He looked back, drawn by the sirens turning down this street. Could the police have tracked him? Unlikely anything would match up so quickly. Of course Bruno must have left fingerprints all over the kid's car. Dean looked to the tainted blood and turned his hand over. Would his fingerprints still be his? Damned little else had stayed his. The Abby girl was right: it was a devil's trade.

Bobby. He would make it all worthwhile. His son would live.

A police car screeched around the corner. Another and one more. Their sirens sped toward Alice Fairbain's. No, past that, to where Bobby's girlfriend lived. Dean listened until the sirens stopped, then stood to work through tangles, ticks, palmettos, muckwater and snakes. At the sight of his house he thought of the first day he and Annie came down—without Bobby—to look at real estate. What a wondrous life they'd planned. And how many times had they made it to the beach? Two. Two was better than none, he philosophically decided. Wouldn't you say, Friend Wittgenstein?

The world, the world is all we know.

No, Friend Wittgenstein, there needs to be something else. That would be too unfair, to leave us with just this rat-hole. A palmetto tip cut his arm. Blood trickled its familiar black-rennet mix. Reaching the road, he looked where the police had gone, but fog still hung and a bend kept the Beasley house from view. He walked across blacktop to his old gate—locked—the realtor wouldn't tell him who bought it, but he guessed—who the hell besides Fairbain would care to keep her name from him? He climbed the gate and hopped down to the grass. It had been freshly cut and the smell was pleasant, almost like a watermelon.

Another siren. He stood listening, watching the empty house. *Annie*, he thought. *Annie.* He could hear growing laughter from inside his own skull. *Why are you laughing, Bruno? Isn't this all part of your life too?* The laughter kept growing and there was a simple word:

Cain.

Then Bruno was gone. Dean checked his shotgun for the ninetieth time and thumbed the safety. He looked at his pants and shoes, soaked from traveling through swamp. He saw blood, coagulated and completely black. Were his senses shutting down? A year, the spell promised a year. It had been only eight months. Again, he pushed the safety to make sure it was off. If he saw Fairbain, that would be it, then come death.

The siren was nearing. Dean ran as best he could to the carport; he could see that Fairbain was using his old house to warehouse her statues. Somehow, he knew, Bobby had something to do with these. But what? It couldn't be anything good. Just the fact that Fairbain was behind it told him that.

A noise from the barn. Fairbain? Dean sprinted again. What the hell happened to the barn's door? It looked like someone had rammed through it from inside. He peeked through recently broken pieces of hanging wood: a rancid death odor assailed him, and as he went in toward the hayloft ladder, he wondered if someone else—someone really living, for instance—would find this odor unbearable and have to turn back. By the ladder he heard a noise outside and pressed against a wall. The noise was a hard wheezing like you'd expect in a lung cancer ward. He decided to chance it and inspect the loft first. Keeping the hacksawed barrel above his head, he could use his right elbow to help him climb. He fully hoped for Fairbain at the top of the steps, he fully hoped to pull the trigger.

Half his expectation came true as he fired at a pale fat midget with dangerous black eyes who swung a glistening hatchet: the shotgun scattered the midget over the floor in ridiculous plaster pieces. Dean shook his head: for all the world it looked like one of Fairbain's statues. Then he gasped, for five, six hundred more stood along the floor. Several opened their eyes and wobbled; the rest remained still. The few that turned picked up tools or boards and began walking toward him. Forgetting the ladder, he dropped onto the barn's dirt floor and ran.

Then he saw her.

"Annie?"

The woman fruitlessly digging outside with a ridiculous pitchfork looked up. Her dress was ripped in so many places that it looked like an ante-bellum drape.

"Annie!" Dean ran forward but stopped within five feet, seeing flies swarming about her, even as she resumed digging, though she still looked at him, tilting her head like a curious pup.

"Annie, it's me, Dean. You recognize me, don't you? Oh God, Annie. Bobby was right. Oh God, oh God, why didn't I believe him."

She edged to look around him and raised her arm. Dean turned to see that several statues had waddled out of the barn. They stopped, looking to the sky. One squat male in white bib overalls continued, wobbling forward with a claw hammer while shielding his black-dot eyes. As he neared, Annie whimpered and Dean swung the barrel of the shotgun against his head, cracking it and leaving an oozing dirty oil to drain down its side. Still, it kept coming, swinging wildly with its hammer. Dean backed off and heard a gurgling behind.

Annie lunged heavily with the pitchfork, leaving black gush to spew as the statue dropped, shivered, then lay still. Dean reached for Annie, but she shook her head violently and turned the pitchfork over so she could write with its shaft on the sand she'd been digging.

A.F. will have Bobby soon and make him like me. She stumbled, caught herself, then wrote, *Or worse.*

Dean closed his eyes momentarily. She was telling him what he already knew, what he'd known from the night he'd stabbed his leg in his apartment. Then he looked at her. "Can't you speak?" he asked, seeing her skin sloughing.

She shook her head and pointed at what she'd written before she swept that spot clean. Evidently the motion's momentum carried her, for she swept several more times, as if she'd forgotten he was there. Dean cast a worried glance to the barn, but the statues were backed from the door now. The noise in the loft had resumed. On the street, yet one more siren.

"Annie, we've—"

But she drew away, managing to gargle out a wet 'No.' Then she wrote more.

Thought I'd killed you. Could not help self A.F.'s spell. Drugs.

She looked to see that he'd read. He nodded and she wrote more.

Dying now. Zombie? Save Bobby before same

She looked at him again. He nodded, lifting the shotgun to show her what he meant to do.

She swept the sand clean again and drew a heart and pointed to Dean. He reached, but she backed off violently. He could see maggots crawling her hairline and he thought some type of white worm was working its way from her lips.

Kill me PLEASE

She twice punched the end of the shaft into the heart she'd drawn, then pointed to the shotgun. When Dean shook his head, she lunged and pulled the short barrel upwards, her mouth opening with the exertion to retch black bile mixed with worms, twigs and dirt. Dean could feel her jerk the gun. He placed his finger on the trigger and closed his eyes. She jerked again.

A loud boom and a soft fall came what seemed like months later.

Cain! Cain! Cain!

He dragged Annie into some cypress and noticed he was sweating a sour milky substance. He was wiping this off with disgust when he saw Aaron running toward the noise in the barn. Minutes later, the noise there ceased and Aaron emerged to inspect a large hole near where Annie had been digging. He called out a name that sounded like a jackass's bray. *Hyena, Hyena.* Dean crouched, trying to hear. Aaron leaned over the huge hole and tilted his ear as if listening. "E-inna," he called again. He looked around, then kicked sand into the pit and picked up something limp and long. God, it was a patch of Annie's hair. Aaron tossed it into the pit and laughed, heading toward Fairbain's. Dean lifted the shotgun, then changed his mind. It might tip off Fairbain. He waited until Aaron was out of hearing and wondered how he could bury Annie—again. He winced as he grabbed her arms and looked on her face.

A noise at the gate stopped him. Two cops came and walked around the barn. Dean recognized the female cop who looked so sleepy that time he'd seen her. She seemed awake enough now, for both she and her partner had drawn guns. After ten or so minutes of searching and finding nothing, they left.

He eyed Fairbain's estate, partially visible now because she'd cut some trees. Nightfall would be the time. He spotted a blackberry bush, but couldn't really say he was hungry. That worried him, so he forced himself to eat all the berries he could find before continuing his search for a shallow indent for Annie's grave.

8.

Jewel walked down from their room with Lori to buy a newspaper and some coffee. For the last thirty minutes she'd heard sirens and finally had given up on sleep. It was past dawn anyway and though medieval expectation might have been for a witch to finish her work at that time, Jewel knew contemporary Sisters found a 9 to 5 framework more convenient.

"Is there a fire somewhere?" Jewel asked the woman who was making their coffee.

"Gossip is that there's been another murder."

"Another?"

"That's right. A little girl was murdered back there last fall, nearly a year ago. Then her parents died in a house fire. How many creams you want?"

"About ten," Jewel answered. "We were thinking of looking for land around here."

"Well I'd start someplace besides Quail Hollow. A friend of mine told me cops are stopping everyone who comes in or out and searching their cars. There's more cops back there than there are people. There's plenty of nice new developments going up east and west of here, if you got that kind of money."

Jewel nodded and paid.

"I don't think I'd want to live back there, anyways. Bad luck place. Gives me the creeps to drive around. A witch lives back there. The one that did those statues by the pool."

"They kind of strike me as spooky," Lori said.

"That's what I think, truth be known—One for breakfast, sir?"

As the woman picked up a menu to seat the new customer, Jewel and Lori carried the coffees toward the newspaper rack.

"There's someone in the group who's really mad at you," Lori said, shifting the sack of coffees under her arm.

"Beth?"

"I don't know, I can't pinpoint her thoughts. But there's someone."

"That's not good. It means a chink in the Pentad. Have you… you call it 'touched,' right?" Lori nodded, setting the coffee on top of the newspaper rack. "Have you touched with the woman who sat *in absentia* for the Pentad? Nikki Ryan?" Not that Jewel was above using a phone book, but she'd rather get her information through this girl Lori before stooping to banalities.

"I touched something late last night," Lori told her, glancing up as another siren sounded on the highway. "A vision of a snake without a head and a pale statue holding a knife. The statue reminded me of those by the swimming pool. Except it had full black eyes like something painted as a joke turned bad."

Jewel nodded indecisively and bought a paper. When they got to the poolside they saw Becky taking a morning swim while Beth inspected one of the nymphs. Even in water Becky lumbered, her body too large for a woman's, though she was by no means unattractive. If one were able to call a young woman a cuddly bear, Becky would fit that description.

"Coffee?" Lori asked Beth. Beth thanked her, but not without first giving the girl a once-over and Jewel a significant glance.

Jewel wasn't going to blow her cover and Lori's ability by convincing anyone there wasn't some darkly lesbian mother-daughter affair going on. So she smiled back at Beth, who drank her coffee black—symbolically so.

"Would you two care to see something very interesting?" Beth asked. She took a hatpin that belonged to the roaring twenties out of her straw-blonde hair and gave the nearest nymph a scratch on its uplifted heel. Jewel flinched, moving her own foot nervously even as she poured cream into her coffee. Behind, she could hear Becky splashing in the pool. But she forgot Becky and the coffee to lean forward: the nymph's heel was oozing a black blood.

"All four of them bleed," Beth said.

"Could it be something they're made of?" Lori asked.

"That's what Becky suggested. It's too bad neither of you

were raised Catholic like me so you'd appreciate such signs of possession."

"Good God, Beth, no one has raised an army of golems since the middle ages." By Jewel's face it was clear that she wasn't doubting, but amazed. "I don't even think a Pentad could do that these days. The Matrix just isn't moving in that direction."

Beth wiped her hatpin on a napkin from the bag of coffee, considered before sticking it in her hair and then wrapped it in a paper napkin. "I don't think *this* Pentad could, that's for certain."

Beth was good; Jewel had never taken that from her. She was adept and she'd sensed that something was wrong with the Pentad just as Lori had, just as Jewel herself had.

"This Pentad would be lucky to finish a crossword. I think we need to confront your friend that we let in yesterday," Beth said.

Jewel could hear Becky's laughter and more splashes. She'd placed that charming creature in jeopardy with this journey; she'd placed them all in jeopardy. "Beth—you, Lori, and myself will go see her. Anne Marie, Nancy, and Tiffany can go see the woman who makes these—Lori and I were just told she's a witch by the hostess. We were also told that there'd been another murder back there." Jewel gave a nod in the direction they'd been looking last night and raised her eyebrows. Beth made a motion to call Becky, but Jewel said, "Let her swim. She's happy doing that."

"Are you going to leave her with the cups?"

"I think so. Does that seem okay to you?"

"You've asked me for more advice in the last two days than you have in the twelve years we've known one another, Jewel Dawn."

"It's because I'm not sure what's going on, Beth."

Beth gave a smile to Lori. "Don't let her fool you, honey. She didn't get to be Executrix of the entire United States by being a second-rate witch like me. She knows plenty."

Jewel caught Beth's worried look as they left the restaurant and saw her drop the wrapped hatpin in the trash bin they passed heading upstairs. One hour later the sirens subsided and the Pentad went over plans for splitting into groups. Though the position of cup-keeper was an honor, Becky seemed disappointed and her lip lowered in a pout as each of them kissed her special chalice and called out the incantation of opposites *"mors, vita; amor, odium; mihi, tibi."* Jewel was assigned to pass over the *in absentia* cup of Nyx Ryan. As she repeated the Latin incantation of "Death, life; love, hate; for me, for you," she kissed Becky's forehead. The gangly little-more-than-girl turned her loose grin upwards and her brown eyes sparkled.

Jewel returned her smile, though inwardly she was disappointed with the shield of power they'd just summoned. Feigning a slip of the tongue, she'd performed the ceremony a second time: even then the usual aquamarine glow of a pentad's shield was more a sick sea-green. As she walked out, glancing back at Becky sitting on the bed amidst the chalices, happy as a pup after a second kiss on the forehead, she thought: a life to be envied. A life to be spared and held precious. She bit her lip.

9.

"Just what the hell is going on, Aaron?" Alice wanted to know. They were staring out the window at all the police cars in front of the Beasley house.

"How should I know? I've been asleep nearly two

hours—"

"Don't play stupid with me, Wasserstrum. You know damned well I mean in Persephone's Escalator. One of those bitches came at me today—with a sharpened rock, in sunlight. In sunlight, do you hear? And just look at yourself; you're lucky to be alive. Your gun was empty. Did you know that?" Aaron stiffened and looked both surprised at the news and pained by his movement. "You want to know what I think?" Alice continued. "I think you almost didn't make it back."

At the window, Aaron watched another police car pull behind a line of four. Each time he moved, his skin split from a newly discovered cut. Maybe it *was* time to let this *goyische* witch help him down there. She was always bragging about her shields and talismans. He turned to see her milky statues dangling about her adoringly.

"You go down with me tonight. We need to be very careful. Down there they are much more powerful than—" he gestured about the room. "They are hate, pure hate."—*Cain! Cain!*—He pressed his temples. "They fight and kill one another; fight here, fight there, constant." He blinked at Alice. "Now you say one came at you in the daylight?"

"That's right."

Aaron turned, hearing yet another police car, no flashing blue American lights this time. A man carrying camera equipment got out.

"In this country they take pictures when bodies are murdered, *nu?*"

Alice walked over, vaguely irritated that Aaron always called America "this country" even though it was his birthplace. A shotgun blast sounded in the distance toward the Kirby place—no doubt someone shooting a rattlesnake.

There was supposedly some guy who raised tropical fish on the property abutting Kirby's who was always shooting frogs and snakes. The police looked curiously in that direction.

"The children!" Alice exclaimed. "You've got to get over there and deactivate them in case those cops start wandering around. While you were asleep I went to the barn. They're working in the daylight now."

"How can they—"

"The loft windows, they've been blocked off. Maybe the Kirby bitch… I don't know. She's out of our hair anyway; she's rotting. I ordered her to work near the second Persephone; maybe she'll tumble in. They're working in the daylight there too. Because it's dark in the hole, Pie says."

Aaron made a face at the mention of Pie—or was it because his cuts hurt him? Alice couldn't tell.

"See if you can get the Kirby bitch to crawl into that hole—no, just tell her to forget she ever knew us and walk into Tampa. She'll make it halfway and drop. That should give the police a good puzzle, maybe get them off our backs. But above all, go make the children stop—what the hell would the cops think—"

"The *kinder* would kill the cops."

"Too soon. We can't buck the entire Pasco County sheriff's office." Alice pointed: a plainclothesman looking toward the direction of the gunshot got into his car and picked up a microphone.

"Go! Go! Don't stand talking to me."

Aaron obeyed her and thumped down the stairs—but he spent time rummaging his room, Alice noticed, surmising that he was loading his pistol. So he was afraid of the children even up here, outside of Persephone.

"Pie," she whispered. The doll tugged at Alice's blue jeans, looking up with a crimson smile. "What do you think, Pie? Should you follow our friend Aaron or sneak to see what's happening with the police? I'm curious about them, but what if the children kill Aaron? Go, run and watch him. If everything is normal, run to the Beasleys' and come back when you know what's going on over there." Alice leaned to stroke her rag doll's red yarn hair. The doll nudged her fingers like a cat. "Use your scamper legs. Go, Pie, go."

Pie sprinted off and Alice turned to watch the police. Minutes later she heard another gun blast near the Kirby place. Two more cruisers pulled up. She fretted until she saw Pie run past the Beasleys' mailbox. So everything was all right with Aaron. Pie, expert at escaping notice, disappeared.

Half an hour and three patrol cars later, Alice heard Aaron curse. He came upstairs to say that he'd quieted the children and told two nosy cops he was shooting his pistol at a rattlesnake.

He lost his smile and said, "One of the *kinder*, it tried to slash at a cop. I played *mit* my flute and it stopped. The cops, they ask what I'm doing and I say, "Starting a new hobby. I want to be in a Rock and Roll band to become all-full American.""

Alice started to say something to the effect that he should leave joking with the police alone, then thought better of it. Maybe they'd throw him in jail. Just as she was thinking this, his smile returned and he pulled a clump of blonde hair from his pocket.

"*Die Kinder.*" He made a slash across his throat. "They tore the Kirby thing's face apart. I found this hair." He grinned.

"Good," Alice replied. "It wasn't much of a face anyway."

Aaron gave a leer that Alice ignored. He'd heard the two of them panting in bed more than once, she knew.

"Where's her body? The police aren't going to find it too, are they?"

He dropped the hair in a wastebasket. "To find they have to be looking, no?"

Alice tapped the window. "We better make sure, and we'd better learn to get along with one another, Aaron, because it looks like we've had a little mishap at the Beasley residence." She stood aside so Aaron could see the first of the body bags being carried to an ambulance. "You don't suppose the children did that too, do you?"

Aaron grunted, not very happily. Outside, an official-looking car pulled up, followed by two full of what must have been reporters.

"This slows the delivery of the Kirby brat, *nu?*"

"That's putting it mildly, my Jewish friend."

Rex began to bark as someone banged the door knocker and the phone rang. Alice checked her watch. "I'll get the phone up here: it's probably our delivery service wondering what's going on, speaking of the devils. And you get the door. It's no doubt a policeman or so."

Aaron shuffled off downstairs. As Alice picked up the phone, she noticed Pie scrambling carelessly across the street right under the wheels of a backing car.

"Hello?" Her breath was a release, for she could see that Pie made it.

"Miz Fairbain? This is Tim. What the hell's going on with all the cops over there? We could damn near been stopped and searched, except we had the police scanner on."

She caught a glimpse of Pie tumbling through the fence to her property. "I don't know. It just happened. Obviously I would have called—"

"Well obviously we can't come with the kid until the cops

are gone. We're at a hotel an exit up. Let me give you the phone number. We'll stay ten hours, then move. Course this will cost extra…"

"Don't worry about the cost. Buy yourselves lobster dinner tonight. Just stay sober and keep the boy sedated. No food for him. Remember. No food for him. Water only."

"Sounds kinky."

"No food, damnit." Alice heard Aaron walk up the steps as she jotted the room number and promised to call the minute things cleared. As she hung up she looked outside for Pie, but couldn't see her.

"Is the *fraulein* deputy Wiggington and two young cops," Aaron announced. "They want to talk with you and look around the yard."

From her window she could see ambulance attendants were loading a third body bag.

"Good God. Did she tell you what happened?"

"She said they cannot say until the detectives come. What? We don't have eyes?" Aaron stared out the window, shrugged, and walked out.

Alice gave a last glance outside: another damned reporter, a TV station this time. She saw a detective waving off the camerawoman before she even got out of the van. Alice walked downstairs to her living room.

"Officers," she said, smiling at the two young men and giving Diane a nod. Diane always looked sleepy and Alice was certain she had a drug or alcohol habit. Diane didn't mind taking small gifts now and then, which was good, because Alice needed a friend in the sheriff's department after the Settles girl's torso had been dredged from her pond.

"Ms. Fairbain, this is Deputy Shroeder and Deputy Johnston. There's been something terrible happened at your neighbors'. We'd like to look around the yard if we could."

Alice led them through the house to the kitchen's back door. As the two started out, Diane stayed behind with Alice: "I need to talk with you about that church." Alice nodded and said loudly, "I'll put some coffee on for both of you."

They watched the two young cops go into the yard, pet the dog, then walk around the sculptures. When Diane turned, Alice noted that her face had lost its tiredness and her green-flecked eyes were nervous. "What happened over at your neighbor's is going to make matters worse. There'll be two detectives here any minute to grill you and Aaron. Probably more later in the afternoon. It's a mess over there."

"A mess?"

"A mess." With that, Wiggington walked out the door to join the other two.

Alice turned to Aaron, who was peering out a front window. "We're going to have some detectives visiting, so you better get rid of that pistol. The way it's sticking under your shirt could hardly pass for a misplaced penis. Make some coffee to keep our friends happy."

There was a clatter in the turret room overhead, the room where Martin Edmonds had slept two nights before. She and Aaron exchanged glances. "Did you clean the room?"

"With everything that's been going on?" he snapped.

The noise, like birds pecking cardboard boxes, grew and Aaron pulled his gun. But when he stepped on a loose riser in the stair, the noise stopped. They continued. Inside the middle turret room, four sculptures had broken on the wood floor. Others swayed on their support strings, their black eyes glaring. Aaron made an involuntary grunt and backed away, but Alice pointed to the half-open window.

"Edmonds must have left it that way." She looked to Aaron, but he was mesmerized by a twirling fat butcher holding a miniature, razor-sharp knife in his plaster hands, his eyes two black opals. A slight clacking began, as if a breeze had blown the statues vaguely against one another. Moving angrily before Aaron, Alice hissed. "*Never* show any elemental you've raised that you're afraid—even if you summon the Devil himself, don't show fear. Give me the damned gun, Aaron."

He did and she walked into the room, purposefully stepping on a statue that had fallen. Another hung in her way; she slapped it hard with the gun barrel, so that it shattered. The clacking ceased and she closed the window. Grabbing the butcher from its hanger, she shouted for Aaron to catch it.

"Crush it under your boot as soon as you do."

Aaron half-caught and half-dropped the statue, and kicked it into the wall rather than crushing it. Alice pulled two more off and dropped them to the floor to step on them. She rubbed her hands in the resultant black blood and held it up to the others, then to Aaron, then walked out, handing him the pistol. "Hide it—not in this room. We'll have a key made. Some large cats would make good investments too. Go to the pound after we talk with these cops. I'll make the coffee."

Two detectives came ten minutes later, a pair looking as if they'd feel more comfortable sitting at some Tampa sleaze bar. Alice learned as much from them as they learned from her. The older Beasley girl was still alive—she'd spent the night with a friend whose mother had brought her back because she'd forgotten a book for school. The woman was going to take care of the child until the state decided the disposition. Alice liked that word *disposition*, since it reminded her of disposing. She didn't have any particular love for the

older Beasley girl, who was always staring. She even suspected the girl might have some power with the Matrix…

"I'm sorry, what did you say?" she asked the detective
sitting on her left, the one who'd gone through two cups
of coffee and was on his third. Didn't he take a bathroom
break?

"I said we found some plaster like you use in your statues
scattered around the house. Did the Beasleys buy a lot of
your work?"

"I gave the two girls some. It's not always plaster I use,
you know. Sometimes I work in concrete. But to answer your
question, yes, they had some of my work. We're neighbors,
after all." She was lying: the Beasleys had never bought or
even took one sculpture from her.

"We also tracked who we think might have been the killers
over to your land."

"Tracked?"

The detectives exchanged glances. "Just how do you con-
struct your statues—"

"Sculptures," Alice corrected.

"… sculptures, Ms. Fairbain?"

"Like I told you, I used to work in concrete, still do on
larger sculptures. On smaller ones I use a type of plaster of
Paris…" She saw that this answer wouldn't satisfy, so she ex-
panded, "Except that I insert a thick core of tarlike resin that
eventually renders the plaster of Paris much more durable
than ordinarily."

This they bought. In fact, they both sat back in their
chairs, happy to have one mystery solved. Aaron and Alice,
on the other hand, were extremely unhappy and didn't dare
look at one another. While they themselves had no earthly
idea what the tar was, it filled each of her sculptures as the

transformation from plaster to living being took place. Blood of some type, they'd mutually supposed. Liquid hate, it seemed to both of them, for now they knew for sure that the children had killed the Beasleys.

The detectives left to inspect the yard with the three policemen already out there. The youngest blonde cop that Diane had introduced—Shroeder, that was his name—pointed to the drainage pond and they walked over to pick up something. Diane used the time to come to the house and talk:

"What is it they found?" Alice asked her.

"A plaster hand. You got coffee?"

Alice poured Wiggington a cup.

"Thanks. What I wanted to tell you earlier is this: the Ever-lasting Assembly has been phoning in complaints so crazy that the dispatcher won't even bother with most of them. The bulk are coming from Maureen Jackson."

"That's the one who speaks in tongues?"

Diane nodded.

"Well there you go," Alice told her.

"I agree, but other neighbors have been complaining too."

"What are they saying?"

"Most of them say that kids are prowling around… but Maureen's insisting that it's your statues."

"Why doesn't the dispatcher just tell her to talk with them in tongues? Interrogate them or order them to stop?"

Deputy Wiggington shifted so her hand rested on the butt of her pistol. "Well, the upshot is that the neighbors are complaining that kids are sneaking over here to see your statues and using the land as a meeting place for witchcraft and voodoo and drugs and…"

"Screwing off, like kids always do. So is that my fault?"

"The Ever-lasting Assembly thinks so. Scuttle is that

they're planning a petition to keep you from selling statues on this land. I just wanted to tell you."

Schroeder gave a yell and Wiggington waved to indicate she'd come.

"God, what's over there now?"

Diane shrugged, but minutes later she came back.

"Looks like The Ever-lasting Assembly's going to have more fuel. There're signs drawn in the sand around the pond—it does look like witchcraft to me. And some more statue parts, so the kids must be breaking up your work. That pond's been a real trouble spot: maybe you should fence it off and get a couple more big dogs…" The deputy let the thought go as the four other policemen returned and walked through her house and left.

As soon as Alice closed the front door on them, she felt a pinch that made her heart skip. She turned to see Pie grinning. "What is it?" she asked more abruptly than she wanted to, for the rag doll's little moods were to be tolerated, not acknowledged.

Pie, grinning even more seeing that she'd gotten the witch's goat, held up a pad filled with writing: *Even cow and dogs killed. Your statues?*

Alice frowned. Noticing Nyx Ryan's name in the sentence following, she read on with an even larger frown: *The Beasley girl is accompanied by the Edmonds man that was here and by NYX RYAN.*

"I think we're going to have to move on our plans very soon, don't you, Pie? Let's go show your Uncle Aaron this."

Pie made a face at that, and Alice said, "He's a musty old bag of hate with his lousy German, his Nazis and concentration camps, but it's a bad time to be dividing forces. Let's make a temporary pact with him. Temporary." Alice waved the pad in Pie's face until the doll nodded. "Good."

The two of them walked upstairs and found Aaron in his room. There they convinced him to start production in the Kirby barn again—keeping an eye out for police. With more of the children they could find Nyx Ryan, the Beasley girl, and Edmonds, and then kill all three.

The *kinder* will like that," Aaron said. "Maybe it will keep them happy for a while." He grinned and left for the Kirby property, taking his gun and two extra clips of bullets. "Wait!" Alice called. "I'm going to give you a shield of power."

"Magic," the hulk snorted. Nonetheless, he was very attentive as she performed the ceremony, and even bent forward to see if he could make out the Latin.

"How does it work?" he asked, looking at the blue glow on his arm with admiration that he tried to conceal.

"It works best when you see whatever is going to be used against you and keep that in your mind. If one of the children comes at you with a chisel, you think of a chisel."

"And if many of them 'come at' me?" Aaron slipped into his bemused foreigner stance, giving the American idiom special emphasis.

"If many of them do, just think of their hands bouncing away. But it loses effectiveness, the less specific you get." Angered by Aaron's tone, Alice decided not to mention that the shield was completely ineffective after one rotation of the earth. Better to keep some safeguards..

Aaron left and she went back upstairs to check on the progress across the street and noticed that more cops were again at her drainage pond. One uniformed policeman spit a wad of tobacco when no one was looking, and Alice laughed. Not much to do until the cops left but go over the incantations she'd need.

"Scoot, Pie, and see what you can find out. I'm going to do a little research."

Pie smiled, glad for a chance to trip a cop or steal some car keys. Alice gave a wave and pulled out a red velvet book, a copy of an obscure grimoire reputed to have belonged to St. Thomas Aquinas himself (fat chance!). But on checking the very first incantation for securing power over raised spirits, Alice began to wonder if the children were really spirits in the usual sense of the word or if…

One of the policemen must have accidentally hit a siren, and she jumped to look out the window. The cops had thinned; it was noon, she saw, and after spotting Pie letting air out of a reporter's tires, she decided to call the motel, but stopped dialing when she felt an odd coolness that had upset her since a month or so after the Settles' girl's torso had been discovered. She cradled the phone and fetched a mallet off her desk, thinking of the children, and looked around to find only her empty studio and dust motes slipping over one another normally—no, that motion near the window was like a very small dust devil. She looked away nonchalantly, then strode across the room toward a sculpture she'd been working on, the single artistic piece not connected with the children she'd done in well over two years, a three-foot reclining Greco-Roman figurine. She tapped slightly at a granite lock of hair and scanned the room surreptitiously. There! Another swirl of dust! And that chill wasn't her imagination.

She blew dust off her work, keeping an eye on the room. Yes, it *had* been about a month after the Settles girl disappeared that this first started. They'd only found the girl's torso: as far as she knew, the head was still missing… wasn't there an enchantment for invisibility that required a human head and beans? It had never interested her, since the last thing any sculptor wants is invisibility; still, it would interest a certain nosy brat who lived across the street, wouldn't it? Maybe that nosy brat did have some power with the Matrix.

One way to find out… *a web of salt enchantment to catch a wet fog.* That phrase she remembered following the recipe for invisibility. Of course there was a counter-charm—that was the charm of magic, the charm of all of life. Still, she didn't like working in salt—no witch did, as salt was a formidable desiccant to power—which made it just the tool to use to catch a nosy witch… Alice caught another movement by a couple of art books and became certain. She needed to do two things: first, make sure whoever or whatever hung around until she constructed what she needed; second, that whoever or whatever didn't get suspicious as she did the constructing. If it was the Beasley kid—goddess below, what brass, after this morning—it suddenly occurred to Alice that the kid might very well think she'd killed her parents. She checked the clock—twenty after twelve. She'd renewed the shield of power on hearing Aaron screaming in Persephone during the night, so it was still plenty strong. She spotted a sharp oyster knife she used in sculpturing and decided to make sure the little brat—*or whoever, don't be too hasty, Alice*—saw it too and would try to use it if there was to be an attack. She walked to pick it up and gouge at the granite woman's toes for a moment—inconsequential, but you'd have to be right on top of her shoulders to see that—then placed it in an easily accessible spot. Yes indeed, that did bring a little stir from the invisible mist, didn't it?

Knife, knife, knife. Alice implanted the thought in her mind to assure that her shield of power would protect her; then she reached for the phone on the desk, purposefully turning her back on the mist-devil. *Knife, knife.* She dialed the number to the Kirby loft.

"*Ja,*" Aaron answered.

Ja. Goddess below, he probably dreams he's an anti-Hitler, maybe an illegitimate son. "Aaron, can you leave the children alone? We're going to have a small change of plans. Come on over, I think I've found an even quicker way to get to the Ryan woman and her psychologist boyfriend."

"You sure, you sure?" he asked thickly.

"Sure. Come on over right now. Shut the children down again. It'll take us a couple of hours."

"Okay," he answered.

Alice hung up and gathered her thoughts for a moment: *knife, knife, knife.* Was the kid just getting her nerve up, or wasn't revenge her real intent? Or was it even the kid? Time would tell, for though she'd have to check the grimoire for the exact words to the incantation, she could gather everything else before Aaron got here. The trick was to keep the kid guessing, to throw out a red herring. Clay, that would work as well as anything.

Alice momentarily forgot where she'd put the clay and felt a twinge of sadness at abandoning creative work for so long. If that sinkhole in her back yard hadn't opened fifteen months ago… but she assured herself as she searched: *Quit whining. You can chisel as much as you want with all the power and money you're going to have. You'll never have to whore your work out again.* She spotted the clay under a TV tray—of all things. It was unbelievably hard and she reached for the oyster knife— too bad, kid, you missed your chance—to cut out two five-pound blocks. A waste of good clay that would have put her in tears in her more impetuous artistic temper. *Stop it,* she told herself. *Think here and now and what you need to do!*

Knife, knife, knife. Good, now here's the knife again in case you want to grab it, darling whoever you are.

"That should do it just fine," she said aloud, picking up the clay and heading downstairs. It would be best to work outside near the water conditioner—that way whoever was shapeshifting in the invisibility mist wouldn't even notice the salt until too late. Delivery had been made last week, so there were at least two hundred pounds in the shed. As Alice walked downstairs, her spine tingled from a coolish breeze at her back. *Knife, knife.* Her griffins slumbered at the foot of the steps. Too bad they couldn't just slice through the problem right now. She shrugged and carried the clay outside.

The water conditioner sat directly behind the house, enclosed in a plywood shed just large enough to hold it, six bags of salt, and some tools. Alice set the clay on the back porch. Was the shapeshifting mist near? She couldn't be sure. She heard Aaron and waved him over as she walked to the kiln and eyed some rebar used in constructing her largest concrete pieces. Before she bent for it, she pulled one of Pie's pads from her pocket and wrote a note, *We have company listening in. Just play along with whatever I say,* and handed it to Aaron.

"Aaron, here's a list of things I want you to buy at the hardware store. Check to see if you think you can get them." She thought she'd caught sight of the mist. Yes, over by the two hunks of clay. *That's right, dearie, just worry and wonder what in the world I'm doing with old dried-out clay.*

Aaron nodded somberly at the note. "When you want me to leave?"

"Not right away. Help me with this rebar first, will you? Twelve pieces, at least six feet in length, over by that shed."

Aaron bunched his brow but took the first six long metal

bars that were the thickness of a finger over. Alice gathered wire to tie them together, and a wire cutter, then looked for a pair of work gloves—she hated working with rebar; nearly every time she managed to slice herself on its razor edges. Ah, there it was again, that coolness. *Curiosity killed more than the cat, dearie.*

She and Aaron worked intently. "Could you tie them together securely in the shape of a box, Aaron? Something big enough to hold two people, say big enough to go around this small shed, for instance."

"You mean to make it like a cube, *nu*?"

"Exactly. And keep an eye on those two pieces of clay while I run into the house: nothing should touch them, okay? Nothing at all." He nodded. *There, dearie, go run for the clay and paw it as much as you can in the shape you're in.* Alice went upstairs, feeling the coolness as she walked by the clay lumps, unable to hold back a smirk. She found the incantation easily and decided to just rip it out and not bother with copying it, to allay any slips of tongue. Pie! If Pie came around, would she scare the girl off? No, whatever the girl was using was good, damned good. Pie had never sensed her before; the girl would be too cocky to leave just because the rag doll showed. What about Rex? Alice shook her head, wondering about him. Maybe the girl—*Why am I so sure it's the girl? Instinct, trust your instinct. But then, I would never have begun this Persephone's Escalator bit if I'd trusted my instinct.* She remembered how she'd drawn away from it when it first opened last summer solstice…

She went downstairs and helped Aaron join the rebar. Before they finished, she lifted one end of the construction—the shape and size of a large cage, though the gaps between the bars were in feet instead of inches. It wasn't too awfully heavy: they should be able to slip it over the low shed with a minimum of trouble. And unless the girl was very alert and very nimble, that would be her undoing: enough salt to attract her bodyweight and coalesce her vapor, surrounded by enchanted iron bars. As nonchalantly as she could, Alice invoked a magical circle. If the kid did notice, she'd probably just think it was part of the preparation for the bars and the clay—which it was, but—there, finished. Now, one last re-bar strut. She tied it doubly with wire, then shook each end, assuring its stability. She took out the pad again. *Go in the shed and cut all the bags of salt open. Then come out and help me lift this over the shed.*

"There's a rake in the shed, Aaron. I need it." She handed him the note, keeping her body between him and the two lumps of clay. He glanced at the note and walked inside, pulling the door to. She heard the heavy plastic being sliced. "Leave the door open when you come out, Aaron." He came out and they quickly lifted the bar over. *Too late, little one, if you haven't gone by now.*

Alice read loudly.

Spirit or flesh, I command thee:
Give up thy misty cloak.
Into loathsome salt must your essence soak.
Spirit or flesh, I command thee
Spirit or flesh, I command thee
Appear, appear, appear!

There was a shuffling of the salt pellets and a wind blew at their backs. What started as a
low whine of pain ended with:
"Aaaaaaaagh!"
"It's the little Beasley girl," Aaron said, looking on the na-

ked teenager crusting over with a fine, white powder. Coughing, Abby began to scratch ferociously, leaving powdery white streaks of salt that turned red as her skin was abraded. She lunged at the open door but was thrown back at the plane created by the iron rebar.

"Water. Please, I need water." Her face was twisted in pain.

Pie scampered around the far corner of the house, its grin growing as it heard Abby retching after tossing off the water processor's lid and trying to drink its salty content. Some fun was up, the rag doll knew.

10.

Nikki and Martin had taken Abby away before the last detective left the Beasley house. As soon as they were in the car, she'd surprised them by wanting to go to Alice Fairbain's in her invisible state that instant. They argued that any confrontation should wait until Abby was better able to handle the situation without emotion.

"It's not going to be a confrontation. I just want to..." Abby let the sentence dangle, not wanting to speak of what had happened.

"And what would you do if you found out she had killed them, Abby?" Martin had asked.

"I'd—" Abby stopped, seeing Nikki's face studying her in the rearview mirror. "I'd come and tell you two. As long as you help avenge my parents and my sister, I'll come and tell you two everything I do."

"I took a blood oath on that, Abby. I want you to remember—"

"I remember. Will you?"

"I'd think the two of you would want to talk to the police if you found out Fairbain was connected with the crime,"

Martin said.

Abby kicked the back seat. "Witchcraft's not admitted as evidence into court unless you're Black or poor—then the judge would believe anything just to get you behind bars. There's ways a lot better than the police…"

As they turned toward the Settles house, Skull, still in the form of a hawk, flew ahead. As Nikki and Martin glanced to the burned house—it was hard not to stare every time they passed—Abby furtively took one of the beans, grimacing as she discarded a strand of the dead girl Cristy's hair, fighting back tears as she thought of her sister and mother. She quietly cracked the window, chanted her incantation and struck at the air three times. Two hundred yards past the Settles' house she turned into mist.

"Abby? Abby!" Martin foolishly tried to reach into the back seat to grab the gaseous wisp slipping out the window, but wound up only with hands chafed from the cold. Nikki stopped the car and shouted, but Abby's vapor had already dissipated. In the back seat, Martin spotted a note on scrap paper: "Back at six. Meet me at the old Settles house."

"Abby!"

Skull flew, but even he was powerless and soon perched atop Nikki's gray Lincoln, clucking surprisingly like a chicken.

"As long as she stays calm, she'll be fine. She acted calm, didn't she?"

Martin raised his eyebrows, his stomach quivering as he recalled the scene at the Beasley house. "I guess," he said, more to assure Nikki than anything.

What was there to do besides meet where and when Abby's note mentioned? So they drove out of Quail Hollow. Martin decided to call St. Veronica's and pointed to a restaurant at the Day's Inn. They parked. Instead of calling, they

both slumped into a booth until a waiter took their order
for coffee—neither felt particularly hungry after the morning. After a few sips, Martin urged himself up and made the
phone call to St. Veronica's, though he almost wished he
hadn't, for it was bad news atop the already bad.

"Bobby's disappeared," he told Nikki on returning. "A new
nurse reported seeing him walk out of the building with two
male nurses. Trouble is, there's only one male nurse in the
hospital."

"Have they reported him missing?"

"I told them to contact Florida Highway Patrol since
it's reasonable to assume he might come back here—or be
abducted back here. I also told them to give the police Alice
Fairbain's name and address—she claims to be legal guardian,
after all."

Nikki shrugged, keeping half an eye on Martin, half on
the front door, half on the pool where she could see Fairbain's leering statuary. *If only I had one more half I could find
creamer for my coffee*, she thought.

"Are there really rituals that require a male virgin?" Martin
asked. At Nikki's surprised glance he reminded her that was
what Abby had told them.

"I guess a virgin for a ritual is possible, but—" she leaned
forward to fix her eyes on Martin— "look, it's no accident
that nearly every philosopher in history has been a man: what
woman would have the pretension to impose her singular
idea of order on the world? It's the same with the kind of
witchcraft you're asking about, sorcery. It's a skeletal remnant
from when politics and the occult intertwined. We witches
got smart and stopped; male politics remains at the same
primitive level." She gave another glance at the statues. The
cupid stared blankly back with a curious tilt of his white-

washed face. Clouds were gathering to the north and she realized it was July 4th. Summer storms might ruin everyone's holiday parade. But everyone in Quail Hollow already had it ruined. She remembered reading about the Settles' girl and her parents last fall. Now this. Did newspapers make things worse by publicizing these murders so heavily?

Martin shrugged. "You were talking about sorcery. Do you think Fairbain's a female sorcerer? A black witch? That's the right term, isn't it?"

Nikki eyed the cupid. "Black witch, the left-hand path. She's a loner; she's not a regular in any coven I know. Maybe there's a tendency—just like there's a tendency for a loner to be a sexual deviant or other type of criminal—for a lone witch to concentrate her powers that way. Look, I'm not a model white witch, I've done things that would shock most people—simply put, there's enough power in magic to make evil tempting. Power corrupts, right?"

"And absolute power corrupts absolutely."

"No doubt. I've always thought that if there were an individual Godhead, she'd be a stinker."

The waiter refreshed their coffees. Nikki noticed some detectives in the back of the restaurant talking with employees. She could swear Cupid's head inclined a few degrees to face them.

"How long have those statues been there?" she asked the waiter.

He wouldn't even look where she was pointing. "They give me the creeps. They were put in a year ago. One night after they were installed we—well, I'm not supposed to be saying this—we had some serious trouble in one of the motel rooms. Some people love them, though. Who knows?"

"They're by Alice Fairbain, aren't they?"

He nodded. "We've got her brochures out in the lobby. You want me to get one for you?"

"That'd be nice. Thanks."

As the waiter left, Martin spoke: "So, could a witch today think that she needed a virgin? You never really answered that."

"A witch or a mental case? You may not distinguish between the two yet, Doctor, but given time you might."

Martin smiled, and Nikki tapped her coffee mug. Both of them wondered if the two cases might just have coalesced with Alice Fairbain.

"Look, a big part of witchcraft is knowing where your spells, talismans, and incantations will carry you and those around you. Fairbain, she might be operating in a very large field of power. The larger the field, the more the fallout, the more hesitant you need to be. The more you should be, anyway."

"Just like with an atomic bomb."

"Exactly. The fallout might very well blow back in your face. Nuclear winter isn't a pleasant possibility."

The waiter brought two brochures, expensive productions in four-color slick paper, then left.

"So what would make someone take the chance?"

"The cardinal sin. Pride, doctor, pride." Nikki held up her brochure. "I know a woman who met Lincoln—not in a previous life like you're thinking—she's not reincarnated, but more of what you'd call molted, like a snake shedding skin. In the usual reincarnation jag there's no immediate transference of mental identity or memory; in this molting, transference is nearly complete and immediate. Migration is the term we use, a changing of both souls and awareness to a new body. The Sisterhood has a need for such women, so that some methods are guaranteed to be passed along. I guess that goes back to my point about power—"

"Absolute power?"

"Certainly not. Your maleness comes through, you keep thinking in sorcerer's terms."

"Have you done this… migration?" Martin tore needlessly at a sugar pack with a hint of an ironic smile.

Nikki leaned to catch Martin's eyes. Brown, a sad brown. "How quickly skepticism returns after your experience yesterday. Do you see what modern churches are fighting against? A lack of spirituality. It's a wonder they have any congregations."

⊗⅊⊗

Outside the restaurant where Nikki and Martin sat, Jewel, Lori, and Beth were returning from what they presumed was Nikki's house, as the phone had only listed *N. Ryan.* No one had been there, so they'd left a note on the door under a barely discernible hex sign. Lori grabbed Jewel's arm as soon as they pulled into the parking lot; she was sitting between Beth and Jewel. "She's here," Lori said, nodding at the restaurant.

Beth, putting the car into park, gave Lori a glance and wondered, *What is it with this girl?* It wasn't any lesbian mother-daughter affair like they all thought, Beth realized, studying Lori's pale forearm and leg. At least that wasn't the major reason for her presence. Beth got out of the car and looked at the restaurant: two guys were standing by the front door; otherwise she could barely make out the faces of customers inside because of the window's tinting. So how could Lori know Nyx Ryan was here? She looked over as the other car door shut. *Okay, Jewel Dawn, I may not be the witch you are, but we're going to have to be a bit more upfront with one another before you can expect my full cooperation.* Beth tried that out in her mind and liked the way it felt. Should she do it now, in front of the girl, here on the sidewalk? No, later.

Beth dropped that thought as soon as they entered the restaurant, for her specialty was auras, and she immediately spotted Nyx Ryan: the woman had aura enough to light Wrigley Field. Realizing she'd stopped to stare in the middle of the dining room, she continued as best she could, trying to get past that aura to concentrate on the man the woman sat with, but no use.

"Nyx."

Jewel clasped the woman and Beth thought she heard her give the greeting. Beth quickly turned to Lori to whisper, "You're part of the Pentad. Whisper 'Blood and Birth' in her ear and await the same reply."

All four women clasped in turn; then Nikki offered them seats and introduced them to Martin Edmonds. "A psychologist," Nikki said, pulling back a lock of black hair. "But don't let that get in your way. He's learning quickly and I think he's already had a brush with the reason you're all down here." Nikki stopped to look at the two detectives, now seated in a corner near the window with Cupid. They nodded and looked back to their coffee. "Speaking of that, I hope you have a good reason prepared for why you're here," she said. "Something terrible happened last night, and since you're sitting with us, you might very well be questioned."

We're looking to buy a home—all of us, for vacation use."

"This far inland?"

"All we could afford. I'm glad you took a class from me and recommended the place."

Nikki nodded and Jewel leaned forward.

"So what happened? And do you think it has anything to

do with the shifting in the Matrix?" Jewel asked.

"More and more. I'll let Martin tell you what happened to him first, though."

Martin's rehash of the previous day in the barn was interrupted halfway through when the detectives came over to introduce themselves and chitchat with the women. Though they finally returned to their table, they hardly appeared assured.

"Suspicious mi-inds," Beth sang quietly.

Martin continued his story, ending with the death of Walter. Jewel asked few questions, except for a detailed description of Alice Fairbain.

"Even better," Martin said, handing over a brochure with a picture of the woman.

"I've met her," Jewel said. Jewel was known for her remarkable recollection, even more amazing as she'd passed through four migrations. Now and then she'd astound an intimate friend with a description of Abraham and Mary Todd Lincoln, who'd both consulted her about an occult matter—on the QT, to be sure.

Jewel recollected Alice Fairbain: "Nothing remarkable, though she did have an impressive familiar, a rag doll. I've only known three Sisters who've had the desire or ability to use an inanimate object. One recently tried a computer, if you can believe it." Jewel laughed. "All she managed to do was erase the entire hard drive. A technician said lightning hit the machine. Stupidity would be more like it. I suppose Alice's employing a rag doll shows skill and determination; one never knows where the whims of the Matrix will lead—and people do change ever so marvelously, don't they?" Jewel ended by staring directly at Nikki, who simply met her gaze with a smile.

"Well, we'll find out about Ms. Fairbain soon enough," Beth said, "presuming that Anne Marie and the others were able to see her."

"The police have been inspecting every car going in all morning," Martin said. Because of—well, this is where Nikki should take over."

When Nikki voiced her suspicions about the Beasley murders and the statues, Beth told them all about the bleeding nymphs by the pool and her hatpin. Martin pointed to the brochure that Jewel still held and they all looked outside to Cupid, who seemed to be staring back.

"Commanding a single rattlesnake is one thing, but animating a troop of statues? The woman couldn't possibly have that kind of power. No witch does, nor any of the old time sorcerers or alchemists either. Even if you believe what you read about the armies they raised, they—"

"Did you have a young girl with you?" Lori asked suddenly. She was leaning toward Nikki and Martin, who said yes. She turned back: "I'm sorry I interrupted, Professor—I mean, Jewel."

Even as Jewel made a pass of her hand to indicate it was all right, Lori's head suddenly tilted and her eyes widened in fear. Her voice came out in a slow rasp. "Salt inside my veins inside my skull inside my heart. Drying, itching. Thirst. A woman holds a bowl full of water, but a rag doll pours it on the ground. A man is asking me questions. Thirst. Please. Please." Not only was Lori rasping, but she had begun to scratch her face violently. Several tables in the room were staring. Mercifully it thundered outside, wildly, and clouds gathered. And mercifully the detectives had left the restaurant.

"Let's pay and get her out of here," Jewel suggested.

So now Beth knew. A true psychic, for it was obvious from the faces of the psychologist Martin Edmonds and the woman Nikki that Lori's act had hit a soft spot. But who was this girl Lori was talking about? The Beasley girl who'd survived? Had the same things come for her after they'd killed her family?

SKIRMISHES, SORTIES; BETRAYALS, QUESTIONS

(midday Monday, July 3, to late night Tuesday, July 4)

1.

Detective Paulsen had been assigned the guests at Day's Inn. Six women checking in together from Kentucky had been too plush an opportunity for him to pass, so he went to their rooms, finding only Becky. The thirty-three-year-old reminded him of his ex-wife when they first married, her way of smiling at nearly everything; so he lingered, chitchatting about this and that, about the Kentucky Derby he always wanted to go to, about the best beaches around the area, about Disney World. Flirting, flirting, flirting.

"Look, you going to be around tonight?" he asked.

Becky gave her ultra-big smile.

"So I usually go to the Quail Hollow Bar down the road and shoot some pool and drink some beer—but there's plenty of ladies that go there, you know? If you want, show on up and I'll tell you all about wonderful Tampa. Harbor Island's a pretty snazzy place, romantic boat rides and all, and you shouldn't miss Busch Gardens—That bar's right down the road; you can almost see it from your room here."

Becky was in a dress as loose and happy as her smile. She shifted against a bureau and the detective watched her hips. They too were like his ex-wife's. He smiled grandly, Becky's grin being infectious, and said good-bye, warning her to be careful. Getting in his cruiser, he looked forward to something other than a pool game anyway—it was getting so he couldn't tell if the table was green or blue, from all the bar smoke.

"Cain! Cain! Cain! Cain!"

"What the hell is that? Turn your volume down." He shouted over his radio at the dispatcher, who protested he didn't hear a thing, that it must be static from the storm. But the noise only got louder, speaking the same word over again and again. Cursing, the detective said he'd call in from a phone booth.

"Cain! Cain! Cain!" was all he heard for reply as he started his car, giving a last look to Becky's room. Peripherally, he saw what he presumed was some pale Canadian kid, wrapped in a white bath towel, climbing the steps as he drove off. Snowbirds, even in the summer now.

2.

Becky was one of the most effective white witches Jewel had ever met in any of her migrations. Despite this, Jewel was never really sure if Becky truly was a witch, if she even had an occult connection with the Matrix. Rather, Jewel wondered, was it just the girl's personality—so unassuming, so open, so considerate that it forced people into joyful interactions. Then again, maybe that was an occult connection of the most direct kind, after all…

3.

After the detective left, Becky returned to her two favorite things: listening to Handel's *Messiah*, which she had on tape, and consulting the tarot deck, which she did more for the colors and artwork on the cards than any cares about the future. The future will come, she thought, just as the end will. She looked at the card she'd drawn: The Hanged Man. Two aged farmers were staring up at a youth on a gibbet with his tongue lolling, and they were almost laughing. What could they know that the hanged man didn't? The youth's eyes were rolled back, so that Becky imagined their pupils hiding the card's real laughter. A life lived is a life loved, and a short full cup of wine is as happy as a long full cup. She was thinking this and she was thinking about the detective's handsome ruddy face, when she heard a scratching at the door. She got off the bed and opened it to see an albino midget wrapped in a towel. As she smiled and bent, other pale midgets joined their fellow and pushed, knocking her back on the bed, slicing at her with makeshift knives and axes. She pulled the bed sheet up in self-defense. She didn't even scream. The statues sliced and hacked so frantically that they broke one another.

4.

Despite the rain pelting them, Jewel slammed the door to Becky's room shut before even entering. She turned, loose-legged, not even bothering to shield her face from the hard drops: "Lori, our room. Could you walk over and open it, please?" Jewel trembled and her eyes went out of focus as she clutched the doorknob to Becky's room behind her. Lori didn't hear, as she'd been trying to touch Abby mentally by holding Nikki's and Martin's hands after they told her the girl's name. Jewel bit her lip on seeing Lori's blue eyes. She reached into her purse and took out a key to the next room down and handed it to Nikki, pointing vaguely.

"Are you all right?" Nikki asked, turning her attention from Lori.

Jewel only pointed to the far room, concentrating on the cooling rain to keep her from being sick as Nikki walked to open the door. As Jewel looked down at the pool, its surface rippled with miniature waves and a film of sweat broke over her body. She nodded for everyone to follow Nikki, though holding back Beth to whisper.

"Something's happened." Her voice cracked.

"Becky?"

Jewel gripped Beth tightly to prevent her entering. "She's dead, slashed—"

"Are you sure? Are you sure she's not just hurt?"

Jewel nodded sickly.

"But the Pentad's shield of—"

"It was weak, you could feel that, couldn't you? That's why I performed the ritual twice, but it was just as weak the second time." Jewel bent over the rail. Tears welled and fell, joining the rain. She inhaled sharply, lifting her face. After Lincoln had been assassinated she'd seen two men hung in a suburb of Washington. They'd been beaten beforehand. And she'd made the stupid mistake of traveling to Germany in the mid-thirties and had seen a young Jewess being dragged into an alley by three Nazi thugs. Feeling that she'd reached the peak of her powers, she managed a spell to let the girl escape. But a fat butcher opened the alley door—he'd evidently been watching—and killed the girl by beating her head against a stone wall, though he seemed surprised when she suddenly went limp. Then the Nazis arrested him. The Hanged Man. If Jewel hadn't interfered, would the Nazis have been content to rape the girl and let her go? It had been a turning point in her life, for humility mixed with indecision, and that night she'd known the fourth would be her last migration.

"Jewel?"

Jewel looked from the pool to Beth's face as she stood nearby on the balcony. Had Beth lightened her hair coloring? Or was her aura happier, more free? "We have a weak link, Beth. No, not the girl Lori. Someone's changed since yesterday. The Pentad was strong then. Or maybe I'm not concentrating enough—" Lori stuck her head out the door and called for Jewel to get out of the rain. "We're coming," Jewel answered, giving a wave of her hand. "We should have brought our familiars. Damn airplanes, anyway. Beth, somehow we've got to get the goblets out of that room before the police go in. I can't face the room again. Becky was so…"

"The Ryan woman will have the familiar you gave her, if you're sure about trusting her."

"Are you?"

"She seemed very angry and upset about the girl Abby."

"Okay, let's go ask."

When they went inside the room, Nikki and Martin were arguing.

"Calling the police for Abby will do absolutely nothing, Martin," Nikki was nearly shouting. "With the shape-shifter spell she can easily be changed into pure salt for a short time. We can't very well tell the police that a hundredweight of salt is really a kidnapped girl they're looking—" Nikki stopped on seeing Jewel and Beth. "What's happened in the next room?" she asked, her voice becoming dark.

"Becky, our keeper, she's been killed."

"But you had a shield of power: I felt it this morning. I stopped long enough to help—two ceremonies, why? The first was done properly."

Jewel shrugged. Lori, still in contact with Abby, was crying quietly with her head in her hands, occasionally twitching and itching herself. Martin looked at the wall as if he could see clear into the next room and shouted angrily: "The police? Okay? Can we call them now?" He strutted to the phone but Jewel held up her hand. "In a few minutes: believe me, it's not going to make a difference to Becky." She turned to Nikki. "We need your familiar to fetch the goblets. They're still on the bed. You know what would happen if the police started suspecting witchcraft—we'd never have a moment to get to this Fairbain woman's house."

"Well damnit, maybe you shouldn't go there. Has anyone ever thought that maybe no one but the police should?" Martin's voice was shrill and he lifted the phone.

"Outsider," Beth hissed. Before Nikki or Jewel could act she made three passes and threw ground chamomile to slump Martin onto the closest single bed. "He's all right," she assured Nikki. "With that damned shield you've got around him, a falling building wouldn't hurt him. He'll just sleep a few minutes until we get this solved." Beth walked to place her hand on Lori, who was still sobbing.

"Can you summon your familiar?" Jewel asked, turning to grab Nikki's hand.

Nikki nodded and opened the door to whistle Skull in. As a red-tailed hawk he perched on her shoulder, majestically surveying the room. It seemed to Jewel that the bird inclined its head slightly toward her, but maybe that was just her pride…

"Give me the key. I'll have him fly the goblets and any spiritual weapons to a field near the road. We can drive and get them before calling the police." Nikki was interrupted by a moan from Lori. Beth was scratching her shoulders, but the girl's mouth hung loose. "But as soon as we get them we *have* to go see what we can do for Abby. From the looks of Lori, the salt spell she's under is extremely painful."

"What about Anne Marie, Tiffany, and Nancy?" Beth called as Jewel handed Nikki the room key. "If it's Fairbain who has the girl, maybe they can help."

Jewel turned to Lori, who'd laid her head down on a desk, exhausted. "Lori, Lori, you've got to concentrate now. Think back to the girl you were just with. Her name's Abby. Abby. Think Abby." Lori lifted her head; her eyes showed fear.

"Do you have anything to sedate her, Beth?"

"I can't interface when I'm sedated."

Jewel grimaced at the word *interface*. "It hurts when you're touching the girl Abby, I know, but it's important."

Lori nodded.

"Can we use any counter spells?" Beth asked Jewel.

Jewel drew a pentagram and slowly materialized an orange tennis ball of fire. As it floated and began to glow, she spoke, "Lori, I want you to listen. It's important that you see through Abby's eyes again." Lori backed against a wall, but Jewel reassured her: "This time it won't hurt, because I'm going to place this globe in your hand. When the pain comes, I want you to visualize all of it going into the globe. It will glow as you do, and the pain will leave. Don't be afraid, okay?" Jewel moved Martin's inert legs and sat on the bed facing Lori, whose face reflected the orange globe. This combined with an occasional flash of lightning that showed even through the curtains. Jewel touched the globe and it took on a brighter hue; she straightened her shoulders and pulled away after a moment of shivering.

"See? It takes every physical pain away."

"I should have been more alert and not concentrated so much on… it's my fault that girl next door was kill—"

Jewel cut Lori short. "Don't try on my responsibilities, young lady. I assigned Becky as keeper—" All three of them turned to hear a great flapping of wings from outside and noticed that Nikki was no longer there. So her familiar was carrying the goblets to safety. "I was the one," Jewel continued in a whisper. "And I was the one who rushed the ceremony of the shield of power without finding the weak link. Maybe I was afraid to find it." She squeezed Lori's hand. "That little Beasley girl will continue to suffer if we don't get on with this. I want you to be brave, Lori, and concentrate." Jewel motioned for Beth to open her traveling case and mouthed the word *candle*. Beth nodded and lit a blue candle on a telephone book in front of Lori. Less than two minutes passed before Lori clawed at her arm and began rasping again:

"'No, I don't know. Please give me some water. Please.'"

Jewel guided Lori's hand to the orange globe. It fiercely sparked and evidently eased the tightness overtaking the girl's pale body. Her voice became monotone, even when she directly spoke what Abby was saying.

"The woman is scooping water before her. Abby concentrates on the water and the woman's large hands. The woman is asking where Doctor Edmonds and Nyx Ryan are. The girl, who's constantly oozing powdery salt from her pores and her mouth and all her bodily openings, tries to spit and answers she doesn't know, she supposes they're at home. Her speech burns—I don't know how she even speaks, her mouth is so dry. At her answer, a hulking man splashes water on himself while a rag doll tosses pellets of salt around the girl, its face glaring a hateful smile. There's a bolt of lightning behind the woman's head. She screams 'Tarpaulin! Get the tarp from the work shed!' The man lumbers off. There're statues everywhere, white, and a lot of them depict small people. There's something else—I saw it, though the girl barely noticed because of her pain—there's someone watching from behind an outbuilding. He's hunched and watching. There, I see him behind the woman who's now asking when the girl is supposed to meet Nyx Ryan and Martin Edmonds; I see him look to his left at an entire field of statues. He's frightened when he looks at them; he's angry when he looks at the woman. He's holding a short rifle in his hands. The girl just felt raindrops on her body and jumps, because her pain's easing—"

"Of course!" Jewel said. "As the salt dissolves in the rain, the spell loses its power. Rain, Beth, can you guide rain?" Seeing Beth shrug, Jewel directed, "Go see if Nyx can. Hurry."

Beth left without hesitation and Jewel muttered at her back, "You may become a reasonable Sister yet, Beth Lewis." But Lori convulsed and continued speaking, so Jewel turned to pay attention:

"The heavy man is coming back and the woman runs to help him carry the tarpaulin. The girl, she is trying to move from under a warped wood shelf that's keeping drizzle off her, but she can barely shift through all the salt pellets pressing against her. The man and woman are putting the tarp over the enclosure now—the girl is wedged against what looks like a giant diving cylinder—it's growing darker outside, like a gravy thickening. She's watching sheets of rain heading through trees. Now the tarp is moved in place over her head and the pelting rain runs down the sides of the shed. She realizes she's on a concrete slab, so there's no hope of getting wet from the ground. Everything has remained dry except a spot where wind is blowing some rain in. She moves toward it, slowly, for she doesn't want to attract the woman's attention. The other man behind a far shed—I can see him in the rain—this other man must see something, for he crawls back to hide. There, a horn blows. And again. The rag doll peeks under the tarpaulin and spots the small puddle forming near the girl. Splashing with its foot, the doll smiles wildly and closes the wooden door, stopping more rain from entering. I can't see anything now. It's dark.

"Wait. Three car doors slam in the distance. 'Let's see who that is,' the woman says. Abby can hear her plainly. 'Is it dry in there, Pie? Good. After an hour of itching she'll be ready to tell us whatever we want. Come on, Pie, or you'll smell like mold tomorrow. The little bitch will wait.'"

Lori stopped and started to itch herself, but Jewel guided her hand back to the orange globe. Lori smacked her lips and blinked her eyes. Jewel could see her pupils dilating, even though all the lights were on in the motel room. Who turned them on? She realized that she had. Then Lori spoke again:

"There's only the sound of rain. No, there's a small drip. The girl shifts in that direction, though it's hard for her to tell where the salt begins and her body ends. The shed is dark, but she can smell the wet. Somewhere a door opens and closes with a bang. She notices a light, a crack she can use to reach water. She is working toward it." Once more, Lori started to scratch herself and Jewel moved her hand toward the orange globe. Tears were coming out of her eyes, even when she touched the globe this time.

"We summoned up what rain we could, as close as we could figure to Alice Fairbain's." This was spoken by Nikki at the door. Beth stood near.

Jewel motioned them in. "Good. Keep it going as long and hard as you can. They're leaving her alone now. Company came. I'm betting it's Anne Marie and the others, now that the police have cleared out."

Beth pointed to Lori, who was quiet. "Abby must be okay for now. So maybe Lori can leave her and find that weak link or at least see what this Fairbain woman's about. Elimination, Jewel. If it's not me, and if it's not this lady," Beth nodded toward Nikki, "who seems more than powerful enough to take us all on without any conspiracy: I might have raised three drops of that deluge she directed—if it's not us and you say it's not the girl here, and Becky's obviously out—" Beth and Jewel both drew a breath, remembering the matter next door— "then that leaves Nancy, Tiffany, or Ann Marie. Tiffany's too busy planning wardrobes, so that leaves Nancy or Ann Marie. My vote in a whodunit always goes for jealousy and resentment, so that leaves just—"

"You sound like a misguided constable from *Murdoch*, Beth."

"Do I? Or are you letting emotion cover the obvious?"

"CAIN! CAIN! CAIN!" Lori shouted maniacally of a sudden and reached to squeeze the orange globe, which barely helped, as she yanked back to beat her head against the headboard behind until Jewel shook her and Beth ran to blow out the candle. It took all of them a couple of minutes to calm Lori, and they nearly knocked Martin, who was still sedated from the chamomile spell, off the bed.

"For what it's worth," Nikki announced, breathing heavily and still helping hold Lori, "Skull's just taken out the last goblet." Lori went limp and they laid her head on a pillow. Nikki reached into her jeans pocket: "Skull also brought these out. I thought you'd want them." She held up a Tarot deck. "Becky was using only the major arcana. The Hanged Man was the outcome." Nikki turned the card over.

Jewel took it and closed her eyes, oddly relieved, even as she felt Lori's heavy breathing. It was as if she'd been working with this card for the last forty years, maybe for all of her migrations: Great knowledge, through great self-sacrifice. But why should Becky be the sacrifice? Becky, who in her simplicity held a knowledge none of them ever would achieve. Who would hurt that goof-child, that lovable she-bear who had a smile for every moment, everyone, and everything? Who would cut her the way they did? And why? Jewel mulled the Hanged Man, dangling from a golden rope, which of course led to knowledge. She imagined Becky turning over that card. What would her reaction have been? A frown? A smile? Certainly not an ironic one. Irony was beyond, no, it was beneath Becky. And what would her reaction have been to the one who killed her? Or ones? She probably smiled even then.

"You saw that room, didn't you?" Jewel suddenly asked Nikki. But she turned to find Beth standing alone.

"She said to leave you be. That she'd be back in two hours. She said that if we wanted the goblets, they were exactly one mile down the road on the right toward Alice Fairbain's, under a live oak. She said if she couldn't get back, she'd send her daughter Night, who knew a lot about Abby and might even help us more. Her daughter would be wearing a pearl necklace, if that were the case."

"Did she say what to do with that worthy gentleman?" Jewel nodded to Martin, whose arm was still slumped up against the headboard.

"She said that if Fairbain hadn't already disposed of the skeletons in the barn, this might be a good time for him to tell the police about them, leaving out anything they'd find too strange. She said we should include him when we could, that his being a psychologist might add some insight to Fairbain, find a weak link. She told me to be nice to him." Beth gave a little smile as she heard several huge blasts of thunder and looked out at the unnaturally dark storm clouds still drenching the area. "I think I'll do what she asked."

Jewel felt Lori twitching. "God's blood! The girl's having a seizure. Get the doctor out of that trance you put him in. I'm going to call the police and an ambulance."

5.

Damn Abby anyway, Nikki thought as she drove towards Alice Fairbain's. Invisibility. The best I can manage is an upset stomach from ingesting one of those beans, especially after knowing where it's been. And the worst that could happen could be very bad, working blindly with a class enchantment like that...

So. The only way to get into Alice Fairbain's house would be as Night, looking for her friend Abby. That would get Fairbain's curiosity going. Nikki pulled to the side of the road as she reached the outskirts of the heavy rain she'd brought on. She breathed in the wet: five minutes was the fastest she'd ever been able to bring the complete change on. *Pride, Night, pride. Stop it.* She left her flashers going just in case someone happened to drive by. Skull was inside the car with her, his feathers ruffled and his disposition the same from the rain. It was too bad he couldn't migrate into something other than a bird. She looked to him and spoke, "But I don't suppose even a seagull could fly in this mess I've made…"

Skull shook water over the front seat and let out quite a sick croak, for a hawk. Nikki concentrated on making the change, using the drench outside as cover.

6.

Dean Kirby crawled under the awning behind the kiln. As the sky darkened more and more, he noticed statues shuffling nervously, their eyes slitting to show black holes. He hissed and sputtered rain. If it wasn't for that damned carload of women out front he'd already be inside and Fairbain would be material for a newspaper story.

What the hell had she and her pals been doing to that girl by the water conditioner? Was it Abby? He was too far away to tell. He wanted to help but couldn't trust himself to stray from saving Bobby. What if Bruno wound up raping and killing the girl, for instance? Not implausible. His thoughts were interrupted when a squat statue with a fiercely long handlebar mustache took a stumbling step and knocked over a bucket. This caused a wild barking inside the house and the back door to open. Martin saw Aaron stare toward the tarpaulin, then around the yard. Fairbain's dog dove between the man's legs, nearly knocking him over, and ran toward the statue that had kicked the pail, knocking it down. Aaron smiled and closed the door. The dog tore at the statue, which weakly flailed out with a rock or something, until it at last lay still. The dog sniffed, then gave a low growl toward Dean…

But Dean wasn't there. Bruno's eyes lit wildly and he leaned the shotgun against a kiln as the dog bounded through heavy rain. As the dog leaped, he grabbed its neck and fell backwards, flipping it overhead and squeezing ever harder until he could feel vertebrae pop out of place and see the dog's tongue loll, dripping bloody saliva over his hand. He pressed and pressed until his fingers tore through fur and into the flesh. Blood spurted.

Cain! Cain! Cain!

Bruno let the dog lay limply and eyed the tarpaulin where he'd seen a young girl. He walked in that direction. The rips the dog had made in his shirt left him glistening and bare-chested.

7.

Within five minutes of answering the front door, Alice Fairbain had been surrounded with the same self-doubts she always had when attending sabbats. Though not a particularly practiced aura reader, she could see that the ashen gray woman before her was skilled in the Matrix beyond anything she herself had ever hoped for. The hard-looking little brunette named Nancy, too, had powers beyond what she'd dreamed of, and there was even something about the willow named Tiffany that Alice couldn't touch—at least until now and the children. Before the children she would have never attempted holding the girl outside in the salt spell. *Admit it, A.F., you never would have even known the girl was present, you never would have felt that chill and put two and two together. But since Persephone opened over a year ago, something has rubbed off and taken you to a better, a higher order of Sisterhood.*

Alice thought along these lines as the women walked around her house pretending to look at the statuary, even picking one or two small pieces for purchase. She then realized that what she'd been able to accomplish with the children had summoned these witches. There was something big going on in the Matrix, and she was the instigator. Damned if she was going to let some outside coven take over now. Sharing with Aaron was more than enough… Still, she needed to be careful, for these three vixens were no doubt attached to a Pentad.

She caught another look from the ashen one who'd been giving glances about when the other two weren't paying attention, glances that just might indicate she wouldn't mind a little *tête à tête*.

"I'm working on something different upstairs—Greco-Roman. Would you care to see it? I noticed you admiring the griffins is why I asked." *Poor, but then you've never been the epitome of tact, Alice.*

"I'd love to. I'll be right back, girls."

Alice saw the short brunette crinkle her brow at this, but nothing else. The other one was busily trying to get Aaron to pay attention by adjusting her bra strap—she'd obviously prepared for a sunny day and wouldn't let a little deluge rain on her private parade.

At the top of the steps, Alice led Anne Marie into the room where Dean Kirby had spent the night. "The Greco-Roman piece is in the room to our left, if you really care to see it. I thought we could talk about other things more profitably, though."

The chime was blowing in the corner again, and Alice looked from it to the window, which was once more open. This time she was damned sure she'd closed it, though she supposed the Beasley girl might have used it as a possible route of entry and exit. She went to close it and felt something snip at her hair. Twisting, she saw Anne Marie running a long fingernail down one of the mobile statues she'd just passed. The statue squirmed as her fingers cut its chest and belly, leaving the black blood to ooze out.

"You know you really need some help controlling these. This one took a stab at you as you passed. Go ahead, feel your neck."

The wind chime was banging now. Alice felt her neck and looked at blood on her fingertips.

"There's a set of spells for controlling elementals." Anne Marie faced the wind chime and drew a pentangle in the air. Alice could see traces of blue where her fingertip had gone. Then the woman made a motion Alice couldn't catch and the chime subsided. "But then these aren't quite elementals, are they? An interesting class of demi-souls. Do you even know what you've done here?"

"Why don't you tell me?"

"Oh no, I'm not good enough for that. If I were, then I'd be in line for Executrix. As it is, my second migration will be my last."

Alice shifted nervously. She'd never met a witch who'd actually migrated. Oh sure, plenty who claimed to be aware of previous reincarnations. But cats reincarnate. Alice couldn't even truthfully say she was aware of a previous life, and she doubted ninety-nine percent of those who said they were. But migrating… a conscious shift from one life to another, taking all the memories intact. She gazed at the blood on her fingers. Why believe this woman? Because she was angry and because she wanted more, that's why.

"If we make a pact, what? What would make you break with a Pentad to join with me?"

"Personal reasons that you don't need to know a lot about. Leave the Pentad's wrath to me. The Pentad hasn't been too successful so far; it may not be for its entirety as long as a non-sister and an *in absentia* member both are allowed to participate."

"So maybe I could use some help. What assurances can we give one another?"

"The same assurances you and that man Aaron seem to have—you're both a bit unsure about what you've raised. I assure you I'm unsure too, but very interested."

"You think it could give you another migration—it's that powerful?"

"Oh yes indeed. I'm sure the two of us can have enough migrating from this to take us content into the twenty-second century."

There was a yelp outside and they went to the window to watch Rex attack one of the statues. Anne Marie's eyebrows lifted when she saw the two-foot chunk of concrete fighting back, catching Rex in the muzzle, before he bit off its arm.

"They… the children never used to be active in the daylight, even with such a dark storm as this," Alice commented.

"Time's coming when you won't dare send your dog out like that." Rex had the statue down now, but not before yelping twice himself. "That's an interesting spell you have on that covered area with the iron bars. Is it part of what you're doing with these elementals, the children, as you call them?"

"No, it's a young whiz kid witch who learned the spell of invisibility and was spying on me. She could be used for summoning a powerful elemental if she's a virgin, though a male would be better."

"Children not being children these days, we can't be too picky about the sex, can we? Maybe we need to take extra care that the little one you're holding doesn't get away."

"She's bound more than tight."

"I trust your judgment implicitly." Rex was now tearing the statue's chest open. Anne Marie shifted her legs slightly open and made small gestures with her hand as she studied the barred-in area. "Do let's talk about these matters more tonight," she said, turning from the window as the statue shattered suddenly in Rex's jaw. She and Alice walked toward the door.

"Do you want me to send my familiar, my Pie?"

"No." Anne Marie laughed. "Just call. I've written the motel number down already. I had a feeling we'd get along."

"And what are you going to tell the Pentad?"

"Oh, the truth, the truth. I'm going to tell them you're much too dangerous to confront now, that we need to regroup and call in another Pentad or so."

"But—how can that help us?"

"Red tape. A week will be wasted—or gained, from our viewpoint. The Matrix is ready to burst right here; and you, I, and your friend Aaron are going to gather all the little baubles it tosses off. They'll be tossed well within a week, with a few prompts."

8.

Night Ryan pulled into Alice Fairbain's driveway, stopping her car in a conspicuous spot. Plenty of cops still wandered the area—she'd passed two patrol cars—so Fairbain wouldn't dare act. How many disappearing teenagers could the police put up with, after all? *It wouldn't be me who disappeared, if it came to a showdown… Pride, Night, pride*, echoed a voice from somewhere.

As her daughter Night—that is, as what was in essence her first migration—Nikki enjoyed enhanced powers. She'd not understood the reason for this, other than the Matrix was somehow tied to the body. Just because her health science teacher said a woman's sexual life came to its fullest after thirty, didn't necessarily mean the life force was greatest then too. Or did it? Sexual magic was supposed to be the most powerful, after all. Night felt Nikki's hot urge toward Martin Edmonds and worried about him even as she worried about the more immediate problem of her friend Abby. She got out of the car, leaving it running as an extra precaution. *Too bad I didn't choose a chimpanzee for a familiar; he could stay as the getaway driver.* Skull shook water at her—it often seemed he could read her mind even beyond the power of summoning.

Night looked at the two-story house ahead. The statues in the lawn combined with the rain and Spanish moss to make the perfect set for a demento movie. Adjusting to the day's memories for the first time, Night realized what had happened to Abby's family that morning and let out a small moan. It was always this way on changing over: whatever had happened to one of them during the interim would begin etching out its memory, usually in order of considered importance rather than time.

Next came Nikki's plan for her: She'd wanted to go to the house and talk with Fairbain, scare her somehow into letting Abby go, at very least stall her so that Abby could get to water and escape as this deluge continued. That plan seemed stupidly slow to Night. She simply walked around back, as the rain was nearly blinding—besides, Fairbain would be occupied with her visitors. If they were the ones from the Pentad, maybe they'd even help if they realized what was going on.

As Night rounded the corner she saw a man within yards of the tarpaulin, lurching in a way that certainly didn't mean Abby any good. Night impetuously ran forward and shoved him sideways just as he reached the shed's door. She then yanked the tarp nearly off, though it stuck on a concrete block. But she had to run from the man, who got up and lurched at her so slowly that she could think *hands* and ward off his fist with the shield she'd summoned that morning. Still, his blow was much more powerful than she could imagine encountering from a human, so she knew he was some sort of elemental. He came again, telegraphing the use of his head as a battering ram. *Head*, she thought, and the stupid beast dropped after hitting her shield. But his power sapped her own. He charged again. This time they both fell, and Night felt sick. She took deep breaths and was ready when he came again. She feinted another stand-off, then collapsed so that he sailed over her and consequently hit a four-foot statue of a caveman and began ripping at its arms as if he'd forgotten her. To her surprise the statue's eyes glimmered blackly and it fought back. She used the time to remove the tarpaulin and open the shed door.

"Night," Abby rasped, looking up through iron bars.

A great deal of salt was pouring from Abby's body in the form of milky water. Night summoned an even deeper, darker raincloud until she could no longer see the house or the creatures fighting.

"I'm almost free," Abby told her. "Is he still around?"

Night shook her head and pointed in the direction of scuffling. "I'm sorry about your parents and sister," she added, remembering that in the shape of Nikki she'd held the girl all morning and helped her with the police and with some business matters, but still wanting to say something simple as friend Night.

Abby nodded and struggled to reach a hand through the iron. Night took her hand and squeezed, waiting for her friend's complete freedom. She saw a form coming through the rain toward the side of the water conditioner shed. It bumped stupidly into the iron rebar, backed up and bumped again, thrashing angrily and tipping the entire iron cage upwards to land sideways and free of the shed. Two black eyes glimmered within feet of her and she knew another statue had come to life. The creature bumped the shed's wooden side now, then fell. Night pulled Abby out and away, even as the creature stood and smashed into the wood again.

"I think they're what killed my family," Abby said, clasping Night.

"That's right, girl. It wasn't me." Night turned to see Alice Fairbain with her rag doll. Aaron was holding a huge umbrella over them. In his other hand he held a pistol.

Bullet, Night thought, and then saying it aloud so that Abby would hear the word even if she wasn't thinking it.

"You two are marvelously adept for little girls. Too bad I already have a partner. Now what do you suppose would happen if Aaron shot you and I hit you—" Alice produced a heavy red monkey wrench—"and Pie sliced you with a razor, and the statue right behind…"

The girls looked to find no statue behind them, for it had disappeared. Alice laughed at their gullibility. "Why don't you just do as we say, and maybe you won't get hurt at all. All we want is to talk with Nikki Ryan and—you wouldn't happen to be her daughter, would you?"

Night didn't answer, for she was busy summoning lightning. But some force hindered her, an outside force that she wasn't even sure Alice was aware of. Still, with time…

An unearthly scream sounded out front. It repeated, over what must have been a bullhorn, sing-songing a dizzy chant of half meaningless words and screeches. "Llamma, llama wicca. Jee-sus! Jee-sus!" The last was coughed out, then the singsong began again. "Llamma, llama, wicca. Ovnum ores ablo. Miheera onte. Miheera onte altum."

"It's that stupid Jackson bitch!" Fairbain hissed, half-turning to the human lobster beside her.

The voice came from the side of the house and was definitely nearing. A police siren sounded briefly and a car door slammed. Another voice yelled out:

"Mrs. Jackson! You can't go back there. Ms. Fairbain has a restraining order on you, remember."

The pig-Latin voice only got louder. Alice slapped at Aaron's hand when he turned the gun in that direction. Then she quickly told the two girls: "Unless you two want to be prosecuted for trespassing, I suggest you leave by the far side of the house. And I suggest you stay away. And tell your mother, dear, that if she wants to ask questions she should come around herself and not send a girl. And child, I didn't kill your parents. So get that out of your head."

"Jeeeeeeeeeeee-sus! Holy One forever. Agha kata non. Say mal le fructo issum ist omne man."

"Mrs. Jackson!"

"Go on, leave. Now."

"What about the notion that's restraining me?" Night asked.

"What notion?" Alice asked sharply.

Night smiled and ran away with Abby, dodging a swipe from Pie. Once they reached the car, Abby was afraid to get in with the hawk until Night convinced Skull to sit in the back and change into something less threatening. The police had tried to block them from behind, but they simply ran the car through a fence. Abby looked back at the tangled wire and clapped her hands. Night felt the odd restraining spell lift the moment they were off Fairbain's property. And Alice Fairbain hadn't known about it…

"I hate her. I'm going to fix her and her little rag doll both."

"You can't hurt the doll, Abby. You know that. No matter what you do, you can't kill it."

"I'll find a way. Do you believe what she said about not killing my parents?"

"I think the statues killed them."

"That's the same as her, isn't it?"

Her tone carried a meanness that made Night look. Abby's skin bled in many places where she'd scratched at the salt, and she was shivering from the rain and the cuts. Night turned on the heater. As they drove past the Settles' burned-out house Abby burst into tears.

"Mrs. Ryan, I'm hurting so much. I just want to go to sleep."

At the words, "Mrs. Ryan," Night pulled to the side of the road, into what was left of an abandoned orange grove, and held her. Maybe it *would* be as well to change back to Nikki now; a mistake like Abby just made would betray her secret to whoever had placed a restraining notion on her. Was someone from the Pentad collaborating? Night began the change, taking it slowly so as not to disturb Abby who was leaning on her shoulder. The rain slacked now that she wasn't forcing a storm; it was only a regularly blinding Florida rain where one could see a hundred feet ahead by paying close attention. She did pay close attention and saw flashing blue lights. She was relatively certain Fairbain had held her cool, so the woman named Jackson had probably lost hers in the confrontation. Witchcraft had its share of weirdos, but it didn't corner the market: Christianity grabbed plenty off life's remainder table too.

The patrol car slowed. Still mostly Night, she played the

role. She lit a cigarette, spewed the nasty smoke in a stream at her windshield and opened a Coke from the back seat, motioning Skull the cockatiel onto her shoulder. Another world-angry teenager. The cops wouldn't give her a second thought as they drove by… Which they soon did, speeding up as they saw her posing.

After they passed, she threw the cigarette out, coughing. Abby squirmed: "Mrs. Ryan, you know that crazy man you were fighting with? I think it was Dean Kirby."

Kirby? If it truly was Dean Kirby back there, had he caused the call for a back-up patrol car? She didn't have time to pursue the thought, for Abby clung to her, resting her head on her breasts, which Night felt swelling. She wondered how Martin was getting on with the Sisters—and the police. Well, he could take care of himself. No need for Abby to confront the police another time in one day. Her brave little trooper mien was about worn out.

9.

"What the hell are you running down there, anyway? A cop convention? We didn't even bother to get off the inter-state this time. There must of been twenty cops cars at the motel there. Look, you want the kid, you come up here and get him, okay? Soon, 'cause we got another job to get to."

Alice stared at the green telephone receiver. There wasn't a damned thing going right. She'd lost the perfect chance with that Ryan woman's daughter and the Beasley girl; water was flooding Persephone's Escalator and they wouldn't be able to descend for three or four days, which meant they'd have to keep the Kirby brat that long, not to mention picking him up; and there was this new hitch on the scene with this Ann Marie—a good or bad hitch? Was she the one who'd cast a restraining "notion" (what an old-fashioned word for a teenager) on Ryan's daughter? If she did, it didn't seem to do a hell of a lot of good.

"I heard." Alice told the kidnapper on the phone and hung up. She turned to see Aaron posing like a slab of bologna. One more in the long list of problems. What had she gotten herself into? Alice took a breath before speaking to him. He'd been absolutely gleeful as they were tormenting the Beasley girl, but moody after getting scratched by the shouting Jackson woman. Moody even when the second cop on the scene pulled out those new plastic handcuffs to twist on the crazed Christian. What would he do when he found out they'd taken on a new partner? Sing *Deutschland* Über *Alles* and shoot off his gun?

"There's nothing to do but go get the boy." Alice had been holding the receiver button down with her finger, angrily trying to cut the plastic with her nail.

"You should be more careful of the thugs that you hire."

She started to give a withering look but stopped on seeing the dark scowl on his face. Things definitely were getting out of hand. And where the hell was Pie in all this rain?

10.

Pie had waited by the police car, and when the Jackson woman was placed in the back seat she'd hopped in. By the time they turned on Highway 54, Maureen Jackson had beat herself senseless by screaming and hitting her head against the Plexiglas divider. Then Pie climbed up Maureen's sopping wet flower print skirt and poked her until she woke. When Maureen opened her eyes, Pie grinned and slit her throat.

The officer driving saw blood spattering the Plexiglas and jumped onto the curb, bending a no parking sign to a sixty-degree tilt. When he saw the woman's neck he radioed for an ambulance and jumped out of the car, waving over the officer who'd first been on the scene as he opened the back door. Both of them saw something bright red fall from the back seat, but were too busy trying to stop Maureen Jackson's bleeding to search. Before the ambulance arrived, she was dead. They figured that what had fallen from the car must have held the razor she used to cut the plastic cuffs and kill herself. They searched nearly an hour but couldn't find it.

At McDonalds's, a quarter mile back, Pie spotted a woman who lived on the road before Alice Fairbain's. She was with her child, an eight-year-old girl. Pie lay down beside the passenger's door and waited for the girl to pick her up.

"Where'd you get that thing?" the mother asked, eating a french fry as they drove off the lot.

"I found her outside the door."

"It's wet and has ketchup all over it. Throw it out."

"Noooooooooooooooooooo!"

"All right, fine. But you're going to have to wash it as soon as we get home."

"You like French fries, Miss Rag Doll?"

Pie inched its smile upwards for the girl.

11.

The police questioned the five women remaining in the Pentad for four hours that afternoon. During that time four phone calls were made. The first was to Denise Beaufort in Kentucky. Though she'd decided against joining the Pentad, Nancy and Beth were keeping in touch with her—despite the ominous overturned plate and Jewel's admonitions that she were best left out. But the present crisis was important, for the police seemed to be on the verge of detaining all five of them, and Denise and her husband were both lawyers. Within an hour of the conversation, a lawyer friend of the two contacted the chief investigating officer and the threats of jail were allayed. "Right now we're looking for one or two males, clearly psychotic," he admitted. "On the other hand, it does seem an odd coincidence that Ms. Ryan should know all the victims. Two detectives saw her talking with you in the dining room a few hours ago."

"She never met Becky," Jewel corrected. "And she really only knew the girl Abby, not the parents or the sister. And I had her in a class."

The detective nodded. "You understand I have to make links where I can. Ms. Ryan is an airline stewardess. Maybe she met someone…" He opened his palms in a gesture of questioning and Jewel nodded.

The second phone call was from Nikki to the hotel room. The police let her speak with Jewel, though a policeman stood by listening to the conversation, the upshot of which was that Nikki invited all five women to stay at her house. Jewel agreed, thinking, as the policeman took notes, that the Pentad had a better chance of reforming in Nikki's house, away from the influence and aura of what happened to Becky. Near the end of the call, Nikki asked, "Do you think they'll let me talk to Martin?" Martin, of course, was being held with the women, since he originally contacted the police about Becky.

It was often said of Jewel Dawn, in all four of her migrations, that she had remarkable powers of persuasion. Jewel always thanked her admirer and fingered the crystal an adept Philadelphia jeweler had cut for her when she fled to that city as Rebel forces threatened to invade Washington in 1864. The crystal was to have been a gift for Mary Todd Lincoln, but that of course never came to be after the assassination. She'd been fingering this crystal while she talked on the phone and the nearby policeman had been staring at its glittering rays. So when she said, "It would be all right for Ms. Ryan to talk with Dr. Edmonds, wouldn't it?" The policeman naturally answered yes. So she handed the phone to Martin.

"I'm fine," both Jewel and the policeman heard Martin say into the phone. Then they both saw him blush a fine crimson. "Yes I could deal with it… Well, because people are standing here listening, Nikki… No more demented than anyone else right now." Martin laughed nervously, then he stopped to listen intently. "Oh?… Oh. Good God. Do you think she was right?… Okay, okay. I'll tell the police… Of course not… I'll phone the hospital and confirm… Yes, at your place." He blushed again, though in a more distracted way. "Yes, very therapeutic… Really? I'm finding out things every day. You'll convert me yet."

He hung up and said he needed to talk with the head detective. "Abby thought she saw Dean Kirby," he told them. "He's just insane enough that he could be behind all this."

Jewel lifted her brows doubtfully as they trudged two doors down to find the detective, thinking, *It certainly didn't take Nyx Ryan all that time to relay that single bit of information.* Jewel appraised Martin's gait as he walked ahead. He was handsome, she just hoped he wouldn't distract Nikki from the main business at hand. Paul had never done that… until his death.

The third call was from Anne Marie to Alice Fairbain. Anne Marie called by Denny's ladies' room, where no policeman listened in: "There's been a bit going on here at the motel. The cup keeper of the Pentad was killed."

"Killed? I didn't—"

"I know you didn't. Even though the shield we summoned was weak, it wasn't paltry. For what it's worth, I gather the police see some similarity to this girl's death and those of your neighbors."

Silence.

"You do see what I mean about needing more control, don't you?"

Silence.

"I'm going to have to leave for a while," Fairbain told Anne Marie. "It's important for that very control that I do. When do you think the cops will clear out?"

"Clear out? I think they're going to be camping here like Boy Scouts for weeks. If you're worried about being stopped, wait at least three more hours. Sundown is always a pleasant time to drive. I'll do what I can to help from this point. Meanwhile, can't you work some minor spells to shrink your aura? It has a nasty orange tint to it that would even make a cop, as you say, suspicious."

"I'll keep that in mind."

"Good. It's meant as quite serious advice, you know, since I have a vested interest in you. Try light-hued candles and meditation. And some lotion on your hands and some lipstick, mascara, and perfume wouldn't hurt. By the way, I'll be traveling too. We're spending tonight with a woman named Nikki Ryan. Do you know her? Jewel took her in as the *in absentia* member."

"*Nyx* Ryan. Yes. And if you don't mind *my* presumption, partner, you need to be careful around her. Did you leave a spell hovering around my house, say around the water conditioner shed we saw from the window?"

"No," Anne Marie said. "Why do you ask?" she peeled at the blue wallpaper by the ladies room.

"Well if you did, it didn't work, and I think the person it didn't work on was Nyx—Nikki Ryan's daughter."

"Indeed." Anne Marie peeled more vigorously. "I *will* be careful. We'll both be careful. Remember, our little Becky was killed in a very similar fashion to the—Beasleys, is that their name?"

"It was their name," Alice said.

"*Was* is a verb I'd as soon avoid, don't you think, partner?"

On the fourth and last phone call, the detective in charge of the investigation heard that a prisoner en route to the detention center managed to kill herself with a razor blade not a quarter mile from the hotel. Evidently they'd need to place an officer every ten yards in this area to keep it safe. He shook his head and wondered why he just didn't go home and get drunk, blow off a couple of fingers with some fireworks and retire early.

12.

Nikki had several domestic, practical, and magical preparations to make before her guests arrived. On the phone she'd threatened to "crawl all over" Martin's bones if the day ever finished. It had slipped out, and Mother of God knew she needed some kind of release from the mess the day was in. But as soon as she said it, she began to think that some sexual magic might just fit the bill of fare, which was escalating far beyond escargot and Dom Perignon into caviar and LaFitte Rothschild, 1964. She'd have to assure that tonight's sleeping arrangements were cooperative with her plan.

Thinking of that, she peeked in to make sure Abby was still asleep. Yes, and still clutching a large tan teddy bear that Night won at last year's county fair. Her breathing was slow, so Nikki closed the door and walked to where the kitchen looked out on the lake, for she intended to perform a banishing ritual both there and at her front door.

Mist was rising from the lake, since the sun was heating the late afternoon in grand Florida fashion. Her next-door neighbor Agnes was sloshing about. After a rain like this her yard could have no less than an inch of standing water, yet there Agnes stood in house slippers with a paint brush and bucket of paint. It would be a miracle if a moccasin didn't bite her. Nikki laid down a black cloth and lit three candles, but stopped the ceremony to watch her neighbor.

Agnes was just the kind of eccentric who would have been burned as a witch in the Middle Ages. Real witches had enough sense, mostly, to keep their practices hidden, but this woman would have been crackle-fuel. She would have admitted, by the time the Inquisition finished with her, to flying on broomsticks and any other male fantasy the monks and priests concocted. Yes your lordship, the Devil's penis is barbed and red and tinged with hot peppers and spews vinegar. It's a foot and a half long. Of course we all love it, wouldn't you? No offense to your holiness.

Nikki watched the woman slosh to her frog pond, whose concrete lip jutted only inches above ground and threatened to meld with the lake if the water rose any higher. Nikki felt a tinge of guilt for not befriending Agnes more, maybe building up her pond for her; it wouldn't take more than three sacks of concrete mix. Agnes bent to look at something—she had amazingly large goldfish considering that her pond was only six feet in diameter—then she straddled the wall and stepped in the water to—well, it looked like she was talking with a statue that spewed water from its mouth. She patted the statue's head—a caricature of an Irishman with top-hat, wine nose and all; then she dipped her brush and started to paint the statue a godawful crimson, indiscriminately dabbing as if the little Irishman had contracted measles. Nikki swayed at the lunacy of the scene. Suddenly the little man wrested the brush from Agnes to jab at her eye; she clutched and fell head first into the pond…

"No! Mrs. Thompson!"

Nikki ran out the back door, hearing the screen bang behind. When she hit the yard her bare feet splashed warm water. Her neighbor looked up and smiled. She'd laid the can down and was shooing a goldfish. Nikki started, realizing she'd hallucinated the statue's attack.

"Hello, Nikki. I'm going to paint Patrick here a bright green. Do you think he'll like it?"

Only a low row of peppermint azaleas separated their yards. Nikki hopped over these.

"I'd like to be that spry. Do you think I could go to one of these spas and work out and do that?"

Nikki blinked and walked up to Mrs. Thompson's smiling face, her two twinkling eyes.

"What'd you think I was going to do, child? Jump in my pond and drown myself?"

"No, no, not at all." Nikki eyed the goofy, smiling statue: it wasn't one of Fairbain's, but an ancient dime store purchase. "It's really too wet to be painting, Mrs. Thompson. Why don't you come over for a nice cup of hot tea."

"Too wet?" The woman looked around, then down at her feet. "I suppose it is. You say hot tea?"

Nikki nodded and searched for Skull. She spotted him high in a cypress, once more a red-tailed hawk. He was staring at the road.

"Let's go inside, Mrs. Thompson. I'm baking cinnamon bread."

"Cinnamon bread? You mean toast?"

"No, cinnamon bread."

"You do cook the strangest concoctions."

As they walked in, Nikki saw Skull swoop toward the road. He lifted a small snake in his talons.

"How's your daughter, dear? I really wonder why the two of you never come over for dinner together. It's not good for mother and daughter to be apart all the time." Agnes opened the screen door and stepped in to wipe her feet on the black ritual mat, ruining its usefulness. Nikki banged her forehead with her palm. Luckily, there were more mats in the house.

"I've got a friend of hers staying with me. Abby Beasley."

"The same Beasley whose family—"

"You've heard, then?"

"But that just happened this morning. The poor girl must be—"

"That's why she's staying here."

Mrs. Thompson's false teeth combined with her humped back and snowy hair to make her resemble a turnip. "If you've got that little girl, you've got your hands full and don't need to entertain me." She turned to back out the door but Nikki blocked her.

"On the contrary, I need you plenty. I've got to go to the store, and I can't leave the girl alone in her state. If you could talk to her, take her to your house and maybe show her your husband's stone collection. Or even better, bring it over here, because she needs to be somewhere familiar," Nikki paused to sigh, "it would be a great help to both of us."

Agnes Thompson's eyes lit.

Nikki congratulated herself on accomplishing several things: making Mrs. Thompson feel useful, keeping Abby company, getting out to make last minute purchases—and bringing Agnes's semi-precious stone collection in the house. For in it were two of the largest uncut emeralds she'd ever seen. Worth a tidy sum, surely, but worth even more as a double talisman against evil intent…

Two hours later Agnes went home, though Abby, on Nikki's advice, sweet-talked her into leaving the stones. One hour after that, the Pentad joined in Nikki's house. She shooed Martin and Abby into the kitchen and the Pentad was re-formed because of Becky's death. This Pentad was nowhere near as powerful as Nikki felt it could be. She tried to draw on Night's youthful strength and even half-migrated under a heavy cover of make-up, a startling show of control over anything she'd accomplished before, and she mused that her mentor Jewel had somehow inspired her. Midway through the ceremony, Nikki could see that Jewel suspected something, though none of the others did—save maybe Anne Marie, who'd rarely taken her eyes off Nikki since stepping into the house. After the summoning, the Sisters seemed pleased with what they'd done, feeling it far superior to that morning's Pentad and its shield of power. *Let's hope so*, Nikki thought, knowing she'd been right on keeping the emeralds in the house: they allayed the effects of a present evil intent, though even they couldn't work perfectly.

Abracadabra! She turned from witch to hostess and went for tea. Martin, in the kitchen with Abby, was making long distance calls to St. Veronica's and consulting with the Pasco sheriff's office about Dean Kirby. Abby had been peeking around the corner, big-eyed at seeing her first coven ritual. She winked at Nikki, and Nikki wondered if she'd spotted the changeover to Night.

No sooner had she winked, though, than she began bawling, and Martin and Nikki both gathered around her, enclosing her in their own circle of warmth—and power.

At twilight they all sat on the back patio watching July Fourth fireworks. Mrs. Thompson came over, jumping with each blast, and Nikki noticed an amused look on Jewel's face. Catching Jewel alone in a bedroom, Nikki found out that she'd known Agnes from a previous migration.

"She's 90 years old if she's a day. When I first met her she was a firebrand marching for temperance. Now she brings over a bottle of sherry and downs half. It goes to show there's hope in the world: you can migrate even without witchcraft." Jewel picked up a pair of bifocals. "Speaking of migrating, I have a feeling that you've been extremely successful. Where exactly is your daughter now, by the way?"

If anyone would guess besides Abby, it would be Jewel Dawn, who'd tutored Nikki twice, once as Nyx, once as her daughter Night.

"You've become quite a powerful Sister, my young amanuensis. Did you know that Anne Marie and I found out through the cards that she wasn't to be my successor?"

Nikki shook her head.

"Oh yes, we checked it several times, using cards, runes, and even a glass ball—which I've never held in much esteem. All agreed. Anne Marie took it quite nobly at the time."

Jewel ended her phrase, "at the time," in such a way that Nikki looked up, but there was laughter from the kitchen and Abby called her name. Jewel grabbed her wrist.

"Just as Agnes Thompson can change for the better, others can change for the worse. Keep that in mind if I'm not around." At Nikki's questioning look, Jewel simply gave her a kiss on the cheek and urged her to the door. "Your own young amanuensis needs all the affection she can get right now to ensure she doesn't embrace the left hand path and become totally immersed in her plans for vengeance."

At midnight bottle rockets flew over the lake. In the light of the rockets, Nikki glanced to Agnes's frog pond. Was the dime store Irishman still there, or another statue? She searched the trees for Skull but couldn't see him. Near the lake, she thought she saw a cypress stump sway—impossible, of course. Then she spotted the movement of a chalk-white cat—or statue. She felt the muscles in Martin's wiry arm tense as he asked if she had a hammer in the house. So he'd seen it too.

The day finally weighed on everyone. One by one they drifted off to their assigned sleeping areas. Mrs. Thompson invited Abby and Jewel over to her house and Nikki barely managed to slip one of the emeralds from the case before Agnes took the stones back. Nikki looked at the statue in the frog pond; it was the reassuring, laughing Irishman, and the white cat really was a white cat. Skull had changed into an owl and was gently cooing outside behind the Spanish moss, so Nikki felt comfortable with that sleeping arrangement and even more comfortable with the sleeping arrangement in her room.

She led Martin inside. Closing her curtain so that the moon wouldn't show through even though it was waxing, she turned off the light and clasped him. At the same time, she began to migrate. The thought had niggled her for two days that young Night needed help in her maturation as a witch. Night had to lose her virginity to fully participate in the Matrix. Blood and Birth. Love and hate. Life and death. It was a dirty trick to play on Martin—he'd no doubt have to quit the psychologist's union for sleeping with a virgin eighteen-year-old. But then again, she wasn't eighteen in any normal sense of the word, Nikki/Night told herself as she felt Martin's caresses and kisses make her breasts and buttocks tighten, her labia swell and open.

"What does a psychologist have to say about a couple making love after a day like today?" Night worried that her teenage voice might startle Martin. But he was tired enough that he didn't notice.

"The death-sex urge. Freud caught psychiatry up with poetry when he postulated that death and sex ruled human passions. In the Renaissance, a poetic euphemism for making love was *dying*."

"Show me, show me," Night giggled.

"Nikki?" Martin asked, tensing.

Night buried her head in his chest and bit hard enough that he forgot his question. She then bit her own lips to hold back the pain as he penetrated moments later; at the same time she saw a dazzle of lights. "Blood and Birth," she mouthed, welcoming her full power.

As she hoped, Martin proved a kind lover, for a second dazzle swept her thirty minutes later. They held one another a while longer then she stood to go to the bathroom, nearly floating in the change that had come upon Night Ryan's young body. Touching the bathroom door, she halted, seeing/sensing an odd glow from the living room. She peeked around the corner, keeping its warm wood close to her nose. She saw Anne Marie on the couch, bathed in an ugly violet aura, her mouth agape as if she were dead. So Jewel was right in suspecting her. Night saw an exhalation swirling like thin blue cigarette smoke, glowing in the dark. Was she letting her soul out, or evil in? Was there a difference? Anne Marie's body twitched and Night inhaled sharply. Too many emotions pulling now for a confrontation. But that there would be one, she had no doubt.

13.

Quail Hollow Estates was understandably quiet and nervous that night; still, other developments close by had no fear. Rockets and firecrackers from these subdivisions awoke Dean Kirby as July 4 began in earnest. He looked down at his leg to see that his foot had been severed. He gagged in anticipation of pain, but there was none. His entire body, in fact, was amazingly pain-free except for a dull sloughing of his skin and a pervasive odor that hung in his throat to make him thirst for ice. Peripherally, he saw the toes of the severed foot pushing in the wet muck to rejoin his stump. In the light of a half moon the blood covering his foot and stump blended blackly with the muck. Then he remembered:

Cain! Cain! Cain!

No. Not that. Remember: You fought with a girl, but she dodged and you began fighting one of the statues. Remember hitting its skull and watching it burst apart, spreading a black fluid into the rain, onto the ground? While you were laughing, two other statues sliced and stabbed you with rocks and pieces of metal. Then Dean pictured Annie digging, insanely digging the sand, left that way by Alice Fairbain. Annie had been alive the whole time they were in Atlanta. The whole time. Through the tangle of bushes he'd been thrown into, he could see Fairbain's house, lights on in a top turret room and in a lower room to his left. He could make out Aaron lumbering around. Suddenly Dean felt his foot, very cool like a snake's skin, attach itself to his leg. There was a brief shock of pain as cool blood ascended his leg and worked toward his heart.

He swayed, thinking of Annie digging with that pitchfork—no doubt Fairbain's idea of a joke. Tonight he'd kill Fairbain. Then he need only find his son to be released from

~297~

this curse—no, not a curse; it was for Bobby and worth it. A blessing. He saw Fairbain in the window; she was arguing with Aaron.

Cain! Cain! Cain!

The shotgun. Where was it? He tried to remember, but could dredge up only fetid smells, not a memory. *Think.*

A bubbling emerged under the apple tree, in the strange sculpture Fairbain called—what did she call it? God, he had to kill her soon, or he wouldn't remember to remember. He looked past the bubbling to the kiln. There was movement, a small white-gray opossum tearing at something bulky. Oh yes, the dog. He'd killed Fairbain's dog. That's where the gun was. He walked through rising mist, listening to crickets and a grand chorus of frogs from the surrounding wetlands. The opossum was tearing at the dog's lips. It heard him and scuttled off with a hiss. Dean stooped for the shotgun. Scuffling furniture and breaking glass sounded from the far room. Shotgun in hand, he walked in that direction, intent on killing Fairbain and Aaron.

Once there, Dean let out a groan that hung wetly in his throat as if skin were dropping off. Bobby? Could it be him? Yes! Bobby was somehow here, and he was being tied to a chair, but he managed to kick a lamp over even as Fairbain and Aaron tied him. Dean couldn't shoot without hitting his son. Fairbain ran from the room, then back, pushing Aaron aside and spraying Bobby with what looked like a can of hair spray. Bobby howled and gasped for breath. When they finished tying him, the two stood back, coughing themselves. *Now*, Dean thought and pulled the trigger. Nothing happened. Either the shell had gotten soaked or the firing pin had jammed with grit.

Aaron walked over to draw the curtains and Dean ducked.

He could hear them saying they would leave the boy for the night.

"Persephone is too wet, anyway," Aaron said. "We won't be able to take him down."

"What about the new entrance?"

"That ground's even lower than this. Four days, maybe five."

Dean heard furniture being shuffled, then the door closing. He held the gun at an angle to catch moonlight: gritty water dribbled from the breech. Fifteen minutes later, he heard the back door open. He could see Alice Fairbain setting a bowl down.

"Rex? Come on, boy." She called again, then said, "Your loss, Rex, the fire ants' gain." The door closed and the light went out.

Dean stared at the yard. A belch came from the sculpture—Persephone's Elevator, that's what she called it. Another belch as if a giant bubble were forcing its way through rainwater. In the house, one light went out; soon, the last, leaving the yard in darkness except for the moon. Dean tried the window. It wasn't locked, but rain had swollen the wood. He heaved and managed to move it several inches when he heard the back door open. He crouched and watched Aaron step out.

"Rex? Rex, *Kommen sie, hund.*"

Then Aaron walked to the sculptured hole and looked down, tossing something in with a splash. Dean could hear a short curse; then he saw Aaron cut straight through the field, heading for his old place. Was that what Annie'd been standing in front of? A second Persephone, whatever the hell that—was Persephone a hole to hell?

Cain! Cain! Cain!

Dean moved from the hole, surprised to find himself there, when he'd just been at the back window. He had to pay attention. He had to concentrate on Bobby. Something dropped from his tonsil and he caught his breath as it slid down his throat. He heard Bruno laugh and tried to suppress him, but couldn't, so he concentrated on Aaron's receding form, the fog that lifted about his motion. There was another belch from Persephone, and steam rising. *Cain! Cain! Cain!*

Dean hit himself and there was more laughter. As it finally faded Dean ran to the window. In minutes he lifted it and was inside. "Bobby," he called, walking through the room. But his voice rasped and he knew Bobby wouldn't recognize it.

"Bobby, it's me, your father."

There was scuffling and straining from the chair Bobby was tied to, then panting through the gag.

"Bobby, I know why you've been afraid of me." Dean winced at his voice, so wet, like a fan was chopping his words. "You think I'm already dead, and that's partially true. But I planned this. I did it for your sake. You've got to understand that your mother tried to kill me, but that it wasn't her doing; it was Alice Fairbain's. I saw your mom today, Bobby. You were right. She's been alive all this time. She's resting now. She's happy once more, Bobby. Do you understand what I'm telling you? She want—" Dean stopped to swallow— "She wanted me to save you, she knew Fairbain had managed to kidnap you from the hospital, and she wanted me to save you from becoming like her, like me. It was her last wish, Bobby, and it's mine too. I'm going to cut you loose and I'm going to give you a key… to a car." Dean swayed and gasped for air. "A blue Ford Mustang rental car. It's at the Day's Inn. You remember the Day's Inn by the

Interstate? That's where the car's at. You need to go there the moment I cut you loose. I want you to drive to Atlanta and call your grandma. Understand? Don't worry about me or your mother. There's nothing to do now. But you remember us and remember that we loved you, okay?" Dean was wheezing. *Why is it coming so fast? I'm supposed to have a year!* He leaned on a table. His eyes adjusted and he could see Bobby staring. Dean shook, thinking a maggot was creeping down his cheek, but it was a tear. He looked for something to cut the ropes with and found scissors on a bookcase, but on turning with them and seeing the look on his son's face, he quickly put them down.

"All right, son. I'll just undo the knots with my hands. You at least can trust me with that. Nod if you do."

In the faint light, Bobby gave an even fainter nod, so Dean worked silently, leaving Bobby gagged until he was sure he wouldn't yell, thinking a ghoul was the greater evil than Alice Fairbain. At last he could feel the boy relax, so he undid the gag.

"Dad, Dad, you've got to go with me. Maybe someone can help you. Dr. Edmonds in Atlanta is smart. Maybe—"

They could hear a shuffling upstairs. "Aaron?" was called faintly; then steps descended.

Dean threw the ropes back in Bobby's lap and pulled up the gag. He ran to close the window, which fortunately went down easier than it had gone up. Then he picked up the wet shotgun and walked to the door…

Which opened momentarily. "Having nightmares about Momma and Daddy, Bobby-kin?"

Cain! Cain! Cain! Dean managed to hold himself and Bruno back. The door was held open a minute, then shut. The steps ascended the stairs once more and the light went out.

Dean finished freeing Bobby and the two of them started out the window. Bobby made a face when he looked at his father and took the shotgun from him. After climbing out, Dean could see that Bobby wanted to hug him but couldn't bring himself to. *What must I look like?* Dean wondered. He saw where his arm had been cut deeply in the fight with the statues that afternoon. Its skin puffed a lip of blackened flesh and blood. He lifted his hands to his face, feeling another gash on his right cheek. As he did this, he felt the boy about his waist.

"Dad, please come with me. Please. A doctor can take care of you." But Bobby withdrew after hearing Dean breathe.

"Go to your grandma, Bobby. I can't even make it to the motel."

"I'll call an ambulance when I get there. Promise you'll wait by the Settles' house for an ambulance. I'll run all the way to the motel and tell them someone's been run over on Greenwillow. They'll come. Let's walk there now."

Bobby was carrying the gun. Too tired to argue, Dean followed. The creek outside Alice Fairbain's gurgled from the rains. Dean halted and swayed, thinking of Annie. He felt a tug. Ten minutes later Bobby propped him behind the Settles' shed.

"Stick to the road, son. Stick to the road. Anything comes near, you can run and hide. You're a track star, remember. A star—" Dean began coughing again. Bobby's eyes widened.

"Stay, Dad. Stay here. There'll be an ambulance in no time."

Fifteen minutes later, Dean heard a shotgun blast and looked to see that Bobby hadn't taken the gun. He hadn't, so everything was okay, it was okay. It was okay, just someone shooting possums or snakes.

JULY FIFTH, MORNING:
INTERLUDE
JULY SIXTH:
DIES IRAE, DIES IRA

1.

No matter where you were in Pasco County on July 5th, you knew about the murders.

Quail Hollow, wasn't that where the little girl disappeared a year ago?

Not even a year. It was just last November.

Did you hear about that woman killing herself in a police car? Don't cops check people for weapons?

They say she hid a razor blade. But my cousin works for the sheriff's office and said that once the coroner saw her, he couldn't see how she did it all by herself.

You mean the cop did it?

No one knows. He couldn't have; he was driving.

I heard there was another killing at the hotel there. Some woman from Kentucky.

A bunch of them from Kentucky from what I hear. Some women's club or something.

I met Vera Beasley once. She brought her youngest girl, the one that got killed, to swimming lessons.

They say the older daughter, the one who's still alive, is a queer bird.

Do you think she did it? There's so much drugs in the schools that you can't tell up from down now.

Did you hear? Someone else has been killed. A teenage kid prowling around was shot and killed by a woman.

He wasn't killed. He's in the hospital. I think the husband shot the kid, not the woman.

I bet the kid's the one who did it all. We ought to go pull his tubes and save the damned state of Florida some money.

I heard it was that kid they thought did the little Settles' girl in for a while last year.

That professor's kid? I heard that kid had the foulest mouth this side of the Gulf of Mexico.

And no matter where you were or what you thought in Pasco County, you looked to the sky all day long, for clouds formed and re-formed, shifting as if they wanted to let hell loose but couldn't quite do so because sunlight was evaporating the condensing water just a fraction too rapidly.

Some people in Pasco County thought they heard a low chant: *Cain! Cain! Cain!*

The preacher at Everlasting Waters Assembly crossed himself in the dark of his garage. It was something heathen he'd been taught to do by a Catholic uncle. But he did it anyway, feeling the back of his neck tingle as a cloud's shadow scudded over the three orange trees he planned on pruning.

Abby spent the entire day crying, the loss of her family finally hitting her as she heard Nikki making arrangements with the funeral director. Hearing her constant sobs deadened Jewel and the remainder of the Pentad, who thought of Becky. At noon, Denise's husband called to say that she was flying down.

"No!" Jewel shouted into the landline phone.

But Anne Marie, on the other extension, sweetly offered to drive and pick her up, and nothing Jewel could say could change the fact that Denise was already on a plane, her husband said. "She knew you'd try to talk her out of it," he added.

Before Anne Marie left, Nikki sneaked the emerald into the trunk of her Trans-Am, which Anne Marie had asked to take to the airport. The moment Anne Marie started the car, she turned to give Nikki a huge scowl, sensing the emerald. Not only the emerald, but a real doozy of a banishing spell. Nikki waved and smiled. Anne Marie got out of the car. "I think I'll just rent a more sedate car," she said. "This one's much too sporty for me."

Three hours before, Aaron found Rex—by his nose as Prince Hamlet would say. Aaron suspected several *kinder* had killed him, but Alice saw the open window and ran to check on their hostage, whom she found gone. She softly hit her head against the wall and called for Pie, but Pie was nowhere around and hadn't been since the Jackson woman yesterday. Things were disintegrating like salt in rain. "Pie, Pie," Alice sobbed in a singsong. When she first created Pie another witch had warned against it, citing an infamous incident where a witch ordered a doll to watch the front entrance to her hutch, but because of an argument over clothes, the doll purposefully ignored riders approaching the side entrance, rationalizing that its command had been to watch only the front. For a hundred years the doll played over the spot where its mistress died until a local viscount ordered the creature caged, weighted and dropped into the deepest part of a nearby mountain lake.

Was that how the story ended, Alice wondered, watching Aaron put Rex in a wheelbarrow and dump him on a compost pile. "Pie, Pie," she sang softly until Aaron came in. She grew quiet for fear of angering him, and they separately drove the area looking for the boy, though Alice spent her time stopping to inspect scraps of cloth.

2.

No one could blame the sheriff's office for not reporting to Doctor Martin Edmonds that Bobby Kirby had been shot as an intruder and was in critical but stable condition. No one could blame that office, for besides the day's five violent deaths, there had been two unrelated domestic squabbles involving gunplay—one ended in property damage, the other in hospitalization; there had been three hold-ups of convenience stores; there had been a drug-related shootout in Dade City and another in New Port Richey; a hit and run death on S.R. 54; two rapes; six bar fights; at least eight break-ins. Pasco County, like all of Florida and all of America, was on a roll.

So at 5:30, while Jewel was talking with the newcomer Denise and the others and while Mrs. Thompson was showing Abby how to fish, Martin watched the local news to learn that a young boy who had been a suspect in last year's slaying of Cristy Settles was shot and wounded in a development just over the Pasco County line. Martin ran and asked to borrow Nikki's car, telling her why. In the commotion, Anne

Marie walked outside toward Abby and Mrs. Thompson…

3.

The Dade City hospital where Bobby lay was an hour's drive, much of it through vast acreage called Swiftmud Water District, which looked to Martin like farmland. Overhead in a power line perched a giant nest. He scanned it and thought of Nikki's body, so young and soft. In an odd flash he thought he remembered awakening at dawn and seeing Night next to him in bed. Wish fulfillment, Doctor Freud. No, that was a bad joke; it was Nikki who enchanted him, not her teenage daughter. But what could come of a love affair like this, her living in one city, him another. Well, it wasn't like he didn't have money for air fare: St. Veronica's paid well. And if that failed, Nikki could always ride her broom up.

This gave him pause. After what had happened to the man of science in the barn, the man of science had to wonder if the science of psychology wasn't a weak sister in the pantheon. Supposedly, Freud said that if he had his life to live over he'd research only the supernatural. Death-bed wish fulfillment, Herr Freud?

Five cows ambled under an oak to his left to disappear into a cypress stand and Spanish moss. Very symbolic, Martin thought. The veil of Maya. The world is an illusion that we think we know, but really don't. Nothing's real.

His neck cricked and he turned the car's air conditioner down. That's it: he simply needed a manipulation. If he were a chiropractor, this could all be explained by a disjointed joint. If he were a surgeon, it would all be something that could be cut out—a benign tumor pressing his optical nerves, for example. If he were a detective it would be part of some crack cocaine cult a la Charles Manson. If he were a preacher, it would be part of the Devil's machinations. Christ, if he were a hairdresser it'd be too strong a whiff of hair spray.

Martin leaned to peer through the windshield, at first unbelieving. A line of three-foot St. Francises and Holy Virgins were walking the road, at least fifty of them. They were carrying garden implements and their black eyes betrayed their intent. Several veered toward him. *Real or not, this is for Walter.* He gunned his engine and drove over them, skidding off the road. A pickup coming too fast in the opposite direction blew its horn, screeching to a stop but not before hitting one of the Holy Virgins. A young man got out and ran around, shouting, "My god!" A young woman got out from the passenger's side.

"No! Get back in!" Martin yelled through his open window. But the man had already fallen, cut and tripped by the small garden saints crawling over him. The woman went down on the other side of the pickup in a scream. Something hit Martin's head from the roof and a St. Francis with an ear-to-ear grin jumped onto the open window frame jabbing with a garden trowel, gashing Martin's palm. Martin pushed St. Francis off and hit the window button, tromping the gas to get closer to the pickup. But maybe a hundred more Francises and Holy Virgins mingled with a few white lawn jockeys emerged from the cypress. Already a group straddled the young man, sawing at a nearly decapitated head. Three others drug the girl's head and heaved it at him. Martin floored the gas. A Holy Virgin dropped onto his hood—from a tree, he supposed. Even as she fell she scraped the car with a small raking tool, her face most un-virgin, not to mention un-mother-of-God-like. Martin drove over her. She became a white speck in the rearview, then disappeared.

The whole thing had been a Wal-Mart Garden Shop gone berserk. How? Fairbain didn't make those kinds of statues, did she?

Approaching a convenience store and seeing he had cell reception, he started to pull over, but the door's glass and the front windows were broken and goods were strewn in the lot. He rolled down his window. Everything sounded much too quiet, so he drove on. At the hospital he phoned 911 to report an accident on… he didn't know the road's name, but he described it as being near something called Swiftmud. Martin hung up after the dispatcher assured him he knew what road he meant; then Martin called Nikki to warn her of the statues, which couldn't have been more than five miles from her home.

"Denise is here now, but Abby and Mrs. Thompson have disappeared," she said. "The woman named Anne Marie is gone too, disappeared the moment she came back with Denise. Lori says that she kidnapped Abby and Mrs. Thompson. Mrs. Thompson's old Ford is missing."

"I thought your emerald was supposed to prevent all this."

"Technically, they weren't in the house with the emerald."

Martin laughed sharply but Nikki bristled: "If I were a lawyer or atomic scientist you wouldn't laugh; you'd accept that hair-splitting with equanimity, wouldn't you?"

"I'm sorry, Nikki. You're exactly right."

"Okay, everyone's shook up. We were waiting for you to call and we're leaving now. Have you seen the boy yet?"

"No, why? Do you want me to call you back when I see him?" There was a hesitation, and Martin stared at the cut on his palm, it was still bleeding.

"Maybe we *should* wait. He might know something important, eh? We're going to have a confrontation tonight with

Anne Marie and Fairbain and we'll need any information we can get."

"Don't forget Lurch and the five thousand statues."

"No, that would be very unwise."

"Nikki—" Martin broke off for a moment, half from the pain in his hand, half from worry. "Look, Nikki, will you take care of yourself… and Night."

Martin heard silence at the mention of Night. "Same to you… and double," Nikki said, like she was catching her breath.

And double echoed as he walked to the receptionist, who suggested he might want to visit the emergency department. Martin looked at his hand and went to the men's room and returned. With a minimum of hassle from the duty nurse he was able to see Bobby, who evidently had three shotgun pellets hit his throat that caused an inflammation around his larynx. He was using a tablet to write during the brief periods that he had the strength.

"He awoke half an hour ago. He's been getting pretty agitated—"

Bobby recognized Doctor Edmonds and groaned, then motioned for the tablet. *Save my dad* was written on it already. Martin nodded and tore off the paper, handing Bobby the board and a pencil.

"Where is he?" Martin asked.

Settle, Bobby wrote. Martin could see the nurse mouthing the name even as he wrote.

"He's written that fifteen times, tearing it off and dropping it. We finally had to take the board away."

"The Settles house near where you used to live?" Martin asked.

Bobby wrote, *yes*. Then he wrote *A.F. stole me. Dad saved me.*

"Why did Alice Fairbain do that?"

Persefonie's Escalator.

"Did she need—" Martin rephrased his question—"There's something in the escalator, isn't there?"

Cain.

What's Cain?"

Abel. Bobby began to falter and the nurse twisted a knob nearby.

"I think we need to leave him alone now."

"Okay. We're going to help your father, Bobby." But the boy wasn't responding. "Tell him when he awakes that I'm going to help his father. That news will help him too, I think."

The nurse nodded. As Martin walked outside, an ambulance pulled up. The woman on the stretcher had bled through the sheet from head to toe. Her mouth was open in shock and if the attendants hadn't been hurrying so, Martin would have presumed her dead.

He called Nikki on the phone and repeated all that he'd heard.

"Fine. We'll meet you at the Settles. Martin, don't go back on 52. Radio and TV have announced that the road's been closed. You can take the interstate down to 54. Will you recognize everything once you're at the Day's Inn?"

"Too well," Martin answered.

"There's a tire iron in the trunk. Get it out and don't stop for anything."

"You don't have to plead with me on that count. I'm no John Wayne."

"Who knows, Martin? You might turn into an Indiana Jones."

4.

When the sky over Quail Hollow turned overcast Dean Kirby rested; when it became sunny, he cleaned and dry-fired the shotgun. Bobby was still free, he knew, for a frustrated Aaron only an hour ago had driven into the Settles' yard and searched around. And only fifteen minutes ago Fairbain had driven by, home for the night. Now was the time.

He felt something slither down his hairline but didn't even bother to find out what. As long as he could walk and pull the trigger—let the worms feast after that. Bruno seemed content to let nature take its course too; something awful told Dean that his body might still serve that creature even beyond death. But wasn't his body already beyond death?

He trudged, passing and being passed by nothing until he reached Fairbain's. It seemed the statues had doubled, but that could be his memory decaying. He walked carefully through them, not getting near. He hadn't come this far to be foiled again. Fairbain's front door was ajar. Where was her dog? He smiled, remembering exactly where doggie was. No lights were on in the house despite approaching darkness.

"Pie? Pie-o? Pie-y baby?"

Hearing the childlike voice Dean almost hid his gun in embarrassment, then saw Fairbain at the top of the stairs, oblivious to him. He eyed the griffins. Their talons shivered.

"Pie? Pie-oh?"

Dean measured the arc of the two griffins' claws, presuming that they were hinged at the elbow.

"Pie? Pie-oh? Don't you love me anymore?"

He dove, feeling his shirt being torn. He looked back to see that each griffin held a section of his shirt and was bending its head to chew the material.

"Pie? Is that you? Pie, you've come home. I'll never do

anything like this again. I hate the children, hate them. You're right. They're nothing but trouble. We'll let Aaron and that woman do whatever they want as long as they take them away."

Alice was descending the steps. She stopped two-thirds down. Dean was still on his stomach, hidden from her view. He aimed the shotgun at her back through the banisters.

"Pie? Pie!" Alice jumped the last steps and pulled at the shreds from Dean's shirt. She screamed and began hitting the griffin on her right, evidently thinking they'd killed her doll. The one she was hitting nonchalantly continued to chew the rags. Dean could see the other's claw ascend to striking position. He straightened and aimed the shotgun. Alice turned around to see him.

"You! You petty animal. You're the one who let your son free. Shoot me! Shotgun!" she yelled, bringing a blue glow about her body and pushing her chest forward. "Shoot so I can kill you!" Dean pulled the trigger. She was pushed into the griffin behind but only laughed. As he pulled the trigger again, the griffin's paw descended with a slam, all three of it claws penetrating her body and leaving her squirming.

"Shotgun, shotgun," she whispered, blood bubbling in her mouth. Despite that the pellets had indeed fallen harmlessly to the floor, the blue glow around her faded. "Pie?" she asked; then she went limp.

Dean swayed, looking at the dead woman's blood puddling on a tan terrazzo floor.

Finished.

DESCENDING THE ESCALATOR

1.

Before man there had been mist. After man came dirty mist. For with the death of Abel by a cudgel blow from Cain, the earth shifted. Where there had been jeweled caverns "measureless to man," now opened bowels of hatred. For the truth is that Abel had driven Cain to murder with his taunting laughter. The truth is that he had pushed his younger brother into a lake and would have drowned him too, had it not been for Eve's passing by. It was then that Cain acted, it was then that fingers pointed. And with the fate of the marked, Cain stumbled into his old age—alone and forsaken, mistrusted even by his progeny and wife. Soon those same bowels opened to receive a second morsel for slow, everlasting digestion. Hate! Hate! Hate!

Upon Cain's arrival the two brothers immediately fought, and once more Cain was victorious. But when he squatted alone in the hard heat of deep earth, something happened: Abel's body gathered itself and renewed the attack, catching

Cain off guard, though in the end Cain again slaughtered his brother—as he was to do for millennium upon millennium. And during those millenniums, from above, descended others: Adam, Eve, the mysterious Lilith—Methuselah, Nefertiti, Buddha, Caesar, Hammurabi, Ghengis Khan, St. Augustine, Richard the Lion-hearted, Mohammed, Lincoln, Einstein— these and the countless lesser souls, the couriers, courtiers, stenographers and small town gossips that have pervaded history. Cain, still shunned, still soured with hate, would greet each with a sharp cudgel, then retreat to rest until Abel once more sneaked upon him to once more be killed.

It was not really the souls who descended, rather their dark shadows. Freud's id, Jung's animus and anima, Socrates' daimon, voodoo's *ti bon ange*—call them what you will: the darker side of every human, that side suppressed in some, exalted in others. A negative soul, an *ak* instead of the Egyptian *ka*. And having no place to go upon death other than Earth's bowels, there it was that these negative souls raged while the soul proper rested in The Great Plenum.

Then, recently, three particulars concurred in a Jungian nest of coincidence. Alice Fairbain accidentally sculpted several likenesses of recently-buried *ak's*. These *ak's* longed for their surface likenesses and, with their tiny hands, began gouging, gouging, until they collapsed a sinkhole in Fairbain's back yard on a midsummer solstice night. Then a living visitor named Aaron descended into the bowels to spring a new hope, just as the descent of Persephone into Hades had once lightened despair. For while Aaron told the *ak* elementals, those dead minor scribes, cobblers, and grocers of his plan to avenge the Juden (a people Cain knew nothing of and cared less than nothing about), they spotted Bobby in his eyes. Consequently, mad whispers descended to Cain even as he slew Abel for the 30 billionth time: *Cain! Cain!* the voices whispered. *You will have a young body that will grow. You will be able to avenge your name so calumniated for so long. Because Cain, you have a physical twin at last born on earth. We have seen him in this man Aaron's eyes.* Cain nodded, slipping on his brother's broken torso. Blood! He would see it once more. He would see its thick red richness upon grass. He would celebrate flies and stench and decay. How powerful he would be above! He felt his forehead where the X had been seared by Adam and Eve and his ridiculous younger siblings… and he smiled.

Cain! Cain! Cain!

2.

Finished, Dean thought on watching the griffin bite into Alice Fairbain's shoulder to pull away a strip of fabric and flesh.

No! Beginning. Cain! Cain! Cain!

It was Bruno, forcing his way in. Dean saw car keys on the door's sill behind Fairbain's body, but when he started for them, both griffins raised their claws. So he ran through the kitchen and out the back. By the time he came around front and opened the door for the keys, the griffin on the right was chewing Fairbain's hair and scalp. Dean backed away and got into her car.

Cain! Cain! Cain!

No. No, Bruno, not your damned Cain.

Dean had already thought it through. The Hillsborough River was twenty minutes away. With any luck it would carry him to the Gulf within a week. There his body would dissolve and be eaten, spread into the good earth, not into hell.

What would friend Wittgenstein say about all this?

The water is all we know.

Dean drove, giving a last glance to the house that once held so much hope for him, his wife and son. He drove out of the Quail Hollow development, past the Circle K convenience store, onto Highway 54. He drove past Day's Inn, trying to see if the rental car was still there. But he knew if he stopped, even if he found Bobby, he'd be more likely to do harm than good. So he drove, fighting back shouts of *Cain!* He drove to the Morris Park bridge where he and Bobby had fished all of one time.

There was no one on the deserted road as he straddled the concrete bridge and put the shotgun to his mouth. His head would float away, parting from his body. *Separated, Bruno, separated despite what you planned. That should send you back to whatever sick hell you came from. Back to Cain.* Dean took the small likeness of himself, his *ka*, from his pocket, set it down and blasted it. He then barely had the energy to point the warm barrel to his mouth. Maybe, good friend Wittgenstein, just maybe there is something else. "Annie?" he called. And he pulled the trigger.

3.

The old woman had been no problem to Anne Marie, for she was happy to ride anywhere. The girl Abby, though, had used a banishing ritual as soon as she'd seen Anne Marie approach. It was a ritual easily swept away, as Anne Marie flicked her finger and employed the fascianatio she once developed in southern France. Under that evil eye's glance, Abby gave in and followed her to the van. As she did, Nancy and Tiffany called from the front door; Anne Marie simply leered and drove off. The lines were drawn, no use in pretending further. She reached Fairbain's house before dark but stopped on seeing what looked like Alice Fairbain slumped in the doorway.

"Stay here," she ordered the child. The doddering old woman had fallen asleep riding over. Anne Marie got out of the car and walked forward. No aura. Whoever it had been was dead, but there was movement. She expelled a groan as the griffin bit the corpse's shoulder. Getting closer she could see by the corpse's large hands that it had indeed been Alice Fairbain.

"I told you, you needed protection, you sad dumb witch."

A noise behind startled her, and she saw a dark blue truck pop over a hump on the lawn and come to a halt behind the van. She recognized Aaron as he got out, gun in hand.

Bullet, she thought, causing her shield to glow slightly about her in case this partnership worked no better than the last.

Aaron stopped to see the child Abby in the car, sitting in an obvious stupor. Anne Marie saw him tap against the window, though he kept an eye on her too. Evidently satisfied, he turned his attention to her, not yet seeing what was behind her.

"You I recognize from yesterday. Why have you brought this child back?"

He stepped forward and saw Fairbain's body.

"She's more than dead. Hoisted by her own claw, you might say. I told her she should be more careful of the elementals she raised."

"You killed her."

"No, she was my partner. Why would I kill her?" Seeing the surprised, angry scowl on Aaron's face, Anne Marie asked, "Didn't she tell you that we were all three to be partners?"

"We don't need any more partners."

"*Au contraire, mon grand Juif.*" Anne Marie stood aside as the griffin ripped more of Alice Fairbain and began to chew. "As you can clearly see, you're much in need of someone who knows what she's doing with the creatures you're raising."

Aaron aimed his pistol. He looked especially red and angry in the setting sun.

"Go ahead, get it off your chest."

He fired three times and Anne Marie kept smiling.

"Now would you care to talk? I think we should get the girl and old woman inside; and as disgusting as it sounds, I think we should let the griffin finish his meal—no body, no police, you know."

"I have a shield too. She gave it to me." Aaron lowered his gun as Anne Marie stepped off the porch and walked toward him.

"You may have once, but you certainly don't now." She held up a sculptured fingernail near his cheek and he raised the pistol, then checked himself. "Think *nail*," she dared him. His eyes narrowed and she scratched his cheek, drawing blood, showing it to him. "You see? The shield needs to be renewed every twenty-four hours, every rotation of the earth. Didn't she tell you that?"

Aaron shook his head, rubbing off the blood to look at it.

"Let's hope *our* partnership's more open. Now, let's get those two inside and away from anyone happening by. This place is thick with cops. I suppose it would be the height of good taste and sense to close the front door."

Slamming the door to hide the griffins and their actions, they led Agnes and Abby around the house and to the room where Bobby'd been. "Sit, Abby, and stay." Anne Marie looked the child directly in the eyes: "Sit, do you understand?" She dug her nails into the girl's cheek and Aaron winced at the blood issuing forth, though Abby barely moved. "Good." Her powers were working despite the Matrix's conflict between the child's shield of defense and her own fascianato. Well, as Jewel often enough said, even the Matrix can sometimes make a slip. Anne Marie turned to the old lady: "Mrs. Thompson, we're going to spend the night here. Do you want to make us all some tea?"

Mrs. Thompson's head agitated up and down in a palsy, and Anne Marie and Aaron led her to the kitchen. From the dining room Aaron watched the woman stupidly guarding the water until it would boil. He turned to Anne Marie, who whispered back,

"An unexpected but harmless guest. Now tell me what you know about these creatures the once-famous Alice Fairbain was summoning up."

"Her? It was me."

Anne Marie arched an eyebrow. "So, *mon grand Juif*, tell me about them." At Aaron's continued obstinacy, she stood. "Do you remember how Alice performed the ritual that gave you a shield of power?" He nodded and she said, "Good. Just to show my heart's with you I'll do the same now. But mine will be stronger, much stronger, because I'm a much stronger witch than Alice Fairbain ever thought of being." After her third pass, Anne Marie proffered her nail again. "*Now* think nail." Aaron did and she slashed at him with no effect. "Do you care to try it with the pistol?" Aaron shook his head vigorously and she laughed. "Oh ye of little faith. Remember that, *mon grand Juif.* Faith will get you far and you need to be sure of yourself when dealing with elementals. Now tell me like a strong, handsome man."

Aaron rubbed a paw against his cheek and saw that there was no blood. A faint scent of perfume came to him and he watched Anne Marie's eyes. She smiled and rubbed a ruby pendant hanging near her breasts until his eyes rested there. Their breaths briefly matched.

"We'll have plenty of time to celebrate becoming partners," she told him, pursing her lips. "But I'm expecting some not-so friendly guests and we need to prepare, so can you get the children out front while you tell me what they're all about?"

"*Kinder*," he corrected. "She called them 'children'; I call them *kinder*."

"*Kinder*—I like that."

"All right, I get them to watch the house. I think they are ready for that."

He and Anne Marie walked by Agnes, who was humming happily to herself, counting out tea bags.

"Maybe we can keep her on as a cook," Anne Marie said once they were outside. Aaron didn't react to her levity; rather, he pointed to Persephone's Escalator, which had taken on a warm glow.

"It was full of water this morning." They walked over to see that the sculpture's white descending steps were completely dry now. One statue blinked as they approached, and its huge black eyes opened to transform what would have been a comically pot-bellied man into a dope-eyed menace. Aaron motioned for it to go around the house. It stared until he pulled his pistol from under his shirt and waved it. Then it and others began to move until half the back yard was emptied.

"Faith, faith," Anne Marie reminded him, kicking a large statue of a knight and hissing when it momentarily raised a sword. The knight hunched its shoulders and turned quickly away.

"Guard," Aaron growled to it as it passed.

"That's right. Treat them like the dirty plaster they are. Do you have guards around the back too?"

"There is too much swamp, but we can if you think."

"I do."

They walked on and Aaron motioned for more statues to spread out. One attacked him with a club, but he used the shield and the statue beat aimlessly before giving up and walking off. After that, Aaron told Anne Marie what he knew of Persephone's Escalator.

"Ms. Alice had been trying to practice voodoo. Mostly it didn't work, though she made enslaved a woman. But something was not doing right, for this woman rotted while she worked, and two men rotted even before that, like they were too long hanging oranges. Then she found an Egyptian text for something different. *Ka*, she called this something different: to raise life forces from those already died. The first ceremony we did at midnight under the apple tree. The sinkhole ground glowed and six tiny *kinder* walked out, like baby ducks. She called it the Persephone's Escalator. More and more of *kinder* came out soon, *aber* only enough to fill the statues we made each day. That's what *ka* does, she told to me. It is attracted and summoned by a once lifetime resemblance on earth."

Anne Marie stopped Aaron, for she saw a police car pass out front. After a brief time at the Beasleys, it turned and left.

"I thought my dear friends would be here by now. I can't really imagine what's keeping them."

"And these are more witches?"

"And these are more witches, yes. But the *kinder* will give them plenty to think about."

"*Ja*." Aaron laughed.

"*Ka*, you were telling me about that."

"That's what she was summoning. But still even when so many came out, she the big witch, thought only of murderers and thieves. She was fool because she never descended. But I descended. An army, I thought. Three armies." Aaron paused to look at Anne Marie, who was looking around at all the statues in the yard.

"You, already I can tell, think army too."

Anne Marie grinned and grabbed his arm.

"And the cave, it has a voice too. *Cain*, it calls, it shouts. Sometimes down there I go mad. Sometimes I feel my blood seep so it can shout too. It was just last week that I found many life-sized *kinder*. The first one I brought up was a young boy, but it died because the Edmonds professor was here."

"What does he have to do with this?"

"The boy. Bobby Kirby. A virgin, and his zombied mother, she fed him ritual food for us. The tiny *kinder*, they would all shiver when they saw the boy work for us and they told me he would help much. But then that went wrong because the mother didn't kill her husband like she was supposed to. Fairbain got mad and zombified her." Aaron made a drinking motion with his hand and spit out imaginary potion with a half-grin, half sour face. Two statues awoke and Aaron shrugged at them with his shoulder, indicating they should walk toward the back fence. "Everyone of course thought she was dead. So the father and the boy got sad and moved to Atlanta. But Alice sent the boy packets of food telling him how sorry she was about his mother, still preparing him, you see? She thought he was the only one for Cain."

"And Cain is—"

"Cain is a…" he looked around at the steam rising from the ground. "Cain is a heat in the caverns. Ms. Alice said he is the symbol of all blood that has been loosed, that if we sacrifice a virgin to him the *kinder* will follow us from the caverns and listen to our commands. So we prepare Bobby.

"But I was the one fighting the tiny *kinder* night after night. I knew they don't care for rituals and witchery and incenses and fine Latin song-chants. Blood *ist* their care. So *Ich* promise blood every time I went *unter*. Blood is what has awoked them."

Anne Marie winced at her *grand Juif's* grammar. She looked at his huge shoulders and thin waist: those attributes outweighed linguistics by far. She was pleased, for with the possibility—the inevitability—of a third migration and its subsequent power, her sexual feelings had re-blossomed. They would, that is, if Jewel Dawn and the Nyx Ryan woman didn't prevent her. From sudden petulance, she loosed a curse, one she knew would ineffectively bounce off both Jewel and the Ryan woman, though it might cause minor discomfort to the others in the Pentad.

Aaron was setting more *kinder* in motion. Anne Marie was surprised at how many there were. One thousand? More? Numbers were hardly her forte. She asked Aaron and he laughed.

"As many as sands in the beaches. They will come up soon when the sacrifice is made. For now, three thousand between this property and the Kirby property." He fell suddenly as one of the children tripped him. Others nearby turned at the commotion and watched, unsure. Aaron cursed and pulled his pistol, but Anne Marie shouted "No, the police!" So he stood and shattered the statue with the pistol's grip.

"Go!" he shouted to the others, kicking shards at them.

"Guard!"

"I think that we need to go soon too. Whatever good fortune is keeping the Pentad away from us can't last. We need to take the girl and descend Persephone."

"It's not midnight. And someone has to stay atop to play the flute. That is what brings the *kinder* up."

"Have you ever thought of playing a recording?"

Aaron blushed, thinking of the caverns where he'd hoarded *kinder* by using a portable recorder. "Alice said it had to be *ein* live, real flute," he lied, knowing the evening dark surrounding them afforded ample camouflage for his face.

"But you said all the *kinder* are interested in is blood. Alice is dead, you're alive." They both stopped, hearing a car make a turn, another patrol car no doubt, then Anne Marie said, "I think the *kinder* will come to a recording. I think they'd come to a recording of a cat fight or even Lawrence Welk's polka music. Aaron, we need to be nice to one another."

As Anne Marie rubbed against Aaron, he felt his pulse moving. "Nice, yes. Then we should take the girl like you say and go make a sacrifice to Cain. Blood, *ja?*"

"Blood. *Ja.*"

They walked to the house, seeing nothing, hearing nothing from the road. The silence made Anne Marie nervous. At the back door she smelled sugar or honey baking. Through the screen she could see the old woman prodding in the oven— and was shocked to see the Abby girl sitting at a small kitchen table, dully rubbing against something that dropped to the floor. She shouldered past Aaron.

"What are you doing out of the room?" she hissed at the girl.

"I carried her out," the old woman said, closing the oven door. "I was getting lonely and she wouldn't come out."

Anne Marie relaxed on hearing that her fascianatio trance had remained effective. And though she was irritated at the Thompson woman, it was better not to let on. "I hope she kept you company?"

"She wouldn't talk. Just stared, so I'm making her some cookies."

"Isn't that nice. We're going to take her on a little walk right now. I think she needs some fresh air."

"What?" the old woman asked.

"Fresh air!" Anne Marie shouted near the woman's left ear. Aaron laughed and walked to his room for extra clips of bullets.

"Can she take some cookies too? They're nearly done."

"If they're done by the time Aaron gets back she can, but we can't wait." Anne Marie squirmed as she looked out the front window, for the munching griffin dropping one of Fairbain's legs distracted even her. Minutes later Aaron was back, wearing tall boots and thick pants. She nodded and tapped Abby's shoulder. The girl looked up. "Come along now and keep quiet."

"These cookies will keep her quiet," Agnes said, handing Abby a small brown bagful as she passed.

"What about her?" Aaron asked, nodding at the old woman.

"Maybe she'll go talk with one of the griffins while we're gone."

He chuckled a *ja* as they walked onto the back porch and headed toward Persephone's Escalator, which had already begun to glow.

Seconds later, there was scuffling near Agnes Thompson's baggy stockings and she bent down to look at the rag doll. "It's a good thing I found you in that nasty freezer, isn't it, honey?"

The doll nodded, staring out into the yard at the three receding figures.

"Who would ever be mean enough to lock you there?"

The rag doll pointed to Aaron's back.

"Are you going out too?"

The doll nodded again, its smile everlasting.

Agnes reached into her gray bun of hair. "A lady never goes out without money to phone home and one of these." She pulled out a three inch hatpin, but the rag doll showed her two of its own, each considerably longer, with rubies on their ends. "That's a good girl. You were brought up right. And do you have a quarter?"

The doll shook its head, so Agnes fished in a tiny coin purse. "Here. As shiny as can be. I don't like that Marie woman or that nasty smelly man at all, do you?" she asked.

The doll shook its head emphatically then pushed open the screen door after Agnes tousled its hair.

4.

They piled into two cars the moment they received Martin's second call warning them that Dean Kirby might be at the Settles house and that Bobby had insisted that something called Cain was threatening.

"Cain, as in Cain and Abel?" Jewel asked as they drove.

Nikki affirmed that was what Martin had said. "You don't suppose there really were a Cain and Abel and that Alice Fairbain has managed to summon them?"

"If she has, she's out of her league."

"She might be out of all our leagues, if she has. Can you imagine the power those two souls would have accreted, given the possibility they once were real?"

Tiffany was filing her nails in the back seat. "Mmm, I'd like to meet them. I'd like to meet Cain anyway."

Nancy groaned as she braked for a stoplight. Denise and Beth were following in Night's Trans-Am. Instead of braking, Beth gunned the TransAm's engine and nearly rear-ended them, unfamiliar with the car's power.

"Ur-males. Splendid, Tiffany. We can't even civilize modern men," Nancy commented, opening the window and shaking her finger at Beth. Denise, still dressed to the nines since she'd been researching in the law library when she'd had a sort of "feeling" about the Pentad and booked the next flight down, had her head in her hands. Nancy couldn't tell whether she was hiding from laughter or fear.

"Would they still even be human after that long?" Nikki said. "Ur-males might be exactly right. Even if you're a strict Biblicist, you're talking six millennia for Cain and Abel. More likely thirty or forty thousand years. Ugh. A hugely long time to bear a grudge."

The traffic light changed.

"At the time they lived, what would humans have looked like?" Nancy wondered.

It was a good question that no one tried to answer.

"Mmm, I still wouldn't mind meeting them."

"The great unwashed," Nancy commented toward Tiffany.

Lori sat in the back next to Tiffany. She closed her eyes as Tiffany's nail file scraped, trying to mentally touch with Abby. She thought she saw a blue tea kettle. Curious, she listened to Tiffany's scraping file and tried to focus on the kettle. Yes, there were voices in another room. A hand pulled down four teacups and turned to look briefly at a large white freezer underneath cabinets.

—What a nice freezer. If I had that, I'd shoot an alligator, law or

no law, and eat it year-round.

—Hello, Mrs. Thompson. It's me, Lori.

—The albino girl? Where are you? How are you talking to me? I don't see you. You need to hide.

Lori saw a frantic searching of the room as Mrs. Thompson shifted her gaze about. It was a large kitchen and there was a dining room to her right in which she thought she saw a man and a woman and something strange hanging behind them. It was moving or twisting. Mrs. Thompson had forgotten her glasses.

—No, I have them with me. How are you talking to me?

—I like you, Mrs. Thompson, so I can talk to you this way. Is Abby with you?

—Yes, but she's sick. I think that woman did something to her.

—Alice Fairbain or Anne Marie?

—I don't know any Alice Fairbain.

—So Anne Marie did something to her.

—She stared at her and started giving orders. When I was a girl, people in the mountains used the Evil Eye. I saw an old man use it once so I knew better than to look, I just acted senile and stupid.

—Can you put your glasses on, Mrs. Thompson?

—I can but I don't want to. There's something in the other room I don't want to see.

—What is it?

—If I don't want to see it, why should I want to talk about it, young lady?

—I'm sorry. Don't get mad, because I can't talk with you then. Ms. Ryan's here—

—Put her on the line.

—It's not a phone, Mrs. Thompson, but I can tell you each what the other says if you help me concentrate. Can you go back and stare at the teakettle? That helped.

—A watched pot never boils.

—Yes, ma'am. But that helped me.

—All right. It's stupid, though.

Lori saw the blue kettle as Mrs. Thompson bent close, then backed off, then twisted to get it in focus.

"I've found Mrs. Thompson and Abby," Lori announced to everyone in the car.

Tiffany even stopped filing her nails at that.

"They're okay for now. They're in a large house with Anne Marie and some man. Mrs. Thompson's in the kitchen making tea for them."

"What's the kitchen look like?" Tiffany asked.

"It's a huge gas stove and there's a large white freezer with yellow shelves—"

"Alice Fairbain's house."

Lori nodded, looking from Tiffany to the two women in front seat. "Mrs. Thompson thinks Anne Marie put an Evil Eye on Abby."

"She could have," Jewel said. "She used that in her former migration, though she'd supposedly given up the left-hand path."

"Garlic," Nikki said. "A good reason to eat it."

"I can tell Mrs. Thompson that."

It hadn't dawned on Nikki or Jewel to use Lori to communicate directly. They nodded and Lori told Mrs. Thompson.

"Tell her to sneak it to Abby and not let Anne Marie smell it."

"Anne Marie's got asthma anyway," Jewel commented. "But you're right, she should be careful."

—Can you give Abby some garlic, Mrs. Thompson? It'll get rid of the Evil Eye.

—Sure. There's plenty of spices in this kitchen. Why didn't I think

of that?

Mrs. Thompson moved from the tea kettle and Lori lost contact. They were nearing their turn-off from Highway 54 when she regained it.

—Mrs. Thompson, you have to be sure that Anne Marie doesn't smell the garlic or she won't let—

—I may not have dealt with many witches in my life, but I've run into plenty of bitches. I'll take care of Miss Marie's nose.

—Try not to get mad, Mrs. Thompson, I lose you when you do. Nikki wants to know about Alice Fairbain. Is she around?

—Tell Nikki that Alice Fairbain won't be bothering anyone anymore if she was the owner of this house. But tell her that this ugly man and Anne Marie know you're coming and are doing something mean out in the yard. From the window I can see little creatures sneaking around that are almost as white as you are.

Lori huffed at that and her own vision blurred. The last she saw was Mrs. Thompson fiddling with the top to the freezer, prying it open. She recovered and told everyone in the car what Mrs. Thompson had said about Anne Marie and Aaron sending out the statues.

"Pull in at that convenience store. Your doctor friend will have to pass here to get to the Settles' house, won't he?"

Nikki nodded.

"Just who is it that takes care of your teenage daughter?" Nancy asked suddenly.

Nikki laughed. "That's why I need a husband. I'm a rotten mother."

Nancy, who'd had two alcoholic parents, didn't return the laugh but walked into the store to buy coffee. While Tiffany finished her nails and Lori concentrated on regaining touch with Mrs. Thompson, Jewel commented quietly:

"On the contrary, I think you'd make a fine mother if you

ever decide to become one."

Nikki was quiet for a moment. "You never did, did you? It takes away your power."

"There's power and there's power." Jewel said. "You seem to have more than enough to go around."

Within ten minutes, Martin pulled in. After a brief conferral, they drove on in two cars, Nikki in Mrs. Thompson's car with Martin, Beth and Denise, and Jewel in the Trans-Am with Lori, Nancy and Tiffany.

A mile from the Settles' house, they encountered a swarm of the children crossing the road and had to stop. The children were surrounding a house on the left, clambering atop one another's shoulders to break its windows with their fists. An elderly man and woman stood dazed at a picture window. He was holding a shotgun at port arms.

"Why doesn't he use it?" Nancy asked on getting out and joining the others.

"I bet this is the guy who accidentally shot Bobby. He's afraid to now." As Martin spoke, a squat statue broke the window so that it sheared off, neatly cutting the statue in chalky, chunky halves. Then the man began firing, causing the statues to scurry back. The moment he turned to his wife for more shells, though, they began their march forward.

Nikki, Jewel and Beth stepped forward and threw bolts of blue electricity that crashed into the middle of them. Martin took a tire iron to several straggling late-comers trying to join the march, while Denise, Nancy and Tiffany worked to cast a banishing pentagram around the house. Skull, floating overhead, kept watch in a farther direction—the Kirby barn and Persephone's Escalator.

"There are so many," Jewel said.

Nikki felt the Pentad's shield being summoned. At nearly

the same time she heard the blast of a shotgun. "The guy's shooting at us now! Martin! Think bullets or whatever the hell shotguns shoot!"

If Martin heard he didn't indicate. The side window to Night's Trans-Am shattered and Nikki heard another blast. Lori was inside, but barely fazed since the Pentad's shield of power was working well. Another blast and two statues fighting beside the house were both shattered. At least the guy had returned to shooting the real threats. As Nikki directed a globe of blue destruction at four miniature white farmers in bibs waddling toward a window, she heard a thunk and turned to see Martin's glib smile over a bleeding statue of Cupid a few feet from her back. He lifted his tire iron in a wave.

"Martin, don't worry about me. I've got the Pentad. You're the one who needs to get away from this guy's shotgun. Your shield's powerful, but you'd still get hurt."

An electric blue glaze buzzed around the house and two plaster elves tumbled from the porch. Nancy, Tiffany and Denise had succeeded with their banishing ritual. Fortunately, the man inside was occupied with a few children who'd gotten in, and though they'd be completely harmless now, he had no way of knowing this and was busily blasting away. Nikki could hear plates crash after a shotgun blast. The man's wife screamed. So much for the good china.

Now that the statues were unable to attack their primary target, many fought one another or scavenged aimlessly, resembling the random motion of ping pong balls in a Lotto machine. Nikki saw one pale ballerina bump a bayonet palm's sharp fronds, angrily working herself into a comi-tragical frenzy. *What tunes them in and out?* She wondered. Then she remembered how intensely Lori'd been staring. Had she tried to contact the statues? Looking back, she could see Lori sitting stiffly near the car's back window, quite frightened. Nikki ran, calling to Martin and Jewel. She reached the car to find sweat pouring off Lori as she blankly stared at a Santa Claus-like statue working its way warily around a German Shepherd dog at the edge of the yard.

"Lori?" There was no response, so she had to call again. "Lori?"

"Cain is telling them to kill, to work terror for preparation of his coming. 'Blood, red blood,' he howls at them. And then his name. 'Cain! Cain! Cain!'" Sweat soaked Lori's blouse, just as if she'd dove into the murky swamp water that pervaded the area.

"It's all right, Lori. That's fine for now," Jewel, who'd just reached the car, said. "Don't interface anymore."

"Cain! Cain!" Lori screamed. She was staring at the poor dog and they all turned: five statues had gathered around it, though it crippled one with its teeth. In a widening circle, more were enclosing, twenty, thirty. The dog jumped fiercely at the closest, then howled as they closed in. Even as Jewel and Nikki did what they could, fur was shred over the grass. Finally Nikki summoned a large blue globe of destruction and burned the area, putting both animal and statues out of their misery.

"Jew-el! Hurry!" It was Tiffany, screaming from a large pine in the far left boundary of the yard where she, Nancy and Denise had triangulated to cast a banishing shield around the house. Nancy, already close, ran, then stopped a few feet away and put her hands to her face.

"It's Denise, I know it's Denise." Jewel ran over, her black ceremonial robe trailing behind.

Nikki reached them a step later. Denise was lying behind

a pine tree on a pile of cones gathered for long term mulch. She was dead, her expensive suit slashed and covered with blood, viciously cut just as Becky had been, just as the Beasleys had been. Nikki heard footsteps and looked to see Martin leading Lori: Nikki emphatically waved him back. The girl was upset enough; she didn't need to see this too. Nancy pointed at what those nearest could see: a purple glow on Denise's ear. Nancy bent to touch an earring of a jade Buddha, pulled back in pain, then turned Denise's jaw, which appeared cool and stiff already. A second jade earring glowed with the same evil aura. Nancy didn't touch this one.

"Anne Marie gave her those last solstice," Jewel said. "If she hadn't been so damned sentimental…" Jewel, standing tall and pulling her black robe about her, looked from the corpse to the sky. She closed her eyes and called in a quiet chant: *"Mori, Venifica. Mori, Venifica. Mori, Venifica."*

Nikki screamed "No, Jewel! Stop!"

But Jewel continued, her eyes not even quavering until a bright orange ectoplasm spewed from her mouth to gather into a globe ten feet overhead. Skull, as an eagle, screed and hovered protectively until Nikki assured it with a hand signal. He then flew to a nearby pine.

"Call it back, Jewel. There's still time. You know that."

"I'm tired of the Hanged Man, Nikki. It's my time."

The globe was buzzing wildly, as if caging several bolts of lightning against their will. In a moment, Jewel passed her hands and called, *"Ite, Ite, Ite.* Go," she whispered. "Go. Go."

The globe shot upwards, reaching the apex of its arc some half mile off. They could clearly see, because of the low Florida horizon, as it began its descent toward Anne Marie, in Alice Fairbain's house.

Jewel swayed, spent, and nearly fell. Nikki directed Tiffany and Nancy to take her to the car where Lori and Martin were now waiting. She and Beth stared at Denise's body as Jewel was led away.

"Jewel Dawn just signed her own death warrant," Nikki said, when they were out of hearing.

"It doesn't have to work that way," Beth replied.

"No, nothing in the Matrix has to work any way. That's its beauty—and terror." Nikki sighed, looking back to the corpse of Denise at their feet. "She's married with children, right?" Beth nodded. "I don't think they need to see her this way. Will you give me your hand?"

Beth looked suspiciously at the eagle still perched in the pine, its white head and beak twisting viciously, but at last proffered her left hand. Nikki shook her head and Beth replaced it with her right, stiffening with surprise at the strength in the lithe woman's grip.

"What was her last name?"

"Beaufort. Denise Mellicent Beaufort."

"I sum-mon you who were once Denise Mellicent Beaufort. I sum-mon you who were once Denise Mellicent Beaufort. I summon you who are parting from this body, to stay. I summon you not to yet look to the West. I summon you to stay beyond your appointed time and cleanse the clay here at our feet. I sum-mon you to do this in the name of those who are left behind, those whom you loved, those whom you still love. It is a small fa-vor, a small delay. I sum-mon you."

Beth tried to concentrate as Nikki summoned, though she wasn't sure what or whom Nikki was summoning—still she couldn't help seeing five of the living statues turn toward Nikki's vatic voice. No surprise, for she felt it pass along the earth to vibrate her toes. What was surprising was how each statue took no more than a step forward before re-appraising and turning quickly to wobble away with fearful circumspection.

Beth felt another stirring at her feet and looked to the corpse of Denise. It was making a sound like you might hear in a forest on a wet spring day, when you imagine you can hear flowers and grasses and tree shoots push through the ground, urged by Persephone to grow, to live once more and free themselves from the clasp of old Hades' winter. She caught her breath as dried blood turned wet, then reversed its flow. The facial gashes healed, a finger that had broken into a compound fracture righted itself as the protruding bone withdrew beneath flesh. The eyes, still open in a frenzy of fear, closed, as did the jaw. Some odd angle about the body as a whole—Beth couldn't tell exactly what—righted itself, so that what was once Denise seemed to slumber. And for a small moment, color returned to the flesh and Beth thought she saw a rise in the chest.

"No, you must go," Nikki quietly cautioned.

Beth felt Nikki let her hand go; at the same time she saw the chest fall and felt a cool air ascend. As it caressed her body, she gave a start of surprise as something pinched her. She rubbed her arm, looking wide-eyed at the corpse.

"Neesey?" she called. She bit her lips as she continued rubbing her arm. She then looked to Nikki in quiet awe: "Neesey—Denise—would always pinch my left arm hard enough to leave a red spot, and say that was my retribution for ever using the left-hand path."

"It's your right arm she pinched."

"Yeah. Yeah it was." Beth bent to brush Denise's hair, then looked at Nikki. "I have no idea how you did that, but I thank you. It will be easier on her husband and kids."

"We need to go," Nikki said, indicating the cars. Beth gave

Denise a last kiss, then stood to walk with Nikki.

5.

"I've always read that the recently dead are extremely volatile and dangerous to handle," Jewel commented once Nikki and Beth reached the car.

"How did you—" Nikki asked.

"I could see the aura of the soul materialize and descend. I've never seen that in any of my migrations. What were you trying to do? Surely not bring her back?"

"No, I have no misconceptions about my limitations. I merely made the soul heal the body to what it was before the mutilations. I just wish there'd been time to do that before Abby saw her family."

"I felt her, Jewel. She told us all good-bye. She pinched my arm like she used to." Beth decided to keep quiet about the moment Denise tried to stay and breathe life back into her body. Then the old man from the house came out and shouted something. Sirens sounded in the distance.

Jewel looked weak, no doubt from the curse she'd thrown. "Nikki, I'm glad your powers exceed my teachings. We're going to need something more powerful even than the Pentad, maybe. Get in the car and listen to what else Lori told us from her contact."

As they drove, Lori repeated that the statues only had the word "Cain!" and the taste of blood in their minds, nothing else at all. "This blood taste comes from the one being supreme among them all—Cain. They fear him, he takes pleasure when they slash and draw blood. He felt me touching with two little statues of girls back there. He laughed so loud that my head throbbed and he spat all sorts of horrible things at me. Leathery winged things, eggs with jaws that dripped blood, rats with razor claws, deformed people whose humps had fingers groping from them. They all reached for my face to leave a slime that burned and left pustules. I screamed and he told me there was no death, only dying, and he laughed and laughed and laughed and laughed and laughed and laughed—"

Martin was in the back seat with Lori. He shook her until she began to sob. Nancy slowed the car by what had been the Settles' house, on seeing three white bishops clubbing something with tiny plaster crosiers.

"My god, they're attacking a vulture," Jewel commented. They watched the black bird hop and throw up its wings only to have black feathers yanked out.

"Mrs. Thompson says it's okay to come on now," Lori said out of the blue, giving a sniff. "She says that none of the statues stayed to guard like Aaron commanded, that they all left."

Jewel nodded, and Nancy put the car in gear, but Nikki told her to wait. "I want to see something," she said, getting out and releasing Skull, who'd turned into a hawk to fit in the car. He swooped and blinded one plaster bishop. The two others shook their fists and looked up; Skull obliged by swooping and blinding them. They stumbled about, one falling after a minute.

"I think we can cut down on the problem," Nikki said, giving a shrill whistle for Skull, who homed onto her shoulder, his red tail fluffing out then folding in. "There are plenty of hawks in this area." Nikki again talked with Skull who took off after some loud screeches and flapping.

"The only Sister in the world whose familiar argues with her," she said, getting into the car and shaking her head, mystified.

"Really?" Jewel asked, raising an eyebrow.

"Really."

"I've seen flashes of greens and violets for the last two hours," Beth commented. Like the earth itself is giving off a bad aura." As she spoke, two more statues, these resembling brides at a wedding, tumbled into the road ahead, fighting one another.

"Hold on, I'll just run them over." But the car nose-dived, not to move again, though its back wheels spun hotly on the asphalt. Nancy rolled down her window and looked out, to scream, "Jump the hell out—now!"

As everyone did, the hood buckled and the rear end lifted so that Lori had to jump three feet. From a crack in the road, two scaly green claws pulled the car like it was a sandwich.

"A present from Anne Marie," Beth said.

"I don't think so. It's an elemental, but if Anne Marie'd left it, it would be attacking us now, not the car, right?"

"It's from Cain's mind," Lori said, holding her temples. "It's from all the minds that stay down there with him."

Beth threw a tentative globe of blue at the claw, which twitched and shook, knocking asphalt about before withdrawing into the ground with half the car.

"It's susceptible to pain anyway."

"Mrs. Thompson needs us. We've got to hurry," Lori told them.

They piled into the second car, sitting on one another's laps, and drove around the great pothole. Pulling into Fairbain's drive, they could see the front door smashed open. What remained was one griffin, chewing on what looked like a human leg.

"Mrs.—" Nikki started from the car, but Lori assured her:

"No, she's alive. She says not to worry about her now, but

to go into the hole in the back, that's where they took Abby. She thinks they're going to kill her."

Jewel unloaded two suitcases while keeping an eye on the griffin and looking for the source of an odd chugging sound. *Chit-chit-chit,* it went

"Can you find Mrs. Thompson, Lori?" Nikki asked.

Lori looked around the yard at scattered white shards of statuary. "She was scared by something and I lost her, but I think she's okay. I know for sure she doesn't want us to come after her."

There was a motion to their right under an ancient oak. A hulk roared and started for them, but tripped over a broken statue.

"It's the other griffin Fairbain kept by the door," Martin whispered.

"What happened to its eyes?"

The griffin's eyes were covered with red splotches, but no one had time to answer for the creature homed in on their voices and stumbled toward them. Beth lifted her left hand and threw a bolt of blue. As she did she held her side, wincing, even as the griffin held its own before falling over dead.

"Denise always told me that what goes around comes around," Beth said, straightening and breathing heavily.

"Are you okay?"

"I've been better, but let's go. I sure won't put so much into the next globe I throw—Damn. What *is* that noise?" she asked as they walked around back toward Persephone's Escalator.

They listened: *chitchitchit-chit, chitchitchit-chit.* No one ventured a guess. Though the grass in the yard was soggy, when they reached Persephone's Elevator a dry heat steadily moved from the mouth of the sculpture. They spotted occasional roving statues; still, most of the yard was empty except for the blocks that had served as bases. Even the oddball statues of frogs and giant snakes or birds were gone. Adding to the eeriness, to their far right, by the cypress near the drainage pond, the *chitchitchit-chit* continued strongly.

A gust of hot air blew up from the opening of Persephone.

"Was that a scream?" Tiffany asked, peering into the opening.

"We need to hurry," Nikki said.

"Fools rush in," Jewel said, holding up her arm. "Let's have some quick preparations. Lori, you're the youngest and strongest, I think you should carry this suitcase. It's full of our chalices and a few practical items like flashlights and wine. If we need to set up an altar, the suitcase can serve as the base. The other suitcase," Jewel gave a smile as she opened it, "holds daggers and two very unSisterlylike guns. I've always held that the Matrix involves everything, including technology—so why not take a short-cut now and then? There are several clips for each gun. Unless anyone objects, I think Martin and Lori are the best candidates, seeing as neither are as yet magically inclined—unless you think you can psychoanalyze the statues out of their aggressions, Doctor?"

"Psychologist," Martin mumbled, "not a psychiatrist." But he took the gun somberly.

"I also brought some goodies. Spices for Beth." Jewel handed over what looked like a small sewing kit. "Jewels for Tiffany, including the three largest rubies I could afford—you'll need a bit of black magic down there, I'm afraid." Jewel paused at an iron set of runes. "They were for Denise. She loved words and shapes and symbols." Jewel passed over them for the next box, a thick clear plastic, handing it to Nancy. "Crystals and oils. If you can, fabricate an extra protective salve. Who knows? Judging from what happened in the road we might need invisibility against dragons." She handed the case over, then looked to Nikki. "And you… Nikki." There was a pause in Jewel's voice that everyone noticed. "Even though I initiated both you and your 'daughter' Night—" her tone was noted only by Nikki—" I have no idea what your specialty is, or if you even have one. Maybe you're a pre-enlightenment Sister, a Bacon or Paracelsus of the female brand. Maybe I'll live to see… maybe I won't."

She turned abruptly. "Tiffany, Beth, Nancy—I want you to witness for the rest of our Sisterhood what instinct tells me." Jewel gathered her black cloak and clasped it with a finger bone. She kissed Nikki full on the lips, then knelt and embraced her mid-section. "You must tell me to rise," she told a surprised Nikki.

Nikki did.

"You're the new Executrix. Half the ritual is over. An abridged version, but it will do. The other half will come at my death."

Nikki stared from Jewel to the others, who all smiled, evidently pleased with Jewel's choice.

"We'd better go," Nikki said.

6.

Ten feet in they stopped, seemingly confronted with a solid rock wall. Then Nikki and Jewel laughed simultaneously, pushing their hands through the illusion. "Good enough to stop the police, anyway," Nikki commented. "Shall we?" They all walked through, even wide-eyed Martin and Lori.

Just as the floor and walls of Persephone's Escalator were dry, so was the air—extremely dry, more like Texas desert than Florida swamp. Nikki commented on this as they entered, saying it was a bonus, for if the passageway had been humid it would be intolerable after thirty steps.

They took many more than thirty steps. After the first slight turn the passage dimmed and they were forced to use flashlights from the suitcase.

"Aren't there gasses and things in mines?" Tiffany asked.

"We're nowhere near deep enough. Old-time miners used to use a parakeet; when it suffocated they'd back off."

There was rubble ahead, a pile of statues. When intact, these must have been appreciably taller than any they'd encountered yet. Also, their texture differed. Their white was so pure that it glowed hideous and blatant, an example of why some cultures chose white, not black, to represent death. And they emanated light like radioactive dials or glow-in-the-dark crucifixes of a bloody Christ. Their shells were thin, more like shards of china than bones, and they crunched easily underfoot.

"Wait a minute, there're things moving in the middle of the pile."

"No, the pile itself is moving."

As they gazed at the rubble, shells of hands crawled over hands, shells of legs over legs, apparently working their slow way toward the respective torsos.

Cain! Cain! Cain!

"What was that?" Lori asked.

Nikki held her flashlight from one blank face to another. "No one else heard anything?" she asked with puzzlement.

"I smell gunpowder," Nancy said.

"That means that Anne Marie and—What's his name?"

"Aaron, Lurch, Lover boy," Martin answered Jewel. He moved close to Nikki, thinking he saw another glow ahead.

The walls?

"Gunpowder means they've been here. This fight must have slowed them considerably." Jewel stepped through the pile and something grabbed her ankle. She grunted and kicked, then shone her light down on a disembodied hand. The others grimaced, shaking off groping fingers and who knew what. Slowly as they walked, with their barely noticing, the walls of the passage took on a reddish glow. And there was something else that no one could quite digest… occasionally someone would stop and look around in befuddlement, until another in the group would have to go back and get her like a bewildered child at a carnival.

Nikki did this to Martin. "We're all hearing some Pied Piper calling us at different times, aren't we? That's it, isn't it?"

Everyone remained too unsure to answer.

A quarter mile farther, the glow had increased so much that they could see without flashlights. A wall shifted, tumbling down rocks and dust to reveal a fissure which emanated a slithering, almost liquid sloshing. Nikki discerned scales moving. "It's like what grabbed our car." More rocks tumbled and the scales wriggled upward, knocking rocks from the wall before them.

"It must be eating its way through the earth."

They hugged the opposite wall and walked on, occasionally looking back as more rocks fell.

"What if this cavern caves in on us because of that thing?"

"Hell, what if there's another thing behind *this* wall?" Nancy slapped the nearby rock, surprised by its warmth. *Cain! Cain! Cain!* Nancy froze.

"Nancy, you always have a delightful outlook," Jewel said; then, noticing her blowing her hand, she asked, "Are you all right?"

"All right?" Nancy asked, shaking herself.

"Listen!" Martin said. "Shots!"

Indeed there were four shots. No other sound. Nancy nodded that she was okay, so they hurried on, hoping more pearly elementals ahead were slowing Anne Marie and Aaron. When they'd taken a slight bend and descended what appeared to be several natural steps it appeared that their hopes were fulfilled, for bullet shells littered the passage, though there weren't any of the elementals in sight.

Martin stopped to touch the wall: "I think vibration makes it warm."

Cain! Cain! Cain! The cavern lit up and Martin momentarily leaned as if he might meld with the wall, but he recoiled as a large male head pushed by two hands bumped into his ankle, then was rolled around him. Then he saw where the head was being pushed, toward a torso and a litter of other shards half-hidden in a recess. Martin moved his foot to kick the head, but couldn't bring himself to do it. "Never to die," he said, watching the head being bumped over the floor.

"What?" Nikki asked, coming back for him.

Martin pointed at the sneering head on the ground, and the recess full of shards.

Jewel had come back too. She watched momentarily as the armless, legless torso lunged ineffectively toward the head. Then the head hit a rock equal to its size, leaving it gummy with a black resin. The hands pushed on fruitlessly while the eyes, nuggets of death, opened to locate the obstruction. *"My name is Ozymandias, king of kings; Look on my works, ye Mighty, and despair!* But I don't think Shelley meant it quite like this," Jewel commented. The three of them hurried on for the others.

Soon all of them came to a point where the passage seemed to end. Lori said she'd just contacted Abby, who confirmed that she, Aaron and Anne Marie had been slowed by fighting. Abby insisted that the passage only *seemed* to end, for that was where they'd nearly been killed. They weren't too far beyond it now. Aaron and Anne Marie both were limping, she told Lori.

"Tell her to eat the cookies if she still has them," Nikki whispered, keeping her eye on a movement to her far left. "Tell her the garlic in the sack will work as an antidote against the Evil Eye. Its odor must already be affecting her if she can talk with us."

Lori shook her head. "She's scared, so her thoughts aren't strong. Anne Marie and Aaron are fighting the *kinder* again. I know that much."

"*Kinder?*"

"That's what Abby says Aaron calls these things."

There were more gunshots. Tiffany pointed to the wall on their right. The other walls were nearly translucent, they were so red. This one was a shiny black. She stepped to touch it, withdrawing with an exclamation of disgust, her fingers and palm sticky with the blackened liquid.

Nikki came over. "My god, it all couldn't be blood, could it?" A movement above attracted her. "It's a ledge and there's another pile of—*kinder?*" She could see Lori nod, her face dull red in the light. "Aaron and Anne Marie must have fought hundreds as they climbed. No wonder they're limping."

The wall crumbled behind, and a red glow revealed the ledge above them. A huge python slithered out and crawled up to hang from a stalactite. A second animal like a double-size great Dane with two heads emerged. The snake dropped and the two fought, thrashing so heavily on the stone floor that the vibrations transmitted.

A midget, whitened monk peeked from the new fissure to stare at the fighting creatures. His silly grin dropped on seeing Nikki and the others. Nikki cast a bluish globe, which skittered off the wall to hit the fighting creatures, then charred the peeping tom monk.

An ivory hand fell at their feet, to immediately finger its way up the wall. As they watched, they noticed that the sheet of oily blood was flowing slowly upwards too. A small step revealed itself as the blood once covering it crept upwards. More shots came from above.

"We need to join the crowd, don't we?" Jewel said. Despite everyone's squeamishness they started up, finding it not as difficult as it looked, for steps and handholds were hidden underneath the thick blood. But it was still a hands-and-knees affair, and they felt disgusted by the time they reached the top, which consisted of a mini plateau the size of a small house, completely littered with shards of dead *kinder*. This second pile was much more active than the last and emanated piglike grunting.

"It'd be hard to find a smarmier place, a smarmier co-ven—or a smarmier psychologist," Jewel commented, taking the pearly shell of a head in her hand and holding it to let viscous black fluid drip. She tossed the luminous head with disgust. Was there a scream as she did? A headless body slith-ered through the rubble and grabbed at her ankles, though the Pentad's shield of power protected her, for the *kinder's* fingers turned brittle and snapped. Its legs kept kicking, how-ever, and she hit its ivory body with her fist where a heart should be, but only a hollow thunk sounded. Finally she cast a blue globe, and black blood spattered all of them as the elemental exploded.

Beth looked at her arm where a shard had imbedded. "I'm bleeding, damn it. This shouldn't be. We re-formed the Pentad without Anne Marie and I'm not wearing any of her damned jewelry. This shouldn't be happening." She stared angrily and backed from the rest of them. "Maybe it's your little girlfriend there, Jewel. Or maybe it's having a damned bad-luck man along." She huffed at Martin, who looked on helplessly. "I'm going back! Screw you all, this is ridiculous!"

The plateau's cavern caught her last word and *ridiculous* echoed about. The walls turned a cherry red. Beth straightened at the echo; then her shoulders slumped as it died away. She shivered and looked at her friends, then at Lori and Martin. "Sorry, you two. I can't believe I just said those things." She took a deep breath and turned to Jewel, holding out her bleeding forearm, trying to control her voice. "But what *is* going on, Jewel? We've got to get the Pentad right or we won't be able to fight these slimy *kinder* or whatever they are, much less Anne Marie and whatever else is down here. We won't be able to do anything for that poor girl ahead, much less get out of here alive ourselves."

"God, all our auras are a mess," Tiffany said before Jewel could answer. "Jewel, maybe Beth's right, maybe we should stop here for a moment and use some of Nancy's oils."

Jewel nodded, so Nancy squatted to mix a salve. "Oil of lemon, oil of garlic—banish one another as you banish us from the enemy's sight. Oil of lemon, oil of garlic—join one another as we enjoin with the enemy when it is our delight. Oil of lemon, oil of garlic—take the sight that is taken, give it to us that we may awaken." Nancy looked up, holding the salve upwards.

"Vinegar," Beth commented, walking over.

Jewel made a face, but held her peace.

"To give us strength."

Nancy nodded and let Beth pour vinegar over the mixture. "We should face the direction we perceive our enemy and make an earth pentagram—all of us," Nancy added, indicating Lori and Martin. "I'll show you what to do."

Lori and Martin imitated Nancy even as behind them on the level below, another wall burst forth another demon. "Don't look; concentrate," Nancy warned. They did and she passed the salve so that each person could rub it over her eyes, ears, nose, mouth and fingertips. When they finished, a Tyrannosaurus Rex was watching them, its teeth level with the ledge's floor. Lolling its head from side to side, it looked curiously through them then turned and walked away.

"Congratulations, Nancy," Martin whispered, feeling a chill pass.

"Sh!" Nikki pointed ahead. Maybe a quarter mile into the narrowing passage stood a group of people.

"It's Anne Marie and Aaron and the girl."

"Are you sure, Jewel? Then who are the others with them?"

"Maybe they've gathered some elementals already. That's what they're down here for, isn't it?"

"They look like they see us. We need to be careful."

"No, they wouldn't see us because of the oils, I'm sure. Maybe they saw the dinosaur behind us—"

"One way or another we have to confront them. If they are gathering elementals, we should do that as soon as possible." Jewel said.

Agreeing, they walked forward. Shots sounded, though from where was anyone's guess because of the echoing. Every few steps they came upon one or more elementals, struggling as always to reclaim its life.

"Shouldn't we kick these shells apart as we come on them?" Martin asked. "As distasteful as it seems, that might be our ticket to getting out on the way back. Otherwise they may all reshape."

"Double apologies," Beth commented, giving an elemental's ivory legs a good kick that sent them skittering down a crevasse. "I never thought I'd hear a psychologist give practical advice." She smiled at Martin.

"Look! The group's gotten closer to us somehow," Nancy said.

And when they looked they could see that the group ahead had halved their distance.

"Isn't the girl Abby shorter than that?" Jewel wondered, bunching her eyes.

"Maybe she's behind them."

"Maybe she managed to get away without their noticing and they're searching for her."

"Is that her? I saw something on a ledge."

"They see her too. They're pointing." Beth raised her arm to throw a globe of destruction, but Nikki jumped to hold her back.

"Something… I think… I think we should wait. After all, they won't see us for a bit. When we're close, we'll be more alarming to them."

Beth nodded and they continued walking, keeping a wary eye on the group ahead, another wary eye on the walls.

"Lori, can you try to contact Abby again?" someone whispered.

Lori concentrated on the sounds of their footsteps, though groans from the walls made her twitch and grimace.

"Maybe we should stop, maybe that would help her," Jewel

said.

Martin stooped to crush a torso with a rock.

Cain! Cain! Cain!

"Aaagh!" Lori fell to her knees, screaming and thrashing. They gathered about her.

"My good god." Martin pointed straight ahead.

Nikki turned. "By the mother of the All."

The others turned to stare with similar shock: the group they'd seen was yards away now and clearly visible. It was their own doubles, returning their stares in similar wonder and awe.

"NOOOOOOO!" Lori shouted. As she did this, the doubles disappeared and three cave mouths opened. The first was puritanical white, more like polished granite than any natural cave. The second was dusty and nondescript as if made of sand. The last was steamy and cast a violet hue one could look on with anger, sorrow, or any number of in-between passions.

"Watch her!" Martin shouted, pointing to Lori.

Beth grabbed Lori just as she was about to hit her forehead against a protruding rock. From a gash, they saw she'd already done it once. "Her blood—it's streaked with black," Beth said. Lori moaned as she fought to get free of Beth.

"TAKE ME, TAKE THE REASONABLE PATH," a voice called, filling the cavern with the lilting, maddening exactitude of a computerized voice in some airport. It came from the middle cave.

"YEA, THOUGH I WALK THROUGH THE VALLEY OF THE SHADOW OF DEATH, I WILL FEAR NO EVIL; FOR THOU ART WITH ME; THY ROD AND THY STAFF COMFORT ME." This voice carried the mixture of bathos and threat a father might use as he slaps his child and draws blood. Rocks fell around the first cave, from where this paternal voice sounded.

The third cave simply began a banshee wail that occasionally turned into a cackle.

"Noooooo!" Lori shouted again.

Martin tore his shirt to dab blood from her forehead, leaving her milk-white skin pale pink. Beth let go her grip on the girl as Jewel, Nikki, Nancy and Tiffany motioned.

"Our instincts tell us the third path," Jewel whispered when Beth reached her side.

Steam spewed from that cave's mouth.

"And you think *I* have a negative outlook?" Beth studied the dank opening, the steam from it carrying the sad-happy mystical wail. She nodded reluctant agreement and walked back to Martin and Lori. The two other caves disappeared, leaving the familiar glowing red rocks and walls. From the remaining cave came a cackle and once more their twins appeared, summoning them.

"We think that going into the third one would—"

"Noooo!" Lori tried to break free from Martin, who held her tightly. "No! The bad me is there. Can't you see her? I'll kill myself. We'll all kill ourselves. You can't fight yourself! No!"

"It's all right, it's all right," Martin cooed. "Look, is it absolutely necessary that she travels to complete the—Pentad?"

"Jewel," Nikki said. "Anne Marie couldn't be much farther ahead. Let Lori stay here."

Jewel looked from Nikki to Lori, who was shivering now, even though the ambient temperature was mid-nineties. "I've already turned this fight between myself and Anne Marie into a vendetta, so I have to go. And you, with your powers, have to go. After all, it may not be only Anne Marie who we're going to fight." Jewel turned toward their doppelgang-ers, standing in the mouth of the third cave and waving their arms like pieces of seaweed. In a mix of voices, from Nancy's gruff cough to Lori's excitable soprano to Martin's reasonable, clinical assurance, the cavern was calling "*Veni, veni, veni.* Come, come, come."

"What do you think?" Jewel pointedly asked Nikki.

"The two of us," she answered. "Beth, Nancy, and Tiffany can set up an altar here. We'll need it if…" she shrugged at their doppelgangers. "Lori can be useful here too. She can tell us if we're heading for Abby, she can—can you do this, Lori?"

Martin indicated with his hand and his mouth that Nikki should tone down. She bit her lip for being so excitable. Was Night coming out? She tried again, leaning to touch Lori's forehead. "Can you wait here and contact Abby and also keep your thoughts trained on Jewel and me?" Nikki worked hard to let her voice take on a mother-daughter tone, and something stirred in her. "Lori?" Lori nodded, wiping at her gash but withdrawing when she caught an image of her double through Nikki's legs.

"I want to go," Martin said. "We've already seen how handy guns can be—it's bullets, not magic that've stopped all these things. If I go and Lori stays there'll be a gun here and a gun with you."

Hearing Martin, Jewel momentarily thought of Paul and grabbed Nikki's arm. "Besides the gun, it would also be good to have yin and yang facing whatever's ahead. There's power and there's power, remember what I told you?"

Nikki did remember. And she thought of how she'd just felt a surge of power when talking with Lori as if she were a daughter. She turned to look at their doppelgangers, now motionless. "All right then, the three of us. And the four of you set up an altar with the suitcases. The Matrix will understand a bit of slovenly work now and then. Mother of God knows this place is slipshod enough."

Tiffany stood from squatting and concentrating on something. "Here, one for each of you." She handed over three rubies. "Whatever you turn it toward must die the way you're thinking—one time only," she warned. "If you try a second time, it will turn on you. You need to bring them back. You need to bring yourselves back. Please." She looked at Jewel as if she were going to stomp her foot petulantly. "Jewel, it doesn't have to turn out the other way and you know it. Tarot isn't final and neither are—"

"I know," Jewel said, mustering the best smile she could and turning to Nancy, who was waiting to give her something.

"Crystals for clarity of decision and foresight," she said, handing one to each of them. "That cavern is going to try to take clarity away from you in more ways than mist and steam."

7.

So the three of them walked forward. As they did, the doppelgangers of the others faded. They looked back to see Tiffany and Nancy constructing an altar while Beth consoled Lori. They looked forward to see the three remaining doppelgangers at the mouth of the cave, grinning and waving them onwards. Their eyes locked on their respective doubles and they all became absorbed in wondering what their opposites were like. *Not friendly*, each might have thought.

Martin nervously fingered his ruby, as did Jewel.

"Use the ruby to kill part of ourselves?" Nikki asked. "I

don't think so. I think facing ourselves is the solution to this crisis." A last few steps and they were close enough to touch. The enigmatic grins remained. With a heavy inhalation, Nikki stepped into the mist. Once inside, she heard herself laugh maniacally, a laughter so loud that her other senses were overcome and she dizzied—falling? She couldn't even be sure of that.

You and your 'white' magic. You and your pimply teenage migration.

The word *migration* blasted through Nikki's head. She concentrated on breathing. Unlike the rest of the cavern's air, this air was cool, even with a hint of must.

If you were a real woman, you'd show them. If you were a wicca like your ancestors. Abby will show them; you know it too. You know that she's already tamed the black art. The black art is the real art.

Cool air, moisture. A pleasant moisture, if she thought about it. So she did, as hard as she could.

War, not peace. Blood, not sweetmilk.

A dazzle of colors assaulted her closed eyes. Crimsons, violets, oranges, and purples pressed in globules. Were the colors real? She couldn't tell, for she couldn't force her eyes to open—or to close, if they were open now. She couldn't make any changes for fear of losing control.

Then something bumped her.

"Martin? Jewel?"

More laughter, coming from every side.

I must migrate, she thought. *I must become Night.* She concentrated on softening her skin, she concentrated on the pain of losing her virginity—so very recently—she concentrated on firming her breasts, she concentrated on letting her mind jump valleys and mountains instead of lumbering old-fogey fashion through logic and *Dare I do this* or *Dare I do that.*

"Just tell the jerk bitch to go away."

On hearing her voice so youthful, Nikki jumped. Then she laughed, she laughed as Night Ryan, her teenage daughter, she laughed as a woman with the vigor of youth backed by experience of age.

"Scram," Night said to the colors. "Get out of my face." She opened her eyes to see Martin groping about a wall, dangerously near an abyss. She ran to grab him, spotting Jewel squatted near the mouth of the cave. Behind her the glowing red of the outside cavern highlighted Jewel's body in a terrifying way, but Night didn't dare let Martin go, for he was thrashing, babbling. Maybe, she decided, that was his way of coping with his double. Regression therapy.

"Just tell the jerk to go away, Martin. Do it. Just tell the jerk to scram. Blow him a big kiss, Martin. Do it." Night shook Martin, which was harder than she expected, for though he was thin, his frame was solid muscle. What the hell did the guy do during office hours—bench press both patient and couch? "Do it, Martin. Do it."

She looked around. Besides the mist and relative dark, something was different in here. She thought she saw Abby's face hanging over the abyss where Martin had nearly fallen, but it was only a protruding rock. Then the rock shifted into a smooth surface, as if someone had cut through limestone and granite for an interstate. Where had the abyss gone? No longer there; instead, a solid wall. Well no, not quite solid, for it emitted a gurgling. She could even see an emerald spray.

"Damn you, Martin Edmonds, open your damned eyes or I'll grab your you-know-whats and put a death grip on them that'll make Hulk Hogan look like a ginger snap." She shook Martin as hard as she could. Finally he opened his eyes.

"Nik—Night." His voice dropped and he looked around to spot Jewel, still squatting and shivering. He turned back to

Night. "Okay, Night-Nikki. You need to level with me. Do you always travel with your mother? Are you some kind of astro body or something?"

"Astral, Doctor. And no I'm not. I am my mother; my mother is me. You and Jewel are going to have to be the only ones besides Abby—*Mother of God, the secret's hardly a secret these days*—who know. I have more power as Night. I don't know why I have more power and right now is hardly the time for speculation. I just do. So I changed. If I hadn't changed I'm not sure I would ever have been free of my other self—you felt the same struggle with your doppelganger?"

Martin nodded.

"All right, so let's not question a good turn; let's snap Jewel out of her private battle and see if we can find Abby."

Night checked the wall—no Abby there, still smooth granite and that cooling green spray. But a fissure was forming, down from the top some two stories above.

"I slept with you the other night, not your mother, right?"

Night looked back sharply, then away. "Martin, now's not the time. It was important."

"It's important that we're truthful with one another too, isn't it?"

"Look at it from my viewpoint, Martin. It's just a streamlined younger version of me. Why not use that body style, so to speak?—no more tricks, I promise. It was important, believe me. There's power in sex; you're Freudian enough to realize that. Reich's orgone box and all—"

"So wise for a youngster."

"Come on, we've got to get the old—Jewel."

"The old biddy? You're not completely you, are you Night-Nikki?"

"No," Night sighed. "It takes time for the change to complete, for me to assimilate everything that my mother has done. Okay? It didn't take much time to assimilate her—my—feelings for you, though. Okay?" Night tugged at Martin, who stood.

As they shook Jewel and broke her embattled trance with her double, they heard a single gunshot—very close, and for every Trans-Am in America Night would have guessed it originated behind the wall where she'd seen Abby's face, behind what she'd first taken to be a drop-off. She took Nancy's crystal from her waistband and pressed it to her forehead. Martin and Jewel looked at her.

"Earlier I saw Abby's face there when Martin was leaning over what looked like an abyss. Now both are gone too and there's just this green spray and sheer granite." Night concentrated on the crystal's clarifying powers, then spoke: "What if that wall isn't there at all? What if it's just a projection of our doppelgangers? Like the opening to the escalator, but a lot better?"

"Night?" Jewel asked, appraising the youth before her. "Nikki?"

Night motioned Martin to explain while she approached the wall, gingerly pushing the granite aside like a thick London fog. Two gunshots and three quick globes of destruction crashed against her, knocking her backwards onto Jewel and Martin.

"Sti-ll a-live. Im-pressive." A great witching voice quavered to scatter green mist about in slipstreams. "Ver-y impressive. So we'll play hide and seek. Bring the 'old biddy' along, I've a score to settle with her."

Night lunged and stuck her hand out. The granite wall turned into a sheet of flame, but she kept her hand steadily against it until there was a yell from within. She smiled as she caught sight of Anne Marie deep inside the false granite, shaking her own hand fervently. But her smile disappeared as she saw Aaron holding onto Abby too. Then they disappeared. "Come on," Night told Martin and Jewel. As she spoke, the flame disappeared, as did the granite. Before them instead loomed the mouth to a great cavern with stalagmites the size of cathedral spires. Its ceiling was a quarter mile high, its floor a mile or more long. As they stepped onto that floor, its consistency became a mushy gray-pink that gave off oils around their shoes. Night pointed to a rising ledge where she saw Anne Marie and Abby. But where was Aaron?

"Think bullet," she warned Martin as they walked along a shallow creek bed, oozing a reddish fluid. Shots echoed about, but they never felt them. Night intercepted a globe of destruction with her own, Jewel did the same to another. Then silence. They hugged the ledge's wall and listened, looking about at the sharp-edged rocks that were mostly a dark gray, though the pinkish glow penetrated occasional cracks to bathe the area in light. One crack would close and another would open, playing shadows.

"Everything in here, it's all moving, isn't it?" Jewel whispered.

They climbed the ledge's gradual incline. After half an hour, Martin peered over the side to where they'd stood, some hundred feet below. "From here the floor looks like a brain—I saw an autopsy once, once was plenty enough…" Martin's voice trailed off.

Night noticed a distant, tall patch of fog approaching from the cavern's interior, scudding like a cloud. When she looked back at Martin he was leaning so far over the ledge that she jerked him back. "You'd better curb your scientific curiosity; you're giving Aaron and Anne Marie a beautiful target."

Martin turned to Jewel, his crouch being the only indication that he'd heard Night: "That orange thing that shot from your mouth on the road earlier, it wouldn't do anything like turn into a puppet, would it?"

"No, nothing like that. It's biding its time; it's my astral projection and can think and scheme."

"Well there's a puppet walking around on the floor or brain or whatever is down there," Martin said.

"You mean another one of the *kinder*?"

"No, it had red hair and looked up at me and smiled. It's heading in the direction that last blue globe thing came from. Into the fog."

Another blue globe of destruction whizzed by them to hit the floor below with a thud.

Cain! Cain! Cain!

Reddish liquid spewed from the crater where the globe had dug, and a convulsion shook the cavern until a huge boulder burst some fifty yards away. Left in its place was a beast that appeared to be an elephant rearing on its hind legs. But instead of a trunk, tentacles grasped the air, twirling boneless, all of them sniffing—or were they searching like eyes? Catching movement on the cavern wall the eyes lurched, carrying the beast forward, though it became mired after a few steps. It worked to loosen itself from the soft floor, erupting a geyser of what gave every appearance of being blood.

Cain! Cain! Cain!

Several blue globes arced toward the beast, bursting around it, evidently only angering it.

Night pointed to where the globes came from, a ledge some hundred yards higher, a continuation of the one they were on. She could make out three figures, one considerably shorter than the others. More globes blasted at the behemoth below until it collapsed.

A vatic witching voice rumbled from the ledge above. "Cain. I sum-mon you by my power. Cain, see that my power is great. I have killed the beast that cruel-ly trampled your brain. I can give—" There was a brief pause. "*We* can give you a key to the upper world where you can revel in slaughter and riches both. Cain, Cain, Cain. I sum-mon you to come forth."

Jewel cued on the voice and walked up the ledge until a patch of mist shrouded her. Despite its thickness, a terrible orange light glowed about her body.

"Jewel," Night whispered, pleaded.

"It's time to pay the Hanged Man," she whispered back. "I've cheated him all my four lives. There's power and there's power, young wise girl. Don't lose sight of one for the other. Blood and Birth."

An uncannily bright orange globe melted its way from inside a nearby boulder. Jewel's body was sucked into the globe. It arced upwards and immediately there was a loud cry cutting across the mist.

"Jew-el, you bitch! I can't believe you'd be so stupid. I had everything!"

"So we do die together after all," floated over the wet air. There was a brief orange burst, strangely silent except for the refrains "Blood and Birth, Blood and Birth; there's power and there's power, there's power and there's power; don't lose sight of one for the other, don't lose sight of one for the other."

Night held her head, swaying with the chanting. The mist swept about, hugging her. Martin pulled her from the ledge and led her up the path as quietly as he could, past the heavy ozone of Jewel's transformation, over a shifting section of wall that fell to clatter like broken slate. He kicked a hunk of metal—oddly out of place, until he realized it was a clip from Aaron's gun.

"Night, are—"

Night caught Martin's lips and whispered in his ear: "Quiet. Jewel's revenge globe would have killed only Anne Marie, the one it was aimed for." Night shook herself and began to climb with the sureness of a goat. Mist rose from the floor far below like heavy steam until they were nearly blinded; still they climbed on by keeping touch with the ledge's wall. On and on and on they climbed, until—

"I have the girl."

They tried to locate the voice. No use, though, for the mist's very thickness made the voice come from every side.

"It's too late to save her. Cain has been summoned. I can feel him coming through the earth below. You can too, *nu*?" Aaron waited.

Night and Martin could feel a trembling even through the soles of their shoes. They could hear bubbles spewing from the heating floor, though the mist was too thick for them to see down there.

"Yes, I can feel it." Night squeezed Martin's arm to keep him quiet, and he understood that surprise was part of her game—two of them, not just one.

"Good." The voice answered. "You were the one Ms. Alice was afraid of all along. But then she was killed maybe by this dead one here—" there was a kicking sound. From above? From below?— "and now you are the one who is left alive. So will you be powerful enough to help me with Cain?"

"Why would I want to help you?"

"To be empress of the world. You have someone with you, *nu?* See how my senses have sharpened by being near Cain, by being his favorite? I can smell that you have a male with you, a *goyische* male psychologist like the ones who experimented on my people and my father and the ones who raped my mother."

Night fumbled for her crystal. Finding it, she held it to her forehead and cleared her mind. "Did your mother tell you that?"

"Of course. And she told me my father died in the concentration camp with the demented German psychologists putting him naked with women to see how long he could live. Two Gestapo, they raped her before she came over. They raped her twice to make her pay for two tickets they said, because she was four months pregnant with me."

—He is ten feet beyond and above you. He is waiting for Martin to speak so he can shoot him.

Lori? Night felt for Martin's face and put her finger to his lips until she felt him nod.

—Yes. Be careful. Cain is—

Night could feel fear, and she recoiled as did Lori. She purposefully directed her voice away from where Lori told her Aaron was perched.

"When did the boat leave, Aaron?" Night leaned forward to see if she could focus on his voice.

"In 1936. They raped her in a cold storage shed ten days before Chanukah. Can you help with Cain? You will be empress and I will be emperor of the entire world. Cain is so powerful; you would not believe the things he knows. He helps me see that you and your Edmonds are looking for me, and that you are talking to locate my voice. Do you know what I do? I smell that on you and I toss my voice about. But it's okay that you do that, for it gives you time to think how powerful I am become and how powerful Cain is. Why do you smell so young—as young as the one I have here?"

"When were you born, Aaron?"

"Again with questions. I was born the last part of Elul, the 20th of August, 1937. What about my question? Cain might mistake you—"

"Then how could your mother have already been four months pregnant, Aaron?"

"What are you asking? Why won't you answer my question? What are you telling me?" There was a muffled shout that Night recognized as Abby's squeal.

"If you were born in August and your mother left Germany in December, how can she have already been four months pregnant? You would have had to have been born in April or—"

"You lying bitch! If Cain wasn't coming for this girl I would kill her and you and your ridiculous Nazi doctor, the three."

"Aaron, your mother was only trying to protect you, she loved you. She couldn't help what the Gestapo… you are your father's son in many ways—"

"Bitch, bitch. Lying *goy* bitch. Cain will start with—aht!"

There was a silence and Night eased forward, whispering for Martin to think *bullet* as he climbed up.

"No! I haven't done anything to you. Leave me alone." It was Abby's voice, pleading.

Even as they hurried toward it, laughter pervaded the cavern. Night saw it actually bubbling in a mini-cyclone on the floor below. Hearing Abby scream Night clambered up the ledge's wall, but slipped back as a thick fluid oozed out. She scrambled up again. Martin continued edging along the trail, a switchback. That would take too long. She gripped loose rocks that fell to sound only of laughter, as if they themselves were mocking her.

"CAIN! CAIN! CAIN!" came in a chant. A small rock at her eye level opened and closed, mouthing the words.

"Get away!"

It was Abby's scream again, and Night slipped against the oozing ledge as some cottony fabric brushed her hand. The grin of the small tumbling creature never stopped, even as it grasped at Night's hair, then lost its grip and fell to the floor below where it bounced upwards as if from a springboard. Pie. It had been Pie. Night continued climbing, giving no more thought to that. There was a whimper as she reached the ledge. Pulling herself up, she saw a lumbering form and readied a globe of destruction. But Abby was clinging to the form, not running away. Martin! And on the ground—the motionless hulk of Aaron, a hatpin sticking in his left eye, his skin a bright oxygen-starved blue even in the mist. Nearby was the burn spot where Anne Marie and Jewel must have combusted, brought down by the eye-for-an eye curse.

Pride, Night, pride. You were so sure of your mountain goat abilities. Mists scattered momentarily in a wind so she ran forward, fearing she would lose her bearings otherwise. *Cain! Cain! Cain!* She heard laughter and saw entire walls crumble. She tugged Martin and Abby as close to her Pentad's Shield of Power as she could, though it was quickly fading, for the Pentad was no longer a fivesome with the death of Jewel. She looked down at Aaron: there was no doubt he was dead.

"The rag doll, Alice Fairbain's rag doll stuck him with the hat pin. Then she was coming after me when Dr. Edmonds came up the path and kicked her and she fell."

A slab dropped behind them, actually lifting them off the

ground and compressing their spines. Night was glad for her present younger body; she noticed Martin grimace and hold his back in pain. Then everything but the wind and mist stopped. Three more doppelgangers appeared on the path's downside with grins as fierce as Pie's; this time Abby's was included. So their retreat was blocked.

"*Who summoned me?*"

The voice bounced from the roof of the cavern, easily a hundred yards above. Night saw stalactites loosening as the voice repeated its question. Several fell, and there was a frenzied scream, half-laugher, half pain, as the stalactites speared the cavern's floor and blood spurted upwards.

"*Who… summoned… me?*"

Martin pointed below. The mists had cleared, and on the oozing gray-pink surface of the floor stood a naked, frowning man whose height was no more than five feet, though he was more of a square than a rectangle. He was so heavy that his stubby feet sank to their ankles in the porous floor.

"*Who summoned me? You?*"

Night could feel the creature's stare, so she answered, using her vatic witching voice: "The one who sum-moned you is dead. We have neither quarrel with, nor fav-or to ask you." Though her Great Voice filled the cavern and bounced from above, she fretted.

"Sorceress," the figure below sneered. "There were two who summoned me. Are you the assistant? Did you kill the other?"

"Bow-th who summon-ned you are dead. We have nei-ther quarrel with, nor fav-or to ask you."

"*Who killed them, then? I will talk with that one.*"

A myriad of stalactites fell as that voice thundered. When the trembling stopped, Night stepped to the edge to look down on the squat figure. With her hand she performed a banishing ritual. Looking at the gritty form below didn't inspire the best conditions for concentration, though, especially as it began beating the ground with a club to elicit more falling rocks.

"My good God," Martin said behind her. "His face, it looks just like Bobby Kirby's, pimples and all."

She saw Pie on the cavern floor, crouching to the left of the man-beast. And directly behind she saw the man beast's double crawling along the gray-pink ground, using what rocks were available for cover. In this one's hand was also a club.

"Who? Speak."

"The one who killed the first woman, she in turn died from the use of her powers. The one who killed the man is now directly to your left. It—"

The man-beast had already turned and was making toward Pie. Seeing what it was, the man-beast laughed so loudly that the roof shifted with a crack that sent Night and Martin and Abby to their knees.

"A doll. Is this the bold thinker to replace the human race? My mother gave me a doll, the woman you call Eve—in her motley sentiment she gave me a doll. Do you know what my brother Abel did to it?" Instantly, Cain's eyes were level with their own; he had tenfolded in size. He bent to the cavern's pink floor and picked up Pie, who stabbed him futilely with a pin. Snorting, he put Pie in his mouth and bit off its head, tossing the body at Abby.

"You're the one they brought for me. A fine virgin. A start until the Kirby child is mine." Cain reached, but Night threw the largest globe of destruction she could muster directly into his eyes. He screamed wildly, and they ran down the path, though

once again they were brought short by their own doppel-gangers.

"Here," Night said. She handed Abby a bean she'd taken from her sack. "Make yourself invisible."

"What about us?" Martin asked.

"We haven't done the ritual, so the beans wouldn't help."

"Can't we do the ritual?"

Roars filled the cavern, and Cain beat at the ledge where they'd stood with his gigantic club, pulverizing that path.

"No. We don't have the skull with us."

"The skull," Martin said matter-of-factly.

Abby was already transforming. "I'll thry my bethst to haalp," she whispered in Night's ear, joining the mist floating about.

"Down the sides then," Martin said, pointing.

Night nodded, looking forward to the doppelgangers and behind to Cain, who was still wiping his eyes. She threw another globe, which Cain caught, laughing loudly. He made to throw it back and Night warned Martin, "Think of electrici-ty."

The blue globe exploded, knocking them over the side of the incline to the next lowest path, where they picked them-selves up. Their doppelgangers once more blocked the way below. Cain's amused laughter was great.

"Weaklings," he taunted. "When I find the virgin girl I'll ascend for the boy Bobby, and then I'll slaughter you all. My mark will be powerful once more; a true race of humans will breed again." He raised his club and taunted, "Do something good, do-gooders. Tell me where the virgin girl and the vir-gin boy are. Save them the agony of the wait."

Martin righted himself and fired the gun wildly. The bul-lets thunked loudly into Cain's huge chest but did little else.

Night raised Tiffany's ruby and pointed it at Cain, thinking suffocation. A blinding ray flashed. To her amazement, Cain grew. In a cobweb of her mind she remembered what black magic she'd studied: the ruby worked off cumulative hatred. Exactly the wrong thing to throw at this elemental of elementals. Then she spotted movement on the floor below; she again saw the double of Cain—Abel?—emerging from underneath an overhang. He too had grown along with his brother. And so had his club.

Night looked at the ruby in her hand. *There's power and there's power. Blood AND Birth*, she remembered Jewel telling her. "Stop firing," she told Martin, who looked at her oddly, nonetheless doing as she requested.

"Remember, Martin: I *am* Nikki. I want you to kiss me, hard, and think of the other night. Think of that and think of tomorrow night when we'll listen to frogs and owls and watch the full moon lap the water in the lake out back."

Night bent forward despite Martin's surprise. Through her blouse her body pressed against his. Both of them were sweating, but a coolness underneath the sweat engulfed them. She slid her tongue deep into his throat, and writhed. Martin stared wide-eyed.

"Noooooo! Impossible! You can't do that down here! You can't do that in front of me! It's wrong, it's evil! Noooooo! Noooooo!"

Understanding the creature's sudden fear and revulsion, Martin grasped Night tightly and returned her kiss.

"Noooooo! Noooooo!"

A tremendous thunk and howl arose. Night and Martin turned together to see that Cain had been cleaved into two neat halves. Behind stood his twin Abel, who looked in amazement at what he had done, his mouth open, his eyes wild. A more absolute stillness than Night had ever experienced trotted through the cavern, as if earth itself had crunched to a halt, wondering which way it should now spin.

"*I have done what I have been unable to do for the passing of a billion moons.*" The second creature said, though his mouth wasn't moving. "*Leave me and my brother to sort our wonder. We will stay buried where we belong to ponder these things. You three must leave to live.*" Abel picked up his brother's halves and drug them toward a dark opening in the distance. Below, Pie's body, underneath a rock, managed to free itself. It turned to them, then to the receding figure of Abel, and finally to Cain, in whose stomach its head rested. It scrambled over boulders that had fallen from Cain's yell and headed toward him.

EPILOGUE TO A PROLOGUE

1.

Once Cain died, the entire cavern shifted so drastically and so often that they barely made it back to Lori and the others waiting on the plateau. Each turn they took depended on Lori's telepathic powers and Beth's magical scents. When they finally reached the four, they were shocked to find the state they were in. The Pentad's power had slowly worn down after Jewel's death and the *kinder* elementals had attacked again and again, thrown off only by Beth's globes of destruction and Lori's gun.

"No time for talk or hugs, we need to go," Nikki said. No one argued. All the *kinder* throughout the cavern were now lifeless, though Nikki thought that would last only as long as it took Cain's halves to rejoin. Then the process would begin again, forever and forever and…

No one's watch had worked since they'd been in Persephone's, but as nearly as they could figure a night and a day had passed, though day or night, it hardly mattered. Were the walls redder? Duller? Who could say? They settled on night because they came to a section where they needed their flashlights. This made them happy, for they remembered this section to be near the opening.

Whose beam hit the figure first? Each person said it was hers, his. Blocking their paths weren't *kinder* or more chimerical monsters or even Cain. Blocking their paths were seven god-spit images of themselves. They sat down, the images sat down. They whispered and planned, the images smiled.

Nikki thought about changing to Night again. Was it worth exposing herself? Even useful? She remembered Night's rashly youthful "Tell the jerk to hit the road." Well, that wouldn't do now. There was no road to hit, was there? Except the one leading out, the one behind the doppelgangers. Nikki could see her antagonistic self smiling from the amid the other group.

There's power and there's power. Blood and Birth. It ran through her mind, but didn't make sense.

Martin spoke, keeping an eye on his doppelganger. "They're us," he said. "So they have to go with us."

This was not greeted with the enthusiasm that several Big Macs and fries would have raised.

"I'm telling you," he insisted, "something down here has separated our respective anima and animus—our ids, our black selves, our darker drives or whatever you wish to call them—from ourselves. That's all Cain is—or at least that's all he was until Abel killed him."

"Maybe you're right," Nikki said. "There's black magic, white magic and gray magic—why should we be surprised to see our lighter and darker selves embodied down here? If we look at the bright side, we're getting a free view and saving years of psychoanalysis and lots of money."

"Is *that* what you show people in your psychoanalysis?" Tiffany asked, clasping an emerald hung about her neck.

"Psychologist," Martin mumbled. He had to admit that what he saw of himself wasn't too pleasing. Still, hadn't that something come in handy in the barn with Walter? Hadn't it gritted its teeth and climbed the cliff to find Abby and stop Pie hours ago? And was it all the good Doctor Martin Edmonds clasping Night Ryan? Or wasn't there the hint of a hot, dank breath involved under the sheets?

"I'm going," he announced. "If I'm right, you can follow. If I'm wrong—Tiffany, would you do me the honor of blasting me through to the next cavern with your ruby?"

Tiffany was taken aback.

Nikki shook her head and reached for Tiffany's ruby. "Martin, if anyone besides you is going to make that decision…" she said.

Martin nodded and kissed her. "Umm. Not bad for an old lady," he whispered. As he walked forward, his doppelganger, which had stood apart from the others, opened its mouth and arms in something of a death throe. As Martin closed in, he almost danced with it, a crazy waltz of whirling and dips, until it slowly immersed into his body, causing him to stumble against the wall. "Blood and Birth," he called back to the others, breathing heavily and wiping blood from his mouth where he'd cut it on the wall. "That's your motto, and I think it's a good one." He motioned with his hands.

One by one, they all walked forward to dance the awkward dance.

2.

"It's been three days," Mrs. Thompson told them. She was still spattered with pink splotches from where she'd painted over the eyes of every statue she could find.

"Spray painting? That was the chugging sound?" Nikki asked.

Mrs. Thompson nodded, passing a plate of cookies. "I heard a commotion in the barn and went over there too. Your friend here was quite a help, weren't you? A lot more than the police, whom we kept avoiding." She offered Skull a cookie and he ruffled his wings, giving Agnes's finger a friendly peck.

They were still in Fairbain's home. Martin walked down the steps into the dining room, giving a quick glance to the empty spots where the griffins had stood. "All the statues have dissolved of their own will or have been destroyed, but the hospital where Bobby's admitted is packed with what the physicians are calling mass hysteria. I volunteered my services."

"So, are you a good one?" Nikki asked.

"A good what?"

"You know, the psy-word."

"Psychologist."

"Mmm-humm," Nikki said, chewing half the cookie Skull had taken.

"Just about as good as you are at being a witch. Blood and Birth, that's what you've got to know, isn't it?"

Nikki swallowed her cookie with a grin while Beth mixed a potion she guaranteed would relax them all. Of course she added vinegar.

www.ingramcontent.com/pod-product-compliance
Lightning Source LLC
Chambersburg PA
CBHW021235190726
48289CB00005B/1331